S.J. MARTIN

Resurgence

Rage. Revenge. Redemption

This book was professionally typeset on Reedsy.
Find out more at reedsy.com

Contents

Chapter One

June 1102 – Stafford Castle

Stafford Castle had finally fallen to King Maredudd of Powys, and the Welsh forces were jubilant. Taking and looting the town had been easy, but the castle was well-defended, with high palisades and desperate defenders fighting for their lives. It had taken longer to capture and had been brutal and bloody.

The sudden disappearance from their camp of his hot-headed brother, Prince Iorwerth, and his five hundred men had been a blow to the Welsh king at a time when he needed as many men as possible to attack the castle. However, two things had helped Maredudd: Sir Nicholas of Stafford had fled in the night, abandoning his captains and men to defend the castle on their own. Then, to balance the desertion of Prince Iorwerth and to Maredudd's relief, the great warrior, Sir Raoul de Tosny, had arrived at Stafford with over six hundred trained men.

This had been the last straw for the disheartened men attempting to hold the castle, and they had negotiated a surrender in return for being allowed to disarm and leave. However, once they reached the forests, Raoul de Tosny's men were waiting for them, and they were all slaughtered. Maredudd was shocked at first, as he had given his word for their safety, but as De Tosny pointed out, he had not given his word to allow them to escape through the forests. He pointed out that these men would only re-arm and fight for the King, so better to kill them now. Maredudd had reluctantly agreed whilst he ordered the clearing of the castle and removal of the bodies on both sides. He intended to occupy the castle and hold it for Robert de Belleme, the powerful and wealthy Earl of Shrewsbury to whom he owed homage. King Maredudd was pleased with their success at Stafford, as was De Tosny; both men knew this would send shock waves through the King's council and advisors.

Two days later, just as the celebrations had begun in earnest at Stafford Castle, Prince Iorwerth had ridden into camp with the despondent and crushed remains of his five-hundred-strong army, back to face the anger and contempt of his brothers, King Maredudd and Cadwgan. His impulsive decision to attack Tamworth had led to his being badly defeated by Lord Robert Beaumont and his forces, and he had lost most of his men.

Prince Iorwerth, pride wounded, now found himself on his knees before his brother, King Maredudd of Powys. This was a humbling position—one he swore he would never assume again before any man or king. However, he hoped this act of submission would set in motion a chain of events that would change his life and the course of their kingdom, as he needed to be back in his brother's court to know their plans.

The Great Hall in Stafford's castle was crowded with hundreds of men, and Iorwerth, hearing the jibes and insults openly muttered and then shouted against him, felt his anger rise. However, to gain what he wanted long-term, he had to bend a knee to show subservience and repentance for his admittedly rash actions.

'So, Iorwerth, you return to my hall with less than a third of the men of Powys who rode out with you. Your foolish and reckless actions have decimated your forces. What say you to this?' Maredudd demanded in a tone that was not conciliatory in the slightest nor took account of his humility in falling to his knees in front of his brother.

'You have the right of it, and I should have listened to you, Brother; I was angry and hurt that you favoured a blackguard and rogue such as Owen ap Cynan over your own flesh and blood. I admit it was foolhardy. I did not use my head, and I was too driven by my emotions. I underestimated how well Tamworth was protected. I expected them to surrender at the sight of our forces. I ask for your forgiveness. It was a rash move, which I regret,' he replied, hoping this would soften his brother's righteous anger.

'As do the families of the men whom Beaumont and his forces slaughtered because of your mistakes, Iorwerth ap Bleddyn, not that you deserve that great name; I am sure that those widows and children regret your rash actions,' growled a deeper voice that alarmed the Prince.

From the shadows behind Maredudd, a huge grizzled figure appeared. Iorwerth felt himself go cold at the sight of this man, for he knew who he was: Raoul II de Tosny. In his sixties now, he looked twenty years younger as he was all sinew and muscle. His long, thick, grey-streaked, dark hair was tied behind, and his hand rested on his sword hilt as usual. However, the Prince swallowed hard and found his voice.

3

'Do you think I don't realise that, De Tosny? These were my men, from my valleys in South Powys, and I will mourn them with their families,' argued Iorwerth, but the big warrior scoffed at this.

'Easy words after the event. I have walked among the survivors out there, huddled around the campfires—the bleeding, the lame, the wounded—they will not forget. You were caught napping, Iorwerth ap Bleddyn. You laid siege to a castle that would have taken two months at least to fall, with no siege equipment, not even scaling ladders, and I have been told by your disheartened serjeants that you were careless and had not set enough scouts and sentries. These are the mistakes made by a green boy who cannot control his anger and jealousy, not a warrior in his late forties. If I was your brother...,' he said, pausing, and with a nod of his head indicated a frowning Maredudd, 'I would put you in the deepest dungeon I had, where you could do no more harm, as we all still wonder why Beaumont did not kill you immediately you were taken. The Castellan of Tamworth would have paid much silver to have your head on a spike above his gates.'

Iorwerth felt cut to the quick by those words, and his mouth was dry as his panic built, but he had to say something to save himself.

'They beat me, bound me tightly and put me on the ground with the other prisoners. Philip de Braose stood over me, his foot on my neck and mentioned a price on my head, but Beaumont wanted to kill me to send a message, for they knew you were attacking Stafford. It was purely by chance that night when two of my men freed themselves from their bonds and cut me loose. We swam the river in the darkness while others escaped behind me, or I would be in that dark cell, waiting for the axe to fall.'

King Maredudd curled his lip in scorn.

'But not enough was set free; they still have at least a hundred and fifty of our men taken captive, men we needed, and many of the men you brought limping back will not be fit to fight for at least a month. Do you not understand what you have done, Iorwerth? The wound is deep indeed and all the more painful when your own flesh and blood fail you with their irresponsible and ill-judged decisions. Even more so when that brother disgraces the brave warrior reputation of Ap Bleddyn of Powys with their incompetence.'

For the first time, Iorwerth felt real fear. He raised his eyes to look up at his brother, who had sat back and was now deep in thought; his face was grim. Would his brother listen to Raoul de Tosny's words? He knew that Maredudd truly respected and listened to the older warrior. This dangerous Norman lord had seen and fought in more rebellions in his lifetime than they would ever see. Iorwerth knew he had been King William's standard bearer as a young man and fought alongside him at Hastings. Finally, Maredudd spoke.

'I do not want you near me at the moment, Iorwerth. I cannot bear even seeing you, knowing the damage you have done by your foolish actions. I will send you back to our court at Mathrafal for at least a month. You may return when your men are again fit for action. Meanwhile, you now owe us hundreds of men. Send your serjeants out to your lands and recruit more.'

The King said this with a finality Iorwerth couldn't argue against, so he pushed himself to his feet and bowed. However, as he turned away, he looked back.

'One thing more, Brother, the Normans have half a dozen spies and informers in this court. I heard them talking. Sir Philip de Braose knew all about my argument with the mercenary, Owen, and that they were safe to attack our camp at Tamworth as you would not ride out to help me.'

There was silence in the hall at Stafford as they all waited for the King's response.

'Two of those informers were hung this morning, Iorwerth, and we will find the others. Now go, tell your men they leave for Powys at first light.'

Iorwerth trudged back to his men. This banishment back to Mathrafal was not ideal for what his new masters demanded of him. He'd promised Robert Beaumont and Count Richard de Clare much to save his life, and they would expect him to deliver. For now, he'd find the extra men his brother wanted, and then he would return to Stafford and do his utmost to bring King Maredudd down, family or not.

His brother, Cadwgan, followed him out and confronted him outside the hall.

'What were you thinking? Or was it that the red mist descended, and you were not thinking at all, Iorwerth? Do you not realise that your selfish attack on Tamworth stains us all? It damages our reputation and makes people question our credibility as allies and even as rulers of Powys.'

This was too much for Iorwerth after the humiliating and frightening experience in the hall, he turned and, with a vicious punch, knocked his older brother to the ground.

'You will regret those words, Cadwgan. I swear by all the gods that you and Maredudd will pay for how you have treated me,' he snarled, fists clenched.

He then realised he was saying too much by letting him

see his anger, so he turned away. However, Cadwgan saw real hatred in his brother's eyes for the first time, far more than the usual sibling animosity, and he felt apprehensive. He determined to speak to the King about him, but he had to wait until the next day as the celebrations for the taking of Stafford Castle went on late into the night.

Early the next morning, Cadwgan found Maredudd and Raoul de Tosny deep in conversation outside the keep's great doors. He bowed to both and joined them.

'I tell you, Maredudd, my dead brother, the great Robert Stafford, would be turning in his grave if he knew that his son, Nicholas, had fled from this castle and gone over to Henry. The shame of a De Stafford, my nephew, supporting Henry Beauclerc, the usurper, the Oathbreaker, is almost too much to bear. I will never recognise Henry as king as long as Duke Robert of Normandy lives,' Raoul de Tosny proclaimed.

At that moment, Iorwerth and his dispirited men rode out of the camp on their way back to the royal court of Powys. He bowed his head in recognition of the King on the steps, but Cadwgan could see his younger brother was stony-faced. A dozen carts carrying the wounded and the lame followed them.

'A disgraceful sight,' growled De Tosny.

'Talking of shame and anger, I am worried by what I see in Iorwerth; there was pure hatred in his face last night when he attacked me,' murmured Cadwgan to the King.

Maredudd glanced down at Cadwgan. He considered his brother an astute and observant man, one worth listening to, and De Tosny agreed.

'Yes, you should listen to Cadwgan as I think perhaps that tree will need pruning, Maredudd. It is often family or friends who slide the fateful dagger between your ribs.'

Maredudd watched his brother leave the camp through narrowed eyes. He knew they were right, but Iorwerth was family. He remembered the time when they were younger, and he had loved his hot-headed brother.

'Do not fear. I hear and heed your words. There are few that I trust, and I have had eyes and ears on all of you for some time,' he said. He laughed to see their expressions at this, but De Tosny nodded in approval

'My informers tell me that Beaumont is leaving Tamworth in a few days. This could be our chance, Maredudd. They will no doubt go northeast to meet Henry at Tickhill, and their force will be strung out along the road. It would be an ideal time to ambush him and his men—to take our revenge for what he did to Iorwerth and our men at Tamworth.'

Maredudd waved them back inside the keep.

'Let us discuss this further in the solar, but any mention of this plan stays between us three for now.'

De Tosny nodded and smiled in satisfaction. He had an old and large debt to settle with Robert Beaumont; he was determined to take his head or die trying, and now, he might get that chance and deliver a blow against the forces of Henry, the Oathbreaker, at the same time.

June 1102 - Tamworth

Rhodri wondered if he would ever get the smell of burning corpses out of his clothes as he stripped off on the riverbank to dive in and at least get it out of his hair. Robert Beaumont had ordered the bodies of the enemy to be placed in several large pyres; these were set alight while the priest buried the few men they had lost in the attack. This was normal, and at first, there was no problem. But then, the wind changed, and the smoke and ash from the pyres covered the camp until, finally, they had subsided to smouldering mounds, still giving off the rank smell of burning fat.

Rhodri emerged from the river refreshed and was rubbing himself dry with a piece of rough cloth when Richard de Clare and Conn Fitz Malvais approached. Although he had his own full-length coloured tattoo on his back, Conn tended to forget about Rhodri's tattoos, which were mainly covered by his leather Horse Warrior jerkin. Now, in the bright sunlight, they were there in all their splendour, from his broad chest to his muscled thighs. De Clare, however, seemed oblivious to the large blue Celtic swirls and designs before him as he launched into the news.

'A messenger from the King has arrived for Beaumont. We are going to his pavilion now to get our orders, and it seems likely that we will leave early tomorrow. Find Serjeant Fox and Gracchus for me, Rhodri; I believe they have gone hunting. Tell them to alert their men to make ready to leave. Some have village women to get rid of and send back to their husbands, and their horses must be groomed and fed.'

Rhodri laughed, but he was pleased to be doing something. They had been here too long at Tamworth despite the better food readily supplied by the relieved and grateful Castellan.

De Clare and Malvais entered Beaumont's pavilion to find Sir Philip de Braose and Urse d'Abetot, the Sheriff of Worcester, with him. They learnt that the Sheriff was to stay with his men in the area to deal with further forays or attacks from the Welsh; he also had the captives to deal with. Beaumont waved them both to camp chairs.

'As you no doubt know, the King's messenger arrived, and we are ordered to join the King at Tickhill. The castle there is currently under siege by the Bishop of Lincoln for the King, as Henry is determined to take as many of Robert de Belleme's castles as possible.'

De Clare concurred. 'It is what we expected. Do we have any further news of Iorwerth? I cannot imagine his brother welcoming him back with open arms.'

Sir Philip de Braose nodded. 'My man, Kenric, rode in this morning. Our tame prince received a frosty reception and was returned to the royal court of Mathrafal in disgrace. This gives us breathing space as it reduces the forces in Stafford, and Iorwerth will be allowed to return. That is when he may become very useful to us, for as we know, Raoul de Tosny has joined the King Maredudd, bringing several hundred men. An old adversary of yours, I believe, Sire.'

Beaumont smiled cynically. 'Yes, we are old, sworn enemies and were fated to meet again on the battlefield someday; he is a loyal supporter of the Duke of Normandy. However, the good news is that Henry has summoned the fyrd in the surrounding counties, which will more than double our numbers.'

De Clare snorted derision, which made Beaumont raise an eyebrow.

'I am sorry, Sire, if that does not raise hope in my breast— rows of men from the fields with pikes and pitchforks facing armoured knights on horseback. In the past, all it has ever done is slow the charge of the cavalry as they trampled and cut the peasants down.'

Malvais thought this was a brave but risky comment, and his eyes flew to Beaumont's face to see how he would take it. To his relief, their leader laughed.

'Yes, you are right in some ways, but if one of these pikes manages to pierce the breast of a charger, bringing a knight down, the pike man's compatriots will hack him to death. That is one less knight we have to deal with. Now repeat that across the rows of the fyrd, and they might bring ten or fifteen knights down; do not dismiss them out of hand, De Clare, as they can be useful. Now go and prepare your men. We will leave tomorrow morning after the men break their fast. We need to do at Tickhill what we have done at Tamworth, and I, for one, relish the task, especially if Robert de Belleme is holed up inside as we suspect.'

Sir Philip de Braose raised a hand. 'No, Sire, he is not; I have more news on that.' He glanced significantly at the others in the tent, and to De Clare's annoyance, Beaumont waved them out.

'Young De Braose seems to be carving a niche in there for himself, and apparently, we were not worthy enough to hear it,' he said to Malvais in annoyance, who shrugged and headed for his men. De Clare watched him go with concern; he could see the pain there in his friend's face and demeanour but could do nothing to lessen it until Chatillon's man, Edvard, arrived from Oxford, for only then could they tell Malvais the truth.

Conn didn't care about De Braose; he had his own demons to wrestle with, which were far more significant than a young, ambitious knight trying to gain influence. His squire, Darius, had been murdered, and he blamed himself for his death. His friend, Georgio, who was an adopted brother, was kidnapped and held in God knows what conditions, and now his month-old son was dead. That thought returned, and the image of Rohese holding his child filled his mind. His son was dead. He shook his head to try and get rid of the image; he knew

11

he had to snap out of this. His men depended on him, but it was proving difficult; the pain of it all was too raw. However, he had other obligations, for he was also an informer, a spy beyond suspicion, hidden in King Henry's camp. He headed to the wagons, where the baskets of pigeons were kept, to send a bird to Piers de Chatillon, the Papal Envoy, French lord and assassin. Chatillon was his mentor and patron, and Conn knew he'd want to know everything about the attacks on Tamworth and Tickhill.

Chapter Two

June 1102- Chatillon-sous-Bagneux, France.

The whole family was assembled in the great hall that evening. They were finishing dinner, and there was much laughter and conversation.

The large, long, wooden shutters had been open all morning to let in the brilliant summer sunshine, and the hall was swept clean and new rushes laid. However, from midday, the weather had begun to change. Ahmed, their physician and friend who had chosen to live with them at the chateau, had cast a gimlet eye at the amassing dark clouds in the distance, moving in fast from the west. Holding a finger in the air, he'd pointed them out to Isabella, Chatillon's beautiful Genoese wife.

She smiled and, ever an optimist, shook her head.

'It may blow over, but I will warn the Steward to be ready to close the hall shutters.'

'You will need to fasten the shutters and bolt them. Can you not feel the stillness and the temperature change? Have I taught you nothing?' he said, shaking his bird-like head at her in semi-amusement before he continued. 'Look at the very tops of the trees, Isabella—they are beginning to wave. I believe we are in for a heavy summer storm, and I can feel the humidity in the air,' he said, holding his hand in the air and rubbing his finger and thumb together.

Watching him, Isabella thought Ahmed looked well. He'd be sixty-six this year and had been a major part of their lives since she married Piers de Chatillon. However, she knew her husband's friendship with the learned Arab doctor and apothecary went back further than that to Chatillon's days as a sixteen-year-old squire in the court of King Philip in Paris. Ahmed had only been in his early thirties then, but he'd helped save Piers' life and had introduced him, and then her, to the most useful and lethal poisons in the world. She could never imagine not having Ahmed in their lives; she'd become not only his willing apprentice but was also almost a daughter to him.

Now, she smiled down the table at him as the wind rattled the shutters and the lashing rain followed.

'You were right, as usual,' she said, as he inclined his head in acknowledgement, and her son, Gabriel, jumped in.

'Cormac and I locked all the youngsters away in the stable block; we thought this storm would frighten them. We also put the mares and foals in the large loose boxes,' said Gabriel, and was pleased when his father nodded his approval both to him and to Cormac, Finian's eldest boy, who desperately missed his father.

'Hopefully, this will blow out tonight as you are to leave for the Royal Court at Ghent tomorrow. What do you think, Ahmed? Will tomorrow be clear?' asked Isabella.

'It is a fast-moving wind, so yes, the storm will move, but there may still be rain. However, I happen to know that this young man does not melt in the rain,' said Ahmed, with a twinkle in his eye.

Gabriel gave a shout of laughter.

'You will never let me forget that and still try to blame me even though I swore I did not leave the gate open. I spent hours in the forests trying to make sure those goats did not end up in the belly of a wolf.'

'We know. We were all there, soaked to the skin, trying to find the stupid, stubborn creatures,' added Dion, Finian's young widow.

Watching her, Chatillon thought Dion was regaining her beauty, with her long dark hair and large, arresting green eyes. She was still only thirty, but Finian's sudden killing had taken its toll as she had faded into the shadows of grief for well over a year, and they had all worried for her. There were a few silver hairs at her temples now, and at times she still carried an air of sadness about her as she watched over their two-year-old daughter, Finnuala, whom Finian Ui Neill, the great Irish warrior, had never seen.

Gabriel shook his head after the jibes and glanced at his laughing mother. He was excited to be going to Ghent, where he would join the court musicians and become one of the many court squires. However, he was also apprehensive about leaving his mother, as he had lost her for so many years when she was kidnapped, and he remembered the agony of not knowing if she was alive or dead. This had affected Gabriel more than his twin brother, Gironde, so now, he leaned forward and held his mother's fingers.

'I could stay until the autumn to see my brother or sister born,' he said hopefully.

She saw the concern on his face, and she saw he was scared, this sensitive boy of theirs. He feared she might die in childbed, as women sometimes did, and he wouldn't be here to say goodbye. She shook her head.

'No, we have already put this off once before. Your brother, Gironde, is serving the French king, and you are leaving tomorrow to serve Count Robert of Flanders. You need to spread your wings, Gabriel, but you will return to us for Yuletide, and with God's grace, the babe will be four months old then and more interesting than a wrapped bundle in a crib,' she said, squeezing his hand.

Gabriel glanced across at his father's face but saw the amused, sardonic smile on his lips. He knew it was hopeless; there was no help there. He would leave tomorrow for Flanders and a new life away from his home, whatever the weather.

Suddenly, the great dyer hounds which had been sleeping in front of the fire were on their feet growling, their hackles raised. Chatillon put his goblet down. The dogs were never wrong. He had his first pair of these great Saxon hunting hounds as a gift from Luc de Malvais twenty years before, and these four were the fifth generation at the chateau. He pushed his chair back as they began to bark and howl while waving his captain, Daniel and his men to the door where his steward was already standing. They were not expecting anyone, especially in this foul weather, but they knew from bitter experience that they could never be too careful; Piers de Chatillon had dozens of enemies. The steward's eyes went from Daniel's face to his master. He was not expecting trouble, but they were always cautious since the attack on the chateau several years ago.

Chatillon nodded, and the bolts were drawn back while ten of Daniel's men stood in a semi-circle, armed and ready as the heavy doors were pulled open. Two men appeared first, and then two wet and bedraggled cloaked figures. The man at the front threw back his hood, showering the floor with droplets. Daniel recognised him immediately as one of Edvard's senior men; he sheathed his sword and told his men to stand down.

'Well met, Saul. This is foul weather for you to be on the roads. Is Sir Edvard with you?' he asked, looking out into the dark, rain-lashed courtyard beyond.

'No, only the four of us. Edvard sent us on our journey and then rode back to Oxford; he may still be there.'

The others had dropped their hoods. Dion, seeing there were two women, hastened forward, waving the servants to take their cloaks before she ushered them to seats by the great fireplace. It was then she realised that the younger woman had a babe strapped to her chest. She called for warming mulled cider to be brought for them as she wondered who they were and why Edvard had sent them.

Having divested himself of his dripping cloak, Saul took a folded piece of vellum from his doublet and, bowing, he handed it to Lord Chatillon. Piers read its contents twice while glancing at the two women and the child. All eyes watched him and waited. Then he shook his head in amazement and laughed aloud.

'The fragile and precious package, which Edvard assured me was on its way to us and which we had mistakenly thought was possibly some delicate Venetian glass, has arrived,' he said, indicating the young woman and babe.

At this, Edvard's wife, Mishna, glanced with concern at the young woman and prayed they were not Edvard's mistress and child. She then chastised herself for such a thought, knowing that Edvard would never do that to her.

Seeing his family's surprise and confusion about this package from Edvard, Chatillon smiled and finally told them who this was.

'Meet young Darius Fitz Malvais, the infant son of Conn and Rohese de Courcy. However, his presence and parentage must be kept secret for now. The child's life was in danger, and the mother's life still may be, but until it is decided otherwise, young Darius will be brought up here at the chateau amongst our children. Now, I must go and send a message to Edvard saying they have arrived safely,' he said, leaving the group clustered around the fire to see and welcome Conn's child.

When he reached his study, Piers sat behind the table, the rain lashing the leaded glass windows behind him as he poured himself a glass of wine and his eyes travelled to a previous message from Pope Paschal. The Holy See felt that King Henry was not keeping his promises to them, and Paschal wanted Chatillon to ensure that the King's war with Robert de Belleme was not an easy win—he wanted it sabotaged. Chatillon sighed and ran his hands through his hair as he thought of the options and the main players on the board. Would removing one or two of them be significant, he wondered, and if so, which one? He would think on it, weighing up the pros and cons, and he'd then send a message to Edvard in a few days.

In the hall, Ahmed called for warm blankets to wrap the child in and keep the bedraggled, shivering women warm. He then lifted the babe from the wet nurse and, unwrapping him, held him up in the firelight. Isabella saw the shock of dark hair and blue eyes as he blinked at Ahmed, and she laughed.

'I can see why they sent him to us; I have never seen Lady Rohese, but the babe is very like Conn.'

Isabella had read the message to Piers from Edvard, which also explained who the two women were, so she waved the housekeeper, Madame Chambord, over and explained about the wet nurse who would join the servants in the nursery. However, Joan was a little more complex; she was a cousin and companion of the Grandesmil women and was one of those poor, in-between relatives of the powerful Norman families, often existing, along with the priest and the tutor, in the middle layer of the great houses. However, Joan solved it as she watched Lady Isabella standing there pondering what to do with her.

'I will be no trouble, my lady. I promised my cousin, Lady Adeline, that I would stay with the babe for his first five years, that is if you find that acceptable. I was a companion and tutor to both my cousins, as my father, a younger brother of Sir Hugh Grandesmil, insisted on having me educated alongside my brother. I read, write, cypher and speak Greek and Latin. I also know the classics, history, and geography, so I will not be a burden on you and could assist your tutor. I will be as happy in the servant's quarters as anywhere.'

Isabella, taken aback at first, liked her all the more for this speech as she had also been educated with her brothers. She assured Joan that she was very welcome, that she would find her a room, and that her services would be very useful, especially with Fergus, Finian and Dion's son, who had run wild since his tutor left for Rome months before. With that, Madame Chambord took them all off to the kitchen for some warming food.

Ahmed was sitting by the fire with Mishna, crooning a soft song to the babe in his arms. Watching the scene, Isabella smiled; there was no doubt that the child would be loved and cossetted here, but the last sentence in the missive from Edvard troubled her. Both parents still believed that the child had died.... Her heart bled for them, for having lost two

19

children—both of them murdered at a young age—she knew the pain they would be enduring.

Mid-June 1102 – Oxford

Sir Nigel D'Oyly warmly welcomed Edvard of Silesia when he entered the Great Hall at Oxford Castle. He waved him to the seat beside him to take some of the nuncheon repast laid out.

'With Beaumont and all his knights gone, the castle has returned to being the home we enjoy, and I am not tripping over yet another knight or squire every time I turn a corner. How was your mission?' he asked, lowering his voice for that last sentence.

'Very successful. I would've been here sooner, but I had business for Chatillon at Winchester. However, my man met me outside the stables with the message that the package we sent to France arrived safely,' replied Edvard.

Sir Nigel nodded in satisfaction. Although their actions were harsh, they had deemed them necessary.

'Are you still determined to tell Rohese the truth? She has broken her heart over the death of that child and the departure of Malvais; I have never seen grief like it.'

Edvard, having recently and unexpectedly become a father himself, could understand it, but to Rohese, it was more than that—the child had been a link, a part of the man whom she truly loved.

'Yes, I will tell her tomorrow; I will ensure her sister, Lady Adeline, is with her as I am sure it will be a shock.'

Sir Nigel looked sceptical. 'If you must, but I am not sure. It could create further difficulties and sadness. The child she is mourning is suddenly alive but being raised by others; a child she will probably never see.'

'Yes, but a child who is alive. We both know De Courcy would have killed him,' whispered Edvard, conscious of servants hovering.

Sir Nigel was prevented from answering by the sound of horns being blown.

'God's blood, what now? Surely, this is not Beaumont back again so soon; Adeline will not be pleased!' he said, pushing himself from his chair and reluctantly walking across the stone-flagged hall to greet the newcomers outside.

Edvard followed and found the courtyard full of men, horses, colourful pennants, and flags, but at first, Edvard did not recognise the livery.

'This is all we need. You certainly cannot tell her about the babe while he is here,' Sir Nigel said in an aside to Edvard, who now recognised the lord, who was pulling his chain mail coif off his head before dismounting.

Sir Robert de Courcy, Royal Steward and husband of Rohese, had finally arrived to see his grieving wife. He mounted the steps and greeted Sir Nigel, but Edvard saw his expression of surprise as he recognised him.

'Edvard of Silesia! To what do we owe this pleasure? Is your master, Chatillon, here as well? The King does like to know when the Papal Envoy is in his country.'

Edvard gave a thin smile that didn't reach his eyes and ignored the jibe.

'No, Lord Chatillon is in France but will leave for Rome shortly. Pope Paschal is somewhat concerned that he has heard nothing from King Henry. Especially as he made such promises to the Holy See when we supported his claim to the throne. While Archbishop Anselm of Canterbury seems to have been struck dumb; it has been so long since he contacted Rome. Many believe Anselm is too old for such a prestigious post, and I know the Pope has several candidates in mind to replace him.'

De Courcy scowled; these were not comments he could answer, but he would make sure that the King heard of what were such veiled threats to him. He was also distracted by his son, William, who arrived and dropped to his knees in front of him for his father's blessing, which De Courcy gave, placing his hand on the boy's head. William had changed; he'd grown since his father had last seen him ten months earlier—inheriting the Grandesmil height. He'd hardly have recognised him as the boy got to his feet and looked him in the eye.

'I see you are in Sir Nigel's livery, William; I hope you are regularly training in the pell yard as well?'

'Every day, Father, I am proud to wear Sir Nigel's livery.'

'Yes, I am sure, and it was good of Sir Nigel to provide this as an interim measure, but I have other plans for you, William. We will speak later as I must see your mother.'

'I will send a servant to let her know you are here. Rohese is not coping well with your son's death. Meanwhile, come and broach a sack of wine with us, and you can tell us the news and what progress the King is making against Robert de Belleme.'

Once seated, De Courcy, still smarting from their last conversation, turned on Edvard again.

'What are you doing here in Oxford if your master is in France?' he asked.

'I am here to arrange and possibly pay the ransom demanded by Owen ap Cynan for the kidnapped Horse Warrior. The

King has agreed with Beaumont for us to pursue this,' replied Edvard.

'It seems a lot of fuss and wasted manpower to me for a mere Horse Warrior. We are in the middle of a civil war here in England, more important issues,' De Courcy sneered.

Edvard controlled his anger and took a long draft of his wine before replying while Sir Nigel's eyes moved nervously from one face to the other. He knew what Edvard was capable of, but he reasoned that he'd not kill the Royal Steward in his great hall as it would break the laws of hospitality, which were sacrosanct. Edvard wiped his hand across his mouth and sighed.

'You seem to have a very short memory, De Courcy, as Sir Georgio di Milan, whom you dismiss as a mere Horse Warrior, was on a mission for the King. He was one of your men when he was kidnapped by a black-hearted Welsh mercenary, a man whom you had foolishly employed and trusted. Owen also betrayed the King, deserting with Beaumont's silver in his saddlebags before the battle had begun,' he said, pinning the Royal Steward with a hard stare.

De Courcy dropped his eyes as he had no answer to this, so Edvard continued.

'Also, Georgio di Milan is one of the finest Horse Warriors I have seen. Trained by Luc de Malvais himself, he left at sixteen to fight in Spain, riding alongside El Cid against the Berber hordes. He then went to Byzantium to fight alongside Conn Fitz Malvais for Emperor Alexios, facing the barbarous Seljuk Turks on a daily basis. All this while you were cowering in the palaces of kings in a livery that never saw a bloodstain, with a sword that was rarely drawn in anger.'

With that, he pushed his chair back and rose to leave, but at the last moment, he turned to lean into De Courcy's face, and Sir Nigel blanched as he leaned back out of the way.

'One more thing. If I hear you belittling or disparaging Georgio di Milan again, I swear I will come in the night while you sleep and cut your tongue out.'

De Courcy, white-faced, had pressed himself as far back into his chair as he could, but now he blustered with outrage and humiliation as Edvard strode away. Sir Nigel let him protest and rage for a short time, but then the Castellan had had enough of him and held up his hand before the Royal Steward's face in annoyance, and De Courcy stilled.

'Edvard of Silesia is not a man many would ever challenge or take on; I am told he can kill a man with his staff before his opponent's sword is out of its scabbard. Your words to him were reckless and were made to offend, so what did you expect? He was right about Georgio di Milan—he is a brave and honourable knight, and many here pray that he can rescue him and kill Owen ap Cynan, who you may now remember also attacked your wife. She nearly died, Robert. Thankfully, Abbot Columbanus saved her.'

De Courcy felt chastised and humiliated by both men, so by the time his wife Rohese arrived with Lady Adeline, he was in no good humour. His greeting to his wife was cursory and cold, and as Adeline expected, he was certainly no comfort to her. De Courcy was shocked by his wife's appearance; she was much thinner, with dark shadows beneath her eyes; her clothes hung on her, and her hair was unkempt. She no longer resembled the beautiful, shapely lady-in-waiting for Queen Matilda with whom he'd fallen in love. As the child was dead, perhaps now was the time to put her away and find another wife. He pondered this for a while as he knew there were ways and means of doing this with the right amount of bribes.

Adeline watched De Courcy like a hawk; his offhand demeanour and narrowed eyes told their own tale when he looked at Rohese. So, later that evening, Adeline forced Rohese to make an effort, brushing her hair until it shone. She then used the tried and tested method of old bread crumbs and a rough cloth to exfoliate her sister's skin before applying egg white and honey for an hour to freshen and reduce any redness. Finally, she dressed her in her finest gown, and rubbed a mixture of hen fat, rose oil and juniper gum into her face, décolletage and arms. Adeline was pleased with the result as she led Rohese down to join the evening company for the first time since the babe's death.

To De Courcy's disgust, Edvard was on the dais nearer the staircase. He immediately stood, taking Rohese by the arm and leading her to her seat.

'You look very beautiful, and when your husband leaves Oxford, I have some heart-lifting news for you,' he whispered.

De Courcy was surprised but pleased by his wife's transformation, and he reminded himself of why he'd married her. Maybe he shouldn't be so hasty—after all, she was a Grandesmil, which counted for much. So he smiled, filled her goblet, and chose the finest morsels to put on her platter—all attention to her suddenly, which had consequences that neither Rohese nor Adeline had expected or wanted.

Rohese retired early; she was tired, and more than that, she was weary as she removed her gown. As she curled up in a large chair by the fire in her linen shift, she felt she had done her duty to be at her husband's side that evening. It was peaceful in the flickering firelight, and before long, she had fallen asleep. She was woken by the sound of the large wooden bolts banging into place on the door. She looked up, blinking, to see her husband standing there. He walked over to her, stood behind her and ran his fingers through the long, dark, auburn tresses, which fell almost to her waist. He came to stand in front of her and pulled her to her feet, holding her tight against his body. She could smell the strong sour wine smell on his breath as he kissed her. She tried to pull away, but his tongue was in her mouth, and his hands gripped her head. Finally, she twisted out of his arms, and he laughed.

'Why the surprise? Surely, you expected and wished for your husband back in your bed after so long apart. We have another child to make as you have lost yet another one, and with God's help, this next one will live. I need another son, Rohese—one is not enough for any man. Now, take off that shift and get into bed.'

'No, Robert, I cannot. You do not understand; it was a difficult birth, and then our babe died. I am not ready for this; I am still ill and grieving for our son. I will not do this!' she exclaimed. The slap when it came was not unexpected, as this was his way, but she still staggered back against the bed.

'Have you forgotten who you are addressing, Madame? I am your husband and will do what I will with you tonight and again tomorrow morning. I may stay several days with this pleasure to look forward to every day.'

Rohese knew he was right. She could do nothing, but anger was building inside her as she pulled her linen shift over her head and flung it on the floor. *I hope he dies in this battle,* she thought, as she laid her head down on the bolster. Through narrowed eyes, she watched him undress until, closing her eyes, she felt him climbing into the bed.

Chapter Three

Mid-June – Oxford

The next morning in the pell yard, De Courcy arrived to watch his son training and was quite impressed at the blows young William delivered to the pell, all of which would build muscle in his young arms. He was about to go and join him when he saw Edvard of Silesia on the far side, training a group of about ten men. He watched it all with a wary eye. De Courcy had heard that Piers de Chatillon insisted he and his men train every morning without fail, and Sir Nicholas was right—the big man was formidable with either sword or staff, moving with a swiftness and lightness on his feet that took him by surprise. William was excited to see his father watching him and redoubled his efforts to show him what he could do, but when he drew breath and turned, hoping for praise, his father was gone.

That night, they gathered again for dinner, and Adeline was concerned about the dangerous look in her sister's eyes as she sat in brooding silence beside her husband. Edvard arrived late into the hall and strode up to the dais to address Sir Nigel.

'I bring news, Sire. The rumours of the battle at Tamworth

are true. In less than a day, Beaumont and his knights defeated the force of Prince Iorwerth. They slaughtered over half of the Welsh rebels and captured the rest. Few of our men were harmed, and we lost none of our knights,' he announced, looking directly at Rohese, who gave him a grateful smile.

The men in the hall cheered at this news, but De Courcy was incensed that the news had come to Edvard of Silesia rather than to him as the King's representative. Yet again, he felt slighted by this man, so he stood to challenge him.

'How do we know this report is either true or accurate?' he shouted, trying to reassert his authority as the cheering faded.

Edvard laughed and turned to the hall.

'My sources of information are never false, Sir Robert, as you imply. Would you like me to list your current mistresses in Winchester and Windsor and where they live, or shall I tell everyone how much you paid for that showy, spavined, grey gelding you rode in on?'

There was much laughter at this, even amongst his own men, for De Courcy might have wealth and position, but he was not liked or popular, and his face darkened as Edvard continued.

'This news of the battle is from the horse's mouth,' he said, at which the men laughed again, getting the jibe.

'My message comes from our very own Gilbert Fitz Richard de Clare, who, with Malvais, led one of the main charges to destroy the rebel camp.'

The men cheered even louder, and Sir Nigel found he had to cover his mouth to hide his smile at De Courcy's discomposure. He glanced left and saw that De Courcy's face was suffused with anger, and his hand was resting on his dagger. Swords were prohibited in the hall, and Sir Nigel quietly reached over and gripped the man's hand, crushing it against the dagger's hilt.

'Not in my hall, De Courcy,' he hissed, as the Royal Steward angrily shook him off.

'You allow some unsavoury people in your hall, Sir Nigel, first Owen ap Cynan, then that damned Horse Warrior, Malvais—I hear he was here for weeks. I would lay silver my loving wife welcomed him more than me. I will be leaving this rat's nest early tomorrow, as King Henry expects me, and I will be taking William with me,' he spat at Rohese, whose mouth dropped open in shock.

'No, do not do that, Robert; I need to have William close, especially now, with the death of our son,' she pleaded, but De Courcy ignored her.

Sir Nigel and Adeline were dismayed but knew they had no say in the decision; De Courcy's word on this, or on anything related to his wife and family, was final.

Moments later, the Royal Steward stood and walked down to confer with his captains about their departure on the following day. Edvard looked at Rohese; her face had drained of the little colour it had, but as her husband left the hall with his captain, she escaped, bowing to Sir Nigel and making for the staircase. Edvard followed her. The noise from the hall covered their conversation as the musicians were getting ready to play.

'I hate him; I want him dead, Edvard. You are an assassin. Can you do that for me?' she pleaded, her face contorted in anger and grief at losing William as well.

He stood looking thoughtfully at her for a few moments as he weighed up the pros and cons of such a killing. He was not blind; he could see the bruises on her arms and wrists.

'The simple answer is no. He is head of the King's household, high in the King's court and favour, and it would make it all too convenient for you and Malvais. Questions would be asked, and glances cast in your direction, which may lead to the ruin of both of you. However, I can make sure he won't trouble you any further tonight or tomorrow.'

Rohese nodded, and unclenching her fists, she mounted the stairs while Edvard watched her go. This was the woman Malvais loved, the mother of his son. He'd do what he could to help her, but it was not the time for a risky assassination. However, anything could happen if the man was ever brave enough to ride out on the battlefield. He could paint a target on De Courcy's back with a purse for the man who struck him down.

Edvard returned to his seat, opened his pouch and extracted a small bottle. He took out the stopper and surreptitiously poured a small amount into the goblet of wine. He then topped it with more wine, and, catching her eye with a nod, he slid it along the table to Adeline. She was on the left-hand side of De Courcy, and she moved it gently into place, taking the original one away. No one saw as the musicians had struck up, and two young men were singing a lively and popular song. All eyes were on them, the men in the crowded hall tapping their feet and hands in time to the song.

Shortly afterwards, De Courcy returned. He was annoyed that his wife had gone to her room, and for an awful moment, he hovered on his feet, glancing at the staircase. It looked to Adeline as if he might follow her, even drag her back to the hall or worse, so she bade him sit back beside her.

'Come, Robert. We see little enough of you, and we love your tales of the happenings at the court. Tell us how the rebel Earl of Shrewsbury, Robert de Belleme, escaped from Arundel. We have not heard the truth of that. I believe Henry was enraged.'

Always susceptible to flattery, De Courcy sat back down, and Adelaide fixed a smile, putting a friendly hand on his arm and encouraging him, saying how much she enjoyed his wit and sallies. Two hours later, De Courcy was not only uproariously drunk but troubled with painful stomach gripes, which meant he couldn't move far from the close stool, and he certainly couldn't mount the stairs. When Adeline rose to leave, he was snoring with his head on the table.

She smiled at Edvard and whispered, 'Thank you.'

Early the next morning, a white-faced De Courcy mounted his horse, he was still bringing up bile, but he was determined to leave and join the King at Leicester.

'Bad meat, Sir Nigel, that is what this is! I suggest you beat your cooks. They are cheating you by buying rotten meat.'

Sir Nigel did not reply; he was too busy saying farewell to William, who was torn between the excitement of riding out with his father and the sadness of leaving his mother, who stood proud and angry at his side, determined not to embarrass her son by crying.

The steward brought out the parting cups, and a toast was raised to the King's success; Adeline handed De Courcy his cup with a smile, knowing what was in it.

'Come back soon, Robert, we do not see enough of you,' she said, forcing sincerity into her voice and expression, for she loathed the man.

The horns were blown to signal the passage of a royal envoy, the standards were raised, and they rode out of the castle, clattering along the streets of Oxford as they headed north to meet King Henry.

Rohese was still burning with anger and filled with despair.

She seemed to have lost everything: her babe, Malvais, and now William, she thought, as she sat in the bright light of the solar window with Adeline helping to repair linen. The door opened, and Sir Nigel and Edvard entered and waved the women to join them. Edvard smiled reassuringly at Rohese.

'What we are about to tell you will come as a shock, Rohese, but it was done for the best possible reasons. I urge you to listen to all that Edvard has to say before you ask the many questions you will have,' said Sir Nigel, in a caring and sympathetic tone that worried her.

She looked at both of them in concern as her mind explored the dire possibilities of what they might impart. Conn was alive, but was he badly injured, or had he married and returned to Brittany to remove himself from her orbit? Seeing the worried expressions flit across her now frowning face, Edvard reached across and placed his hand over hers.

'Do not fear; this is not bad news, but uplifting tidings.'

He then told her the story of the baby's non-existent illness, the swap of her son with a poor babe who had died, and how Joan and the wet nurse had taken her son to France. Rohese didn't speak; she sat stunned, looking at them in wide-eyed shock as she slowly took in what they were telling her. She dropped her head in her hands before running her hands over her face.

'I took flowers to his grave this morning and to the grave of Darius, as I have done every day since they died. You came with me, Adeline, and yet you did not breathe a word; you let me think it was my child I was mourning in that tiny stone cist,' she said, her anger at this heartbreaking deceit building.

Adeline nodded. 'It was not my secret to tell, and we had no choice, Rohese, as De Courcy had to see and believe your grief while he was here. And, we were waiting for a message to tell us that the child had arrived safely in France.'

Rohese looked at her in disbelief. 'Joan is alive as well? She did not die of the pox?' she exclaimed, her last words breaking on a sob for the cousin she had mourned and at the scale of this deception.

'Yes. She did it for you because she loves you. She wanted to go and be with your son. She will stay with him, love and educate him until he wields his first sword and has his own tutor. We had to do this; the babe was the image of Malvais. At the very least, De Courcy would have smothered him in his crib as soon as he set eyes upon him. He already has suspicions about why Malvais was here.'

Rohese, still sobbing, nodded almost absent-mindedly, the next question dominating her mind.

'Does he know? Does Conn know? Was he part of this?'

Edvard shook his head.

'No. His grief and pain are also genuine, and I know the loss of you and his son fills him with sadness. Rhodri, our Welsh druid, has kept in touch with me, and I am leaving today to ride north to Warwick. They will tell me there where De Clare and Malvais are headed after Tamworth. When I find him, I will tell him that his son, young Darius, lives and is alive and well in Chatillon-sous-Bagneux.'

Rohese, her eyes full of tears, looked up at that. 'He is with Piers de Chatillon and his family?'

'Yes. Isabella is expecting a child in August, and my son, Finian, who will be a year soon, is in the nursery, as is Dion's two-year-old daughter. Your son will be raised with them; they will be his friends and family, and he will be trained for knighthood. He will know his heritage, and he will know that you are his mother. I promise, Rohese.'

'You called him Darius. I like that. He was never a Robert—never a De Courcy,' she said with a sad smile.

'One thing you need to know: we thought it might be too dangerous to send him to Conn's family at Morlaix, but there is someone else who worked out the secret of the swap and who knows who his real father is.'

The tension in the room was palpable, as was the fear that they could lose their liberty if this information ever came to light.

'Who?' muttered Sir Nigel.

'Columbanus,' whispered Edvard.

There was shock on all three faces as they looked at one another.

'How does he know? That cunning and manipulative abbot is involved in every aspect of our troubles,' murmured Adeline.

Suddenly, Rohese put a hand over her mouth and, giving a low moan, she rocked forward.

'What is it?' asked Adeline in concern, moving to put her arms around Rohese.

'I can see him. When you said the name, I could suddenly see him—the black Benedictine. He is standing beside Owen on the path. I challenged them about Georgio, and Owen pushed me; he intended to hurt me because of what I had heard. Columbanus turned, and his face showed his shock as he reached out a hand to try and catch me. He was there. Columbanus did not come afterwards and find me—he stood with Owen ap Cynan, arguing over a ransom. He was unhappy that Owen had risked coming to Oxford, but having heard their conversation, I am sure the Abbot knows all about the kidnap.'

Edvard nodded. 'That confirms everything we suspected.

Rhodri was watching him like a hawk. However, I have dealt with the Abbot since, and we have reached an accord that he will not breathe a word about the child, and I will kill Owen for him.'

There was silence as they thought this through.

'But can you trust him?' asked Sir Nigel, who had always disliked the man.

'We have no choice, and he is more frightened of Chatillon. If he breaks his word to us, he knows he will pay. Now I must leave for Warwick,' he said, standing and bowing his head to Sir Nigel.

'Wait!' cried Rohese.

'I need to write to Malvais; I will bring it to you at the stables,' she said, heading for the door.

As it closed behind her, Sir Nigel breathed a sigh of relief.

'That went as well as we could have wished. I own I was worried about telling her, and now I have Columbanus to worry about too. I do not know how I will keep my hands from his throat if he comes here again.'

'I think that is unlikely. I believe he will keep his head down and nurse his wounds. I hope that Malvais takes the news as well as Rohese has. He is likely to land a blow before I have time to hand him the missive from her,' he said, half seriously.

When Edvard reached the stables, his man handed him two messages. The first was frustrating. The men he'd sent to Chester were very good at their job; they had searched the city, questioned and bribed locals, but no one knew of a captive Horse Warrior held there— not even a whisper. They had little more success with Owen's cousin on the sheep farm. With persuasion, he had admitted that Owen was there with his captive. His wife told them slightly more, but both were convinced that Owen was only collecting dues owed him in Chester and was then taking his captive into Wales. So they were no further forward. Yet Rhodri's words resonated—his grandfather, the old druid, was sure the Horse Warrior was held in Chester. He was determined to question Rhodri more when he caught up with him.

The second message was more disturbing; he knew immediately the thin strip of vellum with the coded message was from Chatillon. It was an order for Malvais; Piers wanted him to kill one of the King's men, someone Edvard knew and whom Conn regarded as a compatriot. This would be a real challenge for Malvais, who still wanted to be Chatillon's apprentice assassin, but since that decision, he'd been loaded with grief, more than a man should bear. Edvard was unsure that Conn was in the right emotional place to carry out this kill. He could easily do it for him, but he wouldn't; for all he knew, this might be Chatillon testing Malvais to see if he still had the desire to become an assassin. One thing was certain: he'd tell Conn that his son was alive and well and cared for in Chatillon-sous-Bagneux before showing him this second message.

Chapter Four

Mid-June 1102 – Stafford Castle

It was late in the castle. The torches were guttering in their sconces, and a few dozen men were dozing or snoring in the hall on their pallet beds. The great fire in the centre had almost died, but the castle dogs lay on the rushes as close to its warm embers as possible. It may be June, but it was a dark, cloudy night, and there was a chill breeze outside, enough to make Cadwgan wrap his cloak tight around him as he checked on the sentries and sent the next scouts out on patrol. He was determined that they wouldn't be taken by surprise as his brother, Iorwerth, had been. Entering the hall, he wound his way through the sleeping dogs and men and mounted the solid wooden staircase to the gallery above. At the end was a door to the solar, a large bright room in the daytime with its windows facing south. It was close to midnight when he opened the door, yet a blaze of light met him, lighting up the gallery behind him. Torches blazed in the wall sconces, and at least a dozen candles were lit around the table where several maps were spread.

As he entered, a tall warrior left, whom he vaguely recognised as one of De Tosny's henchmen; an Irish warrior and not a man to meddle with. He watched as his brother, King Maredudd, and Raoul pored over the maps on the table, pointing out features here and there. They argued back and forth over tactics, but De Tosny won as he would be the one to lead the attack on Beaumont and his army. Maredudd waved his brother over to stand with them at the table.

'Only the three of us and Raoul's henchman, O'Brien, know of this attack, and I intend to keep it that way. The men will be told that we are crossing the hills to the north, heading for the old Roman trackway, the Ryknild Way, as we intend to attack Burton-on-Trent. In fact, our men will swing northeast along the valleys and then up into the hills to set up camp on Tatenhill. From there, Raoul and his men can be ready to sweep down in three divisions to attack Beaumont's forces. One of Raoul's men used to live in Branston; there is a ford there, and his father farmed sheep on those hills, and he knows it like the back of his hand. It is an ideal place for an ambush as Beaumont's army will be strung out and vulnerable, easy prey for our men to attack.'

Cadwgan took his brother to one side, dropping into the chairs beside the empty fireplace. He lowered his voice as his eyes darted to De Tosny, who was still poring over the maps of the area.

'Sire, Sir Raoul insists on leading this attack despite our concerns. I am sure you and the whole camp know, there is bad blood between him and Beaumont, and I fear he will be distracted by his hatred of him,' he said, looking his brother directly in the face.

At that point, the large rebel lord, who may have been older but was certainly not deaf, clenched his fists. Turning from the maps, he came and stood over them, glaring at Cadwgan.

'Yes, I hate him—I make no secret of it. In the attack, he is mine—Robert Beaumont's head is mine. I will be the one to find him and kill him! However, my enmity towards him has never affected my planning and leadership; just make sure, Cadwgan, that none of your men kill Beaumont. I will be the person to deliver that last blow!'

Cadwgan could see the man's veins standing out on his temples, his hatred of Beaumont plain to see. But the Welsh prince knew that emotion like this was dangerous in battle. His father had taught him that at a young age, although it was a lesson his brother, Iorwerth, still had to learn.

Maredudd inclined his head towards his brother, raising an eyebrow to indicate he should answer.

'Thank you for your reassurance, Sire. I will ensure that your message goes out to all the serjeants,' said Cadwgan, bowing to the intimidating warrior.

Personally, he thought De Tosny was welcome to him, for he knew Beaumont to be a ferocious fighter who gave no quarter, but there again, so was the great Raoul de Tosny. They were well-matched; the outcome could go either way when those two met in battle.

King Maredudd stood and stretched.

'It is getting late, so let us abed, but go and alert your serjeants before you climb under your blanket; you will leave before dawn, Cadwgan, which will give you the time tomorrow to reach Tatenhill and set up camp. Raoul and I have placed you on the right wing with your cavalry. We want you to smash into the foot soldiers at the back, killing as many as possible. Your men can then loot the carts and wagons for horses, weapons and women. Raoul will be on the far left—cutting the head off the snake is his job. His captain is taking the middle section with the archers and foot soldiers. We will have the element of surprise; they will not know what has hit them. Our scouts have been watching their camp at Tamworth for days; we will know exactly when they leave. With that many carts and wagons, they have no option but to take the road to the west of the River Trent, and we will be waiting for them on the hills above.'

For various reasons, Beaumont's forces left the camp later than expected the following day. Messages arrived to say that Belleme's troops were seen at Dudley, and there was the chance of a counterattack on Tamworth. Vedettes were sent out, galloping southwest to see if any of this was true, while the men waited beside loaded carts and restless horses as the sun began to beat down from a clear blue sky. Rhodri sat under a tree with Conn and their men while De Clare was with Beaumont, waiting for the vedettes to return and confirm or deny what had been heard. The Welsh horse whisperer chewed a grass stem and regarded Conn, sitting, hands clasped, staring at the ground beneath his feet. He strode over and sat beside him on the fallen log.

'Sometimes, things are not as bleak as they seem, Malvais, and in the unlikeliest of places, you can find a little light to lift your spirits. Look over there—the beautiful young blonde woman sitting on the back of that cart swinging her legs, smiling for her husband, who is a serjeant for Philip de Braose.'

Almost unwillingly, Conn raised his eyes and turned to look at the happy sight as the serjeant leaned forward and kissed his wife. She cupped his cheek in affection, and Rhodri nodded in satisfaction.

'We never forget those who have gone, but remember to rejoice in those who still live, those we care for, and who look out for us. When we sat on the slopes of Cair Idris on our way to Lake Bala, I remember King Gruffudd ap Cynan saying that he believes the gods have been looking down on him to allow him to reach his forty-seven years. A short time later, you might remember that his horse suddenly slipped off the narrow track into the scree and slid downwards. Its hooves would not grip, but a quick-thinking Darius leapt from the saddle and grabbed its head collar, whilst anchoring himself on a large rock in the moving scree. Gruffudd laughed it off, but the long drop from that small scree slope over the cliff would have broken every bone in his body. The gods were truly with him on that day, as was Darius.'

Conn looked up again, met Rhodri's eyes and nodded.

'You are right, Rhodri, but the wound is deep when you lose someone close, someone you had responsibility for, and it takes far longer to heal.'

At that moment, a shout came from De Clare, and the horns finally blew as men mounted, and pike men and wagoners alike got to their feet to join the column heading north.

'Do we know how long it will take us?' asked Conn of De Clare whilst looking back at the straggling trail of men and carts, which was already raising quite a dust cloud.

'To Tickhill? It is about two days, I believe. King Henry and his army should be ahead of us now, but they are travelling the eastern route north through Lincoln. I believe the King has business there,' said De Clare, pulling his mail coif back off his head and wiping the sweat from his brow as the day was now becoming very warm.

They had travelled no more than four leagues, as De Clare realised he had forgotten how slow and monotonous it was moving hundreds of men, carts, large ox-drawn wagons carrying the barrels of beer and large pavilions, and the usual ragtag of dozens of camp followers across the country. The knights and cavalry could go no faster than a walking pace as they couldn't risk creating any sizable gaps between them and their foot soldiers. De Clare certainly remembered how the Seljuk Turks had taken advantage of these long columns when he was with Duke Robert on the Crusades. They would cut the columns in two and turn to wipe out the slower foot soldiers. The thought of those attacks unsettled him, and he waved Conn to follow him forward to catch up with Beaumont and Philip de Braose.

As he cantered ahead, De Clare scanned the forests and trees on either side that spread across the Trent Valley. To their west rose a range of hills, some steep, but as he scanned them, nothing stirred. Beaumont had scouts out riding on either side of the column. He could see two of them riding the lower slopes. He also knew that Beaumont would have sent the longer-range vedettes before them, ensuring they were not riding into an ambush.

'All quiet ahead?' he asked, as they reined alongside Beaumont.

'There has been no sign of enemy troop movement. Perhaps our attack on Iorwerth's camp has made them draw their horns in somewhat,' answered Philip de Braose, who was revelling in riding at the great Robert Beaumont's side.

The track had reached a slight rise, and De Clare squinted east across the valley floor. Most of it was covered in trees, and he knew how easily a large force could be hidden beneath their branches.

'I am more worried about where Belleme and his brothers may be as little has been heard of them since they burned Lichfield. He could be creeping up on our eastern wing, waiting for an opportunity to cross the Trent and attack us while we are strung out like this,' responded De Clare.

Beaumont shot Richard de Clare a sharp glance. He respected his opinion as he knew him to be a shrewd and experienced knight who had ridden in the crusade. He turned and ordered De Braose to send more scouts to cross and ride the river banks to the east.

They had covered almost five dusty leagues when they reached the ford at the village of Branston. Beaumont called a halt so they could water the horses and give the men a short rest.

Above them, hidden behind the crest of the hill, the three divisions of Raoul de Tosny's force were patiently waiting; their scouts were ahead, lying hidden in the scrub bushes below, reporting back in soft crow caws and bird whistles. Raoul knew his enemy was below him, but he wanted to wait until every one of Beaumont's knights had dismounted, and then they would attack, catching them off guard. Their horses, knee-deep in water, would be spread across the ford and shallow river sections, the knights and men on foot and therefore vulnerable to attack.

Cadwgan, impatiently waiting with his men for the signal, had finally ridden along behind the ridge to find out what was happening. De Tosny abruptly explained the delay and told him to return at once to his men. They would be attacking imminently, and all three sections must charge at once so the enemy would not, at first, know where to look or counterattack. As he reached his horse and mounted, he noticed a young man he recognised, one of Iorwerth's men. He was lying on the ground, tied and bound tightly, but it was clear that he'd been badly beaten; blood still dripped from his broken nose and mouth. Cadwgan also noticed that several fingers had been severed from his sword hand. He turned to the man holding his horse.

'What happened to him?'

'He was one of the enemy informers—he admitted it. He'd been taking money from an individual called Kenric, who thinks he can wander in and out of our camp at will. But next time, we will be waiting for him. This one made some feeble excuses about a crippled father, but he was riding across the hills to warn them that we were riding to attack Burton on Trent from the north. He nearly pissed himself in fear when he crested the hill and found himself in our camp last night. He tried to turn his pony and flee, but that henchman of De Tosny, the big Irish one with the scarred face, pulled him from the saddle. He sang like a bird when he took a knife to him.'

There was no sympathy now in Cadwgan's gaze as he stared at the bloodied prisoner; no matter his reason for betraying them; he was Welsh, from Powys, and a traitor. He didn't deserve an easy or quick death.

He cantered away and rejoined his men, ensuring they were mounted and ready. He observed the conflicting emotions on the faces of men that could be seen before every battle: excitement, apprehension and the odd flash of fear, quickly hidden while their hands nervously went to the hilts of swords and daggers. The sturdy horses they rode could feel the tension as well, and several had to be tightly circled to calm them so they wouldn't go too soon. Then, the signal came, and they surged over the top and down the steep slopes towards the foot soldiers, carts and heavy wagons trundling on the road towards the ford below.

Cadwgan let out a roar that turned into a screeching battle yell that all of his men joined in with. The men and women below turned to watch in horror at what was charging down the hillside towards them, and then the screams began. Most of the drivers and camp followers had seen the attackers before the foot soldiers, who were marching ahead to the ford. Dozens of women, some of them doxies and whores, some of them wives and sweethearts, ran for cover towards the river banks, many grabbing their children to hide them in the bushes.

The ambush had worked. The hundred pike men barely had time to lower their pikes, or the archers to take up their bows, before the Welsh raiders were on them, their swords slashing down. But despite that, Beaumont's men fought back like demons. This was not the peasant fyrd—these were trained troops who worked together, grabbing and pulling the raiders from their saddles and stabbing without remorse. Before long, however, it was clear that the Welsh horsemen were overwhelming them, and the ground was littered with dead and wounded under their hooves.

Like De Clare, up ahead, Rhodri had been uneasy on the far left wing for some time as they rode towards Branston Ford. He was still just ahead of the middle, escorting the lesser cavalry, but his eyes constantly went to the dark hills on his left, and he could almost feel the menace coming from those slopes. He shook his head at his foolishness, for as he scanned the hills and ridges, not a soul stirred. Then he knew! He reined in and stared intently; there was no sign of any wildlife, not a soaring bird or a rabbit. He kicked his big chestnut Destrier forward, ready to yell a warning to Malvais and De Clare, who were ahead of him at the ford.

Conn was standing on the river bank. He heard the yelling before he saw Rhodri and realised who it was, but he heard the word ambush shouted repeatedly. Then he could see Rhodri over the heads of the men on the crowded riverbank; he was ploughing his way through, people swiftly moving out of his path as he pointed up at the hills. Conn stared intently up at the hills but could see nothing. However, in the short time he had known him, he had come to trust Rhodri's instincts, so he yelled at his men to mount up immediately. He saw De Clare and Beaumont staring at Rhodri in disbelief but not moving.

'Mount! Mount up! To arms! We are under attack!' he shouted at them, and the surrounding knights, which sent them running for their horses.

Then, as Rhodri reined in his big horse beside him, he saw them. Like a wave, the enemy flowed over the crest of the dark hills. They were in three large groups, and he saw immediately that they were already about a third of the way down the steep slopes and would come at speed as they reached the lower slopes and meadow. He knew they would soon be on top of them, crashing into them, and most of their men were still in the water.

He ordered his Horse Warriors into line as he glanced back at the chaos. Men and horses were everywhere, the knights trying to pull their mounts out of the river, some on the banks, some trying to mount from the water, which was always difficult. However, Rhodri's warning had given them a slight advantage, and as the Horse Warriors trotted forward close together in line, he saw Beaumont getting his knights together on the far right. Conn's eyes swept across the hills; he estimated that about eighty cavalry were about to hit the foot soldiers on his left; no doubt the wagons and supplies would also be their target.

De Clare was close behind him, getting his men into some semblance of order.

'We are going back along the road to attack their cavalry on the left wing. Follow us as soon as you can!' shouted Conn.

Beaumont had now successfully rallied most of his men, although some were still in the river.

'We will attack the mounted right-wing, Malvais. De Braose take the middle; they are slower, mainly foot soldiers, bowmen and axe men by the look of them, trample the bastards down,'

'Shields up,' he yelled, as the Welsh bowmen demonstrated their skill with the first flight of arrows arching towards them. Conn heard several horses squeal in pain as the arrows found targets, but he now had his men in formation. They pushed into a canter, six wide rows of thundering hooves as they galloped towards the Welsh raiders on the left who were now in amongst their foot soldiers. Screams and shouts filled the air, along with the clash of swords.

Cadwgan wiped his brow. As he expected, the battle's first moments had been brutal and bloody. He had emerged unscathed, but his horse had a nasty cut on its shoulder, which would need stitching. He wiped the sweat from his eyes with the back of his hand. His men were clearly getting the better of the enemy, and he smiled. Then he heard the thunder of hooves. No doubt some of Beaumont's knights had rallied, so he shouted his men to turn and line up to face them. However, nothing prepared him for what he saw at the meadow's far end galloping towards them, and he stared in alarm.

He had heard the tales of the Breton Horse Warriors since he was young, but most were based on the famous Luc de Malvais, a legend in his own right, no doubt now retired. The cavalry coming towards him was a sight he would never forget. They began in perfect rows, six abreast galloping close in unison, but then, at a shouted order, they spread into longer lines of ten. The size and weight of the huge war Destriers they rode would terrify most men, and there was not a horse under seventeen or eighteen hands high. Every man wore the signature double swords on their backs, and at another order, they knotted their reins and drew both weapons. Cadwgan gave a glance at his cavalry; over half had rallied, but others, imbued with their success, were busy looting the wagons and grabbing the screaming women. Some others were still fighting the valiant foot soldiers who had formed themselves into clumps and were holding off their attackers with a ferocity that spoke of desperation.

'Turn and attack! Turn and attack!' he yelled as the vibration and sounds of the huge hooves filled his ears. He could see the disbelief and shock on his men's faces as they saw what was coming for them.

Cadwgan did the only thing he could; he rallied them as the famous fighting men of Powys, calling on their reputation and courage. Then, realising he couldn't fight with only thirty of his men, he did the unthinkable—he turned and fled, weaving his horse at a gallop back through the trees near the river. The crash as the Horse Warriors hit his men, the screams, and the clash of blades echoed around him as he rode on, trying to shut out the sounds behind him.

I am no better than my coward of a brother, Iorwerth; he thought as he ducked to avoid branches and quickly made his way to a thick copse of trees on a slight rise. He pushed his sturdy Welsh horse through the bushes and into the shade of the trees. From here, on the lower slope, he could see most of the fighting. Close by, he saw that his men stood no chance against the Horse Warriors, and the cheers of the remaining foot soldiers and bowmen were deafening as they renewed their attacks on his men, no doubt buoyed by the reinforcements. Cadwgan had to close his eyes as he watched them cut his men down—his men from Powys whom he'd known and laughed with as they had waited to attack.

He squinted into the distance to where Raoul and his men were engaged, but all he could see was a maelstrom of men and horses fighting; there was no indication of who was getting the upper hand.

'It should be us. We had the element of surprise—we should win this, and if he kills Beaumont and holds up his head, then surely it will be over,' he muttered. He turned sharply as he heard rustling behind him. Had they found him? He drew his sword, but relief filled him as one of his captains and his serjeant pushed their way through the bushes and undergrowth to where he sat on his horse.

'We are undone, Sire; no one can fight against those devils. They are killing our men or trampling them into the ground with the great beasts they ride. I saw two of my men brought down by a great black brute, and its rider was the most ferocious warrior I have ever seen.'

'That will be Malvais! Owen ap Cynan talked about him, the son of the famous Breton Horse Warrior. Yes, it is true they are formidable—but not unbeatable, and we should have been ready for them. Instead, many of our men had dismounted and were looting. They lacked discipline and did not get into line when ordered,' snapped Cadwgan in frustration. The captain reluctantly agreed and hung his head in shame, for he had tried to rally them away from the wagons to no avail.

'Look, Sire, our troops and bowmen in the middle are swinging left to attack Beaumont and his men. We may win yet. Should we ride out and join them?' shouted the serjeant, as he wiped the blood dripping from a deep cut above his eyebrow on the back of his gauntlet.

Cadwgan could see the melee of swords and horses among his men; there would be few cavalry left to join them. Also, he knew that they would be a visible target by galloping across to the far side. However, he was not truly like Iorwerth. His father's blood flowed strongly in his veins, and for all his strategic withdrawal, as he now thought of it, he knew he was not a coward.

'It will be a race, with those devils no doubt on our heels,' he said, looking at his captain, whom he'd known since they were boys.

The man grinned. 'But we are men of Powys, Sire,' he said, shortening his reins.

Cadwgan smiled, dug his spurs in, and they shot out of the copse down the slight rise and raced across the meadow. Lying low along their horse's backs, they galloped towards their own men, listening for the thunder of hooves behind them.

Gracchus, who had rested for a moment, saw them and shouted a warning. Malvais reined Diablo in, wiped the sweat from his face, and narrowed his eyes. He saw better horseflesh and the richly decorated cloak flapping in the wind behind the leader and laughed at the sight.

'Give me ten of your men, Gracchus, and you can clean up here. We are going hunting, for I believe that must be a prince of Powys.

Chapter Five

Mid-June 1102 – Bridgnorth Castle

Robert de Belleme, rebel Earl of Shrewsbury, watched his brother Arnulf pace back and forth across the chamber. Belleme had not paced for some time because of what he called his battle wound, but most people knew the truth, that the injury was inflicted by a woman whom he was trying to rape. To add insult to injury, she had plunged his own long dagger into his thigh, badly chipping the bone and pinning him to the ground. It then splintered, and the wound became infected. It had pained him and given him a slight limp ever since. Now, he let his irritation show.

'God's Blood, Arnulf, I am tired just watching you. Draw up a chair, pour yourself a cup of wine and let us all talk about this sensibly.'

A scowling Arnulf reluctantly came to join his older Montgomery brothers, Robert Belleme and Roger de Poitevin, as he angrily responded.

'I cannot believe Iorwerth would be so stupid. He lost hundreds of men in a reckless gamble.'

'And we have hundreds more. In all, it was less than a sixth of our Welsh forces. I have faith in King Maredudd; he is strong, and he wants the land and silver I promised him. He will not disappoint us. More importantly, what of your Irish allies? Any news?' asked Belleme.

'I have sent our friend, Gerald of Windsor, to my father-in-law, the King of Munster, telling him we need military assistance. A message arrived yesterday saying he'd agreed and that they had set sail for Pembroke.'

'Good, we need to shed no tears over Iorwerth's folly. I believe he has been banished to Mathrafal to recruit more men.'

Arnulf looked mollified by this.

'Do we have any news of what is happening at Tickhill?'

Belleme gave his trademark sneering smile. 'The Bishop of Lincoln has laid siege to the castle there, and with luck, it will keep him and his forces tied up for some time. Henry is going north at a snail's pace, visiting friends and signing charters on the way. At this rate, he might reach Tickhill by Yuletide.'

The brothers laughed at this joke. Henry was not a soldier; he would never be the man to repeat his father's famous forced marches through the night to surprise the enemy.

A knock came on the solar door, and one of their younger knights entered, followed by a dusty messenger.

'My lords, news has come of a battle near Burton on Trent. Raoul de Tosny and his forces have attacked Beaumont's army, which was heading north to join King Henry at Tickhill.'

Arnulf sat forward with a grin. 'It sounds like the arrogant Beaumont has been caught napping himself this time.'

Belleme raised his goblet in a toast.

'See, what did I tell you, Brother? It is only a foolish man, or an oath-breaking king, who dares to take on the might of the Montgomerys. Send a message to our knights and allies that I will give his weight in silver to the man who brings me Robert Beaumont's head.'

'I believe, Brother, there is a long line of those who want to kill Beaumont, and Raoul de Tosny is at the front of the queue—a huge man who weighs so much it may cost you a fortune in silver,' said Roger with a smile.

Belleme turned to the young knight who stood waiting.

'Send for more news at once, as the game will indeed be more interesting with one of the Beaumont brothers dead. Meanwhile, we will stay entrenched here at Bridgnorth for a little longer. Arnulf, I want you to ride to Stafford. It is barely a day's ride. Once there, consult with King Maredudd, as soon we will need to combine our forces and move east in a joint movement to trap Henry and his peasant army.'

Branston ford

Raoul de Tosny had waited for many years for this opportunity to kill or maim his hated enemy. While Cadwgan and his eighty men had galloped down the hill on his right towards the foot soldiers and the wagons, Raoul and his several hundred warriors had descended with a roar on the forces of Robert Beaumont. Those men tried to rally into formation, but dozens were still scrambling to mount their horses.

The noise of the two forces colliding shook the ground and echoed down the valley; shouts, screams, and the clash of blades filled the air. De Tosny's men had the advantage; the downward impetus propelled them forward, crashing into the knights and cavalry of Beaumont's men, slashing and trampling their foes. Before long it became a bloodbath, as the King's forces fought for their lives against the ebullient Welsh raiders who were overwhelming them.

De Tosny could see Beaumont in the centre of a handful of knights. His surcoat was blazoned with his family crest, and his pennant and standard flew above his head.

'We are coming for you, Beaumont!' yelled De Tosny in a scream of rage.

Robert Beaumont heard him and looked up. He saw his enemy's contorted face as he began to cut his way towards him through the rows of men in front. Despite his usual confidence and bravery, he felt his stomach knot, for this encounter had been coming for many years, and now, Raoul de Tosny had the advantage.

Looking down, Beaumont saw his gauntlet was slippery with blood, and he wiped it back and forth on his thigh before he grasped the hilt of his sword whilst taking his dagger in his left hand. He rallied his knights with a booming cry of, 'We are Beaumont men! On me! On me! A boon to any man who takes De Tosny down!'

Hardly were the words out of his mouth before he was fighting for his life as De Tosny and his ten warriors reached them. These men had ridden and fought at De Tosny's side for years, and they were very good. As Beaumont slashed and parried, he saw that his knights were falling to the ground around him, and suddenly, De Tosny was there; his great horse ploughed into Beaumont's mount, which shied away and then tried to rear. Beaumont's reins were knotted and dropped on his horse's neck, but he managed to control it with his knees and turn it away. It made no difference as De Tosny was on him, standing high in his stirrups; the big man was hammering blows down onto his raised sword, and Beaumont's horse was penned in by the press of others around him. His hand and wrist began to feel numb from the constant heavy blows, and suddenly, he knew he was going to die. He prayed that they wouldn't hack his body apart as he lay dying, or drag him away still living, to be impaled on a pole and displayed. He wanted a clean death.

The sheer force of De Tosny's sword from above was now forcing Beaumont's own blade back towards his neck and face. Sweat was running into his eyes. He tried to blink it away, but all he could see was his enemy's crazed grin as he pressed down with his great strength. The strain on Beaumont's arms was telling as he tried to keep the blade from his face, but he knew he couldn't hold it off for much longer.

Suddenly, there was an eruption of noise and crashing blades behind them, enough to cause De Tosny to falter, and Beaumont saw his enemy's gaze shift to something behind them. He took the opportunity to stab his dagger with all his might up into De Tosny's chest. He saw the surprise on the big warrior's face, but it didn't diminish his strength as De Tosny's blade, only a finger's width from his face, didn't waver. The dagger gone, Beaumont had no choice but to grab the blade of his own sword with his left hand, and despite the pain as it sliced into his hand, he pushed back with all his might with his aching arms, and the realisation hit him that he would fall under his enemy's sword.

All at once, another sword came swinging over his head. It brutally sliced into De Tosny's left arm and shoulder, making him reel backwards and freeing Beaumont. He glanced quickly behind in gratitude and saw it was Conn Fitz Malvais on his great black snorting beast. He began to breathe again, but he knew it was not over.

Conn and his men had thundered after Cadwgan and his men and were almost on their heels when a gap opened, and they were absorbed into De Tosny's men. The Horse Warriors found themselves facing a wall of enemy arrows and pikes. Conn swung uphill to go around them and come down behind the Welsh cavalry. He heard Beaumont's loud cry, and from the slope, he could see a big grey-haired warrior and his men cutting through to get to Robert Beaumont. He ordered his men into two rows and came down at a gallop into the crush of men. The Welsh were easier to identify on their smaller, sturdy horses and ponies. They also had longer hair and beards. But he soon realised that De Clare was right about one thing—they were ferocious fighters. It took too long to get to Beaumont, so he signalled his men to keep fighting while he went ahead. He kicked Diablo on. He'd seen the wariness of the enemy to come near the huge, biting, attacking horse, so he used that to force his way through.

Conn slashed left and right, keeping his focus on Beaumont's standard, while Diablo struck at anything in his path, his hooves knocking men flying. Then, looking up, he saw the standard go down, and he hoped and prayed that Beaumont was not dead. As he got closer, he saw that the Norman lord was in a life-or-death struggle with the big warrior. He could see the blade held at his leader's face, but at least a dozen men were fighting between them. He had no choice but to pull Diablo up into a rear. He knew the hooves would slash out at friend and foe alike, but it was worth the risk and could save Beaumont—he had seen how men lose hope and the will to fight if their leader is killed. The huge black horse went into the air on cue, striking out with his hooves at everyone within distance. Then he surged forward, knocking several men to the ground, and riders out of saddles, while blades crashed around them. Conn let out a Breton roar that was answered by his men behind, some of whom were slashing their way through to follow him.

After striking the blow, Conn watched as De Tosny backed away, his left arm hanging, the blood dripping from his fingertips and spreading over his shoulder and chest. He knew the old warrior was badly wounded, so he shouted at Beaumont, who had slumped in his saddle in relief, to finish him. The Norman lord raised his sword and drove his horse at De Tosny's mount, and as it shied around, he swung his sword at the older rebel's neck. As it sliced through flesh and sinew, De Tosny, now mortally wounded, toppled from the saddle and hit the ground as his horse, spattered with blood, pulled back and ran for any gap.

Conn whirled Diablo around to clear a space, then stood in his stirrups and yelled.

'De Tosny is dead! Your leader is dead, killed by the great Lord Beaumont! Lay down your swords or die by the swords of our men!'

He saw the shock register, replaced by panic, on the faces of some of their enemies. Cadwgan, on the far western edge of the crowd, heard it as well and knew all was lost, and it was time to go.

'Retreat! Retreat! Run for the hill and make a stand there if we have to,' he yelled.

His captains and serjeants took up the cry, and before long, it had turned into a rout as men rode or ran back towards the lower hills and the safety of the tree-covered slopes behind them. De Clare and De Braose made to follow them, but a weary and blood-stained Beaumont stopped them with a shout.

'Let them go. We do not want to lose more of our men. Look, they are already forming into groups and will fight like cornered rats to the last man if we pursue them.'

Conn looked around for his men. He was relieved to see the Horse Warriors, with Gracchus, were all there. They were seemingly unhurt or bearing minor wounds, wrapped in a bloody scrap of linen, still mounted and watching the Welsh attackers streaming up and over the hills. He ordered them to ride the horses down into the river to let them drink. The foot soldiers were already killing the enemy wounded, and several knights were chasing a few Welsh stragglers who had missed Cadwgan's call.

At that moment, Rhodri came riding up. He had been responsible for binding and holding the captives near the wagons. However, he now had a woman with him. Her face was tear-stained, her dress torn, and her hands blood-stained. Her blonde hair was tied back in a long woven plait. Conn recognised her from the other day—the girl swinging her legs on the cart, kissing her husband farewell.

Conn raised an eyebrow at him. 'Spoils of war?' he asked his friend, for he knew that Rhodri had a reputation for having a way with women.

'No, just a rescue. They killed her man; he was one of De Braose's men who was trying to protect the women and children. A few rebels had dragged her and another girl into the woods to take turns. I killed two of them; she killed the third with his own dagger, but she needs a physician as her hand is badly cut. I think it may need stitching. I could do it, but he can do a neater job,' he said with a brief smile as he knotted his reins, lifted her down and led her away.

They finally gathered on the river bank again as a blood-spattered Beaumont arrived and announced that it would make sense to camp close to the river for the night. They would bury their dead and see to their wounded men and horses.

'Promise me one thing, Sire: please do not start to burn the bodies until we leave. It took me days to get the smell out of my nostrils,' pleaded Rhodri, who had returned to untack his horse after leaving the woman with the physician.

Conn thought it was good to see Beaumont laugh as he called his squire to treat and bind the deep wound on his left palm. It would leave a scar, one no doubt to remind him how close he came to death at Branston Ford. He now stood and turned to the Welsh druid.

'Well, Rhodri ap Gwyfd, you have given yourself a job: organise a group of the captives with some ropes to drag the bodies of their compatriots over to the meadow and pile them up; we will set fire to them tomorrow as we leave. Serjeant Fox, organise a burial detail for our men and see to other casualties.'

As Rhodri handed his horse to Gracchus to take to the river, the young woman appeared again, her hand now bound with linen strips. She thanked Rhodri for all he'd done and told him she was a healer and had been asked to help the physician with the wounded. He smiled at her and nodded, but she didn't smile back; Conn saw that her face was still haunted by what had happened—the pain of loss was in her eyes.

'She is still in shock. She needs time to mourn, Rhodri. Does she have any family here?'

'No, but she has worked with the physician before. She is Saxon, and so is he, from Sir Philip's lands. He told me her name is Synnove, which means gift of the sun, and he said they had only been married for a few months.'

Conn could understand her pain as he watched her walk back to the river bank, but he noticed that Rhodri's eyes followed her.

June 26th 1102 – Blyth

King Henry had moved far faster in the last few days than Belleme realised, although the main part of his forces was still a day behind him. It was late afternoon when Henry, accompanied by Henry Beaumont and his courtiers, rode into Blyth to spend the night at the Priory, a large Benedictine monastery not far from Tickhill.

'I am enjoying the fact that I am now in the lands of Robert de Belleme. He inherited all of these lands when his older brother, Hugh, was killed, including the castles of Tickhill, Kimberworth, Laughton and Mexborough. I intend to take and hold them all, one by one, every one of his castles in England, so he has nowhere else to run. Any news from Arundel? Has it fallen yet, Warwick?'

Henry Beaumont, Earl of Warwick, shook his head. 'No, Sire, the Castellan there is very loyal to the Montgomerys, but Fitzhamon sent a message to say that he is negotiating a surrender and implying that their lord, Robert de Belleme, has deserted them—that he has left them to their fate to be executed as traitors.'

Henry laughed at this ploy; one his father regularly used when laying siege to a castle, when his Royal Steward, Robert de Courcy, appeared at his side.

'Ah, De Courcy, you have returned. I was sorry to hear of your son's death.'

De Courcy bowed in thanks. 'My Lord King, we are only two leagues from Tickhill. Do you wish me to summon Robert de Bloet, the Bishop of Lincoln, to join you here tomorrow?'

Henry nodded. His troops would begin arriving tomorrow, so he needed the Bishop to give him a clear picture of the siege at Tickhill.

De Bloet arrived the next morning, somewhat disconcerted to find the King already at Blyth, but was reassured by the size of the army filling the fields of the Priory. He found Henry with Beaumont in one of the fields; they were issuing the fyrd with pikes and training them how to use them effectively against cavalry. Bloet was astounded to see the King showing each man, in turn, how to embed it into the ground, holding it in place to wound the horses and bring the knights down. He'd heard it said that King Henry trained his men at Headley Down and Alton last year for the battle against his brother, Robert, but had dismissed it as a rumour.

Henry saw the Bishop of Lincoln hovering and waved him over to join him.

'My Lord Bishop, how goes your taking of Tickhill?' he asked, with a thin smile and a narrow-eyed cold stare that unsettled De Bloet.

'Honestly, Sire? We do not have enough men to lay siege and surround it, as it has a large bailey that runs north. We have launched several attacks, which they have repulsed. The walls are sturdy, and their archers are unfailingly accurate. Also, there are half a dozen hefty postern gates, holes, tunnels and exits from the castle. It is like trying to block a large rabbit warren with not enough nets. They have ample water and supplies and seemingly endless access to more. We could be here for months.'

'Do not fear, De Bloet, the rest of our men should be here by the end of the day, and my Earl of Warwick assures me that Robert Beaumont is on his way with several hundred more. Tomorrow, we march on Tickhill, and I promise that they will answer to their king in blood for their defiance.'

Chapter Six

27th June 1102 – Tickhill Castle

King Henry had ridden in with his entourage and now sat silently on his grey gelding, staring at Tickhill Castle's imposing keep and sturdy walls. The Bishop of Lincoln was beside him.

'As you can see, Sire, the walls are high and solid, the bailey is large, and the motte is one of the highest I have seen. With a solid double-storey keep on top, it is far more formidable than I expected. They put over a dozen archers up there on the walkway of the keep who are highly accurate and have killed several of my men and injured more.'

'No doubt the earth from the deep moat was used to make it that high. I remember Lord Roger de Busli building it. He was immensely proud of it, boasting he had used over a hundred men, and they had completed the first wooden one in only thirty days,' answered Warwick.

The King nodded but didn't take his eyes from the castle towering before them as he replied.

'I remember De Busli well. He was one of the wealthiest men in England, with immense lands and castles that Robert

64

de Belleme inherited. There was a child, was there not? A De Busli heir?'

'Yes, Sire. Sir Roger died in 1099; Belleme's father and he had been close friends. Roger de Busli II was only a babe in arms when his father died, and Robert de Belleme was appointed to the wardship of the child. Suddenly, when approaching his third naming day, the child died. Rumours abounded as Belleme stayed in the castle that night, and with the child's death, all the De Busli lands went to him. The child's family nurse was hysterical when the little boy was found dead, and she swore that Belleme had smothered him. The boy was not ill but had died in his sleep. His mother, Lady Muriel, was distraught, but refused to believe it of Belleme,' explained Warwick.

Henry narrowed his eyes at the figures standing on the keep while weighing up what Warwick had said.

'Given what we know of the Earl of Shrewsbury's ruthless, cruel and sadistic reputation, I would certainly not put it past him,' said the Bishop.

'The mother, Lady Muriel, wasn't she one of the young, pretty ladies-in-waiting around my mother?' asked Henry. 'I seem to remember she was one of my mother's favourites.'

'Yes, my Lord King. She was at least fifteen years younger than her husband, if not more,' answered Warwick.

'She is in there now, Sire,' said De Bloet.

King Henry whirled around to face the Bishop of Lincoln in astonishment.

'The Lady Muriel de Busli is inside the castle we have laid siege to? Why was I not told of this? Even my brother, Robert, refused to attack Winchester because Queen Matilda was there. He received accolades for being so noble. Now, Belleme will

65

accuse me of making war on defenceless noblewomen. Who is her Castellan? Or, God forbid, is she defending the castle on her own?' he demanded.

'Her protector is Fulk of Lisours; I think you know him, Sire, a worthy knight who served her husband and who donated, with Lady Muriel, to the building of St Mary's Priory at Blyth where you were staying,' answered De Bloet.

Henry was quiet and thoughtful for some time. He had to end this siege now. With his Charter of Liberties, he was putting himself forward as a defender of the people, so he had to offer her safe passage before this circumstance became commonly known. He turned and looked around behind him before pointing to a raised bank in front of the trees.

'I want my pavilion erected on there so that I can see everything and they can see me,' he ordered.

The Bishop haltingly intervened. 'Perhaps further back on that crest over there—it is equally high, Sire. The site you have indicated is too exposed and within range of their archers; we lost two sentries who stood within the trees on that spot.'

Henry was about to make a cutting reply when horns began to blow, and the Beaumont flags and pennants appeared on the road, followed by the standards of De Clare and the blue and silver pennants of Malvais.

'Warwick, your brother and his lords have arrived; he will no doubt tell us more of this skirmish he fought near Burton on Trent.'

'I think, Henry, you will find it was far more than a skirmish. The message said he was attacked by over a thousand Welsh raiders, led by Raoul de Tosny, as they made their way north from Tamworth,' replied Warwick.

'Well, let's hear it from the man himself,' said Henry,

watching a dust-covered Robert Beaumont dismount.

The other senior nobles followed him towards the King, while Sir Philip de Braose, seeing De Courcy, asked the Royal Steward where he wanted their men to set up camp and what provisions he could provide, as half of theirs had been looted.

Meanwhile, Robert Beaumont bowed before the King and greeted his brother.

'Well met, Robert. I believe you killed the great Raoul de Tosny, who has been a thorn in both our sides for many years,' said Henry with a welcome smile.

'I did, Sire, but it was a close run. He was only defeated and finally killed with the help of Malvais here, who saved my life. Our men fought bravely against great odds in this surprise attack, and the Horse Warriors put the Welsh Prince Cadwgan to flight, decimating his cavalry.'

Henry nodded his thanks to Malvais and ran his eyes over him, while Warwick congratulated his brother. Henry had not seen Conn Fitz Malvais since the previous year, but he thought the recent tragedies with his men had marked him. Looking at him now, he realised he shouldn't have listened to Ranulph Flambard's wild and manipulative rumour-mongering about him being his sister's child. Tall, broad-shouldered, his skin darkened by the sun, with his dark, shoulder-length hair, he was the image of his father, Luc de Malvais.

Conn was aware of the King's scrutiny and met his eyes with what he hoped was equanimity and calm.

'Piers de Chatillon told me many years ago in Paris that you would prove very useful to me, Conn Fitz Malvais, in the same way that your father and his brother, Morvan, became invaluable to my father. And Chatillon has been proved to be right. I promise I will see that you are rewarded for your service to us.'

Robert Beaumont, weary from the long ride, his muscles still aching from his battle with De Tosny, was pleased for Malvais but had heard enough.

'Sire, the weather is warm, and we have had a long, wearisome ride looking over our shoulders for another attack. Let us find a spot to sit and empty a sack of wine while we tell you of the ambush at Branston,' he said with a rueful smile.

Warwick ordered camp chairs and wine to be brought and placed in the shade of the trees further up the low rise, out of range of Lady Muriel's archers.

An hour later, Henry realised that the attack at Branston was far more serious than he'd first been led to believe.

'Significant planning went into this; they knew the route you would take and where you would be most vulnerable. You tell me they launched nearly a thousand men down the hills at you.'

Robert nodded. 'They were clever and well-hidden. If it had not been for Rhodri ap Gwyfd's instinct and early warning, we would not have known, for none of our scouts or vedettes saw them.'

'How many? How many men did we lose?' asked Warwick, of his brother, with a frown.

'Well over a hundred of our pikemen and foot soldiers; it all happened so quickly. They did their best but could not withstand the onslaught of Cadwgan's cavalry and archers. We lost twenty or so mounted knights and cavalry, and half of our supplies and animals were also driven away on our own carts, but we were helpless to stop them—most of us were fighting for our lives at that point. We have at least another hundred wounded. Most will recover, but as you know, Brother, this will take time.'

'And the enemy? How many did they lose?' asked Henry.

'I would say that Cadwgan lost nearly three-quarters of his cavalry in our attack, about sixty,' answered Conn, as Henry nodded in satisfaction at the damage they had inflicted.

'We burnt several hundred bodies, and there seemed to be large numbers of wounded running for their lives when they heard De Tosny was slain. We took no prisoners nor gave any quarter to the wounded left behind, just the mercy of a quick death. We all know they would have done the same to us,' said Robert Beaumont.

'All in all, I think we destroyed over forty per cent of their force,' commented De Clare.

The King seemed pleased as he took a mouthful of wine and regarded them over the top of his goblet.

'That should mean that with our recent success at Tamworth and now at Branston, we are making holes in the armies of Belleme's Welsh allies. I have been told we have also acquired a Welsh turncoat, a prince of Powys.'

De Clare inclined his head. 'Prince Iorwerth ap Bleddyn. No love is lost between the royal brothers of Powys; I am convinced he will betray them. When we order him to, he will lead King Maredudd and Prince Cadwgan into a trap of our making.'

Henry did not answer immediately but, deep in thought, stared at the walls of Tickhill Castle rising opposite them.

'As long as you are sure, De Clare, that he is not tricking us and that we are not the ones being led into a trap, for that is very much a strategy that Robert de Belleme would use.'

'Do not fear, Sire, for Iorwerth knows the consequences if he betrays us; there is no hole deep enough for him to hide in.'

Henry gave a short, harsh laugh. 'Yet this Welsh brigand, Owen ap Cynan, has done just that; you have still not caught him nor found a trace of the kidnapped Horse Warrior, who is probably kept in such a hole somewhere in Wales.'

De Clare, now tight-lipped, had the grace to look uncomfortable, but Conn was not letting that go, so he stepped forward.

'We have received the ransom note; the Welsh mercenary, Owen, will meet us in Shrewsbury in mid-August and says he will deliver Sir Georgio di Milan. We will be the ones laying the trap then, Sire, but I promise he will pay for his crimes against the Crown and against us,' said Malvais.

'Yes, De Courcy here tells me this renegade, Owen, attacked his wife, Lady Rohese, who, though dangerously ill, still managed to give birth. Then the child died, no doubt from the shock as is often the case with a bad fall. I had that experience with one of my mistresses,' he said with a knowing smile at Conn, who hadn't realised that the Royal Steward had returned from Oxford and was back with the King.

De Courcy now strode forward from the trees and addressed De Clare.

'Your men are now setting up their tents in the meadow behind the church. There is water and ample grazing for the horses; I have ordered fire pits to be dug to set up the roasting spits. Ignoring Malvais, who stood beside De Clare, he turned to the King.

'We were saddened by the loss of our son, and my wife, Rohese, sends her thanks for your concern and prayers. However, I have an heir who is now in your service.'

At this, he pushed his son, William, forward, who bowed to the King as his father continued with a grin.

'I worked hard before I left Oxford to make sure I planted

another one in her belly.' With that, he made an obscene gesture. They all laughed except Malvais and De Clare, who looked away. Conn's hands were clenched so tightly that his knuckles were white as he stared at the ground, intent on not letting De Courcy see that the barbs were hitting home. Seeing this, De Clare quickly changed the subject.

'Tell us, Sire, what are your plans for the morrow?'

'If my plan comes to fruition, we will not need to attack tomorrow, De Clare. All I want is for you to have your men ready—your knights mounted an hour after dawn. With the fyrd, we have thousands of troops here, and we will ring the castle with men and knights at least twenty lines deep so that Sir Fulk of Lisours and Lady Muriel will see what they are facing.'

With that, he turned to look behind at the group erecting his pavilion and waved a hand. His favourite mistress, one of many, Nest Ferch Rhys, the daughter of Rhys ap Tewdwr, King of the Deheubarth, walked gracefully across the grass. She bowed to the assembled nobles and smiled down at Henry, taking the hand he held out to her. Then she stood quietly, eyes downcast.

Conn had seen this renowned Welsh beauty before, but he'd forgotten how breathtaking she was with her long black hair and grey doe-like eyes. He knew she was still very young, only seventeen or so, as she was a hostage of the English court but had been in Henry's bed for at least two years. He also noticed how De Courcy gazed hungrily at her.

The King's mind was now obviously on other things as he dismissed them, and they made their way to the church to find their men. De Clare could feel the anger emanating from Conn.

'They are only words, Malvais—words deliberately delivered to wound. I doubt it is true, but even if it is, she is his wife, and he has the right.'

'Do you think I do not know that? But I know she will not have done so willingly.'

'So now, you are tormenting yourself with harsh images that probably did not happen. That way, anger and madness lie. I know this isn't easy, but again, I firmly advocate that you stop this affair. It is making both you and her unhappy.'

'I love her, Richard. I have tried to end it, but every time I see her, it feels like only days since we last met, and the desire to hold her in my arms and never let her go is overwhelming .'

'Do you think I did not understand the grip of such a love? I have been in a similar position. On our way to the Crusades, I fell in love with an Italian girl in Turin. Like Nest, she was a dark-eyed beauty with masses of black curling hair, and her father was a wealthy merchant. I pursued her, persuaded her into my bed, and her family disowned her. Francesca had no choice but to come with me, and I was head over heels in love with her despite my wife and children in England. We thought we were invisible, of course. Duke Robert turned a blind eye to her, but Bishop Adhemer, our spiritual leader, castigated me and told me to send her away. My friend, Chatillon, who always had women falling at his feet or into his bed, laughed at her hold on me, but he told me I was mad to keep her, building up trouble for myself. When we reached Lucca, she became big with my child but refused to leave me. When we reached Rome, she could not travel any further. She sobbed for days. I left her with friends of Chatillon and swore I would return for her and the child on the way back if i lived. It was the last time I saw her,'

Conn, moved by the story, was initially unsure what to say

but felt he had to ask.

'You abandoned her and your child?'

'No! Surely, you know I am a more honourable man than that, Malvais. When we reached Bari in southern Italy, a message awaited me. She'd died in childbirth; the child, a boy, only lived for a few days and followed her to the grave. So I know the pain of such love and loss, Malvais, but you are dicing with danger by loving Rohese; De Courcy is a dangerous man.'

There was silence for the rest of their walk to the meadow, each deep in their thoughts. They found Serjeant Fox and Gracchus had settled the men, and the horses were hobbled and grazing at the far end of the large meadow near the stream. The hundred or so men were enjoying the first leisure they had experienced for some time. Many were lying in the grass, sleeping in the warm sun. Several were dicing and betting while several barrels of ale had been broached, and the irresistible smell of roast lamb and pork was now filling the air. Conn stood, hands on hips, and smiled to see them when a cough suddenly came behind him, and young William de Courcy was there. Conn had never noticed before, but he saw the boy had Rohese's eyes.

'Sire, you may remember me...,' he started.

Conn laughed. 'Of course I remember you, William de Courcy. What is amiss?'

'Nothing, Sire. I watched you while you were practising in the pell yard in Oxford, and I wondered if I could train with you and your men while we are here. My mother says only one warrior and swordsman in Europe is better than you on horseback, and that is your father, Luc de Malvais,' he said earnestly.

Conn smiled; he might try to forget her, but here was her son asking for a boon. Behind William, De Clare was shaking his head, but Conn ignored him. Anything that angered Robert de Courcy would give him pleasure at the moment, and the boy came to him unsolicited.

'Of course you may, William, but we are all rallying after dawn tomorrow to surround the castle, so you may find yourself in the battle for Tickhill. If so, stay close to your father; you will be safe there.'

The boy's eyes shone excitedly at this, not appreciating the jibe aimed at his father as he bowed and ran back to the King's encampment. De Clare stood beside Conn and watched the young man go.

'I have said this before, Malvais, and you ignored it then, but I say it again: you are playing with fire. Under that somewhat bland exterior, De Courcy is a nasty piece of work, cunning and manipulative, and he has two important weapons: influence and wealth. Be careful.'

They both turned at the sound of hooves behind them, and a recognisable figure cantered off the track into the meadow with his men: Edvard of Silesia had returned.

'Thank all the gods,' murmured De Clare under his breath as Conn greeted his friend. He prayed that Edvard was here to tell Conn the truth about his son, for he was finding that secret increasingly difficult to keep in the face of his friend's grief. However, none of them knew how Conn would react to finding that his son was, in fact, alive and now being raised in France by Chatillon's family.

Chapter Seven

28th June 1102 – Tickhill

Dawn had not yet broken as King Henry lay wide awake, staring at the flapping roof of his pavilion; it seemed as if he hadn't slept since they retired the night before. He needed Lady Muriel to leave Tickhill Castle today; he needed the castle to fall to show Belleme he meant business. But how to do it was crucial, as he ran and reran the persuasive words he would use with her through his head.

His mistress, Nest, stirred slightly beside him and he glanced down at her; she was a constant joy to him as she revelled in his lovemaking. He slipped his hand down under the cover, and between her legs, he gently began to stroke and caress her, almost absentmindedly, as his brain still looked for better-honeyed words to use to Lady Muriel. Beside him, Nest began to softly moan and squirm, and he threw the cover back and moved her legs further apart so he could give her more pleasure. He heard her breath quicken as his mouth dropped to her breasts, and he gently bit her nipples until she cried out for him to take her. He grinned with anticipation as he spread her legs further and gently inserted himself inside

75

her, but only a half-thumb length as he moved back and forth, tormenting her as she tried to pull him deep inside her. He laughed with delight as she grasped his buttocks and begged him until, without warning, he plunged into her, making her cry out.

He'd never known such a hedonistic mistress who revelled in every caress and would happily beg him to take her several times a day. He reluctantly withdrew as he could hear the camp stirring around them. He kissed her gently and climbed out of the camp bed to pull on his braies and tied his chausses. He called for his squire, who laid out his best red velvet tunic, embroidered at the neck and hem with gold thread, while Henry splashed water on his face, shaking the droplets from his hair. Outside, he could hear the tramp of feet, and he knew, as the dawn light increased, that thousands of his men would be moving into position and encircling the castle of Tickhill.

Lady Muriel de Busli had been summoned by her Castellan, Fulk of Lisours, and now she stood beside him on the keep, watching the King's forces surround her castle.

'Completely encircled like this, my lady, we may last a month or two at the most. We have an endless supply of water from the two wells, but our food stocks will now have to be rationed as I doubt a cat could get through those enemy lines,' he warned, whilst watching her reaction.

However, he knew that Lady Muriel was no willow wand that would bend in the breeze; she was made of far sterner stuff.

'He hopes to intimidate us with this show of strength. He makes this threat, but I see no siege equipment, and keeping an army that size here will test his provisions. I can also see that at least forty per cent of his force is the fyrd, men who will want to be back on the land, with the crops due to be harvested in a month or so. If we wished, we could sit this out; after all, Arundel has not fallen yet. They are still loyal to Robert de Belleme.'

'But do you wish to do that, my lady?' he asked.

'Let us see what happens today. I know Henry. He was always an impatient child, and I do not believe he would be that different as a grown man. He will not want his forces tied up here—he will offer us terms. Also, I remember he was no soldier. He was nicknamed Beauclerc for a reason; his head was always in books and manuscripts.'

'He does not need to be, my lady. He has both Beaumont brothers there and Richard de Clare.'

'Gilbert Fitz Richard de Clare—what a handsome young man he was when we were all at court; we were all a little in love with him. But then he became embroiled in the rebellion of Bishop Odo against William Rufus and paid the price. Now, it appears he is back in favour. Bravo, De Clare, a clever and wise move. If I surrender to anyone, it will be to him.'

While he was casting a satisfied eye over the rows and rows of his troops and knights surrounding Tickhill Castle, Henry saw the figures atop the keep. He hoped this would give them pause for thought, for there must be four times the number of men he'd left with Fitzhamon to lay siege to Arundel. He waved Warwick to his side; he was older and far more statesmanlike than his brother, Robert.

'I need you to set up a parley with the Lady Muriel and Fulk at noon. Be tactful and diplomatic; tell her I was unaware she was in residence. I am offering her, with her Castellan and knights, safe passage to Blyth Priory,' ordered King Henry.

Outside the castle, De Clare sat with Malvais, Edvard, and Rhodri on their mounts beside their Horse Warriors. They laughed at Gracchus, who was trying to explain to Serjeant Fox how siege engines worked. The experienced serjeant, who had been on crusade with De Clare, staying at his side during the long siege of Antioch when they had to eat their horses or starve to death, was humouring the big Greek when the messenger arrived, reining in beside them. He bowed.

'Lord de Clare, the Earl of Warwick asks that you join him immediately in a delegation to request a parley.'

'Wish us luck. If Beaumont's honeyed words to the lady work, we may not have to fight at all,' said De Clare, as he shortened his reins and trotted towards the King's pavilion.

Malvais noted Gracchus' disappointment and that of some of his men at this news.

'Do not fear. I believe there will be many more attacks and skirmishes before this war is done. Robert de Belleme is not a man who will give in if he loses a castle or two,' he reassured them.

'Thirty-five,' added Edvard, while Conn raised a questioning eyebrow at him.

'That is what Belleme said in his speech at the King's Easter court—that he had at least thirty-five castles. How could he be expected to remember what he'd rebuilt at one of them?'

Malvais smiled; Belleme was known for his wit and sarcasm.

'Do you think he can defeat the King, Edvard?' he asked in a lower voice.

'It is all in the balance, Malvais. Both sides have significant numbers of knights and men, and as usual, Chatillon is watching, waiting, and sometimes trying to tip the scales in one direction or the other. But more of that later,' he said as he watched the King's envoys, holding the white flag of parley, ride towards the sturdy gates of the castle.

Lady Muriel, still on the parapet of the keep, watched them approach and, with a slight smile, decided to let them wait outside the gates for a while.

Close to the castle walls, De Clare could see that the moat was indeed deep, almost double the height of a man, with only a foot or so of water in the bottom. However, it was full of vicious spikes. This wouldn't be an easy castle to take, especially when attempting to get over the high palisade walls. They sat in the sun, a few horse lengths from the wooden platform that spanned the moat. It would be another hot day, and De Clare was already sweltering under his chain mail hauberk and coif. He glanced sideways at Henry Beaumont, whose face was becoming redder by the moment, a combination of heat, frustration and anger, as the longer they were made to wait, the bigger the insult to the King.

Finally, the noise of the great wooden bars being lifted and the heavy nail-studded gates being pulled open told them their wait was over. Dozens of archers appeared, bows at the ready, arrows nocked, standing on the hoardings inside the sturdy palisade. De Clare felt the sweat trickle down his temples inside his coif as he realized that at least twenty arrows were aimed at his heart, most of which could pierce chain mail at that distance.

Half a dozen horses emerged from the gates—a large War Destrier with the black-bearded Fulk of Lisours was at the front, and five armed knights were behind him.

Beaumont was disappointed that Lady Muriel was not there, but he would conduct the King's business with Lisours. He repeated the King's message verbatim, with the promise of safe passage and no recriminations, and he waited for a response, which again seemed a long time coming as Fulk of Lisours weighed up his words.

Finally, he nodded his head in a bow.

'I will pass on the King's message. If Lady Muriel de Busli agrees to the King's request for a parley at noon, we will hang a white flag over the gates. If not, I promise you we will defend this castle to our last breath.'

With that, he turned, and the cavalcade trotted back inside, the heavy gates closing with a thump behind them. De Clare shortened his reins and turned with Beaumont to ride back to the camp. However, he still felt as if he had a target on his back. All it would take would be for one overly eager archer, someone wanting to make a name for himself for killing the great Beaumont or De Clare. He'd seen it happen before. With some relief, they moved out of range and trotted back into their lines, where he pulled the chain mail coif from his head and wiped the rivulets of sweat from his brow and neck. Dismounting, he led his horse back to their position in the lines as he heard Beaumont shouting the order to the serjeants to let the men stand at ease but maintain their position.

'I hope I am not included in the King's delegation again. I was not sure we would get back alive,' he murmured to Edvard and Malvais.

'Do not fear; they would never kill you under the flag of parley; these are knights of honour,' said Philip de Braose, who had walked up to join them.

This certainty, with a touch of arrogance from an inexperienced knight, was too much for De Clare.

'What an ideal world you live in, Philip, where knightly honour, loyalty and trust abound. I have seen parleys broken and messengers killed on at least six occasions; one of them even stabbed through using the parley flag pole itself. Our King has broken every one of those knightly principles over the last few years. Why would anyone trust him now?' he asked in almost a whisper.

Sir Philip frowned at this stain on King Henry and was about to reply when Edvard raised a hand.

'Let us have no more talk such as this. We may all be trusted friends here, but those around us with flapping ears are not, and I have a far more important question. Why is Rhodri, our Welsh warrior, carrying a full trug of herbs?' he asked, watching the white druid emerging from the tree line behind them.

Then Synnove appeared behind him with another flat trug basket piled just as high, and Edvard gave a low whistle.

'Ah, all is revealed—a Saxon or Norse beauty, I would venture to guess. Rhodri does have a way with the fairer sex; I hear he left a string of broken hearts behind him in Oxford.'

Malvais smiled and tried to excuse him.

'They are friends only; her husband was killed at Branston, and he sees himself as her rescuer and protector.'

Edvard laughed again. 'So, we are looking at a mirror image of myself and Mishna? I was her rescuer and protector for almost a year before I became her lover. Look at us now, husband, wife, and parents of a demanding little boy.'

They all laughed at his expression as he pretended that he had no say or control over those events when they all knew he had immediately fallen in love with Mishna as he helped nurse her back to health.

The temperature rose over the next hour, and there was little shade for men or horses as they all waited for Lady Muriel's reply to the King's overtures. Malvais and De Clare ordered the squires and grooms to bring the leather buckets of water for the horses, whose heads were hung low in the heat, flicking the annoying clouds of flies from their ears and eyes.

Finally, just after noon, the large white parley flag, a linen sheet, was hung over the gate, and they all breathed a sigh of relief, for it meant Lady Muriel would speak to the King. It was still possible that they would have to attack the castle and set to building siege ladders and towers, but most hoped that the King's appeal for them to surrender and save their lives would work. Beaumont ordered all the troops back to their feet, and the knights remounted. The parley this time was all pomp and circumstance, as is often the case. The horns were blown on both sides, standards and pennants abounded, and De Clare was summoned again, this time by Robert Beaumont. He went reluctantly with his squire at his side, proudly flying his long-tailed gonfalon with its red chevronels.

'The Lady Muriel has requested you to be there specifically, De Clare. Is that because you were also once a rebel, or is it because of some long-ago dalliance?' he said, cynically.

'I would like to think it was because we were friends long ago at court, and she knows she can trust my word. How many can say that of you, Beaumont?' he said, with such an engaging smile that Robert was not sure it was said in jest or with any serious intent.

Again, Sir Fulk of Lisours led the way on his war horse, but beside him rode the Lady Muriel on a dun-coloured palfrey. They stopped on the bridge, close enough to go quickly back through their gates if necessary, and waited for the King's party to approach. De Clare noticed that the archers were back in position, but in deference to parley with the King, the bows were on their shoulders, and the arrows un-nocked. The King rode slowly on his favourite dappled grey gelding, flanked by both Beaumont brothers, who were ever watchful, their hands resting on the hilt of their swords. They halted two lengths away and regarded each other in silence until Lady Muriel finally inclined her head in a bow as Fulk made his announcement.

'You have requested a parley, and we are here to listen. Lady Muriel de Busli is the aggrieved party here as she has done you no wrong. Yet you have sent troops to assail a defenceless woman in her home. Is this what you promised when you were crowned as King? Will this be the legacy of King Henry of England?'

Henry could feel his anger building at those words. He wanted the Beaumonts to strike this knight down, but they were in parley, and he could not do that.

'My lady, we have not met for some time, but I have happy memories of you in my mother's court. I was not told that you were in residence here at Tickhill, but as I am sure you are aware, Robert de Belleme has rebelled against the Crown and brought in foreign troops and Welsh mercenaries. They have occupied Stafford Castle, and we were expecting to find his brothers Arnulf Montgomery and Roger de Poitevin here at Tickhill. Even so, I am surprised you had not surrendered the castle to the Bishop of Lincoln, as your King ordered you to do.'

'As I am sure you will realise, Henry, I am in a difficult position. My liege lord, Robert de Belleme, ordered me to

83

hold this castle in the same way as the castellan of Arundel has been ordered. The De Busli motto is '*fides et honor*'. That is what we were taught to believe in. We have lived up to that motto, and we swore our loyalty to the Earl of Shrewsbury many years ago when he had the wardship of my son. We are not in the habit of breaking oaths; they are important to us, and our word and honour are everything.'

Henry heard Robert Beaumont growl beside him at these words and their implications, and he felt the heat rise to his cheeks. However, his anger would not achieve what he wanted here, so he took a deep breath and forced a smile to his lips.

'Lady Muriel, in only days, we can, if forced, bring siege towers and engines while our battering rams will destroy your gates. I have several thousand men who will storm your walls, looting, pillaging, and slaughtering your people. They will follow my orders to give no quarter, and they will kill all inside, even you. I will spare none, for I spent many years watching my father, and I assure you that I am his son in many ways when my will is blatantly thwarted. What use then, as you lay dying, is your motto of '*fides et honour*'? Will that sustain you or your ladies as they are passed from man to man?'

De Clare was shocked at the King's words, although from past experience, he knew how ruthless Henry could be. He noticed that Fulk and Lady Muriel had paled at those words, so now he risked the King's anger as he pushed his horse forward and saw the archers above unshoulder their bows.

'Lady Muriel, the King understands your dilemma, and I assure you that he was genuinely shocked to find you here in the castle. Even Robert de Belleme would never expect you to sacrifice your life and that of your people against a force several thousand strong; at Arundel, he faced only hundreds, but he still ran and escaped. Your courage is noted and applauded by all who hear it. Your loyalty is unquestionable as you have managed to hold out for so long. Please consider the King's generous offer for you and your people to go free with safe passage if they lay down their weapons. None will be hurt if they leave; you have the King's word on that,' he said, turning and looking Henry full in the face. The cold, hard-eyed stare that met him gave him pause for a few moments, and he prayed Henry wouldn't now reject it out of hand. Then, the King nodded with a thin-lipped smile.

'What De Clare says is true, and in front of all these witnesses here, I give you my word. You will no doubt need time to consider this,' he said, shortening his reins and getting ready to leave.

'No, Henry, I will take your offer. Tomorrow morning, I will open the castle gates, and we will leave. However, I will only surrender to Count Gilbert Fitz Richard de Clare, who will escort Sir Fulk, my knights and me to Blyth Priory.'

With that, she turned her palfrey and rode back through the gates, which closed behind her. An apprehensive De Clare stared after her, wondering if, by saving her, he'd destroyed himself. Would he now face the King's wrath?

Chapter Eight

29th June 1102 – Tickhill

Despite Lady Muriel's agreement to surrender the castle, King Henry felt slightly nervous the next morning, but he hid it well as he waited with the Beaumont brothers and De Clare for the castle gates to open. It would be the utmost humiliation if she refused to leave after his threats, and despite De Clare's protests, Henry had insisted on lining the road south on either side with mounted knights and pikemen as a show of strength.

Malvais and Richard de Clare were to one side, ready to ride forward and greet them as they emerged to accept the keys to the castle. This was a token gesture but an important one. Finally, the large, heavy wooden gates were pulled open, and the knights and garrison of Tickhill Castle came out in surrender. They made a show of dropping their weapons in the appointed place, but Malvais was sure that every man there would still have a dagger or probably two secreted about their person.

In the centre was Lady Muriel, with her ladies and courtiers around her, all dressed in their finery to show their status as part of the once wealthy and powerful De Busli family. De

Clare rode out to greet her with Malvais at his side, and as the column stopped, they bowed to her in respect. The traces of the court beauty she once was were still there, and with her head held high, she looked positively regal as she held out the heavy keys to him.

'I know how difficult this must be for you, but by doing this, we are saving lives on both sides,' he said as she smiled and, leaning over, took his hand.

'I would have surrendered to no one else but you, Richard de Clare. This warrior beside you must be Conn Fitz Malvais. I have heard much of you, and you are the image of your uncle,' she whispered.

The words startled both of them and seeing the surprise and shock on their faces, she gave a tinkling laugh before whispering again.

'Yes, I knew about your birth and rescue, but I was the only one of the Queen's ladies who did. We were in Normandy that summer, and I was with Queen Matilda when she escorted your mother, Constance, to Falaise. It was heartbreaking but necessary. King William would have exploded in wrath if he had found out his daughter was with child, and he would probably have killed your real father, Morvan. Now, let us go. I need your escort for my people and me to the priory at Blyth, for I put no trust in Henry Beauclerc.'

With that, she gently kicked her horse on and rode proudly forward, giving King Henry only a slight bow of the head as she rode past him and the Beaumont brothers. It took some time for the long column of troops, archers and local people to leave. No one would risk staying behind in the castle, so they took all their worldly goods. Carts and mules were piled high with everything from furniture to cages of chickens, and

Conn could see how nervous they were, their eyes darting back and forth as they ran the gauntlet of the long line of Henry's troops on either side.

As the last of the column passed by him, Henry glanced up with satisfaction at the castle that was now his, the first of many he would take from Robert de Belleme. He turned to Robert Beaumont.

'The men may go in and loot—they will no doubt find the wine and ale stored there—but nothing is to be destroyed or burnt; make sure the serjeants and captains keep some control over the men. I will initially install Robert de Bloet to hold it for me until I appoint a new Castellan.'

'What now, my Lord King? Do we move onto those castles nearby?' asked Warwick.

To his surprise, Henry did not answer for some time, still staring up at Tickhill Castle before turning his horse away and returning to his pavilion.

'I will call a council for noon, then decide what and when our next move will be.'

Once they had completed their escort of Lady Muriel and had seen her people and men settled into the meadows around the Priory, De Clare went to take their leave of her. She was sitting in the sunshine of the cloisters, and Fulk of Lisours stood watch over her.

'I bid you farewell, my lady,' said De Clare, taking her hand.

'Where will you go now?' asked Malvais.

'I will go with my cousin, Fulk, to Sprotborough and reside there until this civil war is resolved; it is a peaceful place and will be far removed from what occurs next. Henry will no doubt push us out of his mind. I have sent a messenger to Belleme to tell him what has occurred here, as I have no doubt King Henry will now take Mexborough and Kimberworth castles. Once he has escorted us, Fulk will take our men, and he will join Belleme at Bridgnorth; they will be more useful there. As I said to King Henry, we keep our oaths. My people will no doubt wait until Henry's troops have vented their fury on the castle, and then they will return to the village below to try to salvage their lives and homes. I have no doubt that De Bloet will be put in charge, and he will still need servants and artisans, so many will return to Tickhill.'

With that, they clasped arms with Fulk in farewell and left them to make their plans.

'Will Henry leave them alone?' asked Malvais as they mounted to ride back.

De Clare nodded. 'For a while, yes, but Fulk has lands in York and Nottinghamshire, and once Henry finds he has gone to fight for Belleme, they will be forfeited, and he will be forced, like many, to return to his lands in Normandy. Henry is particularly unforgiving to those who rebel against him.'

They arrived back in time to be called to the King's Council. To the astonishment of many, no sooner were they gathered than the King announced he was disbanding the army for a time. There were several gasps at this, and Robert Beaumont, unable to contain himself, stepped forward. The exasperation was clear in his voice as he ignored his brother's warning frown.

'Sire, are you sure this is wise? We have defeated their Welsh forces twice and taken one of his castles, and there is no doubt that we will have Robert de Belleme worried. This pause will give him time to regroup and bring in further mercenaries!' he exclaimed.

Henry raised an eyebrow at Beaumont. 'You are questioning my wisdom?' he asked in a tone that was a clear warning.

Henry Beaumont, glaring at his brother, stepped in.

'My Lord King, my brother Robert has borne the brunt of the last two battles. He has fought bravely for you and bears injuries from those clashes. I can understand his frustration when we feel we have delivered crushing blows that we should build on, but perhaps that is because he does not see your larger plan or strategy.'

To De Clare's surprise, Henry conceded, presumably because he valued the Beaumont brothers and didn't want to alienate either of them.

'Perhaps you are right, Warwick—further explanation would help. I summoned the fyrd, but now I am sending them home at an important time of the year to tend to their crops and animals. This pause will give us all breathing space, and I intend to reconvene our forces in August. Once I have discovered Robert de Belleme's whereabouts, we will launch an attack on him and his brothers,' he said, in a finality that prevented further challenge or comment.

However, Philip de Braose, ignoring the warning signs, bravely stepped forward.

'Sire, as you know, I have a large ring of informers in the Welsh camp and amongst the Montgomerys. I received news this morning that Arnulf Montgomery is at Stafford Castle with King Maredudd. Robert Belleme and his brother, Roger, are at Bridgnorth, but I have been told that Arnulf will leave Stafford to join them there in a few days. We could lay an ambush and kill or capture him.'

Henry stared at the young knight and considered it. They could see he was torn, but he shook his head again and turned to Henry Beaumont.

'No, Henry, you can return to Warwick with your garrison, train your men and prepare, for if Belleme remains at Bridgnorth, that will be our next target in a few months. Robert, if you are keen on action, you, De Clare, Malvais, and De Braose can take the other two smaller castles at Kimberworth and Mexborough. De Courcy has told me they have small garrisons, which should be no problem after what happened here at Tickhill.'

Robert Beaumont bowed in assent, but as the King turned away, Robert glared at De Courcy, who was no soldier or strategist. *So this is who is dripping poison into the King's ear,* he thought, throwing his hands up in frustration as the Royal Steward, De Courcy, continued.

'The King will leave today for Stamford. From there, we will go to Rockingham to hunt in the Royal Forest; any of you not otherwise engaged may join him there if you wish. He will then go to Woodstock, and finally, he will join the Queen and Princess Matilda at Winchester.'

Malvais was another who saw De Courcy's self-satisfied smirk. He knew they would now be engaged in hot and troublesome sieges for the next months. As he turned to follow Beaumont and De Clare out of the King's large pavilion, he noticed that Edvard and Rhodri were on the periphery and he waved them outside.

'You heard?' he asked.

Edvard raised his eyebrows and shook his head at the news.

'He has been badly advised, as this will also give Belleme the chance he needs. The King should be holding this position, consolidating while he has the advantage to strike now. That's what his father and even Duke Robert would have done;

William would force march an army overnight and still win the battle when he appeared from nowhere the next morning.'

De Clare sighed. 'I think someone wants to be back in the comfort and safety of the royal palaces where he never gets his hands dirty or, God forbid, bloodied,' he said.

Just then, De Courcy emerged from the pavilion behind them, and they all burst into laughter when they saw him. He coloured up, knowing that it was directed at him. He stopped and glared at them, trying to find something cutting to say.

Rhodri, unable to resist, turned to Malvais.

'If we can, after taking these smaller castles, which will apparently open their gates to us, we should go back to Oxford for a few weeks; we both have unfinished business there and graves to visit.'

Malvais couldn't resist a side glance at De Courcy, who, red-faced and tight-lipped, turned and strode away. Edvard frowned at Rhodri.

'That was foolish, my Welsh friend, for he is not a man who will forget a comment like that. Be careful around him, Rhodri ap Gwyfd. Do not underestimate him,' he said, but Rhodri laughed it off.

All was bustle and preparation for the king's departure. Tents and pavilions were dismantled, and caparisons were unfolded and brushed down, ready to decorate the King's horses and entourage with his crest. Warwick and Robert Beaumont were with their captains, explaining their plans and giving orders to round up the men still disporting themselves in the castle. The Bishop of Lincoln, Robert de Bloet, came to find the Beaumont brothers to complain of the mayhem and debauchery that had been unleashed on what would be his home for the next few months. Neither of the brothers appreciated his comments, and Robert Beaumont's temper was only lightly reined in.

'We are clearing the castle over the next hour or so, my Lord Bishop, but I would remind you that they are in there on the King's orders; the men need their rewards, small though they may be,' he snapped at the prelate.

The Bishop was not to be appeased as he turned away, muttering about the sights he'd seen when he ventured into the keep and the toll that men's baser instincts would take on the local people.

Malvais was surprised but pleased that most of his men were still in the camp. It was mainly De Clare's and Beaumont's men who had gone into Tickhill Castle to see what loot was to be had. He shared the plans with them and was leading Diablo out of the horse lines to groom when William de Courcy appeared at his side again.

'I have come to take my leave of you, Sire, and thank you, but unfortunately, we ride to Stamford, so I will not be able to take you up on your offer of training.'

Malvais could see the disappointment on the boy's face as he walked over to Diablo and, reaching up, stroked the big horse's neck. To Conn's surprise, the big Destrier did not snap his teeth at him. William saw his surprise and grinned.

'Darius used to let me help groom him before he was killed, and after that, I helped Rhodri with both horses.'

'Well, young William de Courcy, you are one of only five people who have ever done that without being bitten or kicked. You must also be a horse whisperer,' he said, lowering his voice as if it were a secret.

This delighted the boy, who glanced over his shoulder as he heard his father shouting for him. His face fell.

'I must go, but I wish I was your squire—that I was coming with you to attack the next castle,' he said before turning away to trot towards his father, who cuffed him hard on the ear and gripped him by the shoulder.

'You have kept us waiting while we looked for you. What were you doing over there?' he growled.

'Taking my leave. I trained in the pell yard with them in Oxford, and sometimes, I helped groom Diablo. I want a horse just like him when I become a Horse Warrior; my mother says that Malvais will get me one,' he said with an air of defiance.

De Courcy spat on the ground in contempt.

'A Horse Warrior? A sell-sword mercenary? No, William. You will become a knight and rise high in the King's favour, following in my footsteps. If you want a better horse, I will get it for you. Stay away from them, or you will be punished.'

However, the Grandesmil blood flowed hot in the young squire's veins; he was his mother's son.

'Those men are knights as well, but they fight and earn the title. Malvais is my mother's friend; he saved her life when Flambard's men attacked her in the King's camp, and he rode hell for leather to get the medicine for Abbot Columbanus that brought her out of the stupor after the fall,' he said with a stubborn look that reminded De Courcy of Rohese, before he cuffed the boy even harder, making him stumble and nearly fall.

'You never go near them again. I am your father; you obey me. Do you understand?' he said forcefully, and William reluctantly nodded.

However, as they walked towards the mounted column of the King's knights, De Courcy's mind was working overtime. Malvais was at Oxford with Rohese for weeks, but she was in seclusion, injured, and about to give birth; he couldn't possibly have seen her. He put his arm around his son and softened his tone.

'You know I only want what is best for you, William. I will appoint a swordmaster for you when we reach Winchester, and one day you will be a great lord like Warwick, leading the King's army out to the field.'

He saw hope kindle in his son's face and smiled while pressing home his advantage.

'Yes, there is no doubt that Malvais is a great warrior, and I know he has been a friend to our family. Tell me, William, did he see your mother once your new brother was born?'

William was apprehensive and hesitated, unsure what to say, but his father encouraged him.

'Once or twice, I think. My room was beside hers, and he had a distinctive voice, but the knock and Aunt Adeline's voice woke me; he only wanted to see if my mother was recovering and to see my new little brother.'

They had reached the horses by then, where his sour-faced, older squire was waiting, having wasted some time searching for the boy. De Courcy could not question his son further in front of the squire, but an unwelcome seed had been planted in his mind. The horns blew, and the King's entourage, including several hundred men and at least a dozen knights, set off along the dusty, rutted roads to Stamford while the dozens of carts and spare horses trundled in their wake. His mind occupied by what he'd heard, De Courcy threw the unwelcome thought back and forth as he trotted along beside his son, not far behind the King. Suddenly, he jerked the reins hard and pulled his horse out of line.

'I have forgotten something; I will catch up shortly,' he

shouted at his squire.

He pushed his horse into a canter to the rear, where the wagons with the King's pavilion, furniture, hangings, and wine were following on sturdy wagons.

Three men were escorting the wagons. They were not guards or soldiers but men he'd found several years ago when Henry was first crowned king. He'd found them in a tavern near the Thames in London, an unsavoury place, but he had hired them no questions asked, and they had proved invaluable to him ever since. He didn't doubt that they had several ways of making extra money, as some of the supplies slipped into their sacks and were sold, but he was happy to turn a blind eye. Now, he waved them out to one side.

'I have a task for you—a purse is yours when it is done.' He saw the sudden gleam of interest in their eyes, but then he paused.

His original plan had been for them to attack Malvais, to beat and cripple him somehow, breaking his legs so he could never ride again, as the thought that the babe may not have been his child was now eating into him. However, he was astute and realised that Malvais might be too difficult a target. What would happen if he killed two of these men, which he could well do? De Courcy had seen him in the pell yard, taking on four at a time; Malvais might then capture and question the third, who would no doubt squeal like a pig under his blade.

Instead, he would hurt Malvais by attacking one of his friends, the big Greek man, Gracchus or Edvard of Silesia, but no sooner did he have the names than he dismissed them as he knew Edvard could kill all three of his men. As for Malvais, anything could happen in war. He could pay half a dozen men to paint a target on the Horse Warrior's back. And, of course, there was still Owen ap Cynan—the man owed him. He could promise the Welsh mercenary liberty and freedom from pursuit. He knew the man had no loyalty to any side, no patron, so he could use him while convincing King Henry that he had been a spy for them all along. Suddenly, he smiled as he realised which of Conn's men he'd target.

The three men watched him, uneasily glancing at each other in the long silence while waiting for him to speak. Finally, he explained what he wanted and gave them the name.

'I want him beaten so badly, he will not be able to stand. Break as many bones as possible, but make sure you are not caught. Tell Beaumont that I have sent you to guard his supply wagons after what happened at Branston; he will undoubtedly be grateful.'

With that, he threw them a purse and promised the rest of the silver after the job was done before turning and galloping off after the King. The three men stared after him with smiles on their faces. This broke the monotony of guarding wagons and could prove very lucrative.

Chapter Nine

30th June 1102 – Kimberworth

It was only half a day's ride to Kimberworth, not much under three leagues, but they were late in starting, as many of the men were hung over from the celebrations the day before. They had finally found the huge butts of ale, and rich barrels of Burgundy wine, in the large buttery next to the storerooms of the keep.

'Bishop Bloet will be very disappointed; he hoped the fine wines Lady Muriel had stored would be locked away, that the men would not find them,' said De Clare with a grin as he had no great liking for the man.

'Do you think a mere lock would have kept a hundred thirsty men out?' asked Edvard, laughing as he saw the sorry state of some of the men.

They had followed the old Roman road, for Rhodri knew there was a ford over the River Don where they could water the horses. Beaumont was taking no chances after Branston, and he'd sent out a dozen vedettes to search the area and the roads ahead, placing even more sentries around the column as it snaked ahead. De Clare reassured him that these lands were held by Baron Nigel Fossard, loyal to King Henry.

'Only when we head north to Kimberworth do we cross into the lands that Belleme took from De Busli.'

'I want you and Malvais to ride ahead, scout out this castle, see how it is defended and how many men they have deployed, for that will influence where we camp tonight.'

De Clare nodded and went to break the news to their men.

'We need about twenty or so Horse Warriors—where is Gracchus?' he asked, scanning the group, but Rhodri answered.

'He is down at the ford, supposedly watering the horses, but he has been there for a long time, and I think he has an audience in some of Beaumont's men for a few of his wilder tales.'

Conn narrowed his eyes at the group standing on the bank. He didn't recognise the men, but Gracchus was laughing and joking with them.

'Go and tell him we must leave now,' he ordered.

Rhodri strolled down in time to hear the end of the story about Emperor Alexius' pet lion being killed in the attack on the palace in Constantinople. The men were fully engrossed, but he knew Gracchus to be a good storyteller. He clapped the big man on the shoulder and nodded to the men with him.

'Come, big man, we must go; we are riding out immediately.'

He was turning to go when the largest man, a thick-set individual, put a hand on his bare arm. Rhodri looked at the hand in surprise and then up into the man's face. He had a deep scar above his eye that spoke of an old but significant wound. However, the man was smiling as he removed his hand.

'Are you the one they call the white druid?' he asked.

Rhodri did not answer but looked with interest at the other two, one of whom looked away, unable to meet his eyes.

99

'Is it true that you can do magic?' asked the man who appeared to be their leader.

'Druids do not do magic; they merely harness what has been given to us by nature, and we call on the spirits of the earth, the mountains, the trees and streams to help us. Sometimes it works, sometimes it doesn't. Like some women, the spirits can be fickle.'

'Warts!' exclaimed the man as Rhodri, taken aback, raised his eyebrows in surprise.

'There are more and more of them. Can you harness these powers to cure them? They say that druids can cure them,' he said, holding out his hand. There must have been ten warts, many badly bitten as the man had tried to chew or scrape them off.

'Warts spread if you bite them or make them bleed; they are very contagious and could spread to your lips or mouth.'

The big man looked worried and wiped his mouth hard on his tunic.

'I will ask the physician to mix a potion of cider vinegar and dandelion sap. Put it on them daily without fail; it will kill the hard skin, gradually making them disappear.'

The big man cocked his head and gave him a long, thoughtful look and then thanked him. As they left, Rhodri turned to Gracchus.

'Not the usual people I see you spending time with. Do you know them?'

'I have seen them before—they were at the King's camp way back at Alton. But there seems no harm in them; they are hired swords to protect the supplies. Beaumont does not want to lose his wine again,' he laughed.

Behind them, the three men led their horses from the water

and walked them back to the carts and wagons. 'Is that the one?' asked Samuel, the tow-headed man in his late thirties, a well-muscled individual.

Wilken Crick, the big man with the warts, nodded. 'I want you to watch his habits. Where does he go? Who is he friendly with? But pin a different expression on your face. You look nervous. It's not a good look, as it gets you noticed and makes you look shifty.'

'It's the word druid; no one mentioned that he is a druid. I heard stories about them as a boy—human sacrifices and everything. There are some things you don't meddle with, Crick.'

'And, he's one of them Horse Warriors. I've seen them train. I wouldn't want to take them on if they came after us,' said the third, and youngest of the three.

'Like old women you are, frightened by a few tales of bogeymen or riders with two swords on their backs.'

They had the grace to look sheepish as they mounted, but Samuel was not done.

'There's no smoke without fire, Crick. That's all I am saying about those druids.'

Crick shook his head at them and made to trot on, then cast a comment over his shoulder.

'Get friendly with the big Greek; he will know all about this Welshman. Admire the horses; they spend a ridiculous amount of time cleaning them up. We get to know his habits, and then we have him.'

Late June 1102 – Bridgnorth

It was silent in the room and had been for some time as Arnulf and Roger Montgomery exchanged nervous glances. Arnulf had recently returned from Stafford Castle, and the news was not what Belleme wanted to hear. He hadn't said a word yet; he had limped to the stone-mullioned window and stood, gripping the sill whilst staring out over the manor fields and forests beyond. They had seen Belleme in a rage several times over the years, and usually, he tended to strike out at anyone near, but this was different. They could feel the anger emanating from him in a cold fury.

Arnulf finally plucked up the courage. 'What do you want us to do?' he asked in a barely audible voice.

'Do? What can we do when incompetents surround us?' Belleme exclaimed, in such an icy voice that the brothers exchanged glances again as he turned and faced them.

'A month ago, our army outnumbered the King's by two to one: Montgomery forces, Welsh allies from Powys, Raoul de Tosny and his five hundred trained men. Yes, Henry summoned the fyrd, but our army would have cut down his men from the fields with pitchforks. I felt then that our victory was certain. Now, I find Iorwerth let his troops be almost wiped out at Tamworth, and what should have been a victory for us, with an ambush at Branston, turned into a rout. De Tosny was slain, and over half of his men were killed or taken. The damned Horse Warriors almost obliterated Cadwgan's cavalry, and now Henry is laying siege to Tickhill castle with over a thousand men.'

Roger de Poitevin was more optimistic than his brothers, and he tried to lift Belleme's dark mood.

'Come, Brother. Yes, I agree, these numbers are not negligible, but I believe we still have the advantage. Arundel has not fallen, and Fitzhamon is still tied up there. We burnt and looted Lichfield, and King Maredudd has taken Stafford with little resistance. The King's men are tied up in sieges while more of our men are pouring into Bridgnorth and Shrewsbury daily. We need to stay with our original plan to attack Leicester, which had been promised to Robert Beaumont, Count of Meulan. Let us do that now and burn it to the ground while Henry's troops are split and tied up elsewhere; let us leave bare a stick or stone standing.'

Belleme regarded his brothers through narrowed eyes. They were right. At present, they did have the advantage. Why not use it? Ravaging an area that Beaumont coveted appealed to him. He was opening his mouth to agree when a knock came on the solar's door, and a squire appeared in the doorway to announce a visitor. Sir Fulk of Lisours appeared looking hot, tired, and dusty. They could see as he bowed to Belleme that he'd ridden hard.

'My lords,' he said, bowing again as he took a message from the leather tube he carried and handed it to Robert de Belleme.

'It is from the Lady Muriel de Busli. I am ashamed to say that Tickhill has fallen, but we were vastly outnumbered.'

Belleme closed his eyes for a few moments in frustration at this news before unrolling the missive.

My Lord Earl and dear friend,

I have done my duty for as long as possible, holding Tickhill Castle for nearly a month for you, but the odds are overwhelming as Henry has brought thousands of men to surround us. I have no choice but to leave tomorrow

morning. He has offered us all safe passage as long as we disarm. Fulk has done his best, and his archers have killed dozens of the King's men, but it is just a drop in the lake to the huge horde that Henry has gathered. I have asked De Clare to escort us to Blyth Priory safely, but Sir Fulk of Lisours will ride on to bring this to you at all speed, and he and his men will join your service. I give you good luck, Robert. May God be with you in this quest to destroy the Oathbreaker and restore the rightful king, Robert of Normandy, to the throne.

Lady Muriel de Busli

Belleme looked thoughtful for several moments before he passed it to his brothers to read, and then turned to his guest.

'You and your men are very welcome, Sir Fulk. Arnulf, arrange for my armourer to supply Fulk and his men with whatever they need.' Fulk nodded his thanks to Belleme; he'd served with him several times before.

'How many men are with you?' asked Roger de Poitevin.

'Almost a hundred and thirty, plus twenty of the best archers,' he said, wiping the sweat and dust from his brow.

'So King Henry kept his word, and the castle was allowed to empty unchallenged,' commented Roger.

Fulk nodded. 'Henry made a great play of not attacking a woman once he discovered she was still in residence.'

Belleme gave a harsh laugh. 'Copying the ploy he used on Duke Robert at Winchester. The Duke decided he couldn't attack Winchester and seize the treasury, which would have ensured him the throne of England because Queen Matilda was in residence and was with child. The truth was that the babe inside her must have been no bigger than a walnut, but Robert refused to attack, and it lost him the crown.'

Fulk shook his head at the foolishness of that decision as he'd been there with Duke Robert's forces in Hampshire.

'However, Sire, I have further news for you. Lady Muriel sent one of our informers from the King's camp to gallop after me. Henry has decided to disband his army.'

Belleme blinked in astonishment. Looking at his brother's faces, he saw the same shock and surprise registered there.

'Disbanded?' questioned Belleme in a tone of disbelief.

'Yes, Sire, the fyrd has been sent home, back to their fields, and the King was leaving for Stamford before returning to Winchester.'

'What of the Beaumonts? Where are they?' demanded Arnulf.

'Henry has been ordered to return to Warwick, and Robert goes with De Clare to take two more of your castles at Kimberworth and Mexborough. Neither of them was happy with the decision to disband,' replied Fulk.

Belleme limped to a chair, waving the exhausted Fulk to another, and signalled Arnulf to pour them all wine. With his chin on his fist, he considered this sudden, unexpected move.

'Why? What is Henry's thinking? Why has he done this? Has he given up? Or could he possibly no longer see me as a threat?'

His brothers had no answer for him, as they were as surprised and puzzled as he was.

'I believe a breathing space was mentioned,' added Fulk.

'A breathing space in the middle of a civil war? What nonsense! This could be Henry's undoing; he has become overconfident given his unexpected victories at Branston and Tamworth,' declared Roger.

The characteristic cynical smile appeared on Belleme's face

for the first time.

'This could indeed be the biggest mistake Henry has made. Send messages to our captains and to King Maredudd with this news. Henry may need a breathing space, but we certainly do not; we will recruit, train and rearm. Then, I will unleash our forces on him. Meanwhile, I am about to shut down one large ring of informers, as I have recently discovered who supplies King Henry with much of his information. I have paid a high fee for the removal of a far too busy knight who is confident and arrogant enough to think he is one step ahead of us. He is on dangerous ground, which is about to open up and swallow him.'

Chapter Ten

30th June 1102 – Kimberworth

De Clare and Malvais sat in the shade of the trees, staring at Kimberworth. This was a smaller castle than Tickhill, but De Busli had been busy again. This keep was of stone, and again, it was surrounded by a high, sturdy palisade. The gates were firmly closed, and the houses in the small village looked empty, with their doors and shutters barred. Not a soul stirred, and not even a village dog barked.

'They knew we were coming and are prepared,' murmured De Clare.

'I can see about a dozen men on the hoardings but no archers yet,' replied Conn.

'Let us ride around it and see if a relieving force is camped anywhere in the forest or meadows over that hill. Maybe if we are lucky, we are only dealing with the castle's occupants.'

They sent out scouts and rode around the manor lands and fields, but there were no signs of any reinforcements.

'Do we know who the Castellan is? If not, can we find out?' De Clare asked Serjeant Fox.

He took two men and cantered towards the mill he saw on

the hill nearby. The sails were turning, so the miller would no doubt be there. An hour later, he trotted back to find them on the western banks of the River Don, where Beaumont had decided to set up camp, only a short ride from the castle.

'The miller tells me the Castellan is an older knight—Sir Geoffrey Ware. He and his family came over with King William at the conquest and have held the lands around here ever since,' reported Serjeant Fox. Beaumont frowned at this news.

'I know the name but cannot place him. A lesser knight of no consequence—this should not be a problem. Water your horses. We will ride there in an hour; a hundred men should suffice. We will see if Sir Geoffrey will parley. If, as you say, the castle is in defensive mode, then we must presume that he is Belleme's man.'

'Not necessarily. Remember, these were De Busli's lands, another knight who rode with King William at Hastings. I would lay money, Sire, that Sir Geoffrey was one of his friends or compatriots,' interrupted an ebullient Sir Philip de Braose.

De Clare raised an eyebrow. Young De Braose had become very familiar with Robert Beaumont to challenge him like that. He had noticed, several times, how he seemed to take this senior lord to one side to impart news or ask for orders. But Philip was ambitious, and De Clare didn't blame him. He probably should have done more of that and built powerful allies at that age.

Two hours later, they were outside Kimberworth Castle. Malvais and the Horse Warriors were in formation behind Beaumont and De Clare. Philip rode beside them carrying a flag of parley. They were an impressive force with flags and pennants flying. De Clare raised his eyes to the hoardings above, but Conn was right—there seemed to be no archers, only armed men with spears. Beaumont waved Sir Philip forward, and only a few horses' lengths from the gates, he made his announcement.

'Sir Robert Beaumont, Count of Meulan and envoy of King Henry of England, calls for Sir Geoffrey de Ware to account for his actions in denying access to the King's representative.'

Malvais saw a grey-haired figure appear on the hoardings. A dark, younger man was beside him as they stared down at the armed force in front of their castle.

'I do not open my gate to a group of armed warriors who come to rape, pillage and loot as they did at Tickhill. I promised my people my sword and my protection, and I would give my life to do my utmost to keep that promise. And if I should fail or fall in battle, my son will do the same.'

Robert Beaumont sighed and rode forward to rein in beside Sir Philip.

'Sir Geoffrey, you have my word that it did not happen like that at Tickhill. The Lady Muriel, Sir Fulk of Lisours and all their men and villagers were given safe passage, and we would offer you nothing less.'

The old knight turned to one side and consulted with his son for several moments.

'I rode with your father, Roger Beaumont, who was the King's cousin—a great man who was terrifying in battle with his great black beard. Your father was a man you could trust. I have not heard the same of you, young Beaumont. There is too much at stake here to take you at your word.'

De Clare saw they were about to turn away, so he pulled off his coif and rode forward beside Beaumont, for he'd recognised the old man and realised who he was.

'I swear, as God is my witness, that you can trust Robert

Beaumont's word because it is the word of King Henry himself. You were a friend of my father; you fought alongside him. I cannot understand why you now risk your life for the likes of Robert de Belleme, who was no doubt involved in the death of the young De Busli heir. Your king is asking for your loyalty instead, and if you denounce Belleme as he asks, you and your family will remain unmolested on your lands.'

Beaumont frowned at De Clare, who had not been permitted to offer so much. It was quiet for some time, and Malvais watched with interest as the figures disappeared from the hoardings. He glanced at De Clare, who was rigid with tension, as so much depended on the old knight believing him. Malvais wondered if his friend had overplayed his hand this time, for Robert Beaumont did not look happy.

'You had no right to do that,' Beaumont hissed at De Clare.

'This old knight saved the King at Hastings. When William's horse was speared with a pike from under him, Sir Geoffrey and his men put a ring of swords around the King to protect him from the Saxon axe-men until another horse was brought. Do you want to be the man who attacked and dragged this knight out of his castle in chains? Henry is trying to win over the people of England with his Charter of Liberties, not leave a trail of fear and slaughter.'

Beaumont grunted in reluctant acceptance. Part of him knew that De Clare was right and that sometimes a velvet glove was better than a mailed fist.

'I accept that here you may have acted wisely, but as you well know, fear and slaughter are often needed as well to keep control.'

De Clare allowed himself a small smile as he knew he'd won, but he prayed Sir Geoffrey would listen and understand the message he was trying to convey. Shortly afterwards, the gates were pulled open, and Sir Geoffrey and his son rode out to halt in front of them. The old knight bowed formally to Beaumont but smiled at De Clare.

'Gilbert Fitz Richard de Clare, I remember you as a highly annoying child, always full of mischief, always in trouble. I was astounded when I heard you had joined Robert Curthose to ride in battle against his father, King William, at Gerberoi. More worryingly, you drove King William off, his first defeat at the hands of his son and his friends. I remember your father was mortified by what you had done and retreated to his estates in Suffolk.'

De Clare smiled. 'It took me a few years to win my father round. Fortunately, King William forgave Robert and pardoned the rest of us cadet sons, which helped.'

Sir Geoffrey nodded and indicated the man at his side.

'My son, John, and I have discussed your offer, and you are right—we have no love for Robert de Belleme, a vicious and sadistic man who takes after his mother, Mabel, one of the cruellest women I ever met, who would put the eyes out of any tenant who challenged her. Yet his father, Roger Montgomery, was like your father, Beaumont, one of the greatest men in England. So, we will declare for the King and swear allegiance.'

At that, he rode forward and clasped arms with De Clare and Beaumont. Malvais noticed, however, that the son, John de Ware, did not. He remained aloof.

'We would like you to be our guests tonight. I am sure that a real bed, good food and wine will be more attractive than another night in your tent, and I look forward to hearing the news and the truth of what occurred at Branston, for rumours abound.'

De Clare could see that, despite all his initial discontent, Beaumont was pleased with the result as he accepted the offer of hospitality. Malvais, however, was watching Sir Geoffrey's son, obviously a knight in his own right, but his eyes shifted, and he could see he was nervous. Malvais felt uneasy; something about this man didn't feel right, and for some reason, he recognised him. He had a distinctive thin white streak of hair in amongst the black, obviously from a head wound at some point, and he knew he'd seen that before but was unsure where. However, he knew such streaks of white were common in knights and soldiers who had suffered a cut to the scalp, so he thought no more about it. After all, for all he knew, the man may have ridden for Duke Robert last summer and who wouldn't be nervous with a force this size outside their home?

It was with a much lighter heart that, having settled the camp, they rode through the gates of Kimberworth castle that evening.

'I will be glad of a decent bed under a roof for a few days,' said De Clare as they dismounted. Beaumont laughed.

'You are growing soft, De Clare.'

Richard de Clare bridled at this.

'Soft! While you were in your brother's comfortable castle at Warwick, we three were defending the fort at Erddig in all weathers against the Welsh raiders or riding into dangerous territory on Ynys Mon. We have spent almost a year in the saddle and sleeping on the ground, so do not deny me a small amount of comfort when it is offered.'

Beaumont laughed again and slapped him on the back—he did like and respect the Count de Clare.

'Why do you think we sent you, De Clare? Because you get

the job done, and you can charm the birds from the trees with that golden tongue of yours. We have seen in the past week how people trust your word and not mine. I am cut to the bone by that.'

This made De Clare laugh out loud, and even Malvais smiled as he walked to the stables to untack Diablo, as his horse didn't get any better with strange stable boys. This brought young William to mind, and he wondered how he was getting on in Stamford. This, in turn, made him think of Rohese. As he took off the bridle, replacing it with a soft halter and hay net, a wave of sadness came over him at losing both her and his son.

It was not long before the sadness was replaced by a growing anger at fate, but in particular, at Owen ap Cynan, the Welsh mercenary. His hatred of him was a flame that burned inside him. No matter how far or how long he rode, nor how many hours he spent smashing aside his opponents in the pell yard, that anger never dissipated—it grew until it occupied most of his waking thoughts. It all came to mind as he rubbed Diablo down... The attack on Gracchus, the capture of Georgio—God only knew if his friend was still alive, the attack on Rohese, and the death of his child. These went round and round in his head. He also found himself reliving the death of Darius over and over again in his mind as if he was there, watching his squire dropping over the wall thinking he was safe, and then the smacking blow with the spade that must have killed him and toppled his body into the water. His stomach knotted, for the young man had built a special place in his affections.

He stopped what he was doing, clenched his fists, closed his eyes, and let out a growl of pure fury. The veins stood out on his arms and neck as he shook with emotion and anger. Just inside the stable doorway, Rhodri stood watching, shaking his head at what he saw. He quietly walked away rather than letting the Horse Warrior know he was there. Meanwhile, Conn took several deep breaths, walked into the stable yard, splashed cold water onto his face, and entered the castle. He could see De Clare and the others at the long table on the dais, so he made his way through the trestle tables in the hall.

Beaumont had only brought about fifteen of his men with him into the hall, but Conn was surprised at the small number of Sir Geoffrey's men—there were only about thirty-five of them. Was this what he was hoping to defend the castle with? He reached the front trestle and rested a hand on Rhodri's shoulder before handing him a rolled-up bundle. This was a blue tunic with the silver Malvais badge, and Rhodri was overcome by the gift he'd been given, murmuring that he hoped he deserved to wear it.

'I am sure you will. Is all well?' Conn said softly, glancing round the hall, for he trusted the Welshman's instincts.

Rhodri shrugged and lowered his voice.

'The food and ale are good. The black-haired beauty beside the son is Sir Geoffrey's second wife, and she must be thirty years younger. She has given him two daughters, who their nurse has just taken out, but are they his? They bore an un-canny resemblance to the stepson, John de Ware. Something is afoot there—he is more like a lover, and his hand constantly strokes her under the table.'

Conn glanced in their direction and inwardly smiled at what Rhodri had discovered already.

'None of our business, Rhodri. We have weightier matters to deal with. In a few days, we move on to Mexborough, and then we are free agents until the King summons us again. We may well do what you suggest and visit the graves in Oxford.'

As Malvais took his seat beside De Clare, Rhodri inwardly groaned, for one of those graves did not contain Conn's son but a poor baby from the hovels by the River Thames. He didn't understand why Conn hadn't yet been told that his son lived—he wondered what De Clare and Edvard were thinking. He determined to tell Conn himself, if they had not done so by the time they reached Mexborough, for he could see and feel the pent-up anger radiating from the Horse Warrior, and someone would feel the brunt of that anger. He stroked the expensive cloth of his new tunic and prayed it wouldn't be him when Conn heard the truth.

Although approaching his sixtieth birthday, Sir Geoffrey still had sharp eyes, and he leaned forward to welcome Conn as he took his seat.

'I recognise that blue tunic and silver badge—you must be Malvais. However, I would have recognised you in a trice. You are the image of your grandfather, I rode with him several times into Maine and Anjou. I also saw him fall at the battle of Hastings, a fine and courageous warrior, and I hear your father is the same.'

Conn bowed his head in thanks but, realising how hungry he was, applied himself to slicing the large joint of venison for his trencher. He was still preoccupied despite the conversations, toasts, and shouts of laughter around him. The thought of killing Owen and his captain, Rhys, with his bare hands, tearing them limb from limb for what they had done, still filled his head.

The jugglers and fools appeared as the guests at the top table downed goblet after goblet of rich Burgundy wine. Beaumont smacked his lips in appreciation of the quality of the food and wine while De Clare laughed at the fact that entertainers could appear at these castles, even when a civil war was in progress, but they had to earn a living.

At that moment, the jugglers were forming a tower of men; the speed with which they climbed on each other's shoulders and balanced showed this was well practised. Then, they scooped up the small, unsuspecting fool and passed him to the top of the tower. Everyone watched as he teetered on the top, crying out in alarm, clearly terrified, especially when they let go of his arms. Inevitably, he wavered and fell backwards, crashing into the trestle tables behind and covering its occupants with beer from their tankards. Everyone roared with laughter, and even Conn smiled until he heard a distinctive, high-pitched laugh, and he whirled around to find it was John de Ware. Suddenly, he knew where he'd seen him last—the badger streak, the baying, thin laughter—in his mind, he could see him riding at Raoul de Tosny's side. He remembered the high-pitched laugh as the man had almost beheaded one of Beaumont's young knights, Fitz Robert, who was trying to protect his lord. John de Ware was one of the enemies who had fought against them at Branston.

Conn drained his goblet and made the excuse that he needed to piss. He waved Rhodri to follow him as the garde de robe was just off the hall and would give them privacy for a few moments. He told him what he'd discovered.

'Go and look around outside. I suspect this is a trap. Surely, no man could change his allegiance that quickly. If you see anything suspicious, ride for the camp and bring Gracchus, Serjeant Fox, and our men back.'

Rhodri nodded and slowly made his way down the hall, stopping to talk to a few of the men here and there. Then, he slipped out of the hall and down the steps into the shadows of the courtyard. He stayed still for some time against the wall, holding his breath as he listened and watched. He could hear the slight rumble of the guard's conversation on the gates at the far end of the bailey but nothing else. He crept along the wall to the stables, but there was no sound, and he wondered if Malvais had got it wrong. On the other side of the courtyard was a long, low building; it was a warm night, and the shutters were open so he could see the light of a few guttering candles inside. He retreated into the stable doorway and waited again, but nothing stirred, so he quickly tacked up his big chestnut gelding, just in case, and then went to check if the coast was clear to return to the hall. He could see very few men, and the gates stood open—surely, if this were a trap, they would be locked and guarded by more men.

He had just decided to loosen the girth when he heard a creaking sound that resonated across the courtyard. He crept back into the shadows of the large double doors and tried to work out what it was—an old shutter perhaps or a door. Then he saw them. A long line of men came in from what was a rarely used postern gate, hence the creaking. He watched as they ran low in the shadows of the high palisade and entered the barrack room opposite. There must have been forty or fifty of them, all armed. As the last one entered, the door was closed behind them, and he heard the wooden bar slide into place. A figure appeared at the open window and closed the shutters.

Wasting no more time, Rhodri led his big Destrier out of the stable and down onto the grass of the bailey, where its hooves wouldn't ring out as he trotted down to the gates. The guards looked at him in surprise as he rode through, and one man half-heartedly stepped out as if to challenge him but then jumped back out of the way of the great beast. After all, they had no orders to stop anyone from leaving, only anymore coming in.

Rhodri smiled as he pushed his horse into a canter through the trees towards the camp; he'd be back shortly, and they would have no chance of stopping forty Horse Warriors coming through those gates.

Chapter Eleven

June/July 1102 – Kimberworth

In the hall, the copious amount of drink was beginning to have its effect; the men were clapping along with the musicians and raucously singing along to the refrain of some well-known songs. Glancing at Beaumont, who had also imbibed freely of the rich red wine, Malvais realised he'd have to act soon, or they would be too drunk to fight their way out.

On reaching the camp, Rhodri had found the serjeant first, told him what he'd discovered and sent him to the castle, to tell Malvais that he was right about the trap. Serjeant Fox had pretended to be a drunken archer coming through the gate, looking for the serving girl he'd followed out and lost. As he staggered about and made his way inside, the guards laughed at him, as he was no threat. He collapsed on the bailey grass and lay there until they stopped watching him and then he crept towards the hall.

Malvais was impatiently waiting for Rhodri's signal when he suddenly saw movement at the back of the hall. With some relief, he saw Serjeant Fox appear in the arched doorway. He gave Malvais a significant look and a quick nod to confirm the

Horse Warrior's suspicions, and then he slipped back into the shadows and disappeared.

Sticking to the shadows and using a large wooden barrel, Serjeant Fox climbed onto the stable roof and took out his tinder box. Fitting an arrow to the bow, he set it alight and fired it high into the sky. It didn't take long before he could hear the thunder of hooves, and he smiled as he climbed down.

Meanwhile, on the dais, Conn proceeded to drop his knife. Reaching down between the chairs, he tugged at De Clare's belt. Moving his chair to give him room and intending to help, De Clare looked down at him in surprise, but his expression changed as he heard the whispered words.

'I have sent for the men; it's a trap. The son rode against us with De Tosny at Branston and was in the attack on Beaumont.'

De Clare sat up straight, his mind whirling, his eyes darting around the hall. Then he picked up his goblet, and raised it in a toast to the wisdom and loyalty of Sir Geoffrey, which everyone on the top tables joined in with. Taking barely a sip, he quickly put his goblet down and picked up his dagger lying on the table. As Sir John beside him replaced his goblet on the table, De Clare slammed the dagger up to the hilt through the knight's right hand, pinning him to the table. The wine goblet flew off the table, scattering its remaining contents and hitting the stone flags with a clatter. The knight uttered a high-pitched scream like a rabbit caught in the fangs of a stoat. His stepmother beside him began screeching as she saw the dagger and the blood, and Sir Geoffrey pushed his heavy carved chair back so quickly, in shock, that it fell over and crashed to the floor, and he followed it. De Clare knocked the enemy's dagger out of reach. It went skittering across the floor, and one of Beaumont's men picked it up, staring in surprise at the top table and wrongly assuming it was an argument that had escalated.

∽⟨⟩∾

In the camp, Rhodri had rallied the Horse Warriors and sent them to wait in the tree line before the castle as he tried to find Gracchus and Edvard. Finding the former, he told him about the signal of the flaming arrow he'd arranged with Serjeant Fox, and warned him that the rebel men would pour from the barracks in the courtyard. The order was that no quarter was to be given, as they would have slaughtered Beaumont and his lords in their beds. With that, he sent Gracchus to lead them, but he couldn't find Edvard, so he remounted his horse to ride after them until a hand clasped on his calf stopped him. He recognised the slightly stooped, grey-bearded man, the physician.

'Sire, you must come and help your friend; two men have taken Synnove. They said they were leading her to someone who was wounded, but I recognised these untrustworthy, dangerous men from the King's camp last year, and I do not trust them or believe their tale. They mean to do her harm.'

Rhodri paused momentarily, torn between his duty to Malvais and to the young woman he was falling in love with. He knew that Malvais had faith in Gracchus, his Greek captain, so he made his choice; he jumped from the saddle, gave the reins to the physician and ran along the river bank in the direction the man indicated. Before long, the trees thinned slightly, and he could hear her cries ahead. The sun was in its final throes of setting, but there was enough light to see them in a clearing that ran down to the river. The stocky older man—the one with the warts on his hands—held her in front of him. His left forearm was tight across her throat, choking her as she gasped for breath, a dagger in his hand close to her face. Her gown had been ripped open, and the man's right hand was on her naked breasts. Rhodri couldn't see the second man as he gave a growl of rage, running at the man holding her captive.

At the last minute, Crick threw her aside, and she dropped to her knees, retching and sobbing on the river bank. Rhodri was at a full run, his sword in his hand, when he was tripped by a cord stretched across the path, and the first blows descended from nowhere. The other two men had been hidden in the undergrowth and now laid into Rhodri from both sides with heavy clubs. Synnove, still on her hands and knees, let out a piercing scream, for she could do nothing; she had no weapon to stop them from beating him to death in front of her. Having listened to the men as they dragged her away, she didn't doubt that they intended to kill him. She took a deep breath and began to scream again, but Crick grabbed her by the hair and clamped a hand over her mouth, cutting off the cry and silencing her.

Rhodri had rolled himself into a ball, his arms on his head, trying to protect himself as the blows and kicks continued. He heard the distinctive crack as his wrist broke, and he prayed to all his gods that someone would come—that someone had heard her screams or that the physician would bring help. He could now hear a whooshing sound; he thought it was the blood rushing in his ears, as a blow landed on his ribs that took his breath away. All he could feel was pain, a sea of pain, and he knew he was about to pass out. But he heard his grandfather's voice telling him to push the pain out of his head and survive.

The whooshing sound grew louder, and suddenly, the blows stopped, and he heard men crying out in pain. Crick let go of Synnove and, swearing loudly, drew his sword to help his men against the dark figure who was brutally laying into them. He ran forward to stab him from behind. Then, the clouds moved, and the last rays of the sun lit the scene. The man turned slightly and glanced back, and Crick met his eyes. He instantly realised who was attacking them, and with a sharp intake of breath, he turned to run, praying that his men could do the same. However, a backward glance showed Sam on the ground, blood streaming from a broken nose—even in this dying light, he could see his head was lying at an unnatural angle.

The younger man, still holding the club, was swinging it wildly at his attacker whilst backing into the undergrowth to escape the whirling staff. His left arm hung numb and useless at his side; he knew it was broken as the blow from the staff had almost lifted him off his feet. He saw Crick beckoning and then disappearing, and he wanted to run, but the big man in front of him, his face a mask of fury, was relentless. As the club was sent flying from his right hand, he scrabbled frantically to draw the long dagger in his belt, and with some relief his hand closed on the hilt, as he hoped to rush the big man. However, as he pulled it out and bent forward to run, the next whirling blow crashed into his temple. He was dead as he hit the ground.

Edvard had been walking back towards camp when he heard Synnove's scream; he broke into a run and, seeing at once what was happening, had attacked. Now, having dealt with the first two, he looked for the third—the older man with the sword—but he had fled. Edvard walked to the dead man on the ground, nudged him with his foot and recognised the shaggy tow-coloured hair. These were the three men from De Courcy's train in Oxford, the ones sent to guard the wagons for Beaumont. Instead, De Courcy had sent them here to kill Rhodri as a punishment for his foolish words and, no doubt, also to inflict more pain on Malvais.

Edvard, a skilled physician in his own right after years spent with Ahmed at the chateau, knelt on the ground beside a groaning Rhodri, who found it agonising even to try to uncurl and couldn't push himself up as his right hand hung uselessly from a broken wrist. Synnove came over, her tear-stained face full of concern while holding her torn dress together. Edvard did what he could for his new friend, told him to lie still and sent her to bring back the physician and men to help carry Rhodri in a blanket. Only when they got the white druid back to camp, and laid him gently down, did Edvard hear of the trap that had been laid at the castle, as Rhodri whispered what Malvais had discovered.

Filled with foreboding, Edvard left Rhodri in their capable hands as they poured theriac down the injured man's throat. He ran for his horse, praying that Gracchus and Serjeant Fox had reached the castle in time, and that the gates had not been locked against them. If that had happened, and from what Rhodri had told him, Beaumont had far too few men to defend themselves against the rebels.

In the hall, there was shock. Beaumont was now on his feet,

shouting in disbelief as he pulled a shaken Sir Geoffrey to his feet.

'Have they run mad? What are they doing?'

Philip de Braose looked equally stunned and stared at De Clare, usually the calmest of knights. He shook his head at Beaumont to absolve himself of any knowledge but couldn't find any words to answer him. Malvais replied to Beaumont while moving swiftly behind John de Ware to hold a dagger to his throat.

'No, Sire, we have not run mad. This was a trap, and we were all their target; they would have killed us and our men in our beds, having got us sufficiently drunk and complacent with their lies. John de Ware, here, rode at De Tosny's side at Branston; he killed several knights who were trying to defend you while you were battling with De Tosny, including your protégé, young Fitz Robert.'

Beaumont's face was suffused with anger as he stepped forward, but by now, De Ware's men were on their feet. As ordered, they had drunk little and now drew their swords while Beaumont's men had scrambled to protect their lord, forming a semi-circle before him, outnumbered, as these men advanced. To Conn's relief, at that point, sounds of fighting and cries could be heard from outside.

'Call it off, De Ware; tell the men here to disarm. That sound you can hear is our Horse Warriors in the courtyard, and they will kill the men there and then come in here. Tell your men to drop their weapons if they want to live.' De Ware had little choice as he felt the sharp blade pierce the skin of his neck, and a line of blood ran down, staining his light blue tunic.

De Clare, who was now on his feet, sword drawn, facing the hall, had seen the shock on Sir Geoffrey's face and realised that he was not part of this plot, although he still cried out for mercy for his son.

John reluctantly ordered his men to drop their weapons. Not a moment too soon, as the hall doors burst open, and Gracchus and his men surged into the hall. De Clare met Conn's eyes and saw the cold anger and the harsh lines on his friend's face, so he ordered him to remove his dagger from De Ware's throat. De Clare didn't like what he could see, and for a second, he honestly believed Conn was going to slit the traitor's throat. It was not Malvais' decision to be an executioner—that was Beaumont's privilege—and he felt relief as Conn reluctantly stood back.

Sir Geoffrey was angry and shouting as De Clare pulled his dagger from De Ware's hand.

'I knew nothing of this betrayal, Beaumont! I swear on the Holy Sepulchre in Jerusalem!'

He then berated his son for blackening the family name and despoiling its honour, but his son's head was not bowed. Despite his predicament, his spirit was not broken as he turned on his stepmother, who had collapsed into her chair, sobbing and shaking.

'She was as involved in this as much as me. It was her idea to kill Beaumont in his bed as he slept,' he spat at her.

She stood and drew herself up to her full height, and stepping forward, she slapped him hard before Malvais pulled her back.

'You lie! You threatened me, you forced yourself on me, came to my bed night after night, then you blackmailed me, threatening to tell my husband the children were not his, which was not true. Now, you try to transfer the blame for your evil plans and drag me down with you.'

'Bind their hands and imprison them both until we find the truth of this; he will talk at the hands of the King's gaolers,' ordered De Clare, as a shaking Sir Geoffrey dropped back into a chair, a hand over his eyes.

De Braose organised the taking of prisoners in the hall, with the help of Gracchus, while Beaumont now pulling himself together, walked over, and put a hand on the older knight's shoulder, who looked up at him, brushing away the tears in his eyes.

'It is the betrayal from both of them that I cannot take— not only of the King and of our word, but of our family,' he murmured. Beaumont nodded in understanding for this brave old warrior.

'I am returning to camp, but I will leave Serjeant Fox and his men to control the castle and the prisoners for a while. I suggest your first move is to find out who in the castle remains loyal to you. Then, discover which of your armed men were not part of this betrayal. Who among them were following your son's orders, who had no choice? Also, see to your daughters; they will be frightened by all this and will need your reassurance. The fate of your wife and son is out of your hands now; they are guilty of treason and will be dealt with by the King. You must prepare for the worst, as he does not treat traitors lightly.'

Chapter Twelve

July 1102 – Kimberworth Castle

As Edvard galloped through the open gates of the castle, he noticed a dozen bodies lying on the grass of the bailey. He slowed to check they were not Horse Warriors and rode on with relief into the courtyard. He found Serjeant Fox there with his men, guarding dozens of prisoners who sat on the cobbles with bound hands; several were bloodied, and dark, sullen looks were thrown in his direction.

'I would kill them all. They have risen in rebellion against their king; we should be giving no quarter,' he shouted at Serjeant Fox as he dismounted, which spread a wave of panic across the men—they didn't know who this man was, but he seemed to have influence.

'That order may yet come, Sire; a bird has been sent to Winchester, and I am told that the King is in no mood for mercy,' answered Serjeant Fox with an expression of satisfaction. He cast an eye over the captured men, who would have murdered Beaumont and his lord, Richard de Clare, in their beds in cold blood; he'd happily slaughter the lot of them.

Edvard thanked him with a slap on the shoulder; he had a

lot of time for the intuitive, no-nonsense Serjeant. He ran up the steps to the hall, relieved that his friends were unharmed. He saw them grouped on the dais, and as he approached, he caught the end of Beaumont's conversation with Sir Geoffrey.

'As you declared your loyalty to the King and had no part in this plot, I will allow you to stay on your lands, although Serjeant Fox will remain with his men for a week or so until the fate of your son and wife is resolved. Sir Philip de Braose will escort them both as prisoners to the King, who is currently at Windsor. You need to accept that your son will likely be executed.'

Sir Geoffrey was now resigned to this, and he thanked Beaumont for his mercy and generosity towards him. Looking even older, his shoulders bowed, he walked away towards the nursery to comfort his daughters.

Malvais and De Clare had seen Edvard arrive, and, noticing his concerned face, they reassured him that no one was hurt. Edvard told them of the vicious attack on Rhodri.

'He is in a bad way, with at least a broken wrist, several broken ribs, covered in cuts, swelling and blackening bruises. I thank God I did not arrive any later, for I do not know if their orders were to kill him, but I could see the frenzy on their faces, and if I had not stepped in, they would truly have beaten him to death. However, Rhodri is fit, relatively young, and will recover, given time. I suggest you leave him here with Serjeant Fox to let his bones knit. Fortunately, it was not his sword hand that was broken.'

He then lowered his voice, telling them he'd recognised the attackers as De Courcy's men.

'I killed two of them, but their leader escaped.'

Beaumont, close by with his captain, had heard most of it

and stepped up beside them.

'No doubt this was meant as a warning to you, Malvais. De Courcy was consumed with jealousy when he heard you had been at Oxford for several weeks. Your affair with the Lady Rohese was common knowledge in the court and, on the whole, accepted with a smile, even by the King. However, De Courcy is a proud and vengeful man—not the type to turn a blind eye when being cuckolded. I was at the baby's baptism, and even I could see that several people realised the child was yours and not De Courcy's; that sort of information has a habit of getting out. I advise you to take care, especially if you mean to continue this liaison.'

With that, to the Horse Warrior's surprise, he placed a friendly arm around Conn's shoulder.

'More importantly—yet again, Conn Fitz Malvais, you have saved my life, and the lives of my knights, with your quick thinking and courage. They say that things come in threes, so I hope you will be there if my life is in danger again. I promise I will reward you for this. We will have a few rest days as there are many loose ends to tie up here, but we will leave for Mexborough Castle in three days' time. Hopefully, the castle there will be easier to take than the first two.'

Conn thanked him and assured him he needed no reward to save lives—that was his job—but Beaumont would have none of it as he walked away.

De Clare laughed. 'Well, Malvais, I think you may have edged Sir Philip de Braose out of his position as top dog and sent him back into his kennel.'

Conn playfully punched him while shaking his head.

'Come, De Clare, all is resolved here at present. Let us go and see how Rhodri is doing.'

July 1102 – Windsor

Robert de Courcy had taken his son with him when he'd ridden out on business that afternoon. The conversation at Tickhill had rankled when the boy revealed his wish to be a Horse Warrior, so he endeavoured to spend more time with him and appointed a swordmaster and tutor for him. He found his son intelligent and inquisitive, but the constant questions began to wear on him as they rode back into Windsor. He saw with relief that there had been an arrival; twenty or so knights and men were dismounting in the inner ward. He recognised the crest of Philip de Braose on the pennants, so he surmised that it was news from Beaumont. Dismounting, he handed his horse to the groom and sent William to his tutor while he made his way to the King's chamber to be in his place, by his side, when De Braose presented himself.

Henry's father had built Windsor Castle as part of a ring of defensive fortifications. It was important because of its proximity to the River Thames and its position on a bluff above the river. De Courcy disliked it; he thought it resembled Arundel's double-storey keep on a high mound—a place he'd never liked. Like many of King William's castles, it was basic and martial in nature, with little comfort. Henry often preferred to stay in old Windsor at the palace of the Saxon kings, which was ideal for hunting in Windsor forest and far more comfortable, but he had important business here at the castle, so they were here for another week.

As De Courcy passed through the gates of the inner palisade, he heard his name called. Turning, he saw one of the men he had hired. He'd been chatting to the gatekeepers, and now he bowed and moved to one side, away from the guards. De

Courcy reluctantly followed.

'Crick. I hope you have good news for me, but make it quick, I go to the King,' he said, glancing over his shoulder to ensure no one could hear their conversation.

'Yes and no, Sire. We carried out your bidding, and the Welsh druid will not be going anywhere for a while—that's if he lives, which is unlikely. However, we were attacked, and my two men were killed. Do you want me to recruit more?'

De Courcy sucked his breath through gritted teeth at this alarming news.

'Attacked! By whom? Malvais? Are you sure your men are dead? If he were to question them....'

'I assure you, Sire, they are dead, and it was the big man with the oak staff; nothing could stand against that. He killed them both in minutes.'

'Edvard of Silesia! He's still here in England and interfering in our business. Maybe we should have targeted him.'

Crick looked alarmed. 'You would need ten men to bring him down. He is as strong as an ox and lethal with staff or sword. However, I carried out your instructions, and I think it has delivered your message to the Horse Warrior.'

De Courcy met Crick's eyes and saw the cunning glint in them. The man knew too much. He pondered for a moment whether he should kill or threaten him. He decided on the latter, for, after all, he could be very useful.

'Breathe not a word of this, Crick, or I will know; my informers are everywhere, and if I hear a whisper, I will arrange for your body to slide into the Thames one night.'

Crick dropped his eyes and inclined his head in subservience; he knew this man's influence.

'Yes, recruit more, but find us three or more likely men,

perhaps a bit handier with their fists and daggers.' So saying, he reached for his belt, unhooked his purse and threw it to his henchman.

While bowing low to the Royal Steward, Crick grinned at the thought that this purse would not now be split amongst three men. De Courcy watched him go through narrowed eyes. He was pleased that they had taught the Welshman a lesson, and he smiled as he thought of the anger of Malvais, who would, of course, see the attack for what it was. If he had his way, it would only be the beginning. He needed that Horse Warrior dead or disgraced and out of England.

He climbed the steep wooden steps up to the keep and entered the hall to find it crowded. Crick had delayed him, so Sir Philip was already addressing the King while a bound prisoner was on the floor before Henry. He skirted the crowd to stand at the front beside Henry Beaumont, Earl of Warwick.

'Who is the prisoner, Sire?' he whispered.

'John de Ware, a rebel knight, son to Sir Geoffrey Ware. My brother, Robert, had taken Kimberworth without an arrow being fired, but he and his stepmother set it as a trap. If it had not been for Malvais, both Beaumont and De Clare, along with their knights and men, would have been slaughtered in their beds.'

Robert de Courcy closed his eyes and tightened his grip on his sword hilt as the anger flooded his body. Malvais! Yet again, that damned Horse Warrior had triumphed. He opened his eyes as the King stood and, descending from the dais, stopped in front of the prisoner. Reaching down, he gripped the man's chin hard, raising his face to look into his eyes.

'You rode with De Tosny to try and kill Beaumont and his men in a cowardly ambush at Branston. You then try a more despicable and underhand trick by breaking all the sacrosanct laws of hospitality at Kimberworth, duping your father to kill my nobles in their beds. What say you, John de Ware?'

The prisoner shook off Henry's hold on him and struggled to his knees.

'Guilty of what? Of attacking the troops of the man who stole his brother's crown and, if the rumours are true, arranged the murder of his other brother, William Rufus.'

There was a sharp intake of breath in the hall at this, but De Ware continued, showing no humility or remorse for his actions or words. In some ways, Henry Beaumont had to admire his courage and spirit, but there was no doubt that his words had condemned him to a cruel death.

'I call what I did justice against a Norman prince guilty of oath-breaking and probably fratricide. Robert de Belleme shows the meaning of loyalty to his liege lord, the true king, Duke Robert of Normandy, and he is twice the man you are.'

Beaumont saw that Henry's face was white, his lips clamped shut in a thin line as he half turned away from the prisoner and then turned back and swung a blow to his head that sent the man flying across the floor.

'Today, here in the bailey, you will be blinded and castrated. And then tomorrow, you will be taken to the Tower in London, where I promise you will have a slow and agonising death. The pieces of your body will be displayed to show the people of England what happens to traitors. De Courcy, ensure it is done, and now get him out of my sight.'

De Courcy had the prisoner dragged down the steps towards the bailey, but his mind was not on the agonising punishments John de Ware was about to receive. It was full of Conn Fitz Malvais, the Horse Warrior who had taken and despoiled his wife under his nose in Henry's camp, who was the hero of Branston, and now again, his name was on the King's lips as the saviour of Kimberworth. Malvais could seem to do no wrong while De Courcy was here, day in and day out, serving the King's every need with little recognition or thanks. As the prisoner was strapped down onto a wooden table that had been dragged out, De Courcy's mind was on the grave in the churchyard in Oxford.

Was it his child who was in that grave, or was it the bastard child of Malvais?

He knew he could hardly dig it up, but he had ways of getting the truth out of his wife and her sanctimonious sister. First, however, he needed to deal with Malvais. Suddenly, he thought again of Owen ap Cynan and remembered a ransom would be delivered for the kidnapped Horse Warrior next month. This could be the opportunity he needed. The screams from the prisoner filled the bailey but they hardly registered with De Courcy, who left his men to it and went to find a groom to take a message to Crick. He needed the man to travel north to find the Welsh mercenary in the enemy camp.

A thoughtful Henry Beaumont had watched the prisoner being dragged from the hall. Why did an unpleasant and sadistic man like Robert de Belleme inspire such loyalty in some men? Was it truly that he kept his word and his oaths? Or was it that King Henry was still so despised by sections of the Norman and English nobility? They would find out where people's loyalty really lay when their forces finally met in battle in the next month.

King Henry was an astute man, and he saw the puzzled frown on his chief advisor's face; Warwick led his Council, and if he had concerns, he wanted to hear them, so he invited him to join him on the battlements of the keep, to watch the punishment of John de Ware below them.

'Did I see a moment of misgiving or apprehension at my punishments?' asked Henry, searching his loyal friend's face.

'Not at all, my liege. I merely wondered why men like this followed Belleme. What is it about him that they give their lives? John de Ware could have begged for mercy and offered you his allegiance, yet he chose to stay true to his liege lord, insult you, and suffer this fate,' he said, as the high-pitched screams of the prisoner came up from below.

'Robert de Belleme has been there for most of my life, Beaumont, and for some of yours. He is a complex man, a great mathematician and strategist, and a good musician—I remember him playing the harp as a young man. He was one of my brother's closest friends, and I cannot fault Belleme's constant loyalty to him.'

Beaumont laughed. 'I find the harp playing difficult to imagine, Sire.'

Henry smiled. 'It shows his quick and sharp mind—he can turn his hand to anything—but he was also a great fighter, on horseback or off. You will no doubt remember that Belleme was trained by a Saxon Huscarl of King Harold, a man who gave his sword to Belleme's father, the great Roger Montgomery, after the Battle of Hastings. Yes, Belleme's cruel behaviour revolts as many as it attracts, and his tongue can be vicious and damaging, as our friend Malvais found out, but there is an attraction there, and people follow him. There is also the fact that he is the most powerful and wealthy noble in England, with immense lands in Normandy, from his mother. Together with his brothers, the Montgomerys are a deep thorn in my side that needs to be removed.'

At that moment, a messenger from Fitzhamon interrupted them. Henry took the message and read its contents before smiling and handing it to Henry Beaumont.

'Arundel will finally surrender, but on two conditions. They have heard about my mercy at Tickhill, so they want to disarm and leave the castle unharmed, but they want my word of honour that if I defeat Belleme, he will be allowed to leave England and return to his lands in Normandy unharmed.'

'Again, that unswerving loyalty to Belleme. What will you do?'

Henry placed his hands on the stone in front of him. The prisoner below was still alive but was now beyond screaming and was being dragged away, leaving a bloody trail behind him.

'I will agree; after all, it means I have Arundel, one of the great castles of England. Also, I can bring Fitzhamon and my men back, and if Belleme returns to Normandy, what is that to me? He is there to deal with in the future if I wish while I seize all his lands and revenues in England.'

Henry Beaumont nodded sagely. 'However, there is the matter of defeating him first, Sire.'

'Do you doubt me, Warwick? Your brother, Robert, and his lords have already delivered significant blows to his allies. I feel in here that we will prevail,' he said, placing his hand over his heart.

Warwick hoped so, for, as Henry pointed out, Robert de Belleme, Earl of Shrewsbury, was an experienced strategist in warfare with a host of allies and endless money and resources.

Chapter Thirteen

Late July 1102 – Stafford Castle

To say that King Maredudd was bitterly disappointed in his brothers was an understatement. He did not know how he had kept his temper in check at the jibes of Arnulf Montgomery while he was here at Stafford. Arnulf had pointed out that King Maredudd had promised much to the Earl of Shrewsbury, his liege lord, and to them. Yet, despite outnumbering the enemy on both occasions, they had been soundly defeated at Tamworth and Branston, losing nearly a thousand valuable men and cavalry. He'd suggested that perhaps Maredudd and his brothers should return to their court at Mathrafal while he brought in the Irish mercenaries of his father-in-law, Murtagh O'Brien, to finish the job.

Fortunately, Iorwerth had redeemed himself somewhat by arriving while Arnulf was there with the three hundred men he'd been sent to recruit. Maredudd prayed that the Montgomery brother didn't look too closely at these men, for some were boys who could barely hold the heavy sword in their belt, and several others were grey-bearded men who had seen far too many winters. However, Maredudd used this to reassure Arnulf that they were still loyal to Belleme and a force to be reckoned with. After all, they had defeated and driven off Nicholas de Stafford and still held his castle and lands.

That didn't stop him from berating his brothers once Arnulf left to return to Bridgnorth.

Aggrieved from this verbal lashing and burning with resentment, Iorwerth threw himself into training his new men, knowing that it would only be a matter of time before he was standing in Maredudd's place as King of Powys.

Owen ap Cynan stood with Rhys on the hillside and watched Iorwerth and his new recruits.

'They are saying that the King's men have won not only Tamworth, Branston, and Tickhill, but he has taken Kimberworth, and they are on their way to the next castle. I heard Cadwgan telling his friend. Do you not wonder, Owen, if we are on the right side or even in the right war?' asked Rhys. 'I know we have burnt our boats here in England with King Henry, but as we know, there is always work in Ireland for sell-swords.'

'Ireland can be dicey; they'd cut your throat in the night if you disrespected them in any way. I have never known a race touchier when drink is taken, nor more likely to hold a grudge for generations. However, you are right; there are several minor wars in Europe where they would welcome us with open arms. We have done it before in Germany, but for now, let us see how this plays out, for we have unfinished business here.'

Rhys nodded in agreement. He would always be at Owen's side wherever they went.

Owen chewed the end of a grass stalk while watching a group of Iorwerth's young lads repeatedly attacking the pell post. He knew it would take months to build up the muscle they needed, in their arms and shoulders, if these boys were to wield a sword with any force. However, he also knew they probably only had weeks before King Henry recalled his armies, and they would be thrust into the lines of battle to die against trained knights, or much stronger men with pikes.

Those weeks would also bring him to the Feast of the Assumption in Shrewsbury Abbey in mid-August and the meeting with Malvais and Edvard of Silesia. He certainly didn't underestimate either of them, so his plan had to be foolproof. He needed the ransom money to buy the land he had in mind. Every man knew that land gave you power and status, and Owen craved both. They had been living illegally at Lake Bala, on what was Gwynedd land, which gave King Gruffudd ap Cynan the right to burn down their homes with no restitution. However, Owen had also learned the lesson that the right alliances were needed to gain influence, and he was finally working to do that, to use people more.

To his surprise, two messengers found him that week. Rhys brought the first messenger with a barely concealed grin, for the man had tried to disguise himself as a soldier. However, his sword belt was loose, and the sheath banged on his leg, almost tripping him, while every part of him cried out that he was a monk. Sweat ran down his face from his journey, or through fear, as he constantly looked behind him. He begged for a drink from them.

'It was a far longer and harder journey than I thought,' he gasped. Owen could hear Rhys laughing as he walked away to get some ale. Meanwhile, looking highly suspicious, this 'soldier' dipped his hand into his hauberk and brought out the message.

'I am sure you do not know or recognise me in this garb, but I am the servant of Abbot Columbanus, and this is from him,' he whispered, handing him the folded parchment.

Owen gave a harsh laugh. 'Yes, I recognise you. You looked like a scared rat cowering in the corner of the room in Oxford when I was there,' he said, quietening as he unfolded the message.

He read the contents while Rhys, who had returned with a jug of ale, watched with interest as Owen's eyes widened. He looked up at the monk and then at Rhys.

'Do you know what is in this?' he asked, narrowing his eyes.

'I swear on the tomb of Saint Benedict himself that the seal was unbroken. Only you and the Abbot have seen it, and my orders are to burn it as soon as you have read it.'

Owen nodded to Rhys, who drew out his tinder box. In moments, the flames consumed the small roll of parchment.

'Take him away and get him some food while I think this through, and then I will give you a verbal message for your master,' he ordered.

He watched them walk away, then glanced around the south bailey, where his men were camped, to ensure no other eyes had been on that exchange. He sat down on the camp chair outside his small pavilion and gazed into the distance as he considered the surprising message. Abbot Columbanus, a notoriously grasping and greedy man at the best of times, was now suddenly willing to take only a twenty-five per cent share of the ransom, but only if Owen and his men killed Edvard of Silesia. The big man was Chatillon's representative, the one who would deliver the silver but a dangerous man.

This was interesting to Owen, for he could feel the fear coming off the hastily scribbled words on the parchment. He now had to ask himself what Chatillon's vavasseur, Edvard, had on Abbot Columbanus. Had he somehow discovered the

141

Abbot's role in the plot? An alarming thought suddenly struck him. Had Edvard discovered that Columbanus was holding the kidnapped Horse Warrior in Chester? That would be a disaster. He decided to send a trusted man at once to check that his prisoner was still there, for everything depended on Georgio di Milan being alive and able to stumble into that abbey in Shrewsbury on August 15th.

Rhys brought the man back an hour later, and Owen told him he agreed with his master's request. The man looked relieved and had turned away when Owen shouted him back.

'Wait! Tell him I also want ten Benedictine robes as soon as possible—used, not too new.'

The man nodded and scurried away to the horse lines while Owen updated Rhys on the message's contents.

The second message arrived three days later in the late afternoon as one of his men guided a figure towards their camp. This message was brought by a dubious character, one to definitely be wary of—Owen had recognised him immediately by his scarred, weathered face and stocky figure. He also remembered that this man's hand rarely moved far from the hilt of his dagger or sword; the name Crick came to him.

'You seem to be a long way from home, Crick. Are you lost or just foolish to come into the enemy's camp?' asked Owen, whilst standing outside his pavilion with his hands on his hips, his head cocked on one side as he regarded his visitor.

The man gave a thin smile that didn't reach his eyes and boldly dropped uninvited into one of the camp chairs in the sunshine. Owen noticed that he glanced around the bailey before speaking.

'I presume it is safe to speak here as I bring you news—some good, some bad.'

Owen nodded, indicating to one of his young men that wine was needed. Several spits had been set up as usual in the bailey, and the smell of roasting meat wafted across to them. The man took a deep breath and smacked his lips in anticipation, as he was handed a cup of wine, while Owen waited patiently, sipping from his cup and trying not to look too eager.

'You will no doubt be aware of events at Kimberworth?' he asked, and Owen nodded.

'Well, you may share with King Maredudd that his man, Sir John de Ware, was publicly executed two days hence. It was not pretty, and he lasted far too long, but I know that his stepmother, the Lady de Ware, was King Maredudd's cousin, so he will want to know this. Sir Geoffrey pleaded for her life for the sake of his daughters, and King Henry finally agreed, or it would have been her entrails that were pulled from her ravaged body on Tower Hill. She has been condemned instead to be confined, under lock and key in a closed order of the Cistercians. She is being transported across the channel to Citeaux Abbey, near Dijon, as we speak.'

Owen considered this information and how he could use it. The King of Powys would no doubt be impressed that he could get such information quickly; there had not been a whisper of this yet, which would make him more useful to Maredudd, and Owen hoped to keep and build on this alliance with the Welsh king.

Crick smiled as he saw the thoughts openly flit back and forth across the Welsh mercenary's face.

'You will also be pleased to know that my master has done you a great service, which he expects you to return.'

Once again, Owen became wary, as he'd remembered who this man's master was—not a man to cross, so he sat back, crossed his legs, and took a draught of the wine.

'It all depends on the cost of returning the favour; some favours are unequal, and some hardly worth the effort or the expense.'

Crick smiled. He enjoyed a bit of banter with a similar compatriot and he knew of Owen ap Cynan's ruthless reputation. This was the man who had killed and captured Horse Warriors and had the fearless temerity to attack his master's wife, Lady Rohese. Despite that, his master, De Courcy, wanted to use Owen's services, and it was Crick's job to persuade him to take this mission.

'I think you will be pleased to learn that he ordered a severe beating of the white druid, the one who burnt your mother to death inside your house at Lake Bala—yes, we all heard of the slaughter there. It is highly likely that he may not survive that beating. I like to think we may have broken most of the bones in his body.'

Owen was indeed pleased to hear this. While he got the message that Crick himself and his men had delivered this punishment, he kept his satisfaction hidden, inclined his head in thanks, and waited for the catch.

'My master has placed a bounty on the head of Conn Fitz Malvais. As you know, my master is not short of silver, and the bounty equals what Robert Beaumont paid you and all of your men for your services. He does not care where or when it happens but before autumn. Your intended visit to the Abbey in Shrewsbury may give you the opportunity you need or, better still, in the heart of the forthcoming battle. A few good, well-placed archers could easily bring his horse down and cause his demise from the waiting swords of your men.'

Crick saw the gleam in Owen's eyes and knew that the baited

hook had been taken. He smiled. 'Think it through. I will stay here and enjoy your company tonight, and you can let me have your answer in the morning.'

Owen didn't have to think it through; this could be very lucrative. But he'd talk it through with Rhys. His captain returned shortly afterwards and was thoroughly alarmed to see the man, Crick, nestled in their camp. He knew far more about Crick, his nefarious dealings and his reputation for murder and brutality, than Owen did, so Rhys drank little and watched him like a hawk. However, the man proved to be good company, full of hair-raising tales of happenings on the banks of the River Thames and in the dark, narrow streets of London.

Crick left the next day, waving a hand in farewell to Owen ap Cynan, who, having accepted De Courcy's offer, was almost grinning. However, Rhys was cautious and more apprehensive as he listened to the news Crick brought, and the offer that Owen had accepted for them.

'So let me make sure I have this right. Instead of taking the ransom and fleeing, you are now planning for us to kill two men in August, possibly in Shrewsbury, unless we come to battle before then. But not just any men. Conn Fitz Malvais is a famous warrior—you have seen him fight—and Edvard of Silesia is someone I would never take on unless I had five or six good men behind me.'

Owen raised a hand at Rhys' understandable pessimism and placed it on his shoulder.

'Ah, but that is the nub of it, Rhys. We need more men, but better men, who are good with a blade and who can think for themselves—men like Black Bryn, whom the Horse Warriors murdered in Rye. He could be trusted to carry out any job. These opportunities could be the making of us, Rhys. The money from these, and the ransom, will set us up for life on our own land.'

Rhys was a realist. He could never see Owen ap Cynan settling down on a manor and farming lands—he was far too restless—but he liked the idea of having a base they owned. He still had hopes of finding his wife and children, who had been sold into slavery after the attack on Bala, and this would be somewhere safe to take them. However, he agreed with Owen—they needed better men. So, he stood deep in thought for a while before turning and facing his friend.

'I think I know just the man, one who will be happy to do as we wish for silver, no questions asked. He is leaderless at the moment and has no love for Cadwgan or Iorwerth, so he will not join them. Also, he has a following of half a dozen of his own well-trained men, all very capable.'

'Who?' asked Owen with a frown, trying to work out who he meant.

'Daegal O'Brien. He was Raoul de Tosny's henchman, the big man with a pock-marked face and reddish hair. He is the son of an Irish father and a Welsh mother. I noticed that most of De Tosny's men respected him but stayed clear of him and his men in the same way that people do with us. He was banished from Ireland by Arnulf Montgomery's father-in-law, Murtagh O'Brien. Arnulf saw his worth and sent him to De Tosny a few years ago.'

Owen stared into the distance, mentally bringing O'Brien to mind.

'I know the man. Yes, that may work very well. See what you can arrange, Rhys, and make sure he knows we can afford to pay him a bonus if this comes off as we expect.'

Late July – Chester

Georgio sat and stared at the marks along the bottom of the wall. They didn't lie, or did they? Was he deceiving himself? He had tried during his long and agonising incarceration to keep a daily tally, scraping each mark on the wall, but in the winter, he knew there were many days when he stayed under the blankets and shivered uncontrollably, expecting to die in the ice-cold conditions. So his calculations may be wrong, but he thought he'd now been here for a year or more. The older monk, who had returned to bring his food and water, was no help as he wouldn't answer his questions about how long he'd been there or even what date or month it was.

At first, he had used his small fruit knife to cut his hair and beard, but over the last few months, they had grown longer, and he found he didn't care. He had used the long years of training with the warrior monks, as a child, and later with Malvais and the Horse Warriors, to keep his mind as positive as possible, but now, every day was proving more difficult. The lack of food did not help. He regularly washed and cleaned himself—old habits die hard—but now he could count every rib, and the flesh on what was his hard-muscled thighs was disappearing, despite his daily exercise routine. He was not taken in by their tale of the necessity of fasting three days a week for an anchorite, to bring him closer to God in a state of grace. He knew they were trying to either weaken or kill him slowly by starvation.

He was still writing his letters every three days to Dion, the woman he loved, washing the old ones off the wall and starting again; he found that he had developed as a raconteur, telling her of past escapades and battles. At night, in his bed, staring at the flaking roof, he visited the women in his life, his adopted mothers, Merewyn de Malvais and Ette de Malvais, the women who had cared for and loved him since his rescue from the warrior monks as a child. He now found that he was talking to them as if they were sitting in the anchorite cell, listening to him and answering his questions. At times, he blinked and reached out to touch them, but they were not real, and his eyes filled with tears. At times like this, he wondered if he was finally going mad, losing his mind.

Then, one day, he heard voices. These were not the usual distant mumblings that he heard as people walked past on the other side of the abbey wall. These sounded much closer and almost distinct. He moved to stand under the barred window, which had a hand span gap at the bottom for offerings to the anchorite. However, in all the time he'd been here, no one had ever appeared, as an outer wall had been built, only chest height, on the far side of the small triangular grassy area now ablaze with meadow flowers. The wall deterred casual exploration, and most of the people of Chester knew that the saintly old anchorite who had occupied the cell for decades had died.

Georgio dragged the small wooden stool from his table and stood on it so that his head was level with the gap in the barred window. To his surprise, he could see a young man about fifteen years old and a pretty girl whom he'd somehow persuaded to climb over the wall into the privacy of the small meadow. Georgio feasted his eyes on the two people from the normal world. He found he was holding his breath and had even put his hand over his mouth to stop himself crying for help, for God only knew what that would bring down on his head. He racked his brain for something to say as they moved closer, and the dark-haired boy persuaded her to sit on his cloak on the grass. Step one, he whispered to himself and found that he was smiling at the memory, having done it himself many times before. However, he knew he had to speak soon because he couldn't stand there and watch them make love. He went for the gentlest, monk-like voice he could muster.

'God bless you, my children, on this fine summer's day.'

The boy whirled around, frowning, his careful plans foiled. The girl looked shocked initially, but then modestly lowered her eyes and made to kneel up, a flush of embarrassment flooding her cheeks.

'No, please do not go; I presume you have come to ask for a special intention or dispensation? I am an anchorite who, after a year of isolation and prayer, can now commune directly with St. Werburgh.'

The boy, still annoyed, pulled the girl to her feet, but the girl was interested; she came from a good merchant family in the city. She moved closer and stared through the bars at the bearded monk, who seemed younger than expected with kind, deep brown eyes.

'Do I have to pay for these prayers?' she asked.

'No, of course not. I am here to intercede through St. Werburgh with God, and I cannot accept money, but I can accept donations of food; apples, cheese, bread, simple things.'

The boy, resigned to the situation now became interested.

'How long did you say you have been in there? We were all told you were dead.'

'I have been here for a year, purifying myself, but spread the word that the anchorite is now ready to intercede for them. Bring your family and friends.'

Surprisingly, the boy came forward, bringing a small cloth bundle.

'My mother is ill; she has a falling sickness and pains in her head, and the local physician can do nothing for her,' he explained.

Georgio racked his memory, for in the summer when Chatillon and Malvais had gone to England, he'd stayed behind in France to look after and guard the occupants of the chateau. During those long months, he'd watched and learnt much from Ahmed, probably one of the most famous Arab physicians in Europe. He remembered that the falling sickness was often related to the ears, infection, and blockage in the tubes from the throat.

'I will spend several hours a day offering prayers to the saint and asking her to intercede for you, but you must also find the strongest peppermint you can find. There will be a herbalist at the market. Tell her to heat it with crushed mustard seed, nutmeg, and water. I know these are expensive, but I believe this will work. She must place a cloth over her head and inhale the warm vapours thrice daily.'

The boy initially looked taken aback. He'd only expected prayers, but he thanked Georgio and unwrapped the cloth bundle, revealing two apples, a large chunk of cheese and sliced meats. Georgio's mouth watered at the sight, and he had to restrain himself as the boy divided the picnic into three. They ate in silence, Georgio still balancing on his stool.

When they had finished, the girl brushed away any crumbs from the cheese and rose to her feet.

'What is your name?' she asked.

Georgio thought for a few moments but decided not to risk the truth.

'I am named after a famous saint in my part of the world. St Ambrose of Milan.'

'Well, Ambrose, thank you for helping my friend, and I will tell my family you are here.'

With that, they bade him farewell, and he watched them walk away, the boy lifting the giggling girl back over the wall. She turned and raised a hand to him at the last minute, and that was too much for Georgio, who stepped down from the stool and let the silent tears stream down his face.

The next day and the one after, he found himself on the stool, his hands grasping the bars. He stared hungrily at the wall across the small meadow, but they didn't reappear. However, the following day, he noticed one or two people stopping at the wall to stand on tiptoe and look over, so he surmised that word must be spreading that he was there.

Two days later, he was napping in the close, stifling heat of a summer afternoon when a gruff voice woke him.

'Anchorite, anchorite, are you there?'

He scrambled onto his stool and saw a middle-aged man with a stick limping across the grass. A woman was trotting at his side, and for a moment, he wondered how the limping, injured man had got in until he saw a small wooden ladder propped up against the wall.

'God bless you, sir and mistress, welcome. Have you come to request prayers to the holy saint for an intervention?'

The woman nodded while the man looked sceptical and was resigned to being brought there by his wife.

'They are saying your prayers and wisdom have helped the burgher's wife; I want prayers said for my husband here. He is a master thatcher but had a fall from the roof. The physician says the leg is not broken, but a week later, it is still twice the size, and he cannot work. Our sons are still apprentices and are too young and too inexperienced to take his place. He is limping up and down each day, shouting at them on the roof, but their work is nowhere as good as his, and we will lose custom. We want you to pray to the saint to heal his knee quickly.'

Georgio nodded; this was an easy one for him as he'd dealt with many such swellings in horses. He assured them he would ask St. Werburgh to intercede.

'I will dedicate a full day of prayers to you, but can I ask, is the knee hot to the touch?'

The man nodded. 'Yes, and very painful.'

'You must promise me to stay off it for three days. You have a twisted knee. As the Romans used to say, *rubor, calor, tumor, dolar*—every student physician learns that—in other words, redness, heat, swelling and pain. I want you to raise it high when you rest; the humors need to settle. Mistress, I want you to make an embrocation of crushed mandrake root, rosemary and wintergreen oil. Put it in a cold poultice and wrap it around the knee.'

The woman profusely thanked the anchorite as she delved into her bag and brought out a fresh loaf of bread, which she passed through, followed by a full half of salmon wrapped in a damp cloth. *Of course, it's Friday*, thought Georgio as he blessed them for their gifts of food. They turned to leave, but then the man stopped and gave Georgio a long look.

'You must have worked with horses at some point, as I re-member now that my old grandfather used to use wintergreen oil on the knees of his horses if they had fallen.'

Georgio nodded, his eyes filling with tears as he stepped down from the stool. He wanted to yell at the man, *Yes, I am a Horse Warrior! I am not an anchorite. I am a prisoner here in Chester, held against my will!*

Instead, he carried his bounty to the corner table, carefully placing it out of the old monk's sight line. He unwrapped the large salmon, which would probably last him two days. Then, the man's words echoing in his head, he dropped to sit on his palliasse, and, closing his eyes, he banged his head gently back against the wall.

'I am a Horse Warrior. I am a Breton Horse Warrior,' he repeated, over and over, getting louder and louder until he jumped to his feet, clenched his fists and shouted it at the top of his voice.

'I am a Breton Horse Warrior!'

Chapter Fourteen

July 1102 – Kimberworth Castle

Despite the strapping and the strong dose of theriac, Rhodri spent that first night floating in a sea of pain. He knew how lucky he was to be alive; he'd done his best to deflect the blows as they landed, turning and moving as the heavy clubs descended, but they still had broken bones, and if Edvard hadn't arrived....

He was awake several times during the night, and each time, Synnove was there with a cold cloth for his forehead. He could feel a fever building, and she was determined to keep it down. However, as the first light of dawn touched the sides of the tent, he refused any more theriac because although it dulled the pain, it clouded his thinking. As its effects wore off and the waves of pain increased, he made her learn a list of ingredients.

'This is an infusion for pain that my grandfather makes. Go and find willow bark, radish, bishopwort, wild garlic, wormwood, and cropleek. Pound them up and boil them with red nettle, then strain them into a container.'

'I am sure that the physician has several of these, and I know that wild garlic and bishopwort, which we call betony, grows nearby,' she replied.

He watched her run from the tent, a trug on her arm. He saw the purple bruises darkening on her throat, shoulders and arms, and he swore he'd find Crick and kill him for what he'd done to her. He had not dared to ask if he'd forced himself on her; that conversation would be too painful for both of them. But he swore he would hunt him down and put the fear of God into him before he gave him a slow death. And then he would deal with De Courcy.

By now, the bruises were coming out on him too. His blue tribal druidic tattoos could hardly be seen for the black and blue mottling over most of his arms, back and thighs. He could see there was significant swelling that needed to be brought down, for he didn't intend to lie there like a cripple or bed-bound invalid. As soon as the physician arrived to tut over him for refusing theriac, he held up a hand and told him to make a thick salve of mandrake root, henbane, hemlock and bruised black nightshade leaves. He explained it was a druid staple for reducing swelling and inflammation. The physician was more than happy to listen. He went off positively eager, never before having had access to these druidic cures and potions; two hours later, he reappeared and smeared the salve on every bruised and swollen part of Rhodri's body. Only then did Rhodri give in and agree to rest.

Two nights later, De Clare and Malvais sat around the campfire outside their pavilion, watching and occasionally turning chickens, roasting on two small spits over the glowing embers of the banked fire. Beaumont had told them they were leaving for Mexborough the next day, and neither man was sorry. Several flaming torches had been stuck in the ground to give them light as the sky had clouded over again. As silent as ever, Edvard arrived out of the shadows to join them, and as he pulled up a camp chair, De Clare cast him a significant glance to remind him that now was the time to give Malvais the truth about his son.

He gave De Clare a quick nod and indicated toward the chickens. The fat from the birds was dropping and sizzling in the fire, making his mouth water.

'I hope one of those is for me,' he said.

De Clare laughed. 'Yes, but only one, as we have seen your prodigious appetite, and we have not eaten since we broke our fast this morning.'

Edvard slapped his big frame, which they knew was hard, solid muscle.

'This needs a lot of upkeep, and you and I, De Clare, are not getting younger, so we need more food to stop our muscles from wasting away.'

They all laughed, and the chickens—six in all—were taken from the spits and dropped onto the waiting platters to be pulled apart. In no time at all, only carcasses remained, and the men were licking and wiping the grease from their fingers and mouths. Malvais poured them wine, and De Clare stared pointedly at Edvard again, raising his eyebrows in a question. Getting the hint, Edvard took a deep mouthful of wine and began.

'Malvais, we need to tell you something that you will not like, but I assure you that it was done for the best possible reasons, and the decision to keep this from you was to protect those you love.'

Conn sat back in the camp chair and looked from Edvard's face to De Clare in surprise as he watched Edvard take a deep breath to continue. However, there was a noise behind them, and to their astonishment, Rhodri limped slowly and painfully towards the campfire. He had heard Edvard's opening line while he stood in the shadows, catching his breath and waiting for the pain from his ribs to subside.

'I am glad you are finally telling him, as I was about to do so, but I know I have to be here when you do it, as I played a part in this,' he said, his breathing ragged as it hurt to draw deep breaths.

De Clare leapt to his feet, seeing Rhodri struggling and shaken. He offered to help him into a camp chair, but Rhodri refused.

'There is less pain when I stand; I have a staff to lean on. But please continue, Edvard.'

Conn watched all this, his eyes darting from face to face. He could feel his stomach tightening as whatever this was. It was of import—something they had kept from him. It suggested that it was bad news, something painful. Was it his family? Or were they about to tell him that Georgio was dead? The apprehension built as Edvard began to tell the story of what had taken place in Oxford and what they had done with the child—his son.

Conn felt himself go cold at first as he listened in disbelief. Part of him could not at first grasp what they were saying— that his son was alive and now in France, being brought up and cared for by Isabella de Chatillon and Edvard's wife, Mishna.

Edvard saw the shock register on Conn's face and then the telltale red spots of anger appearing on his pale cheekbones as the Horse Warrior's hands clenched. Edvard had rehearsed this speech many times, but the words were now somehow sticking in his throat.

'It is history repeating itself, Conn. This babe was saved in the same way that you were rescued from certain death and whisked away in the night,' he murmured.

It felt like the right thing to say, but now, even to him, the words sounded hollow. Conn's head was suddenly full of images, the tiny shroud-wrapped body in the small stone coffin—the unbearable grief for him and Rohese. He had so many questions, but he was finding it difficult to catch his breath; his chest felt tight. He stood up, and Edvard saw his friend's confusion and lost expression as he stared wildly into the forest's darkness around them. Then he turned and raised his eyes to Edvard, who had also stood, and they stared at one another for a long, drawn-out moment while De Clare watched them both nervously. Edvard could see that Conn needed to be alone for a while, so he stepped to one side to let him leave and watched as he walked off towards the river bank and the solitude of the darkness there.

De Clare released the breath he'd been holding, and the three men stood in silence until De Clare offered to help Rhodri back to the physician's tent. They made slow progress and found a worried Synnove waiting at the door. She helped him slowly lower Rhodri onto the bed while shaking her head at his foolishness in trying to walk anywhere in such pain. Rhodri reached up and grasped De Clare's hand.

'He had to be told, but it should have been sooner.'

De Clare nodded in agreement. 'You are right, Rhodri, but the time never seemed right with the events at Tickhill and here at Kimberworth. Also, we were waiting for news that the child was safe in France. I am also convinced that your attack was linked to the child. Fortunately, I do not believe De Courcy knows that the child lives, but he does now suspect that it was not his child, and no doubt Rohese will suffer for that. However, you must try and put all of this out of your mind; rest and recover, for we need you back with us.'

Rhodri gave a guilty smile. 'I know, and I will try to move a little each day, or these injuries will stiffen.' Then he lowered his voice to whisper to De Clare. 'I will admit that every step of that walk to your campfire was agony, but I had to be there. I had to look him in the face when we told him what we had done.'

De Clare shook his head at his resilience and determination and began to leave, but he stopped at the tent door and turned with a puzzled look.

'How did you know it was tonight that we would tell him? We were originally going to tell him when we reached Mexborough.'

Rhodri gave him one of his enigmatic smiles. 'I knew,' he said before closing his eyes.

Two hours later, Conn returned. He stood in the shadows for a while and looked at his two friends, and a gamut of emotions went through him; he loved these two men, but he found it difficult to believe they had kept this from him, and now, he needed answers. Both men looked at him with apprehension as he stepped forward from the trees, hands hanging by his sides, his face difficult to read in the flickering firelight. He dropped into a chair, stared at them for a while and then demanded that they tell it all, again, from the beginning. Edvard, pouring him some wine, knew that it was going to be alright at that point.

De Clare spelt out all of Rhodri's difficult tasks that he selflessly carried out for Conn and Rohese: finding a suitably ill baby and persuading the parents to part with its body; finding a safe farm on the outskirts of Oxford and moving the baby, the wet nurse, and Joan there for safety; and then helping Edvard arrange their onward journey to France. At that point, Edvard reassured Conn.

'Your child will be safe there, brought up and educated with the children of the chateau. Joan will stay with him for most of his younger childhood, and no doubt tell him of his beautiful mother and brave warrior father. You will visit him as often as you can and will have the chance to watch him grow. He will always know who his father is.'

Edvard paused, and Conn nodded. However, the frown did not lift, and he seemed absorbed in his thoughts, so Edvard continued.

'We called him Darius Fitz Malvais. It seemed the right thing to do, and we thought you might be pleased.'

At this, Edvard saw Conn's eyes lift and shine with tears in the firelight before he sat forward, his hands clasped, and asked, 'And Rohese? Does she know that our child lives? Or is she still shrouded in grief?'

'She does now. I told her before I left Oxford, and she has written you a letter,' said Edvard, handing him a folded piece of vellum.

'One other thing,' said De Claire, sitting forward, glancing behind him to make sure no one was near and then lowered his voice. 'Sir Nigel de Avery and Lady Adeline know about the child, and they guard your secret well, but there is one other—Abbot Columbanus. He knows that the child is your son and not De Courcy's and that we buried a different child, but he does not know where your child is, and he has no proof of any of this. However, Edvard here, with persuasion, did get him to admit he was working with Owen. He pleaded that he had no choice as Owen had threatened him. I am unsure, but he has promised to help us trap the Welsh mercenary in Shrewsbury Abbey when we deliver the ransom for Georgio.'

'That is now less than a month away, and I would lay odds that it will be when Henry summons the army against Belleme, but despite everything, we must be in that abbey on the 15th of August, waiting for Owen ap Cynan. And then justice and vengeance will be delivered,' said Conn.

'Do not fear. Beaumont knows of the importance of this ransom, and he owes you a debt, Malvais, for saving our lives. He will not miss us for three days. Also, we now know for definite, thanks to Philip de Braose, that Robert de Belleme and the Montgomery brothers are at Bridgnorth with some of their forces. I imagine that Henry will plan to challenge him there, and it is less than a day's ride from Shrewsbury,' said De Clare to reassure him.

It was now very late, and the two men headed for their beds, leaving Conn sitting by the embers of the dying fire; he was still reeling from the shock of the news as wave after wave of emotion washed over him. He felt unbridled joy that his son lived and was now safe in France and that he could claim him as his own. But his heart bled for Rohese, who wouldn't see him growing up. He was determined to share news of him when he could with her sister, Lady Adeline, who would pass it on to Rohese.

However, the cold anger still burned inside him for the death of Darius, his squire; it never diminished, and now Abbot Columbanus, yet again, seemed to be wrapped up in all of this and even knew about his son. He could happily snap the neck of the crow-like Abbot without a second thought. Then he remembered De Clare's words—that the Abbot was working with Owen. Did that mean that he knew the whereabouts of

Georgio? If so, how could Columbanus and Owen possibly afford to let Georgio live? He knew too much.

Everything now depended on what happened in the abbey in Shrewsbury. It needed to be meticulously planned to ensure that they got Georgio out of there alive and that Owen and Rhys would die. There would be nowhere for them or their men to run, as he planned to have his and De Clare's men surrounding the abbey and monastery, and if Columbanus was somehow caught up in it, so much the better. Finally, he stood, stretched, and moved into the pavilion to lay on his bed, but sleep did not come for many hours.

When De Clare woke the next morning, his friend was gone. Edvard, who was breaking his fast outside the tent, did not seem concerned.

'I saw him rise just after dawn. He took his bridle so I would lay silver that he has gone for a gallop to clear his head. Why the concern?'

De Clare gave an exasperated snort at his nonchalance.

'He was already like a coiled spring before we imparted last night's news. I would not put it past him to have gone after Columbanus. I saw his face when I told him that; it was like thunder.'

Edvard tore off another chunk of warm bread from the castle ovens and shook his head.

'He would not do that yet; it is more important to him to get Georgio back—that is if he is still alive. Malvais would not do anything stupid to put that at risk.'

Malvais had been for a hard gallop to get the demons out of him and Diablo. He had also sent a bird off to Chatillon to update him on events at Kimberworth; he knew any information on Henry's forces would be useful to the Papal Envoy. Having returned to camp and rubbed Diablo down, he made his way to see Rhodri.

When he arrived, he stood at the tent door and saw that his friend was fretting. The sounds of the camp being dismantled were all around them, and Synnove was assuring Rhodri that he would be moved to the castle to be with Serjeant Fox and his men and that she would be staying with him. He witnessed a tender moment between them as Rhodri reached for her hand and kissed her fingers. However, he made light of it as he entered.

'Be careful, Synnove—he has a reputation for breaking hearts, even when incapacitated like this.'

She smiled and mixed more of the foul-smelling salve that Rhodri insisted on putting on the bruises daily. Malvais pulled up a stool and was shocked at the extent of the bruising he could see, as Rhodri was bare-chested apart from the tight strapping around his ribs.

'They certainly gave you a working over,' he said in a shocked tone, as hardly an inch of flesh on his shoulders and arms was not bruised.

'I do not doubt that they would have killed me, Malvais. My fault for letting my mouth run away with me and sparking De Courcy's ire and revenge. However, the physician tells me the wrist is a clean break and should heal well. I will wear a hard leather wrist guard for the next six months and try not to punch anyone with that hand,' he said with a laugh.

Conn was astounded that he could laugh and joke so lightly, for he could only imagine the pain he was in.

'I am sorry that you have suffered on my account, but I am here to thank you for what you have done for my son. That was well over the duties of a Horse Warrior; it was the actions of a friend, and I will never forget it. I do promise you that we will find the leader who escaped. I discovered from one of the wagon drivers that his name was Crick, Wilken Crick, a dangerous man who emerged from the back streets of London but in the employ of De Courcy. I am told he is a man to be wary of, quick with his fists and dagger at any slight or insult. But you and I will hunt him down once we have Georgio safe.'

Seeing the hard, cold gleam in Conn's eyes, Rhodri believed him and was pleased.

'For now, rest and recuperate, Rhodri; we will be back from Mexborough in a week or two,' he said, as Synnove returned with a red-coloured liquid, which the druid drained. He dropped back against the bolster and closed his eyes.

'What was that?' Conn asked the young woman.

'His grandfather's infusion. And Rhodri is right—it works fast and reduces inflammation. Alaric, the physician, is elated as they are far more potent and effective than ours.'

That didn't surprise him with what he'd seen of the wise and astute old druid in the mountains. He bade them farewell and emerged into the sunshine to find De Clare waiting for him.

'Beaumont wants to see us,' he said, leading the way.

They found their leader by the river, watching his men watering their horses before they left.

'I hope we will be away from here within the next hour. Will you and your men ride ahead as usual and scout the land? I am not ready for any more surprises in or outside the castle at Mexborough.'

Both men smiled at his sally, bowed their assent and made to turn away, but Robert Beaumont called them back.

'Wait! I promised I would reward you for saving my life

twice, Conn Fitz Malvais, and so I have had one of my clerics draw this up for you.'

He reached out to his squire, who handed him a rolled document. He handed it to Malvais, who unrolled it and read the contents with surprise.

'You are giving this to me, Sire? I do not deserve or expect this. I was only doing what I was trained to do. My men and I are already generously paid for our services by King Henry,' replied Conn, trying to hand it back, but Beaumont brushed away his words.

'If it had not been for your courage and skill with a sword, I would not be here today after what happened at Branston. I know De Tosny would have killed me; my arms were weakening, and I could no longer hold him off. I had prepared myself to die when your sword slashed down between us. You risked your life for me, fighting your way through that throng of De Tosny's men, and that is not something I will forget, Malvais. Then, here at Kimberworth, your gut instinct and quick thinking saved all our lives that night by recognising John de Ware and sending for your men. You rightly deserve this reward.'

Conn gave in gracefully and passed the document to De Clare, who scanned it and raised an eyebrow at the generosity of the gift. Beaumont had given Malvais the lands and manor of Neauphle-le-Chateau. It was in France, not far from Paris and, just as importantly, only a day's ride from Chatillon-sous-Bagneux, where his son was being brought up. For a moment, De Clare searched Beaumont's face for any guile. Could he possibly know the child was alive and where he had gone? But he could see no amusement, or knowledge of it, in the noble's face and dismissed the thought.

'Look at it this way, Malvais, you will actually be doing me a favour by taking it off my hands. I inherited this as part of a large portion of land from my mother's side of the family. The old knight who lived and farmed there as my tenant died without an heir. A bailiff runs it, but I will be honest: I have never set foot on it, and I have neglected it somewhat. The castle and lands are now yours and on record with the French notary at the King's court in Paris. You have been in a better position than I am, for I am tied body and soul by blood and loyalty to King Henry, but as a sell-sword, you have always been able to choose whom you fight for. Now, however, you will owe your tithes and fealty to the French king, but I have never found that a problem. You can send him ten men or the silver instead if you are ever called to pay. However, I need to warn you that things may change if King Philip dies and Louis, the Dauphin, takes the throne. He is a different fish altogether from his indolent father—more like a great pike eating up the smaller prey. He may expect more of you, and we all know he has his eyes on the Norman Vexin area, which he believes should be in France. I need to tell you this so you are prepared.'

Malvais found himself lost for words; he'd never expected anything like this, a pouch of silver, maybe, or new weapons but not land. He knew that when his father, Morvan, died, he would inherit a small estate on the troublesome borders of Maine, which his father received as a reward from King William. Until now, he'd always been a landless knight, one of many who sold their swords to the highest bidder, yet he had just been given ownership of a manor and land in France.

Edvard had arrived to join them by the river as this was happening, and now he frowned as he heard all of this, for the ownership of these lands and fealty to the French king could have implications that Chatillon might not like. He resolved to get De Clare's view and to send a bird off to Piers, who had been in Rome attempting to placate and direct Pope Paschal's policy but was returning home for the birth of his child. Edvard felt this award of land in France may not be welcome news to his master, who had other, more imminent plans for Conn Fitz Malvais.

Chapter Fifteen

Late July 1102 – Mexborough

It was later that morning when they finally set off for Mexborough Castle. The arrival of Sir Philip de Braose and his men from Windsor had delayed them, as he immediately reported to Robert Beaumont and gave him messages from the King. To De Clare's surprise, Sir Philip also had new information about the movement of King Maredudd's forces, which was particularly annoying as he had heard nothing from Prince Iorwerth, who had promised them so much in return for his life and the throne of Powys. He complained bitterly to Malvais and Edvard as they rode along what was known as the Great Roman Ridge, a long defensive structure that was built for defence by the Brigantes against the Romans.

'De Braose must have some highly placed informers in the Powys camp; I hope they are not feeding him disinformation on purpose to lead us yet again into a trap,' muttered De Clare in a disgruntled tone.

'I do not know why you are complaining. We use information from Chatillon on a regular basis, and it has always proved to be trusted and useful,' commented Malvais.

'Yes, exactly! Because it is trusted, and people are afraid of Chatillon and his men. He can squeeze words out of the tightest lips. But what is young De Braose using? His charm and enthusiasm? More importantly, how is he getting this information?'

'Kenric,' said Edvard, who had listened to De Clare's rant in amusement.

De Clare turned in the saddle to look at Edvard in astonishment.

'What? Kenric, his manservant? The dark, handsome lad in his twenties who wants to be a knight?'

Edvard nodded. 'That is the one, but he is highly intelligent, and Philip is very liberal with his money. The one thing Piers de Chatillon found out at an early age is that you get what you pay for. Also, Kenric's mother is Welsh; she is one of the ladies of the court at Mathrafal who serves Maredudd's wife, Hunydd ferch Einudd. So our friend, Kenric, has reason to be there and seems to come and go as he pleases, unmolested, bringing back vital information for our ambitious friend, Sir Philip.'

Malvais gave a snort of laughter, for Edvard, with his constant surveillance and usual judicious questioning, had found out more in a few weeks than De Clare had in months.

'This Kenric must be very good or very lucky, flitting in and out of both camps like a ghost,' said Conn as he pushed a restless, head-shaking Diablo into a controlled canter.

Edvard watched in admiration at the easy way he controlled the big, tempestuous Destrier, which was now cantering sideways, throwing in the odd playful buck and shaking its head up and down to lessen the control and pressure on the bit so he could break into a gallop. Conn refused to let him have his way and constantly turned him in circles on the ridge until they came to the cultivated manor fields and grazing meadows around the castle. Only then did he turn him down the steep bank into the fields and let him go, galloping ahead to scout the route for Beaumont.

A short while later, he was back, and he reined in beside the lead group.

'This ridge goes all the way to the River Don, and there's no sign of troops there, Sire. The castle gates are wide open, with only a small group of frightened villagers seemingly waiting in front of their houses nearby.'

Beaumont signalled for the column to move forward towards the village. The houses were clustered around the road approaching the castle, and at a glance, Beaumont could see that this was much smaller than the previous two they had taken. It was a typical timber motte and bailey castle. The villagers had all dropped to their knees at the sight of the great Robert Beaumont, his pennants and flags flying and what seemed to them, a great host of knights and men behind him. De Clare saw the real fear on their faces as mothers clutched their children closely.

'Who is the Castellan or leader here?' shouted Philip de Braose, having taken it upon himself, again, to be Beaumont's herald.

A thick-set, bald-headed man got to his feet and bowed repeatedly in their direction. De Clare could see the sweat of fear beading his forehead as his wife pushed him forward.

'The Castellan has left, Sire; the news came and spread like wildfire of what had happened at Tickhill and Kimberworth castles. The peddlers brought the news of the proclamation; the one that was read in every market town about the execution of John de Ware. They reckon he was torn apart while he still lived, and that was enough for the Castellan and his family. They packed their goods and abandoned us. He rode off to join the Earl of Shrewsbury, leaving us all to face you and your army,' he said, wiping the sweat from his brow with a scrap of cloth from his jerkin.

De Clare could see the man's hand was shaking, so he rode forward a few steps and stared down at him.

'How long have you been bailiff here?' he asked in a gentler tone.

'Nigh on twelve years now, Sire, but I was his assistant long before that. I do a good job, as the folks here will tell you. John Watkins, firm but fair, that's me,' he said in a slightly more confident tone.

De Clare nodded and encouraged him. 'So, you were De Busli's man.'

Watkins nodded vigorously. 'The Lady Muriel was always very good to us after her lord died, but then Robert de Belleme came and took over the land, raising tithes and taxes. He also took many of the young men away to be soldiers; the sons who the people needed to help work the land. We haven't seen hide or hair of them since.'

De Clare turned to Beaumont and shrugged at this catalogue of woe; the villagers were certainly not on the side of Belleme.

'It seems we will have no opposition here, so let us ride into the castle and make use of what little there is. We will set up our camp inside the bailey, and the men can take over the meadow. I am sure our friend, John Watkins, can slaughter some animals to feed us.'

The bailiff nodded in agreement, the relief on his face plain to see, as Beaumont agreed with De Clare's suggestion. Kicking their horses on, they rode along the village street and up into the bailey of the castle, which overlooked the River Don. As usual, Malvais sent his scouts to ride the fields and woods around, but nothing was found. It seemed the bailiff spoke the truth. However, he and De Clare set up rotas of sentries so they wouldn't be caught napping again.

Out to impress and win the favour of the King's men, the bailiff and the villagers did them proud, and the long trestle tables in the hall groaned under the weight of roast meats, chickens, and fish from the river. The women must have baked all afternoon, as there were dozens of large, warm, round loaves and slabs of golden butter and cheeses.

'The lands around here must be bountiful indeed,' remarked Edvard to John Watkins, who was hovering to make sure all was well for Lord Robert Beaumont and his knights. Edvard waved him to a seat.

'They always have been, Sire. The meadows by the river are rich and lush for the grazing of kine and sheep, but De Croix, the Castellan placed here by Belleme, tried to bleed us dry; he treated freemen and villains alike as serfs. Then he stole our young men, attracting them with tales of war and gallantry and a silver coin for each of them. Two of my sons, he took, who used to help me at the mill.'

Edvard liked the man. He seemed an honest soul buffeted by the winds of fortune, so he raised his cup to him. 'I will say a prayer that this war is over swiftly and they are safely returned to you.'

The bailiff thanked him and went to chivvy the serving girls to bring more ale. The hall was not large, and the men were crammed close on the trestle tables, but the food was good and the relief palpable that they hadn't been called on to fight. Glancing around, Edvard realised that Malvais was missing;

he presumed that, as usual, he'd be checking on the sentries or the horse lines as thoroughly as usual. However, sometime later, he still had not appeared, so Edvard got to his feet and headed for the doors. He paused briefly beside Gracchus and the Horse warriors.

'Has anyone seen Malvais?' he asked, and the big Greek replied.

'He was doing the rounds, but I saw him talking to a local and asking about the small stone church or chapel in the trees.'

Edvard stepped outside and went down the wooden steps towards the bailey. A young woman was coming up, eyes down; she was intent on watching her step while carrying something, so he stepped to one side to let her pass.

'Can you tell me which direction the church is in?' he asked, taking her by surprise.

The woman stopped, flustered by the attention, her arms laden high with warm loaves from the bread ovens.

'It's only a small chapel really, over there in the clearing, named after John the Baptist it is. The bailiff tells us he was christened in it, but we reckon it must have only been a wooden shed in those days,' she said, laughing.

Edvard realised that this was a village joke, so he thanked her with a smile. He could feel the relief of these people after the rumours and horror stories of what had happened at other castles. However, he knew they had reason to be afraid, for over fifty of John de Ware's men had been killed at Kimberworth.

It was dark now, and the lowering clouds threatened rain as he squinted over at the clearing in the direction she indicated and made his way to find the small church. He pushed the door open, dipped his fingers in the holy water of the stoup to cross himself, and walked slowly forward down the nave.

Only one large candle was lit on the altar, so the church was full of shadows. As usual, there were no benches, only a few stools for the old and infirm at the sides. It may be small, but it had been decorated and cared for. At the transept, the church had two separate bye-altars off both sides of the nave for prayers and special intentions to be offered. He noticed the one on the left was dedicated to St John the Baptist, but at first, he could see no sign of Conn. He walked forward to where the nave crossed the small transept when a slight noise caught his attention in the bye-altar on the right. From the light of the candle, he could just see that this altar was dedicated to Our Lady of the Seven Sorrows. What he saw made him step back into the shadows and lean on the nearest pillar, as the Horse Warrior had obviously wanted to be on his own.

Conn had removed his tunic and lay face down in supplication.

Two things struck Edvard. First, Conn never removed his undershirt, yet here he was, naked from the waist up, the vivid colours of the tattoo that covered his back reflected in the light of the candle. Then there was Conn praying—a rare sight. The formative and vicious years with the Warrior Monks, when religion had dominated almost every waking moment, had scarred Conn for life.

Edvard held his breath and waited; he could see and hear that Conn was praying for the people he'd lost, but as he heard the words of the well-known Confiteor prayer, he realised that Conn was acknowledging his guilt and begging for forgiveness for not protecting his men, Andreas, Gracchus, Georgio, Darius and now Rhodri. Edvard froze as Conn stood and began the last lines of *mea culpa, mea maxima culpa.*

However, to add to Edvard's unease, instead of the usual three times, Conn repeated it all *seven* times. Edvard felt the hairs on the back of his neck stand up, and he shivered as he remembered Chatillon talking about Conn's dark side.

Seven times whilst standing in the chapel of the *Seven Sorrows*, and as Conn raised his arms, Edvard suddenly saw the seven drops of blood, bright red, that dripped from the crown of thorns that hung on the full-length, sword-shaped crucifix tattooed on his back. *Seven.* The 'Power of *Seven'* was hammered into the *Seven* chosen young acolytes who were to be sent out into the world as Warriors of Christ to kill and carry out every wish of the twisted Cardinal Dauferio, who became Pope Victor III. A pope whom Chatillon was forced to murder before he destroyed the Holy See with his plans.

Edvard, an expert at not making a sound, slowly backed out of the chapel, for this was something he shouldn't have seen. It had unsettled him, for it showed that even in someone as level-headed and courageous as Conn, when under a huge amount of emotional grief, the indoctrination from six years in the hands of those monks was still there, ingrained.

As Conn came out of the chapel, Edvard walked up to him as if he'd just arrived.

'I heard you were in here. I understand your need to get away at times; you have suffered so much over the last year or so, it is inevitable that it will take its toll.'

Conn gave a grateful nod and clasped arms with his friend and mentor. He trusted Edvard implicitly, and intuitively, he knew that Edvard saw and understood his anguish.

'I need to talk to you, Conn and now is as good a time as any. Come, I have found a particularly fine wine which is waiting for us in your pavilion. Edvard had ordered his man to light a fire, and he and Conn sat for a while, just the two of them, and watched the flames. The raucous noises from the hall drifted down across the bailey occasionally. For the first time in a while, Conn felt at peace. He'd found the ritual in the chapel to be cathartic, and suddenly, the future looked somewhat brighter; his son was alive, and they would rescue Georgio.

'Much has happened since you came to England on the orders of Chatillon, some good, some bad, but because of some of these events, I fear that you are losing sight of your mission here. You begged Chatillon at the paddock rails at the chateau several years ago to take you on as his apprentice. He did so, and reluctantly at first, unsure whether you had the cold instinct of an assassin. However, you proved yourself, again and again, as we fought against Sheikh Ishmael and his men, and Chatillon began to believe he had indeed found an heir to his legacy. Then unexpectedly, there came the murder of Marietta, and blaming yourself for her death, you ran. You fled east to Byzantium, but both Chatillon and I believe that was, in fact, the making of you as you became a great and respected leader in the forces of Emperor Alexios. More importantly, over that year, you learned to live with your grief.'

Edvard paused, taking a large mouthful of wine as he let his words sink in. He needed Conn to realise his importance and his role in how the future would play out. Again, they sat in silence for a while. The threatened rain had blown over, and the night sky was now clear.

'I did love her—Marietta,' murmured Conn.

'Do not punch me if I say this, but I was never convinced; I think you fell in love with the idea of her. You put her on a pedestal because she was beautiful inside and out and totally in love with you, but we did not think you were ready. Afterwards, you were consumed by guilt, but realistically, you could never have reached or saved her or Finian on that night; it was impossible. I think your guilt was because you knew you did not love her enough.'

Conn considered this for a while, and deep inside, thinking of his all-consuming love for Rohese, he knew that Edvard was right. So, he reluctantly inclined his head in agreement.

'Now, you are back in a similar situation, but we have no problem with your anger for the death of Darius and the capture of Georgio. That is normal. You saw Chatillon when his wife and twin sons were taken; he was distraught, consumed with fury and rage. But he turned that anger and anguish into a clear purpose, getting them back and carefully planning his revenge. I have never met another man like him for his ability to remove all emotion from any situation, but he only learnt to do that when he was a similar age to you after horrendous events in Rome and Budapest. I now have two things I need to ask you,' he said, and paused.

Conn shivered slightly. The clear night had brought a chill breeze, but it was more the tone of Edvard's voice, so he waited with some apprehension for the questions.

'You are sending regular information on the movement of the King's troops and Henry's plans to Chatillon. There is no doubt that some of this he will share with Belleme as part of the bigger plan, for I know that Pope Paschal does not want this to be an easy victory for King Henry. He wants to sow doubt and fear, for the last thing Paschal wants is a triumphant, ebullient King of England who has no gratitude, or respect, for the Holy See. He wants Henry to have to fight and struggle to keep the crown he stole from Duke Robert, for that still rankles with the Pope.'

Edvard paused again as he gathered his thoughts, and Conn waited, for he thought he knew what was coming. It was a question that he'd asked himself recently in the dark reaches of the night when sleep would not come.

'In the next month, the delivery of the ransom, the freeing of Georgio and the killing of Owen and his men are of paramount importance. However, once that is over and the fate of England is decided on the battlefield, what do you see for yourself? Do you consider yourself bound by the promises you made to Chatillon several years ago? Since then, you have made a name for yourself here in England with King Henry and the Beaumonts and have been richly rewarded with land in France. Does this pull your loyalty in different directions? Fealty to the French king, allegiance to Beaumont? You can imagine how Chatillon might view this—you do realise that he will expect your loyalty to him to be absolute, don't you?'

This was not the question that Conn was expecting, and it gave him pause as he considered Edvard's words. This was not a flippant question, and he had the right to ask it given his recent actions and behaviour. But now, he had to think how he would phrase his answer. The question had all sorts of implications, so his words had to be chosen carefully before answering.

'I have no allegiance to Beaumont; I merely serve him because the Horse Warriors are in the pay of King Henry. However, I like and respect the man; he is a fighter, not easily frightened. I also have the advantage that he is now in my debt. As for the lands he gave me, I was astounded and have not really had time to think it through. I suppose that, like Chatillon, if my lands are in France, I owe some sort of fealty to King Philip. However, I have always considered that the loyalty of myself and Georgio are to Piers de Chatillon, who never gave up searching for us as captives; we owe him and you our lives. I see him as my liege lord and patron, and now he is raising my son for me.'

Edvard nodded in satisfaction and refilled their cups.

'Chatillon's case is slightly different; he was born in France to an old, wealthy and respected French family that produced statesmen and popes. You are a Breton Horse Warrior, through and through, although you now own these lands, and the French Seneschal is aware of that transfer. However, you can tenant them if you wish, and then the obligation to provide men or money to the French king will be transferred to the knight who takes on the tenancy, but he will also have a responsibility to you as his liege lord,' explained Edvard.

Conn hadn't considered that possibility, but he dismissed it. 'I think I'd like to stand on my own lands first, see exactly what I own and what it consists of. Are there villages? Is there a house or small castle?'

Edvard could understand what that moment would feel like for a landless knight. He had never owned land but spent his life living in the grace and favour of others he served.

'From the second that scroll of ownership was handed over, those lands were yours. Shall I ask Daniel and his men to ride over and check on the bailiff Beaumont has in place? I am sure I heard him use the word neglected, and that tends to give some bailiffs free rein, which in turn can lead to them becoming petty tyrants, some even considering the land their own.'

Conn nodded, and Edvard stood and gave Conn a hand to pull him to his feet. He didn't let it go; instead, he increased his grip and pulled him forward, their faces close.

'The second question depended on your answer to the first. You told Chatillon you wanted to become what he is, to be trained to inherit his legacy. You said you wanted to help him run his informer network, which, as you know, operates in every court and every city in Europe.'

Conn's eyes were fixed on Edvard's face, which was lit eerily from the dancing flames of the fire. He nodded as he wondered what was coming next.

'But more importantly, you begged him to teach you to become the lethal assassin that he is because he recognised the need in you. So I now ask you on his behalf, is that what you still want, Conn Fitz Malvais? Do you still crave the danger and the exhilaration that comes from slipping a knife between a man's ribs in the dark corridor of some palace? Do you want to smile quietly to yourself with satisfaction while watching the poison you dripped into their wine rush through someone's blood as they drop and groan?'

The grip on Conn's hand became tighter. He could feel Edvard's breath on his face as he remembered the day he had begged Chatillon to teach him—the day he realised that he did not only want to be a Horse Warrior and a sell-sword, but also wanted to make a name for himself. He wanted to see the respect, awe, and fear that Piers de Chatillon engendered when he walked into a room. Since then, however, so much has happened. He'd killed so many and lost so many, but was he that same person? he asked himself. The thoughts raced through his mind as the sheer intensity of Edvard's gaze never wavered. Then the realisation came that he still yearned for more than just this. The fighting, the battles, the plaudits and the companionship of his men were all very estimable in their own right, but he knew they were not enough.

'Yes,' he said in a whisper and then again louder. 'Yes, I want that.'

Edvard slowly released his hand and stepped back. Conn found his face difficult to read, but he felt, rather than saw, that this was the right answer.

'I would have expected nothing less from the man who assassinated the great Sir Hugh, the Wolf of Chester. Chatillon has a new assignment for you to be carried out as soon as possible. There is a man who must be removed, and a large amount of silver has been paid for this. Chatillon has agreed that half of it will come to you.'

Conn felt somehow relieved and elated at the same time as he made his decision. The silver would always be useful, but deep down, he knew that was secondary. Chatillon had seen and recognised his darker side, his lust for danger. And, more importantly, his lack of empathy, something which the Warrior Monks had thoroughly erased. Marietta had seen it in him, too; she saw what he was but had still loved him. As for Rohese, she knew he was one of Chatillon's assassins and accepted it. So now, he nodded in acceptance of this new assignment.

'Who is it? Is he here or in one of the enemy camps?' he asked, as Edvard dropped back into the camp chair and poured more wine for them both.

'He is here, which makes it easier as you know him and his movements.'

'Who?' asked Conn, with the first tingle of apprehension; *it is surely not Beaumont or,* God forbid, *De Clare?*

'It is a troublesome, ambitious knight, Sir Philip de Braose, who has been far too busy for someone's liking.' Conn froze for a moment before dropping into the chair beside Edvard.

'Philip?' he murmured, surprised at first, for he considered the man a friend.

However, thinking back to De Clare's comments, he could see why. Philip was supplying a lot of information to the King and Beaumont, but now he was a target and had to die. He felt Edvard's gaze on him, watching his reaction, and so he nodded as he didn't want to raise any doubts about his ability to do this.

'He will be removed,' he said, and drained his cup.

Chapter Sixteen

It always gave Piers de Chatillon a warm feeling when he rode back through the gates and stone archway of his home. It was a large old chateau that had been extended with two larger wings being built over several generations. The original old tower, reinforced with several buttresses and made higher by Chatillon's father, was still there but was now encircled by a defensive wall with embrasures. As he rode into the courtyard with his men, he looked up and saw the figure of his friend, Ahmed, and raised a hand in greeting. Ahmed had happily taken over the care of the carrier pigeons in the coop on the top of the tower as he undertook the deciphering and sending of many messages each day whilst Edvard was in England.

   Piers had been away in Rome for two months, attending and updating Pope Paschal on events and politics across Europe. He found that this pope took far more managing than most because he was a worrier. Piers thought back with nostalgia to the previous popes, including his uncle; all of them had been more able and astute than Paschal. Fortunately, Piers had surrounded this troublesome pope with his own appointees, papal clerics, trained by him not to let the Holy Father make any rash decisions without notifying him first. He had left the Lateran Palace earlier than expected as Isabella was due to give birth in the next few weeks, and he was determined to be back home for that.

Even though he had Ahmed at the chateau, Piers knew that childbirth could be a risky business and dangerous if childbed fever set in, which could take the healthiest and youngest woman in less than a week. However, Isabella seemed unconcerned; she was excited about this unexpected late child despite being nearly thirty-eight years old.

As he reined in outside the great doors, there she was, looking as beautiful as ever, waiting on the steps with Dion and Mishna to greet him as he dismounted. He was hot, dusty, and tired, but he ran up the steps to greet her.

'You are a sight for sore eyes, my love, and you are glowing with health,' he said, stroking the corn-coloured golden hair in which not a grey hair had yet appeared despite the trauma and grief she'd experienced.

Oblivious to anyone else, her eyes feasted on him. She knew she shouldn't, but she worried about him when he made the regular long trips to Rome, which took over a week on horseback or even longer in bad weather. He still took his position as Senior Papal Envoy very seriously, but part of her wished he'd step down; then she laughed at herself for such a thought as she knew he revelled in the power and influence it gave him. He kissed her deeply, and excitement coursed through her. She may be huge with his child, but his very touch still made her senses tingle. He released her and, greeting the other women, he put his arm around his wife's waist and went into his hall where the large dyer hounds thrust their wet noses into his hands as they ecstatically greeted their master. He dropped his aching limbs into a chair.

Ahmed quietly entered the hall, clutching a pouch of messages to his chest. Piers greeted him with a welcoming nod, knowing they would go up to his business room to go through them.

'Is it my imagination, or are you twice the size you were before I left?' he said regarding Isabella. Madame Chambord brought in a tankard of cold ale and a tray of his favourite small honey cakes. She'd worked in the chateau since she was a young girl and had moved up to become his housekeeper and cook many years before. In her eyes, he could do no wrong.

'That's because she is carrying the weight of two. I tell her repeatedly that it is twins again, but she is in denial,' said Ahmed, while Isabella rolled her eyes at him.

'This is my fifth child; I would know if it was twins. This is just a large baby.'

At that moment, Joan appeared from the garden with Dion's youngest and Darius in her arms, now over three months old. Chatillon waved her over and noticed that the boy's eyes followed all movement in the hall.

'Is he thriving? He seems to be,' he asked, taking hold of one of the waving fists that tightly gripped his fingers. 'He certainly seems to have his father's strength,' he laughed.

Isabella smiled; she was pleased that Joan had settled seamlessly into the house. She'd certainly had an impact on Fergus, Dion's middle boy, who had been starting to run wild. Now, he sat at a table each morning for geography, history, Greek, and Latin, and was full of stories of Greek heroes and battles.

Chatillon drained his tankard and, waving Ahmed to follow,

made for the stairs. To his surprise, Isabella followed him, mounting each stair slowly.

'I am not prepared to relinquish sight and sound of you just yet,' she said, and he smiled, taking her arm.

Nearly two dozen messages from all corners of Europe were in Ahmed's hands, and he divided them into two piles. The first pile contained urgent messages and essential information, and the second pile was to be dealt with later. Ahmed placed both piles in chronological order, as he'd seen Edvard do in the past.

Chatillon read and then shook his head at the messages from the court of the Holy Roman Emperor, Henry IV.

Chatillon and his uncle, Pope Urban, had put a lot of time, money, and support into the Emperor's son and heir, Conrad. Unlike his father, who was constantly at war with the Pope, Conrad wanted to embrace a partnership with the Holy See. Conrad had many supporters in Italy, but when he turned against his father, Henry, the Emperor, a ruthless man, acted swiftly and had Conrad formally deposed as his heir. Instead, the Emperor had his second son, Henry, crowned as King of Germany and even made him co-ruler of the empire. Chatillon was now busily working behind the scenes to convert the young Henry back to the Pope and the Holy See.

Isabella saw the frown on Chatillon's face; she guessed it was news about the Emperor. Conrad had died; he'd been poisoned last summer. He was only twenty-seven but he'd become a thorn in his father's side that needed removing.

'Has it worked?' she asked. He knew immediately what she was asking, as she was an astute and intelligent woman who kept her finger on the pulse of European politics.

'It is beginning to gain ground; we paid the young Bavarian

counts a significant amount to influence young Henry and take him under their wing. They have succeeded and now have a plan to depose the Emperor, which will play right into our hands.

'Ahmed, send a message to Henry, King of Germany, to let him know that Pope Paschal offers money and support for his plans and that I am willing to travel to Aachen to discuss this.'

'But, not yet!' snapped Isabella.

'Of course,' he reassured her, but he winked at Ahmed, who laughed.

They worked their way through the diminishing piles of messages until Chatillon reached Edvard's message. He gave a low whistle as he read the contents, and Isabella raised her eyebrows.

'Good news or bad?' she asked.

'Well, it seems young Darius will have an inheritance. Conn has been granted significant lands at Neauphle-le-Chateau as a reward for saving Robert Beaumont's life twice. Edvard suggests we send Daniel and a few of his men over there to see what condition it is in and how it is being managed. I may ride over there with them; it is only a half day's ride,' he said, raising his eyes to hers.

Isabella threw her hands up in exasperation.

'Well, you were missing for the birth of all of our children, so I should not expect you to be here for this one,' she responded in an emotional voice as she struggled to her feet.

Chatillon moved swiftly around the table and held her face in his hands. 'I love you, Isabella, and I swear I will be here.' Her expression softened at that, and she stroked his face before leaving them to it.

Ahmed shook his bird-like head at him. 'She always becomes more and more short-tempered as the time approaches, and I promise, it is twins, so I would not linger there. I estimate five days,' said Ahmed, leaving his friend to read the last message from Edvard on his own. As he scanned the words, Chatillon smiled, for Edvard assured him that Conn had accepted the assignment but was somewhat perturbed by it. Chatillon was not concerned by his being 'perturbed' for he had confidence in his disciple, and would watch and wait with interest to see how he would handle this situation.

For the next three days, Piers busied himself with estate business and spent time with Isabella. However, late the following evening, he waved his captain over. Daniel had been with him for nearly twenty years, ever since he had arrived as a young eighteen-year-old sell-sword looking for work. Piers trusted him implicitly; he was a good man to have at one's back, quick with his sword and intelligent, always thinking on his feet. He had successfully carried out dozens of assignments for Chatillon and had never flinched from being put in danger.

'I am sure you heard me say that Conn has come unexpect-edly into some land at Neauphle-le-Chateau. What do we know about that area? It is only a few leagues from us, I believe.'

Daniel, who was never one to rush into conversation, thought for a few moments before replying.

'I remember they had a few problems when the old lord died. It sits at the end of the Plain of Versailles, close to the western forests of Rambouillet, often the haunt of robbers and deserters. However, I have not heard it mentioned by the passing peddlers or merchants for a while now.'

That triggered Chatillon's memory. 'Ah yes, the new Seneschal who took up the position after the death of Gervais had plans to round up those deserters, and I believe he cleared most of them out, but like rats when left alone for a while, they slink back in. We will ride over there tomorrow. I think five or six men will suffice.'

◦◦◦◦◦

As Piers surmised, it was not far, nearer three leagues, but still under a half day on a fresh horse. They could see the obvious neglect as they rode up the rutted track towards the village and main house. The houses of the villagers and villeins alike were run down, with thatch in desperate need of repair and broken or rotten shutters. A blacksmith's shop was at the end of the row, but it had an empty, unused air as if the fire hadn't been lit for a very long time. There was little sign of life in the village apart from the pigs rooting between the hovels and a small pack of mangy curs that were not even interested enough to give a voice in warning. The fields yonder were unkempt, and the borders of the strips were strewn with weeds, which would never be allowed to happen with any management.

'I think Conn may have his work cut out here,' murmured Daniel as they left the single street of the village and rode towards what he expected to be the manor house, which sat on a slight rise.

The village was named after the chateau, which, although it had a pleasant, double-fronted, open-faced aspect, was barely a third of the size of Chatillon's home. There was no tower, but it was solid, built of old stone, and ivy grew up its walls. As they rode through the gates, they could see the neglect there as well—piles of stinking refuse littering the stable yard to the right. They clattered over the filthy and broken cobbles, and to their surprise, an old ostler appeared in answer to their shouts. He'd obviously just woken up as he blinked his eyes like an owl in the sunlight and rubbed them as if he could barely comprehend what he saw.

'You there, come and take this horse for my lord and then the others. Tie them over there in the shade and make sure they have water,' ordered Daniel.

The man knuckled his forehead and went to take the reins.

'Where is the bailiff? Is he still here at the manor?' asked Chatillon whilst dismounting.

The man twisted his face unto a grimace before answering.

'Oh, he be here alright. He be in there, never any place else. Since the old lord died, four years hence, gone to ruin the place has under his dirty stealing hands,' he said, pointing at the chateau.

Daniel and Chatillon exchanged a meaningful glance before heading for the manor house's doors and mounting the steps.

'You can see this was well built; these are solid, old oak doors, but the handles are loose. Nothing has been maintained here for years. I am surprised that Beaumont has not noticed the fall off in tithes and revenue,' commented Daniel.

'I think that Beaumont only inherited a few years ago, and he has had other things on his mind, Daniel, with Duke Robert's invasion of England and the rebellion. This is probably one of a dozen manors he inherited from his mother. I would lay odds that he has never set foot here; possibly, no one has since the old knight died,' answered Chatillon, pushing the heavy doors open.

The bright sunshine behind them shone into the larger-than-expected hall. It reminded Chatillon of King William's hunting lodge at l'Aigle as it had a beautifully carved wooden staircase to one side, which led to a galleried balcony on three sides. However, here the similarity ended as the smell from the hall hit them. It was filthy—rotting rushes on the floor strewn with mouldy food, chicken bones, and carcasses. It looked as if it had been barely cleaned for years. The trestle tables were still covered in trenchers and leather tankards, all filthy and untouched.

'The bailiff lives in this?' asked Daniel in a shocked tone.

Chatillon's eyes, having roved over the empty hall, went towards the staircase. He waved Daniel and two of their men forward to follow him.

'We will search upstairs. Search the kitchens and outbuildings; gather any servants or villagers you can find in the courtyard,' he ordered the other four men as he took the stairs two at a time with Daniel close behind him.

He pointed the other two men to search the rooms on the other side of the gallery while he and Daniel opened the ones on this side. In every room, there was dust and dirt or soiled pallet beds. They continued to the end and, through an arched opening along a short corridor, flung open the door to the main chamber. The shutters were slightly ajar, letting light spill onto the scene before them.

A large, corpulent, bald man, who obviously liked his food, lay naked and snoring on the bed. Beside him were two women, one plump older one and the other a young woman. Both had been asleep, but the younger one awoke and pulled the soiled cover up to hide her nakedness as she stared in shock at the armed men now striding into the room. She let out a strangled scream, which woke the older woman, who stared in horror while scrambling for a crumpled gown on the floor. The bailiff, meanwhile, snored on, oblivious to what was happening. His bare chest bore evidence of wine stains, and at least two empty wine sacks were on the floor.

'Wake him!' ordered Chatillon to the older woman, who quickly knelt on the bed and vigorously shook the man while the girl still cowered with the cover clutched to her chin.

The bailiff let out a torrent of abuse at the woman and swung a hand, which hit the side of her face. Chatillon sighed and nodded to Daniel, who waved her away and drew his dagger. He moved towards the bed as Chatillon ordered her to throw the shutters wide. The girl sprang from the bed, snatched up her shift and ran for the door, but one of their men caught her by the arm and held her there. Daniel now held his dagger at the rolls of fat around the bailiff's throat.

'Do you want to try raising a hand to me and see what happens?' he growled as the man opened his eyes, gasped, and raised a hand to shade his face from the bright sunlight so he could see his attackers. His face paled as he saw Chatillon, obviously a lord of some consequence, in his fine clothes.

'Pull on your braies and get down to the courtyard where my lord will be waiting to hear why you have let this manor go to wrack and ruin,' snapped Daniel.

Chatillon stared with distaste as the man heaved his white, flaccid body to the side of the bed and put his head in his hands. Wrinkling his nose at the stench of the piss pots in the room, he left Daniel to bring him down and gladly escaped into the fresher air of the courtyard where his men had gathered about twenty unprepossessing people. He stood on the top step and scanned their faces, noting the usual mix of fear, apprehension, and the sullen glances of resentment from the ne'er-do-wells and shirkers. However, he noticed one or two at the back who met his assessing gaze with one of their own. Taking in their stance—slightly better clothes and resigned expression—he thought they were probably freemen by the look of them, ones who didn't expect much from another absent overlord.

Behind him, his men pushed the two women and the half-naked bailiff out of the doors and past him down the steps, where the man fell to his knees in front of the crowd and promptly vomited up the previous night's wine. Some were shocked to see him like this, some grinned, and one or two walked forward and spat on him.

'Take him over there; pour some buckets of water over him to get the stink off him, as my lord will need to question him,' ordered Daniel.

Meanwhile, Chatillon addressed the crowd, telling them in a few sentences about their new lord, a famous warrior who was currently serving the English King Henry but would be coming as soon as he could view his lands and meet his people. When he paused, one of the men at the back stepped forward.

'What do we do in the interim, Sire? What about him, Anton Dubois, known locally as Le Sanglier? He and his cronies bled us to death; dozens of people left, and some even went to work in the city—gave up everything to get away from him, as the previous bailiff fled when he arrived.'

The man suddenly faltered as if his courage had failed, but Chatillon liked his look and waved him forward.

'What is your name?' he asked

'Jean-Loup,' he replied, and Chatillon laughed.

'Well, Jean the Wolf, do you think you can step up and take his role as bailiff? I can hear in your words that you have had an education somewhere.'

The man looked taken aback by the offer, but several others nodded and pushed him forward.

'I can only do my best, Sire. Yes, I was sent to be educated by the Benedictines in Paris, but I left them at sixteen to join the King's Guard; a religious life was not for me. I was forced to come back here two years ago to help my family as my father was injured and then he died, so I am still here and still fighting and defying the likes of him,' he said, pointing at the grey-faced bailiff.

Chatillon was pleased by his choice; he seemed trustworthy. He waved him to the front and told the crowd that Jean-Loup was now in charge of the manor of Neauphle-le-Chateau. They would follow his orders until Sir Conn Fitz Malvais arrived. Daniel pointed to the two women from the chamber and asked if he wanted them punished. Seeing the bruises on the younger girl's arms, Chatillon shook his head.

'No, they can get in there and start the cleanup with their brooms. I want the hall swept clean and every inch of it scrubbed; I expect fresh rushes on the floor the next time I walk through those doors.' They scurried up the steps—anything to avoid the wrath of this lord and his narrow, black-eyed stare.

The bailiff was still on his knees near the water trough.

'Get to your feet,' ordered Daniel as Piers stood, hands on hips, looking at the man with distaste.

'You have cheated your master, Lord Robert Beaumont; shall I send you in chains for him to deal with? Or would that be a waste of his time, for he would only execute you, and we can do that here.'

The man facing him with his stomach hanging over his soiled braies met his eyes, and for a moment, Chatillon was perplexed. He saw no fear. Instead, there was arrogance, a misplaced confidence in something or someone. Why was that, he wondered as he glanced at his captain. Daniel raised an eyebrow in understanding and nodded behind them. When Chatillon turned, he saw three of the sullen men leaning against the stable doors watching; these were his henchmen. Even more unsettling, as he met the gaze of one, he saw him turn away with an amused smile.

'You seem unconcerned at your fate, Dubois. Why is that, I wonder? Where are you from?' he asked.

Again, the man didn't drop his eyes but met Chatillon's directly as he answered.

'I am from Avignon,' he said, and Chatillon heard a note of pride in his voice.

'Avignon, a pit full of vipers and rogues if ever there was one. You are a long way from home, Dubois. Why did you leave, I wonder? Or did someone bring or entice you here? I have a large house in Avignon and many influential friends there at all levels. Do you still have family in Avignon? I assure you, I can find them and make them suffer for your crimes.'

For the first time, the man's eyes flickered in concern. This time, his mouth twisted in a scowl as he asked in a low voice, 'Who are you? I could add to your wealth if you let me. I have friends here. I am not known as Le Sanglier, The Boar, for nothing; I am dangerous when cornered,' he said, waving a hand towards the nearby Rambouillet Forest.

At that moment, Piers understood the man's confidence and gave a short, harsh laugh, further disconcerting the now-sweating man. But it was Daniel who answered his question.

'He is Lord Piers de Chatillon, and I assure you, Dubois, he is the embodiment of your deepest and darkest fears.'

The man's eyes dropped from Daniel's, and his face registered his shock as he stared down at the black-booted legs of the French lord who stood before him. He now realised he had made a terrible mistake, for he knew the name Chatillon. Who didn't, in the robber community of France? Even in Avignon, it was a name that brought dread and fear into the stinking backstreets. They had all heard the stories—this was a man without a soul. Gradually, his eyes travelled up the black velvet tunic to the man who now stood regarding him with a twist of amusement on his lips.

'I am sorry, my lord; I had no idea who you were,' he began and faltered as he clearly saw his fate in the cold, hard face before him.

Chatillon drew his dagger and turned it slowly in his hand so that the light caught on it. It was unusual—long and narrow, with a hilt highly decorated with inlaid amethysts. It was a dagger with a history—an assassin's blade.

'This blade has seen many deaths, yet it was given to me as a gift from a grateful Pope, who rightly thought I would have a use for it. This is the famous blade used to kill King Wenceslas, and I now wonder if it is too good for you. Would your blood tarnish or soil its reputation, Dubois?' he asked while glancing at Daniel.

Knowing his master, Daniel stepped back, leaving the robber bailiff standing helplessly and alone, his hands at his sides. But even knowing what was coming, the man was not done.

'They will come and avenge my death. *He* will come and avenge my death,' he said in a threatening tone.

It happened so fast that some men beside the stable doors almost missed it. The famous blade flashed and opened the large man's abdomen from left to right. Dubois dropped to his knees, his hands trying to hold in his entrails. His head fell back in a howl as the blade returned to slash his throat. He toppled forward, and his blood pumped onto the filthy cobbles. His henchmen stared in horror and backed away, but the men behind them, led by Jean-Loup, were waiting for them.

'Leave one alive; we want to question him about the men in the forest and, in particular, the one who may come and avenge his death,' ordered Chatillon as he rinsed his blade in the nearby water trough.

An hour later, the bodies were dumped to rot in the midden, and Chatillon knew everything he needed to know. He'd included Jean-Loup in the interrogation of the last man, as he'd seen and dealt with the group of deserters that terrorised the area for miles around. When they had finished with him, they dragged him out of the village and threw him down on the track, for Chatillon wanted news of their arrival to filter back to their leader, the man Dubois was paying with silver and goods from the estate.

Chatillon decided to stay there for two days to see what damage had been done to the lands and what he could do to rectify it. Daniel found the original scrolls and well-kept records of the previous landowner and his bailiff in a dust-covered chest in one of the storerooms. As they unrolled them, Chatillon was pleased by the thorough record-keeping and surprised by what he found there.

'There must be seven hides of land here. Nearly a thousand acres, including part of the forest for timber.'

Jean-Loup nodded. 'My father was a freeman before me, and my family has always farmed this land. Then, there were nearly forty villeins and cottars who farmed and worked their strips here or laboured on the manor, and the old lord looked after his people. The brigands in the forest drove the people away, stealing their goods and produce and taking their women. They also took much of our stock; we have less than a quarter of the kine, sheep and goats we had before, as we have not been strong enough to fight back. And we had the safety of our families to think of.'

'I thought the forests had been cleared of brigands and deserters by the King's men?' asked Daniel.

'They did for a while, but by the next autumn, they were drifting back, a few at first and then even more of them, led by some rogue from Avignon. They swooped on the villages on the edge of the forest without warning, raiding and pillaging. Any resistance, and they fired the thatch of the houses.'

Chatillon was thoughtful for some time, and then he sent two birds. One he sent to Ahmed to tell Isabella he'd be here until the end of the week, promising he'd return by Friday. He knew he was cutting it close to Ahmed's estimate of five days before the birth, but there was so much to put in place here. The second bird he sent to the French court in Paris to inform the Seneschal of what he'd found happening at Neauphle-le-Chateau and to request his assistance.

Later that day, in the heart of the Rambouillet Forest on a high bluff overlooking the River Mauldre, a bruised and beaten man, missing several fingers on one hand, staggered into the large, well-guarded camp of the brigands, mumbling about an attack.

'Take him to Le Sudiste; he will want to hear this,' ordered the lookout.

The man named Le Sudiste, the Southerner, was not a big man, but he had a presence. He was intelligent and imbued with a natural cunning and ruthlessness that made him feared and had built his reputation. He listened to the man's tale and sat back with a frown as his men waited, expecting an order to ride out and attack the men who had dared to do this.

'Chatillon. Here in Neauphle-le-Chateau? Piers de Chatillon?' he repeated, looking at the battered and bloody man, who nodded. Le Sudiste certainly knew the name; this was not a man to trifle with.

'How many men?' he asked.

'Only half a dozen but well-trained swordsmen, and he has elected a leader in the village, who has rallied the rest of the villagers. This Chatillon, he gutted Le Sanglier like a pig in seconds without a backward glance at the body.'

He'd expected their leader to be shocked at this news, but Le Sudiste only nodded.

'Yes, he would; I know of him. He kills as other men breathe. We will bide our time, watch, wait, and keep our heads down. Chatillon is powerful and very wealthy, and only a madman would take him on. I imagine he will not stay there long, and then we will punish those who thought to rise up against us.'

The man in question was thinking the same as he stood on the steps of the chateau and watched the sun setting in the west over the forest. He'd sent into Paris to recruit more men to help Jean-Loup, but he knew the renegade in the forest would be smarting at the loss of a lucrative set-up like this, and his pride would be wounded at the death of his man, Dubois, whom he'd placed here to strip it bare. It was only a matter of time before he came to exact his revenge, and Chatillon had to make sure they were ready for that. He smiled as he thought of Isabella; there would be nothing about this situation that she'd like, and they had faced enough danger over the last few years. However, he was determined to do everything he could over the next few days to secure Conn's lands until he finally returned to France with his Horse Warriors in the autumn. And then, this Le Sudiste, whoever he was, wouldn't know what had hit him.

Chapter Seventeen

August 1102 – Chester

Georgio had a new lease of life; he was basking in his newfound fame as an anchorite, and the pile of food and wine on his table in the corner grew daily. At least three or four people, sometimes even more, came each day to ask for prayers for a special intention, for a loved one, or to beg for the ingredients of a potion or tonic like the one that had cured the Burgher's wife. The news of her recovery had raced through the town. His isolation was over, although he tried to look suitably despondent when the stern-faced monk, Brother Alphonse, brought his food on the usual days. However, Georgio was a realist and knew this couldn't last; he'd been told by some of his visitors that the town was now awash with stories of the anchorite, a holy man who was also a healer.

It was not long before it came to a sudden end, as Brother Alphonse was there later one day at an unusual time. He pushed his face into the opening of Georgio's cell, hissing and spitting with fury at what he discovered.

'What are you doing, anchorite? Abbot Columbanus will be furious with us when he hears of this—there is no doubt that he *will* hear of it as the town is abuzz. You were supposed to stay here and pray quietly, not have people queuing in the meadow to come and see you.'

'No, I was supposed to die, Alphonse. Isn't that right? Were they not your orders? It was not for purifying the body and soul; I was aware that you were trying to starve me to death,' answered Georgio in a quiet voice.

For a second, the narrow-faced old monk was silent, for there was little he could answer to the accusation. They both knew it was true, and the old monk still had faith; he wouldn't blatantly lie for Abbot Columbanus. He stepped back slightly from the opening and slowly shook his head.

'We have orders from those above us, and we have to follow them; we do not have a choice. The Abbot can quickly find fault and demote or punish us for any disobedience or for straying from the path that they have chosen.'

Georgio could hear the apologetic note in the monk's voice for a few moments, but he was not in a forgiving mood as he turned on the monk.

'And the path that was chosen for me by Columbanus was that I would slowly become weaker and would die from lack of food. Do you realise that I have done nothing wrong to deserve this? I am a Horse Warrior, kidnapped by the Welsh mercenary, Owen ap Cynan—that is who is giving the Abbot orders, so you are all dancing to the tune of that murdering rogue. There is nothing Christian or godlike about what they are doing. Yet you do have a choice. I do not know how you sleep at night, knowing that you are slowly killing me. I hope for your sake that this comes out in the confessional.'

'I cannot help any of that; it is beyond my control, but you have to stop these people from coming to visit you if you wish to survive. We have received a message that one of Owen's men is being sent to check on you. They will kill you if they find you have told people who you really are,' he whispered, as if someone was at his shoulder listening.

'I have told no one. They think I am Brother Ambrose from Italy and that I have spent years praying and fasting,' he said in a more subdued tone.

'Well, to save your life and mine, Brother Ambrose may become ill with a virulent fever that will keep people away from him. I will place one of the novices on the other side of the wall to discourage people from visiting you.'

With that, Brother Alphonse was gone, leaving Georgio on his own to wonder why Owen was suddenly sending a man to Chester. Was it to finally kill him?'

Two days later, he was woken by voices. At first, as it was dusk, he presumed someone had got past the watchdog outside at the wall and was approaching the anchorite window. Then he realised that the voices were coming from the other side, from the small abbey courtyard.

'Where is he?' asked a voice.

'In the anchorite cell,' was the answer.

Georgio recognised the deep tones of Brother Alphonse.

'Where is the door? How do I get in to see him?' a younger voice asked in a puzzled tone. Georgio thought he recognised the voice but couldn't quite place it, and then he realised the man was Welsh, and a shiver went through him. It must be the man Owen had sent—the man possibly here to end his life.

'You can't get in there; there is no door, and we pass food and things through this long gap here,' he explained in a patient tone.

There was a long pause as the man outside considered this,

and Georgio could almost feel the man's disbelief in the silence before he said the next words.

'He is walled up! You have sealed our prisoner in there for a year, inside a stone tomb. Dear God, is he still alive in there?'

'Very much so; he has recently become something of an attraction. They bring their food offerings to the barred window on the other side, and he offers up prayers for them. But they also come to be cured; he is known as a healer in the town.'

Rhys looked at the old monk in disbelief—that he'd allowed their prisoner to do this.

'Georgio di Milan is an attraction? For pilgrims and the sick to visit? Does Owen or Columbanus know of this?'

The old monk dropped his eyes and shook his head.

'Neither did we for a while, for we try to keep to ourselves within the monastery, following the codes and rules of St. Benedict. We rarely set foot outside. But Brother Paul, who buys fresh food every day, heard lots of people talking about him in the marketplace, and when we looked, we found them lining up on the other side of the meadow wall to visit him.'

'Holy sweet Jesus and all his saints,' spat Rhys before crossing himself for blaspheming.

'Owen will be furious. This man is supposed to be a secret prisoner, out of sight. Columbanus promised Owen that was what would happen—that he'd be hidden away,' he said in a shocked tone whilst staring at the wall of the anchorite cell in front of him.

Rhys moved slightly closer to the opening and looked into the cell. Even though the sun was setting and it was only dimly lit, he stared in shock at the thin, long-haired and bearded figure dressed in a rough wool robe. He was unrecognisable from the tall, strong, muscled Horse Warrior with his Italian good looks and flashing dark eyes that he'd last seen. Rhys remembered that he'd liked the man for his courage, pride, and standing up to Owen despite the punishments he received. Georgio turned into the light on the far side of the cell, and as Rhys examined his face, he could see no fear, but he could see apprehension in his stance and was not surprised. He turned away, shocked at what he'd seen and what they had done to this bold Horse Warrior. Was this all part of Owen's plan, he wondered, as he stood, his hand holding his chin in thought? Then he decided he could no longer leave Georgio in that sealed stone cell; the day of delivering the ransom was not far off, and from what he could see, he couldn't imagine him causing any trouble. He turned to the older monk.

'I will return tomorrow afternoon. I want men waiting to remove that wall; there is no way he can stay here now if what you say is true. I will find some clothes and shackles, and you will ensure that word is spread around the marketplace that the anchorite is ill and will probably not recover. Meanwhile, I will take the prisoner out of Chester when it is dark. I need you to arrange a cart for us, for I do not believe he can ride any great distance.'

'Where will you take him?' asked the monk.

'Probably back to Owen at Stafford Castle. He will decide what to do with him when we get there.'

Late afternoon the next day, Georgio cowered in the far corner of his cell near the latrine drain as the large hammers smashed the wall down. He was filled with an odd excitement mixed with apprehension about what would happen next. Soon, they had made a hole large enough, and Rhys climbed into the stone cell. Georgio recognised him immediately but didn't move out of the corner. He was at first surprised that Owen had sent his captain but reasoned that if he was to die, Owen wanted someone capable of doing it efficiently.

'Have you come to kill me?' he whispered.

Rhys shook his head as he stopped and stared at the writing covering every inch of the walls. He tried to imagine how he would have survived somewhere like this for a year. By looking at this and reading about his exploits, he could see that Georgio had found a way to keep himself sane. He thought that in the same place, he would probably have run mad—a year bricked up alive with no human contact apart from a meal poked through a hole a few times a week. He turned to face the Horse Warrior and held a hand out to pull him to his feet.

'No, Georgio di Milan, I have not come to kill you. I have come to take you south, probably to Stafford Castle. Piers de Chatillon has agreed to pay your ransom to Owen. If all goes well, you will be set free.'

Georgio found these words difficult to take in as he stood staring at Rhys, his hand still clasped firmly in his. He pulled himself to his feet but felt dizzy and unsteady as he was ordered to climb over the smashed stones into the courtyard. Rhys ordered him to take off the stinking robe and wash himself to get the stench of the cell off his skin. Georgio pulled off the black robe and felt the sun on his body for the first time in a year. The Welsh captain stepped back in surprise as the full colourful glory of the sword-cross tattoo on Georgio's back was lit by the sun, as did the two monks with the hammers whose mouths dropped open at the sight. Oblivious to their gaze, Georgio poured a full bucket of water over himself, scrubbed at his skin and, rubbing himself dry with the rough cloth provided, pulled on his braies, chauses, and a belted tunic. It felt strange to be back in normal clothes, but in some ways, it was reassuring. After so long in his dim environment, Georgio was finding everything too bright in the sun-filled courtyard; he blinked repeatedly, holding his hand up to shade his eyes and praying they weren't damaged, as he'd heard of that happening to men who were held for a long time in deep, dark cells.

Suddenly, Rhys stepped towards him, drawing his dagger, and Georgio stepped back in alarm, wondering if all of this had been a ploy and they had only needed him out of a monk's robe before they cut his throat. Instead, Rhys pulled him forward, sliced through the long beard and hacked at the long, matted hair so that he looked close to normal.

Rhys and Brother Alphonse took him to the refectory, where Georgio had his first decent, hot meal since the previous autumn. As he mopped up his platter with a piece of bread, Rhys poured him some ale and addressed him.

'Now we wait here until dark. Then, you will be shackled and put in a cart. We will head south. One word out of place, and I will cut your tongue out. Do you understand, Georgio di Milan?' asked Rhys in a low tone, as other monks were present in the refectory and were looking across at the visitors with interest.

Georgio nodded. Then, sitting spellbound, he gazed up at the high, vaulted roof above him. He felt overwhelmed by the size of the room; he was so unused to space. He glanced across at Rhys, who was now giving instructions to Alphonse, clasped his hands and stared at them for a few moments as if in prayer as he thought through what was happening. He knew he was almost free, but even in his weakened and bemused state, he knew he had to keep his wits about him. He had long ago realised, with a horrible certainty, that Owen wanted him dead. Somehow, he'd collect the ransom and kill him, while Columbanus could certainly not let him live to tell Malvais and Beaumont what he knew about his involvement.

He sat quietly and prayed that Malvais had also realised all of this and that he had a plan. He had survived against all the odds in captivity in an anchorite cell for a year. Life was too precious to have it taken away from him now.

Chapter Eighteen

Early August 1102 - Stafford Castle

As Rhys and his men rode back into the grounds of Stafford Castle with their prisoner, he could feel the change in the atmosphere. More men had arrived, and the meadows outside the castle were now full of tents. He noticed that there seemed to be a sense of urgency; the usual training was taking place but with at least double the numbers. The sounds of clashing blades rang through the air, combined with the harsh noise of the blacksmith's hammers, and blades being sharpened on grindstones.

They rode through the gates and headed for Owen's camp in the corner at the far end of the bailey, which had also filled considerably with more small pavilions; it looked as if all of King Maredudd's allies had been summoned. There was no sign of Owen, but Rhys noticed that Daegal and his men had taken up residence beside them, with the protection of the sturdy palisade at their backs. Rhys smiled, a camp, within a camp, this was so typical of their sort, selling their swords but keeping their fiercely fought for independence.

He wearily dismounted as the cart, escorted by his men,

trundled in to pull up alongside, and he went to unload his captive. He felt the watchful eyes of Daegal and his men on him as he pulled Georgio, who had shackles on his wrists and ankles, from the cart. Rhys had not been prepared to take any risk of his captive escaping, for even in his present debilitated state, he knew Georgio to be intelligent and resourceful.

Georgio, meanwhile, was wide-eyed at what he saw around him; he'd known nothing of recent events until Rhys, to give him his due, had brought him up to date around the campfire one night. He now knew what had occurred at Alton, how King Henry's ploy had paid off and ensured him the crown. He also now had an idea of how this civil war had come about and who was arrayed on both sides. As they entered the castle, Georgio had seen the activity and, from experience, had estimated that they would be moving south to fight within the next week.

He had complacently accepted his fate as a large metal stake was hammered into the ground. He did not doubt that it was for him, but he was still elated at being out of the anchorite cell.

At the end of his first night out of isolation, the noise, the people and the movement all around when travelling from Chester had almost been too much, and the following day, when he was being bounced around in the cart over the hard summer rutted roads, he had occasionally surreptitiously dashed away a tear. Now, glad to be out of the cart, which had left him with numerous bruises, he made himself comfortable on the grass, folded his cloak behind his head, and closed his eyes.

He was awoken by angry voices.

Owen, returning from a council of war with King Maredudd, had stopped in his tracks at the sight of the prisoner chained at the side of his pavilion. He'd whirled around to find Rhys and spotted him and one of his men carrying the tack back from the horse lines. Rhys had spotted the sturdy figure of Owen waiting for him—the anger in his face and his stance clear to see, and he sighed, waiting for the expected storm to break.

'God's Wounds! What is he doing here?'

Rhys went immediately on the attack.

'What else was I supposed to do? You had him locked up in a sealed tomb, for Christ's sake, and he almost starved to death. He only survived by becoming the anchorite you turned him into; people were queuing across the abbey meadow to see him and bring him food. He was becoming famous. Is that what you wanted, Owen?'

The ferocity of this response took Owen aback. Rhys was usually even-tempered. Also, the news of Georgio's success was unsettling. All it needed was one travelling peddler to spread the word of this warrior anchorite in Chester as they headed south to sell their wares. He turned and stared down at his captive, who was awake and regarding him warily. He saw at once how thin and weakened he was; there was none of the bravado in his face that he'd perceived before with this Horse Warrior, but neither was there fear in his eyes as he sat up.

'Well, Georgio di Milan, you are an unexpected problem, but I promise that if you put one foot wrong, I will be delivering your corpse to Shrewsbury Abbey.'

Rhys had to look down to hide a smile as he saw that the Horse Warrior hadn't lost his bite; Georgio glared at Owen and came immediately back at him.

'I thought that was the plan, Owen ap Cynan, for you have

never been a man of your word, and after all, you cannot let me live with what I know about you and the others who were involved in my imprisonment.'

Owen strode towards him, every part of his being ready to kick the insolent Horse Warrior in the face when, out of the corner of his eye, he saw Daegal. The man had stood up and moved forward, and Owen could see the curiosity on his face as he watched and listened, so instead, he bent down and grabbed Georgio by the throat, squeezing hard and lifting him off the ground.

'Don't push me, or I promise I will cut your throat without any hesitation,' he hissed, as he flung him back to the ground.

Daegal O'Brien was very interested in what was playing out before him; he didn't trust Owen either. He'd been reluctantly persuaded by Rhys to join forces with them, as it suited him at the moment, but it hadn't been an easy transition, and they had already clashed and come to blows once or twice. Daegal saw their arrangement as lucrative , aware that he was more than an equal to Owen. However, the Welsh mercenary saw Daegal and his men purely as hired swords, so it had taken a few nights to thrash that out. Now, there was an uneasy peace, as there had been no clear winner. physically, they were evenly matched and both skilled with weapons, but in other ways, they were very different.

Daegal was a warrior through and through. He'd ridden for ten years at Raoul de Tosny's side, a lord whom he'd respected and admired as a great strategist and fierce fighter. His leader's death at Branston had hit him hard, so this arrangement with Owen was a compromise while he decided on his next move. The problem was that he smelled the stink of ambition and greed coming off Owen ap Cynan, and that usually meant a man would sacrifice anyone, or anything, to get what they wanted. So, for now, he would use Owen to fill his coffers, but he didn't trust him one whit.

He watched this new development with interest and wondered who this prisoner was; he immediately saw that Owen was not happy to see him there. The Welshman had been deliberately vague about the plan he was putting in place but needed Daegal's help. He'd given a brief outline of an attack in Shrewsbury that would prove very lucrative for them all. He also hinted that there was even more silver if two of the men they were meeting there were killed, men with a high price on their heads. He'd been close enough to hear the exchange with the prisoner, and it was apparent, with the mention of Shrewsbury, that this troublesome prisoner was somehow the key. He determined to find out why; after all, Rhys and Owen wouldn't be hovering over him all the time.

His chance came the following night; Owen and Rhys were called to the Great Hall for an emergency council. Two messages had arrived, the first to say that Leicester had been attacked and buildings burned at the end of July. Belleme and his brothers were on the offensive, which had pleased the Welsh King of Powys. However, the second message was more worrying. It was a warning that William Pantulf, Baron of Wem, was marching south to retake Stafford Castle. King Maredudd had immediately sent out his brother, Iorwerth, to discover the veracity of this message, and now they were waiting for news but planning to evacuate depending on the size of Pantulf's forces.

Daegal watched and waited until they had gone and then casually wandered over to sit beside Georgio and the guard they had left. The excitement of what was happening in the hall was palpable, and it took him no time at all to offer to guard the prisoner while the man crept into the back of the hall to listen to the news and bring back the information before Owen returned. No sooner had the man's figure faded into the falling dusk than Daegal poured two cups of wine for him and the prisoner. Georgio took it warily and thanked him, for people never made gestures such as this without reason.

'Your arrival seemed to put the cat amongst the pigeons; I have never seen such ire from Owen ap Cynan. So who are you to cause such an outburst?' he asked in a soft voice.

Georgio drained the cup and held it out to be filled again. If he was giving information, it needed paying for, and it was a good quality wine, the like of which he'd not tasted for a long time.

'Tell me who you are first. I find it safer to know who I am dealing with.'

Daegal laughed at the audacity and confidence of a man in shackles, but he warmed to him.

'Well said. We should always be careful. I am Daegal O'Brien, former captain to Lord Raoul de Tosny and now a man without allegiance, so I am lending my sword to King Maredudd by fighting alongside Owen,' he replied.

'O'Brien? One of the descendants of the great Brian Boru, High King of Munster and Leinster? I thought I recognised the Irish accent,' answered Georgio with a smile.

Daegal was surprised. 'You know your Irish history. How is that? No doubt you were taught by Irish monks. They seem to be everywhere in Europe.'

Georgio shook his head and held out his cup again. 'I had a good friend—a great Irish warrior—who told me of it,' answered Georgio.

Daegal raised his eyebrows again; this captive was full of surprises.

'And who might that have been, and with such a friend, how do you now find yourself in shackles for a pig like Owen?'

Georgio instantly understood that this man was no friend of Owen's and could be useful.

'His name was Finian Ui Neill; he was descended from the kings of Tara and, after the leader of the Breton Horse Warriors, Luc de Malvais, one of the most fearsome warriors I have ever seen. He trained us for several years, but unfortunately, he was killed in Italy two years ago.'

Daegal was so startled by this that he paused, his cup halfway to his mouth, and regarded the man sitting on the ground with more respect.

'I know of Ui Neill—show me any Irishman who doesn't. I came up against him once when we were both younger, and I wished I hadn't, but in those days, I was too cocky, too full of myself, thinking I was good enough to take him. He gave me this,' he said, rolling up a sleeve to show a long, old, white scar down his forearm.

'He could have killed me then, like I was nothing, lying injured on the ground, my sword sent flying from my hand. Instead, he laughed at me and throwing my sword at my feet, he walked away. He was a true warrior, and I was saddened to hear of his death. Will you now tell me your name?'

For some reason, Georgio decided to trust this man. He was a frightening sight with his thick, dark, spiky red hair and weathered, scarred face, looking every inch a ruthless sell-sword, but he had a way about him, and one could tell that he'd commanded men.

'My name is Georgio di Milan, and I am a Breton Horse

Warrior; I rode with Conn Fitz Malvais in Spain against the Berbers and for Emperor Alexius in Byzantium. We returned to England last summer to ride for King Henry, until I was attacked on patrol and captured by Owen. Since then, over a year now, he has kept me walled up in a cell in Chester Abbey. Now, at last, he is ready to ransom me, but I do not believe he intends me to be alive when that happens. I think he intends for my comrades and friends to find my corpse.'

Daegal was silent for some time as he considered what he'd been told. It seemed a fantastical tale, and it left him with more questions. *Why did Owen kidnap this man? He is not a great lord to bring a high price. Then, why has he kept him walled up for so long?* There was far more to this than met the eye, and he needed to think it through and work this knowledge to his advantage.

'I know of the Breton Horse Warriors. Indeed, I fought against them at Branston this year; they are truly formidable. Unfortunately for us, their leader rescued Robert Beaumont from certain death at the hands of my lord, Raoul de Tosny and enabled Beaumont to kill him. My men and I were fighting too far away to help him.'

Georgio found he had to swallow and look away at that point. His Horse Warriors had been in a battle, risking life and limb, and he hadn't been there.

'Who won?' he asked in a low voice full of emotion, hoping that his friends had not been killed or badly wounded— especially his squire, Darius, who didn't have much experience in the thick of battle.

'Your Horse Warriors won; they had destroyed Cadwgan's undisciplined cavalry, and we had lost the element of surprise by then. De Tosny's death, a man known as an unbeatable warrior, took the heart out of them, as Beaumont's men and knights rallied and attacked.'

Seeing the wistful expression on the young Horse Warrior's face, Daegal could understand how he felt. The excitement and comradeship of riding knee-to-knee into battle formed a bond between them. However, Daegal needed to know more; there were too many gaps in this tale.

'So, why you? Why did Owen kidnap and imprison you?' he asked, sitting forward.

'I have thought long and hard about that in the dark, bleak confines of my cell, and every time, I come up with only one word: opportunity. He and his men decided to desert from King Henry, and they came upon our campfire by chance. We had been careless, as there were only two of us. He killed my friend, Gracchus, and for some reason, they took me. I think it was originally to torture me, as he hated me for killing Black Bryn, one of his men. And he hated Malvais because he was everything that Owen wasn't. Then he realised that I could be a prize, so he decided to imprison and ransom me. And here we are. Our mentor and friend, Piers de Chatillon, has agreed to pay the ransom, and I believe I will be handed over for a huge amount of silver in Shrewsbury Abbey in a week or so.'

'They are powerful and influential friends you mention, which increases your worth to Owen. However, no one meddles with Piers de Chatillon. Is Owen mad to do so? Is he your real father that he is prepared to pay this ransom?'

Georgio laughed for the first time in a long time at this suggestion, and it felt good.

'No. As I said, he is a friend. He rescued Malvais and me when we were only nine years old, and he has taken us under his wing ever since.'

Daegal was quiet again as he began to see opportunities with this valuable captive. There may be some very grateful people if he managed to stop Owen from killing this Horse Warrior. He turned and glanced across to the keep, but there was no movement from the hall yet.

'I presume that this Breton, Malvais, of whom you speak must be related to the great Luc de Malvais.'

Georgio paused for a moment and then nodded. It was only Conn's secret to tell about his parentage, and very few people knew that it was Morvan de Malvais, who was his father.

'Yes, Conn Fitz Malvais is his son, fast becoming as lethal as his father.'

Daegal O'Brien suddenly ran his hands over his face and through his unruly hair, for a picture had come to his mind of the big, dark-haired warrior on a wild black horse with crossed swords on his back who had attacked them and then fearlessly rode through the thick of the battle to save Beaumont by striking at De Tosny.

'Yes, I have seen him, and I also swore that one day I would find him for wounding my liege lord so badly that Beaumont could kill him.'

Georgio's eyes opened wide in alarm as he prayed he'd not told this man too much. He put down the empty cup and shrank back to the pavilion's sides. Fortunately, behind them, the hall doors opened at that moment, spilling men and noise out into the bailey. The guard came running back to ensure he was there when Owen and Rhys returned. He thanked Daegal for his help, but the big, rangy Irishman shrugged it off. He had much to think about as he walked slowly back to his bed.

However, he'd barely reached it when a hand was laid on his arm, and Rhys was beside him.

'I believe you volunteered to guard the prisoner and sent my man away.'

Daegal could see the hard glitter in the man's eyes, but he decided at first to play it down, so he shrugged.

'It was nothing; I was bored, the guard was bored, it didn't need two of us. I did him a favour,' he said, turning away, but the hand descended again.

'Do not countermand my orders to my men; you have no idea how dangerous this prisoner can be,' he snapped.

Daegal lowered his face towards Rhys.

'Or how valuable! I have heard his story. Were you part of this Rhys, to keep a warrior like us in a sealed stone cell for a year like an animal? I am surprised he is still sane. No wonder so many are queuing up to kill Owen. Now, get your hand off my arm, or I swear I will cut it from your wrist.' His hand moved to the hilt of his dagger.

Rhys backed away, holding his palms facing out towards the Irish mercenary to show he was not armed. Daegal gave a thin smile, spat on the ground, and walked away, leaving Rhys staring after him in apprehension as he realised they might have made a mistake in bringing the big man on board. He knew that, as a younger man, Daegal had been a novice monk and had been defrocked and expelled for raping a serving girl. Because of this, he'd been forced to become a brigand, shunned at first until the local populations began to fear him. Determined to make a name for himself, he became so brutal and notorious that Murtagh O'Brien banished him, so he ended up in England in the service of De Tosny. However, it was clear that Daegal O'Brien had learned a belief in the warrior code of honour and loyalty from his liege lord, it was ingrained in him.

These were not the attributes that Owen or his sell-swords lived by. He decided not to share any of this with Owen. He could imagine the reaction, and he knew they would need Daegal's help at the abbey to take on the warriors bringing the ransom. After that, they would go their separate ways.

Chapter Nineteen

Early August – Windsor Castle

Henry had been basking in his success to date with the news of the surrender of Arundel. The defeat of Belleme's allies at Tamworth and Branston, and the taking of his castles at Tickhill, Kimberworth and Mexborough, gave him immense satisfaction. He was also enjoying his time back in Windsor with his wife Matilda and their daughter, now six months old and beginning to respond to her father. He'd always loved his children; he had at least fifteen at the last count to his many and varied mistresses, and no one could say that he did not provide for his offspring, arranging houses and suitable marriages for them.

However, he was conscious that he needed a legitimate son, so he had bedded his wife every night since he arrived. To give his queen her due, she was no shrinking violet, and he'd taught her to enjoy their lovemaking. He particularly enjoyed early morning bedsport with her, and it was with some regret that he was called out of bed by his Royal Steward, Robert de Courcy, who had urgent news for him.

Henry unashamedly walked naked across the chamber to where De Courcy had unfolded the vellum and weighted it down on the table. Henry read it twice before raising his narrowed eyes to De Courcy.

'Send in my manservant; I will dress immediately. And send the Earl of Warwick to me.'

As Henry strode back into the bedchamber, Matilda could see by his pinched, white face that something was amiss, but she waited for him to tell her as she could see the rising anger in him.

'You would think that Robert de Belleme would respect this respite I have given him, but no, he has sent his brothers to attack Leicester, burning and pillaging. The people outside of the old Roman town walls were slaughtered as they tried to run for safety. He has attacked Leicester with the intent of mocking me.'

Matilda looked puzzled. 'Why Leicester, Sire?'

'The powerful Grandesmils, who ruled the city, rose against me to support Duke Robert, but I was merciful and allowed them to live, giving them hefty fines instead. However, I removed the Sheriff of Leicester title from them and awarded it to Robert Beaumont, a loyal and true follower. Then, Ivo de Grandesmil, brother of Rohese de Courcy, announced that he was going on a new crusade to Jerusalem, which he didn't reach the first time. You may remember he was one of the disgraced and scorned rope danglers, the knights who deserted from Antioch when the enemy approached. He mortgaged his lands to Robert Beaumont to raise the funds for this crusade. Now Robert de Belleme claims that I forced him into this—that I gave Ivo no choice. Because of that, he has launched an attack on what he sees as lands stolen by

Beaumont.'

Matilda came naked from the bed and wrapped her arms around Henry, holding him tightly as she could hear the mounting anger and frustration in his voice, and she knew he needed to be calm to deal with this.

'You need to finish this, my husband. You have declared all of the Montgomery brothers outlaws, so you now need to destroy them once and for all. Bring the peace and prosperity to England that you promised in your Charter of Liberties, and prove to the people of England that you are their protector and that they can trust your word.'

Henry held her at arm's length and gazed into her face. His marriage to Matilda had been a political one. She was a princess of Scotland, and a daughter of the House of Wessex, with immense influence at home and abroad. Just as importantly, she was very religious and devout—a queen who had a close friendship with Anselm, the Archbishop of Canterbury.

Henry had fallen in love with her at first sight when she was under the Abbess of Romsey's—her Aunt Cristina's—wing, and he'd loved her ever since. He kissed her deeply, running his hands over her naked body.

'If I did not have to go, I swear I would pick you up and carry you back to bed,' he said, pulling her close but reluctantly letting her go.

'I would have welcomed it, my Lord King; I need to give you a son—an heir to the throne.'

Henry hesitated, looking at her parted lips, her skin still rosy from their previous lovemaking. He was tempted and could feel himself hardening at the thought. But then he heard De Courcy and his servant enter the outer chamber, and he shook his head at her in dismay, groaning with frustration as she moved quickly to hide under the embroidered cover. He smiled at her as she pulled it up to her chin. Turning to leave, he whispered back over his shoulder, 'Stay there. I promise I will be back soon.'

Closing the door, he went to meet Henry Beaumont, Earl of Warwick, the commander of the King's armies, whose booming voice he could hear in the antechamber as he dressed.

He found Warwick just as infuriated as he was by the news about the attack on Leicester, but now the Earl had more details.

'Fortunately, my brother's quick-thinking Castellan had the sense to close the gates and man the walls, and the townspeople cowered behind them as Belleme's forces burnt, pillaged, and slaughtered all they found in the houses and villages close to the walls. Arnulf Montgomery and Roger de Poitevin are still there, and I am told they have siege ladders, so the people will not be able to hold out for much longer. I have sent a force to try and relieve the town, Sire.'

De Courcy, much to his annoyance, was then waved out of the room by Warwick. Surprised, he glanced at the King, hoping he would countermand the order, but there was no help there.

Once the Royal Steward had left, the Earl came closer to the King and lowered his voice. 'I know you do not want to hear this, Henry, but I have known you and been at your side for twenty years. You know of my service to you and my unswerving loyalty.' Henry nodded; he had an inkling of what was coming and respected Warwick, an experienced and wise advisor.

'You should not listen to the likes of that professional courtier out there, and you are astute enough to see that they have their own agenda, which is not always in your best interests. It was a mistake to dismantle your forces, as I am sure you now realise, and perhaps you honestly believed that Belleme would respect this respite. I did not, and neither did my brother; Belleme is a snake, and it is time we cut his head off. He saw the respite as a sign of weakness and took advantage. Now, we will show him that you are not weak in any way. Summon the fyrd again, Henry—reassemble your armies, and we will undertake a forced march on Bridgnorth without further ado.'

Henry, never one to openly admit a mistake, knew he was right, but he was not about to lose face, so he announced in a voice loud enough to carry to the corridors.

'Assemble my armies, my Lord Earl. Summon the fyrd. We first march for your fortress at Warwick to gather our men, and from there, we march on Belleme's stronghold at Bridgnorth. With luck and God on our side, I will have his head on a spike before the end of August.'

2nd August 1102 – Kimberworth Castle

Serjeant Fox and Rhodri were dicing in the hall at Kimberworth when the sounds of an arrival assailed their ears—the clatter of many hooves on the cobbles, the shouts for squires and grooms. It was the arrival of a large group of men.

Serjeant Fox was pleased to see how quickly Rhodri managed to stand and move towards the large doors, wide open to let the afternoon light into the hall. Rhodri was healing fast; he'd walked and moved like a crippled old man a week before, wincing in pain at every movement. Fox did not doubt the druid was still in pain—broken bones and deep bruising do not heal that quickly—but he'd never seen someone so determined to recover their strength and movement. He'd watched in admiration as the Welsh horseman had pushed his bruised and battered body more with each day that passed. However, Rhodri was still not a prepossessing sight—the black, blue and purple swelling and contusions had gone down and had turned yellow in places, but he now wore a tightly strapped leather wrist guard and a staunch heavy leather doublet to help his ribs heal. The serjeant also knew that the fear of being left behind again had driven him; he was desperate to rejoin Malvais and De Clare, regardless of pain and discomfort.

Fox drained his tankard of ale, pocketed his winnings and lucky dice, and went to join Rhodri on the steps, where he watched the dozens of knights and men pouring into the bailey. Beyond the castle, he could see hundreds more were setting up tents and camps in the adjacent fields. He was pleased to see his liege lord, De Clare, riding beside Beaumont, as the serjeant had now had enough of Kimberworth. Once Sir Geoffrey de Ware had got over the shock of his wife and son's betrayal, he'd found a new lease of life, and the serjeant had helped him weed out and be rid of any disloyal men or servants. He could now assure De Clare that leaving Sir Geoffrey in charge of the castle and lands was safe.

Rhodri, meanwhile, was still scanning the arrivals, and it was with some relief that he saw the distinctive crossed swords and black leather doublets of the Horse Warriors on their huge Destriers. His biggest fear had been that Malvais might be sent on somewhere and not return to Kimberworth, and he would be left here, especially since they had been told Sir William Pantulf was marching south to attack Stafford Castle. As they dismounted, he limped over to greet them. Malvais clasped arms with him and smiled as he looked him up and down.

'You are almost all of the colours of the rainbow, Rhodri, but you look better and seem to be moving well. I am pleased to see you, and hopefully, we will get a decent bed and food tonight.'

'I assure you I am almost recovered. However, I am afraid you will only be here for one night. A bird arrived from Henry Beaumont for his brother, Robert. Orders have arrived, which Serjeant Fox let me have sight of. We are riding back to Warwick. The King has recalled his armies and the fyrd to gather there to launch an attack on Bridgnorth.'

This news gave Conn pause as he watered and then brushed down Diablo. Piers de Chatillon had given him an assignment—to remove Philip de Braose, who was supplying significant information. He had to admit he'd killed dozens of men before—usually in battle and he had been involved in two high-level assassinations without an ounce of regret or conscience. He knew that Chatillon had recognised this quality in him, this coldness and lack of empathy or sympathy. There had only been two instances in his life when he'd halted his blade to give mercy and one of these he had almost instantly regretted. Still, Philip de Braose had become a companion, a comrade with whom he'd ridden and fought alongside. Yes, Philip was an idealist and ambitious, but wasn't every knight in some way?

He'd spent several nights lying awake thinking of how to carry this out, and then something occurred to him. It was not so much Phillip who extracted the information; it was his man, Kenric. Further questions and investigation had shown that the young Welshman ran the web of informers in

Stafford, Mathrafal and Bridgnorth. All Philip did was assess the veracity and usefulness of the information, which he then fed to Robert Beaumont. It was a smooth and clever operation that greatly furthered Philip's career.

As he brushed the mud from Diablo's legs and picked the stones from his hooves, another thought came to him: the wording of Chatillon's orders. Conn had never heard his mentor use the word 'remove' before; it had always been 'kill', which may have given him the leeway he needed. He knew Chatillon had received a large fee for removing this troublesome knight. Therefore, Conn presumed that the request had come from Robert de Belleme, Earl of Shrewsbury, the wealthiest man in England and Normandy. He knew this intended assassination was linked to the civil war. The crucial information Philip provided to Beaumont was damaging to Belleme; once the war ended, Philip would no longer be a threat. He gave Diablo a final rub down and then went to find Rhodri. If he was going to act, it had to be tonight, as once in Warwick Castle, it would be far too difficult, with too many eyes on them.

Rhodri listened to Conn's request with interest and a raised eyebrow. The argument that Malvais put forward was compelling; with Rhodri's help, he would save a knight's life, but Malvais could give him little detail, as other events had to happen first. Rhodri had known Malvais for almost a year now, and he trusted him and his judgement, so he agreed and headed to find Synnove to help him with what he needed.

Conn then headed for Gracchus and his men, who had seen to their horses. Most of them were sitting around a campfire repairing and cleaning their tack.

'No doubt you have heard the news; we leave for Warwick at

first light. That should please you all as it should get you the battle you were so keen on,' he said with a grin.

Gracchus smiled and waved the harness he was cleaning.

'That is why we are doing this now; we have our reputation to consider when we ride into Warwick Castle.'

Conn nodded in satisfaction and was pleased he had instilled pride in their appearance in his men. He knew the horses and tack would shine when they rode through those gates.

'Well, I have a task for you as I know how much you love hunting. Take your bows into the woods and get me two or three bucks. The day is hot again; they will be coming down to the streams to drink and should be easy targets. Our camp servants will hang and prepare the meat, two for you and the men and one for my gathering tonight. Do you still have the iron plates, Gracchus?'

The big man laughed. 'I have one, which is yours for the asking, but I know where to find the other,' he said, with a wink, heading off to reclaim it.

Conn smiled. The big Greek warrior was almost as good as Darius at obtaining food and items in impossible circum-stances. It was Darius who had first rigged the flat metal plate, stolen from an armourer, and placed it over the fire to cook the venison steaks and innards rather than dangling them on spits. Conn then collared De Clare to provide the best wine he could lay his hands on, as he planned on having a feast at their pavilion that night to celebrate their success. He told him to be sure to invite Philip de Braose and a few of their other knights. De Clare was happy to do so—few now wanted to return to eat in Sir Geoffrey's hall in the castle as the planned attack had been too close for comfort.

Rhodri returned to the pavilion an hour before dusk. Malvais was alone outside the large tent, cleaning his tack. Rhodri surreptitiously handed him a very small, stoppered bottle.

'A few drops will suffice. Do not overdose, or he may not wake for days.'

Conn thanked him and placed it inside his doublet.

'Will he show the symptoms I requested?'

Rhodri nodded. 'It is slow acting at first—a very small amount of digitalis, with other ingredients to confuse. He will be slurring and disorientated as if he is drunk, so fill his cup regularly with wine before you dose him. Then, his vision will blur for the next few days, and his balance will go—a type of falling sickness.'

Conn looked thoughtful.

'This is good, as they will have no choice but to leave him behind. Is there a servant you trust, or one who can be bribed to administer a drop of this every three days into the medicine that the physician will leave?'

Again, Rhodri gave him a long stare of appraisal.

'I know of someone who can be paid and trusted, and I presume this is intended for Sir Philip de Braose.'

Conn's eyes widened at this, but then he gave a sardonic smile. Rhodri's acuity and foresight never ceased to astound him. The Welsh druid watched, listened, and absorbed everything, and because of his stillness, he often saw and heard things that others missed.

'You are right, but I am doing this for the right reasons, and you must never breathe a word of what we do as only Edvard, you and I know of this. From what I have learnt, I am very aware that it can be fatal in higher doses. Please assure me he will recover completely once we stop administering it.'

Rhodri inclined his head. 'It may take a month or so for it

to be eradicated from his body, but following that, he should return to normal.'

Conn put a hand on his shoulder to thank him and insisted that he be at their campfire tonight for their celebration, and then he strode away. Watching him, Rhodri hoped that whatever Malvais was involved in was not too dangerous a game.

Rhodri knew that his destiny was tied up with Malvais, and his one wish was to go with him to Morlaix in Brittany, where his brother, Brian, had worked for the family. He needed to have speech with Conn's father, Luc de Malvais, and his uncle, Morvan, for they had hunted down and killed the Warrior Monks, who had murdered his older brother when he delivered the child.

His quest was a spiritual one: he'd been tasked with finding any of Brian ap Gwyfdd's bones, and only Conn's relatives knew the area where they lay, scattered or not. His grand-father, the Arch Druid, said that Brian's spirit was lost and unsettled, and only the return of any of his brother's bones to Ynys Mon would give him peace. Until that moment, Rhodri would stay at Conn's side, riding with him and protecting him when he could.

Chapter Twenty

2nd August 1102 – Eynsham

Abbot Columbanus stood and watched as his monks folded the ten Benedictine robes into neat bundles, to fit into the sacks that would be loaded onto the pack mule behind Brother Peter, who was undertaking the ride to Shrewsbury. On arrival, the robes would be delivered to a trusted sacristan at St Chad's Church on College Hill. Owen and his men could pick them up from there. He did not doubt that these were disguises for the rebels to infiltrate the large crowd in the abbey church on the 15th of August for the feast of the Assumption of the Virgin Mary.

Columbanus hadn't slept at all well since his run-in with Edvard of Silesia. He had no doubt the man would carry out his threats if the captive Horse Warrior were harmed. To make things worse, a message from Brother Alphonse in Chester had arrived, telling him that Owen's henchman had taken the captive away.

That news produced a mixed reaction of relief and fear. Relief that the Horse Warrior was no longer in Chester, as he sent a message to order the anchorite cell to be razed to the ground immediately. For fear that if the Horse Warrior was on the loose travelling the countryside with Rhys, who might he not tell of his year-long incarceration and who was behind it? Anyone he came into contact with on the journey as Rhys could not be with him every moment.

Columbanus was torn by indecision, and his first reaction was flight. For some time, he'd wanted to return to Monte Cassino, the first abbey built for the Benedictine order, founded by Saint Benedict himself. He'd spent a happy few years there as a young monk, and a pilgrimage to Italy over the winter, with a few of his young, novice monks might be exactly what he needed. Then, he could return in a year or so, and hopefully, everything would be resolved and forgotten. Edvard of Silesia and the Horse Warrior would hopefully be dead as arranged, and he could ensure that Owen ap Cynan followed them to the grave. Before he left for Italy, he could, as a loyal supporter of King Henry, contact Robert Beaumont to say that a large group of rebels would be arriving at St Chad's in Shrewsbury on the 14th of August.

However, as he paced back and forth, he was plagued with doubts and felt his ire rising. Why should he give up all he'd achieved when he was still owed a quarter of the ransom? He would not put it past Owen to make off with all of the silver. In that case, should he go to Shrewsbury? He could stay in the background, probably at Saint Chad's, so that Owen knew he was there, looking after his interests and watching the Welsh rogue's every move. If he was clever, playing one person off against the other, then anyone who could implicate him would be dead without him paying even a groat for their deaths.

He watched Brother Peter out of the gates, then walked into his abbey church at Eynsham, sitting quietly, arms folded, in the Bishop's chair on the side of the altar. He closed his eyes and thought through every move. The problem was the unpredictability: Malvais, Edvard of Silesia, and the Italian Horse Warrior himself—who knew what they would do? Georgio di Milan had to be incapacitated somehow before it came to the handing over inside the abbey. If the captive had still been at Chester, he could have ordered his tongue cut out and his fingers broken so he could neither speak nor write; he berated himself for not having thought of that before, for now, God knew where he was or to whom he was talking.

An hour later, he stood, for he now had the germ of an idea and had made a decision. On the 11th of August, he would leave for Shrewsbury to put the plan into play. Owen ap Cynan was not going to get one over on him. He'd be waiting for him at St Chad's and ensure the Horse Warrior was permanently silenced. He smiled at the thought—he would outwit them all.

Kimberworth Castle

The smell of sizzling venison steaks filled the air as the men around the campfire raised toast after toast to their triumphs at Tamworth, Branston and Belleme's three castles in the north. De Clare raided Sir Geoffrey's cellars and found several sacks of strong burgundy wine. As the goblets were repeatedly filled, tales of more exploits came out, and De Clare demanded that Conn tell the tale of his hand-to-hand combat with Mengu Timur in Nicomedia.

With some reluctance, Conn agreed, as only De Clare knew of his time in Anatolia. He made it light-hearted at first, admitting it was his fault for stealing Rhea, the woman of

Mengu, heir to the Pecheneg tribes. This brought several cheers and raised goblets, but they quieted as he became more serious and described the fight, barefoot in the sand with an opponent well versed in this type of fighting with spear and dagger. Conn rarely mentioned his exploits, but he was a good storyteller, and they hung on his words, easily imagining the straining muscles and the sweat dripping from their brows as Conn fought for his life, a dagger at his throat. However, against the odds, he had triumphed and turned the blade on his enemy. He explained how, at the last minute, Darius had galloped in with the evidence of Rhea's betrayal and falsehoods to stop him from killing Mengu, which could have caused a bloodbath with the fierce Pecheneg tribes.

There was silence at the end, and then De Clare filled all the cups and raised a toast to Darius, to fallen comrades, and Georgio, wherever he was. Rhodri lightened the mood by producing a whistle made from elder wood and proved himself to be adept at playing tunes and some well-known songs. At the sound of music, Serjeant Fox, Gracchus and several men walked over to join them, standing and singing along. Someone produced a drum to accompany the whistle, and it soon became quite a party.

Seeing them all so occupied, Conn stood and quietly left the campfire. He stood on the edge of the trees in the shadows and watched them for a while with a smile. Philip de Braose was quite drunk, singing and slapping his thigh in time to the music. Conn had easily slipped a few drops into his cup, and he expected it to take effect soon as he melted away into the gloom of the trees and left them. Seeing him leave, De Clare thought it was probably the mention of Darius and Georgio that caused him to leave. He cursed himself for his carelessness and hoped he would return soon.

Meanwhile, Conn moved swiftly to where the servants and squires were drinking and dicing around their campfire; he called one of De Clare's servants over.

'Sir Philip de Braose wants you to take this pouch of silver to his man, Kenric. His orders are to ride to Stafford immediately as we have news of an attack. Tell him we want to know how they will respond.'

The servant nodded, placed the pouch in his belt, and trotted towards Sir Philip's men camped beneath the trees.

Conn slipped into the darkness and went through the woods to the horse lines in the meadow below. He remembered that Kenric rode a large dark bay with white socks, so it took him only moments to find it, tied at the end of the line. There was a well-worn track through the woods from the camp to the meadow on this side, so he stepped into the gloom of the trees and waited for his quarry. It didn't take long before he heard the sound of someone approaching. There was only a quarter moon, but it was a clear sky, and there was enough light to make sure it was the man he wanted.

Kenric had his bridle over his shoulder, and his arms were full with his saddle, the pouch of coins jangling at his belt as he hurried down the track. Conn let him pass and then moved quickly and silently behind him, doing instinctively what Chatillon had taught him several years before. In seconds, he grabbed Kenric's dark hair and pulled his head back moving a dagger to his throat. The informer, feeling the cold blade on his skin, gasped in shock and dropped the saddle at his feet. He managed to gasp one word. 'Mercy.'

'Unfortunately, it is too late for mercy, Kenric; you were far too good at your job,' growled Conn as he cut his throat and let him drop to the ground.

He wiped his blade and dragged the body deep into the undergrowth. No doubt, the wild animals would quickly dispose of it; foxes, wolves, and boars would all have their fill until little would be left of the handsome young Welshman. Conn recovered his pouch of silver, carried the saddle and bridle to drop near the horse lines, and made his way stealthily back through the woods towards their pavilion in the clearing. De Clare nodded at him with a smile as he dropped back into his camp chair, pleased to see that he had returned so soon.

Rhodri was now playing a haunting lament, which produced a sardonic smile from Conn—a fitting tune for the death of the informer, Kenric, and part of his mind noted that he felt no regret at the young man's death. He noticed that Philip de Braose had fallen from his stool and was drunkenly snoring on the ground.

Conn felt well satisfied with the night's work. He looked across and found Edvard's eyes on him, and he smiled at him, inclining his head with a nod at his friend. He would tell Edvard what had transpired tomorrow morning, hoping that his actions would satisfy Chatillon.

The next morning was bustling with preparations as the camp was packed up, and they prepared to leave for Warwick. De Clare waved him over as he was going to tack up Diablo.

'Sir Philip became ill in the night; at first, his servants thought it was the drink, but he was convulsed with pain, so they called the physician to give him a drench to clear his guts. However, he is still ill today, unable to stand, and appears to be still drunk; he obviously cannot stomach too much strong wine. Beaumont has ordered him to stay behind and join us tomorrow when he recovers.'

Conn nodded, his face painted with the most solicitous expression. Turning, he found Edvard beside him as De Clare left to find Serjeant Fox.

'You heard?' asked Conn. Edvard inclined his head but then watched the chaos in the bailey before turning back.

'That is very convenient,' he said with a smile.

'He will not recover for at least a month, probably longer. I hear that his man, Kenric, has gone missing as well. I am afraid he might have gone over to the other side,' added Conn.

Edvard gave a snort of laughter at the play on words and found himself smiling and nodding in admiration for how Malvais had handled a difficult task. He knew that Chatillon would be pleased with the outcome, so he slapped Conn on the shoulder in approbation and went off to send a bird to Chatillon and another to their client, Robert de Belleme.

An hour later, they rode out of Kimberworth on the road to Warwick.

'I will be happy if I never have to see that place again,' exclaimed De Clare with a shiver.

Both Beaumont and Malvais laughed.

'I think you are getting soft in your old age, De Clare,' jibed Beaumont.

'Perhaps, but I could not ride into that courtyard without thinking we almost died there. I no longer see the castle and a genial Sir Geoffrey de Ware. I see our tomb and our blood-soaked beds.'

For all their bravado and jesting, both men riding beside him realised that what he said was true. They wouldn't be alive now if Conn had not recognised John de Ware. So silence reigned for some time until Beaumont spoke.

'Let us put the recent past behind us. Tomorrow, we will

be in Warwick, and not long after, we will be bearding Robert de Belleme in his lair in Bridgnorth. Then we will see the true test of his mettle, his strength, and resolve against the King's army.'

Conn broke away to ride back and check on his men. Belleme's resolve wouldn't be the only one tested, he thought, as he pulled in alongside Gracchus. It would be King Henry's and how much stomach he had for a civil war, as he'd have to kill Englishmen as well as take on Belleme's Welsh and Irish allies.

Chapter Twenty-one

Belleme unrolled the thin message and smiled with satisfaction as he read that two birds had been killed with one stone. The message was not signed, of course, but it told him that the spy Kenric had been killed and that Sir Phillip de Braose had been removed. It also told him that Beaumont was riding for Warwick, but that did not cause him concern, as they had expected that. He was sending his brother, Roger de Poitevin, to Stafford. He called him over and showed him the message.

'Make sure that King Maredudd knows of this. There is no doubt that Kenric ran a string of informers, and hopefully, with no one to lead or direct them, that should stop the flow of information from his camp to the enemy,' he said.

'I believe that the King of Powys has other concerns, Brother. Sir William Pantulf of Wem has been sent east to try to retake Stafford Castle. Prince Iorwerth has been sent northwest to come around on his flank to assess the size of the force and its position. As soon as I have further news, I will let you know.'

Belleme walked to the window and stared out across the fields, thinking through this news before turning to Roger.

'You will remember, of course, that William Pantulf was accused of killing our mother.'

Roger nodded but said nothing. He could see the emotion on his older brother's face, still there after all these years, but he'd been very close to their mother, her favourite. Her enemies had brutally beheaded her, and the scars left from his mother's death were still deep with Belleme.

'We insisted on a trial by ordeal, but he survived the ordeal, and they cleared Pantulf of his heinous crime. I was never convinced he was innocent, and now, he is riding against us, supporting King Henry. However, from what I remember, he was like an old woman—indecisive. He must be in his sixties now. I am surprised he can still mount a horse; his progress to Stafford will be slow, and he will no doubt leave himself open to attack and ambush. Ride for Stafford with no delay, and make sure you and our Welsh allies stop him, Roger. Avenge our mother by bringing me his head.'

His brother bowed and made for the door, pleased with the prospect of finally crossing swords with the enemy. However, he was stopped at the stairs by the appearance of Arnulf, who was out of breath and clutching a missive; Sir Fulk of Lisours was beside him.

'Brother, King Henry is on the move; he has been clever and stolen a march on us. He left Windsor whilst summoning his army to reassemble, and he recalled the fyrd from the fields; they are joining him en route. Fulk and his scouts have just returned.'

The knight stepped forward and bowed to Belleme.

'My Lord Earl, he has indeed assembled a great host quickly and is moving far faster than expected. My informers tell me he is force marching his men to Warwick, where he will join the Beaumont brothers and their armies.'

Belleme's reaction was unexpected. With a triumphant expression, he slammed his fist into the palm of his left hand.

'This is Leicester; our attacks there have brought him back into the field as we wanted. This could play right into our hands. Roger, ride for Stafford as if the hounds of hell are on your heels; we need Pantulf defeated and his forces destroyed. Give no quarter. Order King Maredudd to begin moving his forces south, as I do not doubt that Henry will attack us at Bridgnorth.

'Arnulf, ride to meet with our Irish allies and bring them over the border into Shropshire. Now that we know where he will strike, we will catch him in a pincer movement from the east and west, and while he is dealing with that, our forces from the north will attack. This is our chance, brothers, to take back the throne for Duke Robert, the rightful King of England. Now go!'

August 6th – Drayton

William Pantulf was indeed taking his time on the roads to Stafford. He had only travelled a third of the way when he halted his forces for the night below the small hamlet of Drayton on the River Tern. This was mainly because he was waiting for more men from his tenants, and the fyrd, to join him. He was not optimistic; Henry was not a popular king— a cleric by nature, and an oathbreaker by reputation—and he still had to prove himself. Sir William Pantulf knew that many knights in England still supported Duke Robert, and considered that Henry had stolen the crown from his older brother; he had to admit he was one of them. But, having fallen out with the Montgomerys over the murder of their mother, a crime of which he was not guilty, he had lost his lands in Shropshire. Having aligned himself with Henry, he prayed that the King would defeat Belleme and, because of his loyalty, the lands the Montgomery's had stolen from him would be returned.

Prince Iorwerth sat hidden within the trees on a slight bluff overlooking the River Tern, watching Pantulf. He had five trusted men with him, as they were only a small scouting party sent to track Pantulf. They sat and patiently watched the activity on the far bank in the camp below them. Before long, it was dusk; the campfires were lit, as the men prepared their food, and the smells of roasting meat wafted across the river. Still, Iorwerth waited. The watery sun was setting as he finally unrolled his white flag of parley and waved his men to follow him down the hill to the ford and into the enemy camp.

They were challenged immediately, but the Welsh Prince of Powys told them he had important messages for Sir William. So, they were escorted to his pavilion, where they dismounted and disarmed. Iorwerth's men were unhappy, but he led the way by dropping his sword and dagger at the serjeants' feet as their arrival was announced.

Belleme was wrong about Pantulf on several counts—he was still only in his late fifties and was a handsome man with a full head of dark hair, kept in the old fashion and tied back. He was also a man who was frustrated by the slow progress they had made today, but they were governed by the pace of the foot soldiers and the carts that regularly broke wheels and axles on the hard rutted roads.

Pantulf was surprised to hear Prince Iorwerth's arrival

announced and immediately wondered what devious ploy the Ap Bleddyn clan was putting into play now. He had spent most of his life fighting on the Welsh borders, and he'd not trust the Welshman one whit. He'd found them to be as cunning and devious as the day was long. He emerged from his pavilion, hands on hips, and ran his eyes over the Prince and his small entourage.

'To what do I owe this great pleasure, Iorwerth? It must be many years since I laid eyes on you—usually riding into the distance, as you raided my lands and that of my tenants to steal their beasts.'

Iorwerth bowed, only acknowledging the jibe with a slight smile.

'The pleasure is all mine, my lord, but I bring you news and information that may work to the advantage of both of us. However, it is for your ears only.'

Sir William stared him down in suspicion, but to give the Prince his due, he met that gaze steadily, and Sir William nodded to his steward to bring him inside.

As the wine was poured, Sir William examined his guest. The Prince had aged since their last encounter, and having his own valuable sources of information, he knew of the disaster that had unfolded at Tamworth and Iorwerth's exile to Mathrafal. He also knew Iorwerth was often at odds with his brother, King Maredudd. As the steward bowed out, leaving them alone, Sir William steepled his fingers and, looking over them, at the Prince he moved straight to the point.

'So, what information do you bring me? I am aware that you are not in your brother's favour at present.'

Iorwerth gave a thin smile at the lack of pleasantries or hospitality and inclined his head to compliment the knight on his knowledge. Then, without further ado, he told him of Tamworth and his promises to De Clare and Robert Beaumont. To his dismay, Sir William gave a bark of laughter, and Iorwerth felt his cheeks flush with anger as the knight sat forward.

'It never ceases to amaze me how a brother can turn on a brother when money, land, or even something as fragile as reputation is at stake. No matter whether you be Welsh, English, Norman or even the wild Picts. What price, family loyalty and honour, then? So, let me have this right: at the moment, you are purely a scouting party for your brother, but you will return to Stafford to report our position and strength. Then, when I reach Shallowford, he plans that you will be waiting with all of your men to ride out and attack me, but in reality, you and your men will join me to help me take Stafford Castle and defeat your brothers.'

Iorwerth gave an angry nod, trying to keep his temper under control as he heard Sir William's mocking tone.

'What makes you think that I cannot take Stafford without your help, defeating you and eliminating the Ap Bleddyn clan from the borderlands?'

'More men arrive at Stafford daily; we have more than twice your number, mainly trained fighters and mercenaries. As we left my brother, we heard from a messenger that Roger de Poitevin was riding for Stafford with a large cohort of men. However, if I bring my five hundred men to your side, we have the element of surprise. They will not know we have changed sides until it is too late.'

'And you are certain that you and your men will be happy to turn and slaughter your brothers, their families and men who were their friends and comrades without a moment's hesitation?' he asked with a raised eyebrow and a doubting sneer.

Iorwerth also sat forward, his face only a hand span from Sir William.

'Yes! My men are all from *my* lands, *my* valleys; when it comes down to it, silver talks, as does land and the offer of homesteads. Belleme has been generous in his payments, so my men will follow my orders. They know I keep my word and will make it worth their while.'

Sir William sat back again, drained his goblet, and looked thoughtful. He knew Iorwerth was right; Stafford Castle would be hard to take, but boosted by turncoat numbers and with Iorwerth's men inside to open the gates, victory could quickly be theirs.

'I will sleep on it. If I agree, we will travel east to Shallowford—you will know it, as it sits on the Meece Brook. You will ride to join us there, but be certain of one thing, Prince Iorwerth ap Bleddyn—if you betray me as easily as you betray your brothers, then I swear that I will find you, string you up, tear your liver out, and eat it in front of you. Do we understand each other?'

Iorwerth, now pale-faced, nodded, and Sir William stood.

'Go back to your camp on the bluff. Yes, we have watched you tracking us. I will send a man at dawn with my decision. You took a big risk riding into my camp tonight, but I wonder if I am taking a bigger risk trusting a man like you.'

Iorwerth gave him any assurances he could, thanked him, and left. Part of him felt elated as he strapped on his sword, and part felt the sting of Sir William's words—loyalty and betrayal of blood. However, he quickly pushed them aside. The gains were too great, and he knew he had to talk to his men here and back at Stafford and win them over to his plan without a word of it leaking out to his brothers or their men, a seemingly impossible task.

As promised, Pantulf's man arrived shortly after dawn and told Iorwerth that Sir William wanted to see him immediately. With a building sense of excitement, he ordered his men to pack up the camp and be ready to leave. Then, he rode down from the bluff on his own to cross the River Tern, where he found the camp already packing up and getting ready to move.

'Well, Iorwerth ap Bleddyn, I have decided to take a risk on you, but more so because I trust Richard de Clare. I've already sent a messenger to him to say that you have approached me and we have reached an agreement. Now, you will sit down and tell me everything I need to know about Stafford Castle and its defences. Then, we will plan the best way for you to betray your brothers to my advantage.'

Iorwerth agreed and spent the next hour outlining numbers, defences in place inside and outside the castle, and his brother's plan for defence and attack. However, lying awake in the early dawn seemed to have given Iorwerth a twinge of conscience.

'I will do anything you say, Sir William, and I will not only help you to take Stafford, and my men and I will even ride with you to support King Henry against Robert de Belleme, Earl of Shrewsbury, but there is one condition.'

Sir William raised an eyebrow. He was unsure that Iorwerth was in any position to make demands, especially if Beaumont and De Clare were controlling him, but he decided to humour him and listen to his plea.

'I want my brothers to live. I am happy to arrange their capture and imprisonment with you, but I do not want them killed. I need a promise from Beaumont that they will not be executed.'

Iorwerth rose slightly in his estimation at that point.

'So you are happy to depose King Maredudd and take the throne of Powys, but you do not want the stain of fratricide on your hands. That is understandable, for some say it never washes off. I will see what I can do; I imagine King Henry would not like to set the precedent of killing kings, so it may not be a problem. Now, we must leave; you have a hard and fast morning ride back to Stafford, and I will move my force to Shallowford, where we will set up camp and await your arrival. I expect to see you by dusk tomorrow evening, or I will presume you have betrayed us all.'

'You have my word, Sir William, and that is still worth something in Powys,' he said, leaving the knight staring after him as he set off at a run to mount his horse and ride back to his men.

Chapter Twenty-two

6th August 1102 – Warwick Castle

Beaumont and his entourage had arrived at Warwick the day before. From the first moment of riding through the gates, and despite the cheers that echoed when they realised it was Robert Beaumont, Conn and De Clare could feel the tense atmosphere of the castle, mixed with the excitement and anticipation of preparing for battle. They had been greeted by cheering crowds, both inside and outside the castle on the streets of the town, that was growing around its walls. Yet again, the meadows and fields around Warwick were full of tents and men while servants and squires seemed to be running everywhere. There was much back-slapping and numerous plaudits given over their successes at Tamworth, Branston, and the taking of Belleme's castles in the north, and the stories became more exciting with each telling. That night in the Great Hall, many toasts were raised to Beaumont and his knights, as well as to the Breton Horse Warriors, for saving Beaumont's life and destroying the Welsh cavalry of Prince Cadwgan.

Looking down the hall, watching his men, Conn saw their reluctance and shyness at first at these compliments; they were self-effacing warriors and not used to such acclaim. Gradually, as more tankards were raised to them, he saw their grins appear, and he was pleased with the recognition being given for their exploits and courage.

De Clare was a much happier man the next morning, and Conn even heard him humming a tune, as they strode out of the castle door to check on their men, who had been sent to water their horses in the River Avon. Conn laughed and slapped his friend on the shoulder.

'What a difference a night under a roof, in a real bed, can make to a man,' he said, as they crossed the bailey.

'Never underestimate the recuperating power of a comfortable night's rest, Malvais, especially as you get older,' De Clare replied with a grin.

At that moment, one of Beaumont's scouts galloped through the gates, and when he saw Robert Beaumont coming down the steps, he skidded to a halt and leapt from the saddle to kneel before him. De Clare and Conn, seeing the urgency, turned back and were close enough to hear what was said when he delivered the news.

'My Lord Count, the King's great host has been seen less than five leagues away; he has force-marched his armies to get here as swiftly as possible. Your captain said to tell you that King Henry will be here before the end of the day if they keep the same pace.'

Seeing his steward emerging from the door behind him, Beaumont waved him to join him.

'Prepare rooms for the King; no doubt your master, Warwick, will be with him and the usual large entourage. Warn the kitchens, slaughter at least a dozen beasts and set up the fire pits here in the bailey. They may well be here before dusk by the sound of it.'

The steward bowed and ran off, calling for the castle servants.

'Well, Sire, this is good news as the King was not expected for days. It seems thatHenry finally means to take the war to Robert de Belleme and attack him in his castle at Bridgnorth,' said De Clare.

'Not before time, De Clare; we need an end to this civil war and the Montgomery brothers. They have been a thorn in all of our sides for far too long,' added Beaumont.

Leaving De Clare with Beaumont, Conn walked over to the stables, where he found Edvard leaning against a stall and talking to Rhodri. He shared the news of the King's imminent arrival. Rhodri stopped brushing his horse's legs and turned to face Conn as he realised what this might mean.

'Does that mean the arrival of De Courcy? I presume he will be with the King as usual, and I have a large debt to repay there, Malvais,' he growled.

Conn was about to reply to Rhodri, hoping to placate him, when Edvard raised a hand to stop him.

'Yes, there is no doubt of that, Rhodri, but not here in Warwick Castle. You need to pick your time and place to take your revenge. It is too well known amongst Beaumont's men that it was De Courcy who ordered your beating. I agree he needs to be punished or die, but it must be elsewhere so it does not come back on you or Malvais.'

Rhodri clenched his fists at this, but he reluctantly saw the sense in Edvard's words; he knew he was right, and he'd never put them at risk because of his actions. They had become good friends over the last year, ones he would trust with his life. But he was not going to put everything aside.

'And Crick? Will he and his men be in De Courcy's train as usual, for that is one debt I can pay with interest?'

Edvard raised his eyebrows and pointedly looked Rhodri up and down while shaking his head at what he saw. The yellowing bruises were fading but still there, showing the deep damage inflicted on his flesh. His wrist and ribs were still strapped up, and they would be for some time yet.

'You know you are in no state to take on a man like Crick, Rhodri. Leave him to me, for I also owe him, but I doubt very much if he will show his face here; he knows we will want to exact our revenge on him.'

By late afternoon, the excitement in the town and castle was palpable, and by the time the first horns were heard in the distance, almost every person in the castle had found a reason to be in the bailey area or on the walls. The King had summoned the fyrd, who had left their fields and homes to join his forces as he marched north. At the same time, his knights brought out their contingents of men to join the King, although some did so reluctantly. This meant the King's army now stretched behind him for well over a league.

Henry Beaumont, Earl of Warwick, rode at the King's side, as did Robert Fitzhamon, Baron of Gloucester and Lord of Glamorgan, who, with the recent fall of Arundel Castle, had brought his troops to join King Henry. Behind them rode dozens of lords and knights, the banners and gonfalons of the great houses of Normandy and England stretched as far as the eye could see—a wide column of bright swirling colours in the sunshine.

The cheers began as soon as the King appeared, and it swelled as thousands inside and outside the castle joined in, many townsfolk hanging out of windows or climbing on each other's shoulders to see the King. Conn, beside De Clare, could see the pleasure on Henry's face as he rode through the gates of the castle and into the bailey. He was not used to this acclaim from his people, having spent the last year defending his right to the throne and trying to shake off the degrading title of 'Oathbreaker'.

Once inside, the King dismounted and strode forward to mount the steps and clasp arms with Robert Beaumont.

'Well met, Count Robert. I heard about your tribulations at Kimberworth, and I believe if it had not been for this man beside you, I would have lost many of my valuable lords and knights,' said the King as he moved to place a hand on the shoulder of Malvais, who bowed deeply.

'Robert Beaumont is again deep in your debt, Conn Fitz Malvais.'

'I assure you, my Lord King, I have been amply rewarded by the Count of Meulan.'

'Rightly so, but not by me,' he turned and beckoned to De Courcy, who was finding it difficult to hide his anger while listening to the accolades for the man he hated, but he mounted the steps to bow in front of the King.

'Ensure that a substantial purse of silver is delivered to Malvais today. We must reward our heroes and saviours who risk their lives in our service, and we will celebrate their deeds and actions. With men such as these riding with us and God on our side, we cannot fail to defeat the Montgomerys.'

De Courcy bowed to the King and turned away, his eyes on the steps as he slowly ascended, his lips now a thin white line because they were clamped so tightly together. This bastard Breton, who had despoiled his wife and probably fathered the dead child, had to die—no matter the cost; Owen ap Cynan had better keep his promise to kill Malvais, or he'd hunt the Welsh mercenary down. Halfway down the steps, he stopped and raised his eyes, his face white except for two spots of anger on his cheekbones. But the first sight he saw across the heads of the crowd was Rhodri, the white druid. He was standing beside Edvard of Silesia, who was watching him with a slightly mocking smile on his lips.

De Courcy narrowed his eyes. So, the arrogant Welshman had survived the beating, which was unfortunate as Crick seemed certain he couldn't. Then he noticed that Rhodri's eyes were closed, his arm was outstretched, and the finger pointed at him. He was not a suspicious man, but as he watched the druid's lips moving, chanting or incanting, De Courcy experienced an involuntary shiver. He dragged his eyes away to follow the King into the castle, but somehow, he couldn't prevent himself from glancing back again; Rhodri was still there, the finger following him as he mounted the steps. He suddenly found he had a cold sweat on his brow, and he impatiently brushed it away as he entered the coolness of the Great Hall. He castigated himself for such weakness—he did not believe in this pagan nonsense—but he couldn't prevent his hand from fingering the small gold crucifix he wore around his neck.

Suddenly, a voice intruded upon his thoughts as they crossed the hall. Richard de Clare was close beside him and had seen his agitation and actions in clutching the crucifix.

'That cross will not help you against a druid curse, as they were here in Europe long before Christ. Theirs is an older magic, which few understand or can access; they guard their secrets, and nothing is written down. However, I have seen what they can do when they summon the spirits of the land

and sky. I stood beside the King of Gwynedd in Wales and saw a house burst into flames on Rhodri's command. It was beyond my understanding. But you brought this on yourself, De Courcy. You chose the wrong man to have beaten to death; Rhodri is the grandson of the most powerful Archdruid in Europe. They will not forgive or forget what you have done. Fortunately for you, Rhodri is not a darach—he will not kill you without reason or unless his grandfather gives the order. But he can certainly make you suffer, to ache in every part of your body, or even worse to inflict impotence on you.'

De Courcy suddenly found he could not speak; his mouth had become bone dry as De Clare moved away, leaving the Royal Steward standing there wishing that Crick had finished the job and killed the Welshman. As the day wore on, De Courcy managed to shrug off the earlier incident, although he realised there were whispers amongst the servants for some reason— he saw them glancing at him and talking with their hands over their mouths. It was late that evening, and the sun was setting when he finally returned to the small room he'd been allocated, to change out of his dust-covered clothes. It had been a long and tiresome day. To his surprise, he found his servant sitting on the floor, his back against the torch-lit wall outside the room.

'Why are you out here? I hope the fire is lit, my clothes are laid out, and the ewer is full of water, or I will be late for dinner.'

'Sire, you do not want to go in there; that is why I am out here. Things have been placed on your bed.'

De Courcy laughed at the man.

'I will not be scared by a dead, eviscerated raven placed on my bolster; do they not know who I am? I am a De Courcy!' he exclaimed, throwing the room door open with a resounding bang as it crashed into the wall.

However, the objects on the bed differed from what he'd expected. There was a small branch of what looked like elder wood and three round flat stones of a size that would fit into your palm. He waved the servant to bring the candle closer, and he noticed that the outline of a large boar, its head facing in different directions, was inscribed on each stone. De Courcy straightened up and turned on his servant.

'Do we know what this signifies?' he murmured, almost to himself.

The servant shook his head. 'No, but I can find out; the woodsman who delivers the logs knew about the white druid cursing you. I heard him frightening the kitchen girls with tales of the druids and how they slaughtered human sacrifices in the woods.'

De Courcy felt his anger rising again that there was talk about him among the common servants.

'Get rid of it all!' he exclaimed.

'In fact, throw it all into the fire. It is pagan nonsense! They think to frighten us like children!'

The servant reluctantly did as he was told before pouring his master a goblet of wine. For all of his bravado, he could see that De Courcy was rattled; he'd been with him for ten years and knew his moods.

That night at dinner, King Henry surprised the Beaumonts with his eagerness and enthusiasm for coming to grips with his enemies. He seemed full of valour and made extensive plans.

'The men will rest tonight and tomorrow, but I want them all prepared to march at dawn on Friday. We will need to cross the River Severn and be in a position to attack Belleme at Bridgnorth the next morning.'

Robert Beaumont agreed. 'That is possible, Sire, but only if we march hard and fast; I suggest you send the wagons ahead tomorrow, a day early, as that is what usually slows us down or holds us up by blocking the narrow tracks through the forests. Belleme has built an impressive bridge at Bridgnorth, but it will be well-guarded or even destroyed when he learns of our approach. However, I believe there is a crossing at Qualford about a league further south. That way, we can swing out away from the Severn and then come back in from a direction he does not expect, attacking out of the dawn mists from the river and trapping him in his castle, which I remember is on a peninsula of land—good for defence but not to escape from.'

King Henry thumped the table in his enthusiasm to endorse this plan.

'What they say is true: if you surround yourself with men of foresight and experience, then you cannot fail. I raise my cup to you, Beaumont.'

Several toasts followed late into the night while De Courcy sat and hardly touched his wine. His eyes had scanned the hall for the white druid, but he couldn't see him. Instead, he found his eyes drawn to Malvais and his friends, laughing and drinking as if they had no cares in the world.

'Your time will come soon enough,' he muttered, hoping Owen ap Cynan was moving south towards Shrewsbury and the trap that would be set. An hour later, he finally made his way to his room. His servant was not in sight, and the fire had gone out. As he passed it, he glanced at the embers. As expected, it was full of wood ash, but he saw that the three stones glowed from the heat as if they were lit from within, and the etching of the boar now stood out in white. The door opened, and his manservant arrived with a jug of wine and some bread and cheese; he knew his master's habits. To his surprise, De Courcy didn't move; he remained staring at the fire, so he placed the items on the table and came to stand at his side.

'Courage and ferocity,' he said.

De Courcy gave him a puzzled look.

'That is what the boar signifies. The woodsman was still there when I went to the kitchens. He is sweet on the cook, so I asked him. He said it was a significant curse to send malevolence to you or someone close to you.'

De Courcy closed his eyes as his hand returned to his cross. He didn't believe any of this, but he was pleased that he had left his son, William, with his tutor at Windsor.

Chapter Twenty-three

6th August 1102- Budebroc near Warwick

Edvard was also missing from the great welcome feast for the King, for he had been active, and it was paying off. His men had been sent out to search the surrounding area since early morning, and they finally rode back in later that afternoon. Most of these men had been with Edvard for ten years, if not longer, making up part of the contingent at Chatillon-sous-Bagneux, and he'd trust them with his life.

Their leader, Jean, glancing around, made sure they watered their horses first to avoid arousing suspicion before walking slowly over to where Edvard was sitting in the late summer sunshine talking to Serjeant Fox, a man he had much time for, as they had ridden together for nearly a year, as they had searched in vain for Georgio di Milan. He dropped to his haunches in front of the two men.

'We have found him,' he announced, knowing De Clare's serjeant could be trusted and was aware of the search.

'As we expected, he and his men have been left outside of Warwick; he knew he could not risk being recognised, for retribution would be swift to follow, so as he always does, he lingers in the shadows, on the outskirts. They are staying at a small insignificant inn in the hamlet of Budebroc, which consists of little else except for a few farms and cottages and a small mill for the villager's use. I expect he and his men intend to join the tail of the army when it moves north. The innkeeper is unhappy; I managed a few words with a serving woman who told me they are drunk every night, causing trouble and driving his few local customers away.'

Edvard nodded in satisfaction. 'Get some food for you and your men—it is plentiful in the hall. Then meet me at dusk, Jean, and we will ride to this hamlet and visit our friend.'

Jean straightened, but then turned back for a second and met Edvard's eyes, as he lowered his voice to only a whisper. 'Do you wish me to tell Rhodri that we have found him?'

'I last saw Rhodri early this morning when we were breaking our fast; I later noticed his horse was gone. I would lay silver that Rhodri is already there, close to that inn, watching our quarry, despite my warning to stay away from him,' said Edvard, glancing significantly at Serjeant Fox.

'Do you need my help? I can make an excuse to slip away for a few hours,' he asked.

'No, I believe that the fewer people involved, the better, but thank you, I will not forget your offer,' replied Edvard.

In truth it had taken no great effort for Rhodri to work out that Crick wouldn't be staying too far away from De Courcy, so that he could be contacted or summoned if he was needed to carry out his dirty work. Rhodri had visited several villages to the north and west of Warwick, as he knew the King's army would leave in that direction. He heard tell of the inn at Budebroc and their unwelcome visitors, and he had placed himself at a distance at first, watching all movement, then stealthily walked all around the building, staying in the trees surrounding it. He saw the number of horses in the open stable stalls, six, including Crick's gelding with the four white socks. Now, Rhodri had established himself at the far side of a small orchard opposite the inn, but with a good view of the front and side doorways, and there he would wait for his chance.

He knew that Edvard was right; he was in no physical condition to engage in combat with Crick, a solid, muscular man, or any of his men, but he couldn't stay away from him, as the desire for revenge was too great. However, he had brought his bow and a quiver full of arrows; his grandfather had ensured that all of his children and grandchildren were competent archers—for their protection and that of their families. Now, Rhodri sat with his back to the orchard wall and waited for the opportunity to fire an arrow into his black heart.

When dusk fell, Rhodri ran, doubled up, behind the chest-high stone wall so that he was in a position to see through the shutters as the candles were lit inside. It had been a warm sunny day, one of the last for a while, he thought, as he watched the distant clouds scudding towards them. Rain was coming; he could feel it in the air, and he prayed they would leave the shutters open. One good shot was all he needed, he thought, as he settled down to wait for darkness.

Rhodri was a good scout, as he had proved in the past; he was also one of the best trackers, with the ability to get very close to an enemy without them ever knowing he was there. He'd been taught by the best, but when a hand was laid on his shoulder, his eyes had been closed, his head resting on the wall, and his heart leapt into his mouth because he'd not heard a sound. He began to leap up, dagger drawn, to kill whoever it was. However, he found his arm grasped in a hard grip, and in the faint light of the last rays of the sun, he recognised Edvard, who shook his head at him and raised a finger to his lips. He waved Rhodri to follow him, as the big man ducked below the low branches of the fruit trees, heading for the gate on the far side.

His heart still thumping, Rhodri watched him slide and sidestep soundlessly between the twigs and dead leaves on the orchard floor. For his size, he moved so lightly. The man was a master of stealth, and Rhodri was not surprised he had not heard his approach. They passed through the gate and joined Edvard's men. His captain, Jean, explained what they knew.

'From what we have discovered and seen through the window, he has five men with him. All look as if they can handle themselves—outlaws, mercenaries or scum from the back streets by the look of them. They seem confident they are safe this far from the town, so they are careless and talkative, and no watch appears to be set outside.'

Edvard looked thoughtful before turning to the Welshman.

'That bow may be useful if you are any good with it, Rhodri. It may shorten the odds somewhat, but under no circumstances do you climb over that wall until I summon you. Malvais would never forgive me if anything happened to you again. Leave Crick to us. I will do my best to make sure he is alive when we bring him to you.'

Rhodri sighed in frustration but nodded in agreement as the men split into two groups. As he turned to move back behind the orchard wall, he suddenly put his hand on Edvard's arm and pulled his head down to whisper.

'One more thing. They go out to the privy, behind the inn—

you cannot see it from here, but all men need to piss.'

Edvard nodded with a smile, and then he and his men melted away into the increasing darkness. Heavy rain clouds had now covered the sky, and not a sliver of the moon nor a star could be seen, which was perfect for Edvard and his men.

Inside the small inn, the taciturn innkeeper and his wife had served a hearty game stew to the men. To appease him, Crick promised they would go hunting on the morrow to replenish their larder; he also wanted to keep his men occupied. They were like unpredictable caged animals cooped up all day and just as difficult to control. He had found himself forced to remind one or two of them who was paying their wages, and punishing blows had been delivered. He had felt the resentful glances today and heard the muttered curses under their breath, and he didn't doubt that one of them would slip a knife between his ribs without a second thought, taking his purse as they left. For a few wistful moments, he missed Sam, his boon companion; it was a crying shame that he'd met his end at Kimberworth, attacking the Welshman.

With their stomachs full, the men settled down to some dicing and gaming—they would bet on two cockroaches given half a chance. So, he gave them something to look forward to the next day by offering a bonus to the first man who brought down a hind or a young boar. He told them the innkeeper had a few hounds they could borrow. The ale flowed free as they fancied their chances and began telling tales of great hunts in the Royal Forest.

'Not so much hunts as poaching then,' suggested Crick, to much laughter.

He sat back, content. The mood seemed to lighten, and he felt he was finally building rapport with these ruffians and

263

outlaws. Suddenly he felt a shiver go through him. He was not cold as he was in the only comfortable chair near the fire. He glanced behind him; the shutters were open, but it was pitch black outside, and he could hear the first pitter-patters of falling rain. He cursed under his breath, for that would make tracking the game in the forest more difficult. However, he still felt a coldness, the type that sent a shiver of apprehension through you, and he rubbed his hands together in front of the fire. He felt unsettled, so he pushed himself up from the chair and went to stand at the open window. There was nothing to be seen out there, no movement or sound.

In the orchard, Rhodri closed his eyes and softly chanted an incantation, like the one directed at De Courcy; it was one of his grandfather's, one of malevolence, a curse. He opened his eyes as he finished and saw the solid, broad shape standing at the window. He knew immediately it was Crick. The man was stock still and staring at the spot where Rhodri was hidden as if he could sense his presence. Now was the moment, and he bent slowly and picked up the bow—the distance was perfect. It would hammer into the man's chest, and surely, he couldn't miss at this distance. He considered the rising wind and rain as he threaded his bow, but then he paused. If, for some reason, Crick moved, or God forbid if he missed, then the whole group would be aware of the attack, and he'd be placing Edvard and his men in danger. They would have lost the element of surprise. As the seconds ticked by, Crick suddenly leant forward and pulled the shutters closed. Rhodri cursed softly and flung his bow on the grass.

Crick gave himself a shake as he turned back into the room, but the hairs were still up on the back of his neck. *Am I getting jumpy for no good reason?* he asked himself. But, ever cautious, he told Todd, one of the quicker and more astute of his rag-tag band, to go and have a scout around outside just in case. Todd stood outside the inn in the darkness; the rain was becoming heavier, and he could hardly see more than a man's length in any direction. Knowing Crick, he did as he was ordered, and he set out at a fast stride around the inn, but not even a rat was stirring in this weather. He headed for the privy, the usual large hole in the ground with an open wooden canopy over it and wooden planks to stand on. He didn't hear a sound as the knife flashed and the blood spurted from his throat. In seconds, he was dropped face down into the depths of the deep cesspit, and the dark sludge swallowed his body.

Crick was wondering where Todd had got to when the door opened, and two men came in, shaking the rain from their cloaks. Crick was initially alarmed, but then he spotted the King's badge on the cloaks they spread to dry over stools near the fire. These were two of King Henry's scouts, no doubt returning to Warwick and getting out of the heavy rain. He motioned to his men to keep the noise down while the scouts stood at the counter in conversation with the innkeeper. He heard the words, *a great host gathered at Warwick...* and he relaxed. They were no threat. They pulled up stools on the other side of the fire, and he asked them how preparations were going, which opened the floodgates. They were happy to describe the thousands of men gathered to finally take the battle to the enemy. He quickly learnt that the King's forces were leaving at dawn on Friday for Bridgnorth, and as they sipped their warm mulled ale, he realised he recognised the younger man of the two, but as Crick had been in the King's camp for many months, that was not unusual.

Finally, with a sigh at the sound of the heavy rain, they

reluctantly stood and reclaimed their steaming cloaks. They threw them over their shoulders, taking time to fasten the clasps when, without warning, they let out a loud, harsh shout. Drawing their swords and daggers, they attacked his men, who moments before had been sitting, dicing and listening to their news. Like him, his men were relaxed; they had been taken in by these men and were unprepared for what happened.

Crick leapt back in shock, knocking his chair to the ground. Behind him, the unlocked shutters were pulled open, and Edvard quickly clambered in, staff in hand, which he swung with lethal effect. Two more of Edvard's men burst through the door and made for Crick, while one of the ruffians managed to make his escape by diving head-first out of the window. As he got to his feet, an arrow took him in the throat, and he dropped like a stone on the soaking ground.

Crick had only just managed to pull his sword from its sheath when it was knocked from his hand by Edvard's men, and he was forced to his knees, a dagger at his throat. He had now recognised his assailants, and with an awful finality, he knew he would die for what they had done to the Welshman. He was foolish to come back into their sphere of influence, but the draw of silver, as ever, had made him minimise the risks, which was his undoing. He merely hoped they would kill him quickly. However, no doubt it would be like for like; he'd be taken outside and beaten to death by Edvard of Silesia's men.

He glanced at them and could see that they were not scum from the riverbanks and the back streets; these were trained mercenaries loyal to their leader. He saw the intelligence in their demeanour, and his fate was reflected in their eyes as they looked at him with scorn. He could see they despised him for what he had done. He hung his head as, in the past, he always ensured he operated in the shadows, never taking the blame, but now they all knew what he'd ordered, and he felt a flicker of shame for the first time.

His eyes travelled around the room of the inn; in his frightened state, he'd become aware of everything—the dead bodies of his men lying around him, their blood seeping through the cracks in the worn floorboards and already beginning to congeal. He saw the innkeeper and his wife cowering behind the rough wooden counter, only a plank really, and suddenly, he wondered what they were all waiting for. Why didn't they just take him outside and kill him, get it over with? Then, with an awful insight, he knew. The door opened, and Rhodri, the white druid came in.

Ironically, the first thing that struck Crick was that he had failed De Courcy; this man, this druid, should be dead. The second was Sam's words, which suddenly returned to him as he thought of the shiver and unnatural cold he had felt at that window.

You don't mess with some things, Crick, and one of them is those druids.

Crick took in the still-yellowing bruising that covered most of the man's body and the stone-cold expressionless face, but he felt and saw the intensity of the man's eyes as he drew his dagger—a long, thin, druid blade. Crick closed his eyes as he now realised he was not going to have an easy death, and his stomach clenched in terror. The Welshman indicated he should be pulled to his feet, and Crick swallowed in fear as he approached. In a quick action, the man used the dagger to split his tunic from neck to hem and tore it off him until Crick stood bare-chested, and a rope was put around his neck. Rhodri then used the dagger to inscribe a thin cross in Crick's skin below his rib cage back and front, and as the blood ran down his stomach from the shallow wounds, it was Edvard who nodded to his men to take him outside. To Crick's surprise, he was lifted and tied over the back of his horse; he'd presumed that they were going to hang him.

It was pitch black as his head bounced against the trotting horse's side. As his body was jolted on the horse, he prayed that they wouldn't torture him, for he knew he'd give De Courcy away, but then he admitted to himself that he'd never liked the man. Giving De Courcy up in exchange for a quick death could be in his best interests. Crick now presumed they would take him to Warwick, where he'd be executed by Beaumont or even at the King's orders as the Welshman was one of their men after all. He knew it would be brutal; he'd watched several drawing and quartering executions in the past.

However, Rhodri was not taking Crick to Warwick; he had other plans. He had ridden this area and talked to the woodsmen, and he knew the track they were now riding down was 'The Woodway', which would lead them onto the main road through the Forest of Arden to Henley and Bridgnorth. The King and his army would come this way from Warwick, and now all Rhodri needed was the right oak tree on that road.

Chapter Twenty-four

8th August 1102 – Road to Bridgnorth

As usual for a force of that size, it took a considerable amount of time to get them moving and on the road. Fortunately, the King had listened to Beaumont's advice, and most of the carts and wagons had set off the previous day. They were essential to any army, carrying everything from extra weapons, armour, tack, hundreds of tents and pavilions, huge casks of beer, sacks of wine, and foodstuffs. Everyone had been up and ready at dawn, but it was still over two hours later that they were on the road to Henley in Arden, where they would water the horses at the ford on the river Aine.

Conn hadn't forgotten the lesson at Branston Ford, and he rode back and forth with Serjeant Fox and his men into both sides of the Forest of Arden, their eyes everywhere to check there was no sign of ambush, while Beaumont scouts rode on ahead. Conn and Serjeant Fox had rejoined the long column and were riding near the back with the archers and crossbowmen when everything stopped. They reined in, chatting to the men, and waited for the column to move again, but to no avail. Finally, they cantered to the front to see what the holdup was.

He saw that the King, Beaumont, and De Clare had dis-mounted, and he wondered if one was ill. They stood close together in an open grove of trees facing the road. At first, he hesitated to join them as a white-faced De Courcy was with them, but De Clare saw him and waved him over. He dismounted, walked into the clearing, and immediately saw why they had stopped as De Clare took him to one side.

'The scouts came galloping back to tell us of it, thinking it was a warning to the King, but both you and I know what this is,' he said in a low voice.

Conn raised his eyes to what held their attention; he'd seen a lot in his life, almost every type of atrocity in warfare from age sixteen onwards—he and Georgio, on the orders of the warrior monks, had killed their first man together, aged only nine—but certain images stay imprinted on your mind, and this would be one of them.

A naked man had been tied to an oak tree. There was a rope around his neck, but it was there to hold his head up, not to strangle him. His arms and feet were roped and pulled behind the great trunk, but the most distinctive sight was the branch that came through the top of the man's stomach, on which he'd been impaled. Conn walked closer with De Clare, and he could see that the thick branch had been sharpened. The man, no doubt, had been pushed onto it, but the side twigs with their leaves still intact had been pulled through the wound, so it looked as though the branch was growing through his body. Blood ran down his torso and slowly dripped onto the ground below.

'He was alive when someone did this to him; it is recent,' murmured Conn to De Clare, who nodded in agreement.

They stepped back to Beaumont and the King while Serjeant Fox, who had now also dismounted, handed the horses to Gracchus to hold and walked over to look at the body on the tree. He gave a slight smile when he realised who this man was before moving to stand behind De Clare.

'Sire, I suggest we ride on rather than leaving all of our men standing in this heat; we have not far to go to Henley. I do not believe that this has anything to do with you or Robert de Belleme, as we have no idea who this man is or why he is here,' insisted Beaumont.

Serjeant Fox stepped forward and bowed to Beaumont, for whom he had a lot of respect.

'His name is Wilken Crick, Sire, and he is one of Sir Robert de Courcy's men.'

The group turned to stare at an ashen-faced De Courcy, who tried to shrug it off at first, but De Clare could see that his fists were clenched, and his knuckles were white.

As the King waited, De Courcy was forced to answer.

'Is it? I would not have recognised him; I hired him and a few of his men to protect the wagons, after what happened at Branston, but I never exchanged more than a few words with him.'

'You had better go and check that it is him. Does he have a wife or family? At the very least, you can give him a decent Christian burial here. See to it, De Courcy,' snapped Beaumont.

They were all stopped in their tracks as they turned away to return to their horses by a groan from the man they had presumed dead, and to De Courcy's dismay, Crick's eyes opened.

'Dear sweet Jesus, he is still alive. How can that be?' murmured King Henry, crossing himself and retreating towards his horse.

Beaumont shook his head in annoyance. He now had his suspicions about who might have done this and why, but deep down, he also knew who was to blame, and he glared at the Royal Steward.

'Put him out of his misery, De Courcy. This is your mess, and it is the least you can do, for I do not doubt that in some way you are responsible for this man's death,' he growled, in a low tone before following the King and waving the column on.

Conn and Serjeant Fox returned to their horses while De Clare moved closer to De Courcy.

'Retribution, De Courcy. The oak tree is significant, and this man is paying, on its trunk, for his heinous crimes, which you ordered. Few will shed tears for this man's demise, but I would be afraid to close my eyes at night if I were you. Now go and finish off the poor bastard.'

De Courcy stumbled towards Crick but quickly realised that he needed his horse; whoever had put him here either had ladders or had been mounted. Deep down, he knew who was responsible, and his blood ran cold. His equally white-faced servant helped him to mount, and then held the horse as De Courcy stood up in his stirrups and drew his dagger. As long as he lived, he'd never forget the grateful look in Wilken Crick's eyes as he slit the man's throat.

'Get some men, cut him down and bury him here,' he said, to his servant, in a shaken voice as he watched the King's column go past.

Word had gone around like wildfire, and it seemed to the Royal Steward that every lord, knight, squire, and servant were whispering behind their hands and judging him as the column moved on. Then, the cohort of Horse Warriors rode past. He froze as he saw Rhodri ap Gwyfd riding at the front beside Gracchus, but the druid didn't even look in his direction. However, Edvard of Silesia did. He reined in and walked his horse slowly over to De Courcy. To Edvard, De Courcy looked as if he was unable to move, transfixed by what he'd seen in the grove of oak trees. He was pleased to see that the man was in shock.

'It should have been you on that tree, De Courcy; he has hung there in agony more than a day, purely because he was the weapon you used to try and kill an innocent man. God will judge you for your actions, and I hope when your time does come, you have a similar, long lingering death,' he said, before kicking his horse on to rejoin the Horse Warriors.

De Courcy felt numb as he sat and watched the men pull the body off the branch and lower it to the ground to be buried. By then, however, his mind was apportioning blame for this situation, which had tarnished his reputation with the Beaumonts and the King. He blamed everyone but himself and concluded that this was his wife's fault, and he would ensure Rohese suffered for it. After all, if she hadn't taken the Breton Horse Warrior as her lover, then Rhodri ap Gwyfd would never have come to his notice. She had brought all of this on them by her adulterous actions, which again seemed to be common knowledge; he'd seen the courtiers whispering behind their hands.

He'd have her interred in a nunnery immediately, a closed order so she'd never see the light of day again. He'd repudiate her and her treacherous Grandesmil family. He would apply to Rome immediately for an annulment on the grounds of her adultery, and he would marry again—a young girl from an influential and wealthy family, one he could mould to his ways and who would be grateful to be aligned with the name of De Courcy.

With this pleasant thought in his mind, he kicked his horse on to join the King's group at the front; he would make his abject policies to the King over this, and all would be well, for Henry could not do without his skills and organisation and he would soon be back in favour.

10th August 1102 – Morlaix, Brittany

As Conn's uncle, Luc de Malvais, and his contingent of Breton Horse Warriors trotted through the large stone archway into the cobbled stableyard late that afternoon, he saw with a smile that there was a welcoming party on the wide stone steps of his home. His wife, Merewyn, and his brother, Morvan, stood side by side outside the great oak doors. As he dismounted, he watched Merewyn run lightly down the steps, still looking as lithe and lovely as she had been many years ago when he had fallen in love with this Saxon rebel in Ravensworth. The silver-blonde hair was lighter now, and the laughter lines at her eyes and mouth were more pronounced, but she was just as beautiful to him. He opened his arms, and she ran into them, ignoring the dirt, dust and mud that liberally covered him and his men. He held her tightly, raising her face to kiss the soft mouth held up to him.

'You have been away far too long. You said a month, but it has been three, and I have missed you so much this time, Luc,' she said, then she glanced back to the steps. 'We have all missed you,' she added, smiling.

Luc kissed her again and raised a hand in greeting to Morvan, whose dark, elfin-like, pretty wife, Minette, had joined him and waved enthusiastically at the whole group, many of whom grinned back at her—Ette, as she was affectionately known, was much loved by the men at Morlaix.

'I will explain all shortly, but first, I must see to Shadow.'

Merewyn sighed and unwrapped her arms from his waist; she knew the horses always came first, but this time, she'd wanted to hold on to Luc as long as possible. It never got any better when these absences stretched on and on, as her worst fears filled her mind in the dark, lonely nights on her own. She mounted the steps and stood beside Morvan and Ette as Luc led the big, steel-grey dappled stallion into his large box stall, where fresh hay and water awaited.

Morvan's eyes followed the big horse. 'You know how I have always loved the pure blacks—after all, his wild grandmother, Midnight, was my horse—but I must admit that Shadow is a stunning horse. That ghost dapple always turns heads.'

'It is because he is so unusual; his mother is pure black, his grandfather—Luc's previous horse, Esprit de Noir—was a steel dapple, but Shadow has the darkest, most perfect dapple I have ever seen, especially with that jet-black mane and tail,' added Merewyn.

Morvan nodded. 'He also has a far better temperament than his brother, Diablo, and we have already had three colts and a filly from him this year.'

Merewyn smiled. The huge War Destriers dominated their lives, and often, their conversations here at Morlaix involved breeding, training, following, or searching for better blood-lines as orders for these horses came in from most of the royal courts of Europe. However, she wished with all her heart that it was all they did instead of Luc and Morvan being regularly called on to repel raiders from Brittany's borders. She was also unsettled because a large pile of messages awaited Luc, some of which were rolled vellum in leather tubes—these were usually serious and never boded well.

Luc was approaching his forty-ninth name day now, although he looked much younger, and he was as fit, if not fitter, than some of his newer and younger Horse Warrior recruits. Although his thick head of hair was just as black, he had silver wings at his temples now, making him look even more handsome to Merewyn. They were also grandparents now; Lusian had married well and had two young boys, and their daughter, Chantal, had a second girl this year. Their youngest son, Garrett, named after her brother, was twenty now and a Horse Warrior through and through, with no interest in settling down yet. He'd repeatedly talked of riding to join Conn and Georgio, especially after their visit to Morlaix last year, when Garrett had sat enthralled listening to their exploits in Byzantium. Merewyn was reluctant to let him go, even though Luc had reminded her that Conn and Georgio had ridden to Spain when they were only sixteen. They were mere boys, she thought, remembering the tears she had shed when they left, as she expected never to see them again. Now, Conn was carving his own reputation as a fearsome Horse Warrior while poor Georgio was a prisoner, God knows where.

Morvan and Ette turned to go into the hall. Mathew, who had been the steward for the Malvais family for at least thirty years, hovered to see what Merewyn wanted him to do. She placed an affectionate hand on his arm. He was a thoughtful, loyal, highly respected man who could control the dozens of servants in the castle with barely a disapproving glance.

'I need a word with Luc, Mathew, but the men will, as usual, be starving, so serve dinner early, in about an hour, if the cook can cope.'

She went down the steps, crossed to the stables, and leant against the door jamb, watching Luc rub the dust from the big stallion's coat. He sent her a quick smile, but she had news for him that he didn't expect, and even after long years of marriage, she was not sure how he would take it. He paused momentarily and raised an eyebrow at her; she was not usually so quiet.

'What is it?' he asked, sensing her nervousness.

She decided to plunge in as she knew he always liked plain speaking.

'Something neither of us was expecting after so long,' she murmured, dropping her eyes and suddenly feeling shy.

It took him a few moments, but then his eyes widened. Dropping the cloth, he stepped forward and pulled her into his arms.

'When?' he asked.

'I think I am about three months. I am sure it was the night before you left; we were so passionate.' Luc laughed, picked her up and swung her around.

'I thought about that night often while we were away; you were indeed like a woman possessed, so passionate. And this is the result—another child to look after us in our dotage. I care not what it is, girl or boy, as long as it is healthy and you are safe and well. I cannot imagine life without you in it, Merewyn Eymer.'

She hugged him tighter. He had not called her by her maiden name for a long time, and it brought back memories of their time in Ravensworth, some good, some best forgotten.

'Come, Mathew is waiting to serve dinner, and your men will no doubt be starving. I expect they are sitting and banging their knives on the table.'

But he still did not let her go, kissing her eyelids and then her mouth before holding her at arm's length.

'Only if you promise me we will have another night of passion tonight, albeit gentler; no more riding for you, my lady.'

She pulled a shocked face and pretended to look around to check that no stableboys had heard before she gave in to laughter. She picked up her skirts and ran swiftly across the yard and up the steps. Luc stopped at the water trough to wash the grime and dust of a full day on the roads of Brittany from his face and hair, but there was a spring in his step as he ran up the steps to the hall. A father again! It was unexpected but filled him with joy.

Dinner was lively, to say the least, with thirty Horse Warriors back in the hall, but the family loved it as it felt normal again. Luc didn't have to say a word about the problems they'd faced on the Maine border, for Garrett was doing it for him as he arrived to take his place. He smiled at his son's enthusiasm, while the women and some of the servants grimaced at the gory details of the raiders they had killed. Watching Garrett and the way his hands moved, he looked the image of his namesake, Merewyn's brother, even down to the dark auburn hair.

As the meal ended and the noise from the hall became less pronounced, Mathew informed Luc that several important messages had arrived, along with numerous messages by bird. Luc reluctantly left the table, waving Morvan to follow him to the business room. Mathew had lit a roaring fire in there, and they were pleased as a cold breeze was coming off the sea that night. He poured their wine and left them to it.

Luc first broke the seals on the rolled vellum, read both briefly, and then, with a grin, handed them to his brother.

'Both of these concern you. I suggest you pack your saddle-bags.'

Morvan gave him a puzzled look. The first was from his friend and old comrade, Robert Curthose, Duke of Normandy. As part of the Treaty of Alton, the royal brothers had agreed to support each other in times of war. King Henry had now ordered his brother, Robert, to attack Belleme's lands and castles in Normandy. Robert desperately needed Morvan's counsel on this, as Belleme was also his friend and his wealthiest and most loyal supporter. However, at the same time, Robert did not want to give his brother, Henry, any excuse for saying that he'd broken the Treaty of Alton.

'Why do I feel as if King Henry's greedy eyes are turning to Normandy?' asked Luc.

Morvan shook his head. 'This is a difficult one, Luc. Belleme and I hate each other since he tried to rape Ette in Scotland, and do not forget, Conn is fighting for King Henry against Belleme in England as we speak. We are on different sides.'

Luc looked thoughtful before he replied. 'Do not forget that Belleme now knows that Conn is your son and not mine, a secret he has kept for you despite being questioned by King Henry. Piers does believe that Belleme has put the feud between you aside. You had better read the next one while you think this over. This is from Chatillon, and interesting news indeed,' he said with a grin.

Morvan unrolled the next message and read its contents. His first reaction was laughter, for Chatillon had known exactly what Duke Robert had written, and offered his advice, but it was the last paragraph that took his breath away. There had been no hint or news of this, and it raised so many questions.

I do not believe you are aware of this, but we have Conn's son, Darius, here at the chateau. This information must stay only with you and your family, or the child could be at risk. Also, Conn has been given an estate a few leagues from here as a reward from Robert Beaumont, but it has its problems. When you leave the Duke at Rouen, I suggest you come here to meet your grandson and help me eliminate the problem of the raiders in the Rambouillet Forest for him. I would say that ten Horse Warriors would suffice.

Yours
Chatillon

Luc, who had sat back to sip his wine, watched the emotions play over his brother's face as he bent forward to put Chatillon's message in the fire. He smiled; old habits die hard, and Chatillon had always insisted on messages being burnt.

'It sounds somewhat of an adventure; I am envious, but much as I would like to ride with you, Merewyn is with child, and I need to be here.'

Morvan gave a shout of laughter at this and raised his goblet high.

'Let us have a toast to me as a grandfather for the first time and to you and Merewyn for a healthy fourth child.'

'Do we know where this child, Darius, came from?' asked Luc.

Morvan shook his head. 'No, this is completely out of the blue, but if the child is in danger, it is like Conn all over again, history repeating itself. But where is the danger coming from this time?'

Both men sat in the flickering light of the fire, thoughtfully remembering the terrible time when Constance was forced to give her child up to be murdered, and the resulting backlash had meant that Morvan and Luc were estranged for several years.

'Whatever the story, Luc, I am prepared to protect young Darius with my life, like you did for Conn. I presume there must be a reason for the child being sent to Chatillon rather than to us, and I will find the answers to all of these questions at Chatillon sous Bagneux. But first, I must go and support Duke Robert. Now let us go and tell our wives the news; I will lay silver that Ette will want to come with me,' he laughed.

But as he followed his brother out, Luc was unsettled. There was far more to all of this than met the eye—the child, the raiders in the forest— he felt uneasy and feared that his brother might be putting himself in danger, not to mention becoming embroiled once again in Duke Robert's turbulent and often disastrous affairs.

Chapter Twenty-five

9th August 1102 – Stafford Castle

Daegal had always been a light sleeper—living among the warlike tribes in the kingdoms of Ireland, you had to be. But it was more than that, and tonight, he found it almost impossible to sleep as he'd been uneasy for most of the day. Even sharing half a sack of wine with Rhys hadn't settled his mind or his stomach.

Daegal had always been a watcher and a listener; whenever he fought, he'd always walk the camp to get a feel for the men and the atmosphere, and now he could feel tension and doubt rather than the expected emotions—anticipation and excitement tinged with a touch of anxiety—before an attack. Prince Iorwerth had ridden back in yesterday shortly after noon, and he was certainly excited—itching to get into battle. Daegal could see it in his face and in every muscle in his body; he was like a coiled spring. He stood beside Owen in the Great Hall to hear the Prince's report to his brother, King Maredudd. Iorwerth had been tracking Sir William Pantulf, and he'd found that, as predicted, Pantulf was slow-moving, and his forces were smaller than expected. Iorwerth thought that the Norman knight was heading for Shallowford and that they could easily ambush and take him, preventing him from attacking Stafford Castle.

Daegal could see that, for once, King Maredudd was pleased with his brother; he praised Iorwerth in front of the assembled courtiers and his brother, Cadwgan. However, that had been the beginning of Daegal's unease, for he'd noticed that Prince Iorwerth couldn't quite meet the eyes of either of his brothers. No doubt some would try to put down his shiftiness to humility at his brother's praise, but Daegal knew there was nothing humble about the Prince—he had known and watched him for several years and would not trust him one whit.

Iorwerth left the court early, saying he had to talk to his men and prepare them for a full attack on the morrow. Daegal strolled slowly along behind him, keeping him in sight, and then standing unobtrusively on the outskirts of the throng. The Prince was clever; he divided his men into groups of about eighty so all could gather around and hear his words without him raising his voice. To Daegal's disappointment, the Prince spoke to his men in their own dialect, one that Daegal didn't fully understand, but he didn't need to, for he saw their faces, the puzzled looks, the frowns, the shaking of their heads. Seeing their reluctance, Prince Iorwerth took out his fat purse and gave each man a piece of silver, more than some of them would earn as labourers toiling on the land in six months or, for some, a year.

Daegal was puzzled; he knew that Iorwerth had been sent away in disgrace, but now he was back and in high favour and seemed eager to win his brother's approval. Why were his men so reluctant to fight that he had to bribe them?

These thoughts went round and round in his head until he

finally threw his blanket off and got to his feet. He couldn't explain it, but his instincts were never wrong, so he shook Owen ap Cynan awake.

'We must leave as soon as possible,' he growled.

Owen, angry at being disturbed, rubbed the sleep from his eyes.

'Are you mad? We are attacking Pantulf tomorrow, for which we will be well paid,' he said, moving to roll back under his blanket.

'You won't live to spend it. I tell you there is treachery afoot; it is a trap, I just know it. Let us take your captive and go south while we can, as I believe that Iorwerth is about to kill his brother, and we will be collateral damage. Mercenaries in the service of the rebels, they will delight in stringing us up.'

This got Owen's attention, but he was still sceptical. He wondered how Daegal O'Brien could know all this. However, when Rhys joined them, he was convinced as he trusted the Irishman's instincts.

'He is right, Owen. I admit that something about Iorwerth's tale did not feel right; he made it all sound too easy. Let us not take the chance.'

Owen reluctantly agreed and stood up, kicking his blanket to one side. But then he gripped Daegal by the shoulder. 'You had better be right, O'Brien, or you will owe me a lot of money.'

'I am rarely wrong about these things, Owen; I can almost taste the betrayal in the air here at Stafford,' he said as he went to roll up his blanket and pack his saddlebags.

An hour later, they were leading their horses out of the camp. There was so much movement of men and horses coming and going that the sleepy guards sitting around the brazier hardly gave them a glance. One of them recognised Owen and his men and waved them on, presuming they were the advance scouts for tomorrow's attack. Owen left one of his men behind, hidden in the trees on the castle bank, where he had a good view of the castle and surrounding fields.

Kicked awake and groggy at first, Georgio now had his wits about him and watched these developments with interest. He wondered how this would affect him and his handover at Shrewsbury Abbey, which was now less than a week away. His stomach clenched in fear at the thought.

He was on a horse being led behind Rhys. His hands were tied in front of him, but his ankles were back in irons under the horse's belly. He prayed he didn't fall off, for with him dangling underneath, the horse would panic, and he would be trampled to death by the horse's hooves as it tried to rid itself of the unusual burden; he gripped the high pommel of the old wooden saddle as if his life depended on it.

Owen headed south, and Daegal, who had been riding and scouting at the rear to ensure they were not being followed, realised that the Welshman was descending through the trees to follow the track by the river. He pulled up alongside him.

'Where are we heading? I presume you have a plan.'

'This is the River Penk on our left. We follow this to Penkridge, where a large community of clerics exists. Abbot Columbanus sent me to do some work for them, clearing the land of troublesome villeins so they could put it to grass and keep sheep. They know me here and will not give us any trouble.'

Daegal glanced behind at the sixty or so mercenaries following them.

'Will they make us welcome when they see how many men we bring?' he asked, doubtfully.

Owen laughed. 'I rarely give these clerics or monks a choice, but we will conveniently change sides. We will camp on the meadows on the banks of the Penk, just below the settlement. There is a large church in Penkridge that is a Royal Chapel. They are proud of that as it gives them independence from the bishop, so we tell them we are going to fight for King Henry against the outlawed Montgomerys, and I promise they will provide us with food. We will ensure the men behave and stay away from the women in the village for the few days we will be there. It will give us a base to finalise our plans; it is only a day and a half ride to Shrewsbury from there.'

Unwillingly, Daegal was impressed; Owen seemed to have thought this through. He glanced at Georgio, who met his look with a steady gaze and a raised questioning eyebrow. He liked the young man, and it still went against all of his principles to see an innocent warrior murdered. Listening to Owen and Rhys, he was more convinced than ever that they didn't intend the Horse Warrior to be alive when he was handed over. But until he was privy to Owen's final plans, he couldn't find any way to help Georgio. Maybe it was better for him to walk away from this and let them do as they wished; why should he risk his life and turn down Owen's silver on a principle? But then he questioned himself again for what was a man without principles. It was Ralph de Tosny who had hammered the warrior's code into him.

But that brought the problem of Malvais to mind, which was another dilemma for him, for it had not been the Horse Warrior who had killed his long-time lord and mentor, Ralph de Tosny—Robert Beaumont had done that. But it was Malvais who had disabled De Tosny, providing Beaumont with the opportunity. He could still see his sword flashing through the air and slicing into De Tosny's shoulder. There was no way his lord could fight Beaumont after that. So, he'd sworn to kill Beaumont and the Horse Warrior, and now he had the opportunity. Owen had assured him that Conn Fitz Malvais would be in Shrewsbury Abbey on the 15th of August, and Owen told him he'd even pay him for killing him.

10th August 1102 – Oxford

Sir Nigel D'Oyly had asked Edvard to keep him posted about events on the King's campaign, as news was slow in coming to them in Oxford. Lady Adeline used to say they received swifter and better news of events in the country from the pedlars. However, Edvard had been true to his word, and several birds had arrived to tell him of Beaumont's successes and the King's forced march to Warwick. He'd shared these messages with Rohese and Adeline, as they always wanted to know where Malvais was.

He knew the King's forces were now marching northwest to Bridgnorth, where they hoped to put an end to the Montgomerys once and for all. As far as he was concerned, there were no winners in a civil war; the killing, burning and destruction of villages and towns could take a decade to recover from. He asked himself what would happen if, by chance, Robert de Belleme won. He certainly had the money and the armies to do so, and he was a clever and experienced strategist in warfare. Although he was known as the King's man, inside, he knew that Henry had stolen the crown from Duke Robert—he saw Henry for the oathbreaker he was, and despised him for it, and as such, Belleme had every right to challenge and kill him.

These treacherous thoughts were interrupted by a knock on the solar's door and the appearance of his steward.

'Sire, a messenger has arrived from the King's camp; he says it is urgent.'

Sir Nigel raised his eyes in surprise. He'd already sent a hundred men to the King; surely he could not be demanding more? However, as the steward ushered in the messenger, he recognised the sour-faced man and the livery. It was De Courcy's squire, the one who never seemed to be good enough to attain his knighthood, and the bitterness of that sat on him like a heavy cloak. He thought he must be nearly thirty years old by now. As he looked him up and down with distaste, he waved him forward and took the rolled vellum from his hand. Anything from De Courcy was anathema to Sir Nigel, particularly after the last unpleasant visit of the Royal Steward. However, as he always remained in the King's favour and was the husband of Rohese, he was forced to tolerate the arrogant man.

He read the brief message with growing disbelief and then read it again before glaring at the Squire.

'Do you know the contents of this?' he asked, throwing it on the table.

'Yes, Sire, I am privy to my master's wishes, and as it states, I have to stay here and escort the Lady Rohese to Wytham Abbey, where the nuns from Helenstow were relocated. I hear they have a small black cross made from one of the nails of the true cross; surely that would be a wonder to behold, and the Lady Rohese should be honoured to be there.'

Sir Nigel narrowed his eyes at the arrogant squire.

'Has your master taken leave of his senses? The Lady Rohese

is a Grandesmil, a member of one of the great houses of England and Normandy. Does the King know of this? If he does not, I will ensure he does, for Rohese is one of Queen Matilda's ladies-in-waiting.'

To Sir Nigel's astonishment, the squire folded his arms and sneered.

'I cannot think my master, the King's Royal Steward, would welcome your interference in his marriage. The Lady Rohese is his property to do with as he wills. The Grandesmils have been proved to be traitors, and she is guilty of adultery and possibly of giving birth to a child that is not from my master's loins, so he has every right to put her away and demand an annulment.'

Sir Nigel found he was suddenly speechless with anger and shot to his feet.

'Does your impudence know no bounds? How dare you stand there and say such things to me when you are no more than a jumped-up servant? To speak so of your betters and masters in such a way deserves a beating. Steward, get him out of here and see to it before I deliver it myself. Give him a room above the stables while we await the return of Lady Rohese. I will send urgent messages to the King and Queen.'

The steward bowed and pushed the shocked and equally angry squire out of the room. He'd never seen his master so red-faced and furious, and he delivered a punch to the squire's head that sent him crashing into the wall.

Sir Nigel dropped into his chair and gulped back the goblet of wine at his side while he thought about what to do. It was obvious that the squire was repeating what he had heard his master say, but that was alarming in itself. Rohese was with Lady Adeline at Bicester, where the latter still held properties.

Her deceased husband, Roger d'Ivry, had been the lifetime boon companion of his brother, Robert D'Oyly, who had built Oxford Castle. They shared the two manors, but it had all come to Adeline on their deaths. She happily went to Bicester a few times a year to administer the manor courts, check the work of her bailiffs and enjoy the peace. They were expected back on Friday, giving him three days to halt this madness. He would send messages as their names still held significant sway, and he would do everything in his power to stop this.

He had to make sure that Rohese never entered the portals of Wytham Abbey, for once in exclusion in a closed order such as Helenstow, they would never get her out, and he didn't doubt that De Courcy would be paying them well to hold and bury her there in isolation. He needed to warn the sisters that they could not return to Oxford. He had to get Rohese away, but to where?

It was no good turning to the family as her father, the Sheriff of Leicester, had died a few years ago, and her brother, Ivo, had been fined for his part in Duke Robert's invasion and had now given up his lands to Beaumont and gone on crusade. However, he remembered that the older brother, Robert de Grandesmil, had inherited all the wealthy lands in Normandy. He sat and wracked his brain for several moments as to where that was, and then it came to him: Saint Evrout de Bois in the Orne region, that was where the impressive castle was situated. The siblings were not close, but surely he'd take his sister in to save her from such a fate.

He moved to the table and, picking up a vellum sheet, began writing a letter to Adeline, telling her to run and explaining why. He told her to take Rohese to Gloucester to his cousin, and he would send money and men to help them. But all must be done quickly and in secret, for he didn't trust De Courcy one whit. The man had deep pockets and a lot of influence, certainly enough to prevent her from leaving the country. He summoned his steward; he needed help only from the servants and men he could trust. He may pay for what he was about to do, but he'd not let this happen to Rohese. She was Adeline's sister, and he'd secretly loved Adeline deeply for many years.

He suddenly thought of Edvard, who had easily got Joan and the child out of England; this was the help he needed, but how could he reach him? He was where no bird could find him, and it would take days to ride there. By then, it would be too late. He stopped pacing suddenly as he thought of a way but dismissed it as madness—it could get him hung. Then he realised that it was his only chance of contacting Edvard. He would send a bird to Belleme and beg him to get an urgent message to Edvard of Silesia, who was riding with the King's forces to lay siege to Bridgnorth. As he voiced his thoughts, he realised how ridiculous it sounded. But there was a chance the rebel Earl would agree to send a messenger, for Sir Nigel knew that Belleme also hated De Courcy with a vengeance.

He prepared the message and explained to his steward what he was doing and what he was risking. He looked shocked at first, but then his loyal servant nodded.

'No one will know of this but you and I, Sire, but you need to know the squire brought four men at arms with him, and they are questioning the stable boys and grooms as to where the Lady Rohese has gone and when she is returning. I fear they may ride out and take her on the road, because the squire realised that you will try to prevent them.' Sir Nigel frowned at this news and handed him the letter for Adeline and a large purse.

'Send our brightest man on our fastest horse; tell him to stay with them to protect them on the road to Gloucester. Meanwhile, do anything you can to stop De Courcy's men from leaving—get them drunk, lame their horses. We have got to get to the Lady Rohese first.'

However, he was back in no time with a worried expression that didn't bode well.

'Sire, I sent the message to Belleme, but I was too late at the stables, as two of them had already left for Bicester. I have given the letter and purse to your young squire. He knows what he has to do and what is at stake.'

'God help us all if this ever comes out,' he muttered, as he dropped into his chair, and ran his hands through his hair in frustration. If anything happened to Adeline, he would tear Robert de Courcy limb from limb.

Chapter Twenty-six

10th August 1102 – Stafford

Owen's man hadn't been the only one watching and awaiting events at Stafford Castle. Belleme's brother, Roger de Poitevin, was following his brother's command and was riding north to join King Maredudd to defeat Pantulf at Stafford when, only half a league away from the castle, his two scouts had come galloping back.

'Sire, I suggest you halt our men here as something is amiss at Stafford; a large force is attacking the castle, far more than only Sir William Pantulf. We captured one of the men trying to escape the slaughter. He said it was Prince Iorwerth of Powys who was attacking and that he had betrayed his brothers, changed sides and joined with Sir William Pantulf.'

Roger de Poitevin tried to take this in as it was not only unexpected but disastrous. He had four hundred men with him, but the plan had been for him to join with Iorwerth to attack Pantulf. He couldn't attack a force of what was now nearly a thousand men on his own, especially if they had already taken King Maredudd by surprise and captured Iorwerth's brother, Cadwgan. he realised that Maredudd's men, inside and outside the castle, wouldn't know which way to turn if their leaders had gone. He turned to his captain.

'Tell the men to rest and water the horses as we have no option but to return to Bridgnorth, but first, I need to see the truth of what is happening at Stafford Castle with my own eyes. If he has betrayed us, I swear I will find and gut Iorwerth ap Bleddyn with my own hands, for he has broken his oath and the promises he made to the Montgomerys, and we never forget or forgive such treachery.'

With that, he rode back to Stafford Castle with the scouts. Owen's man, still hidden in the undergrowth, heard them coming and melted away through the trees to mount his horse, as he'd seen and heard enough to tell Owen that Daegal O'Brien was indeed right; they were giving little quarter down there, and they would have been killed or captured if they had stayed.

Roger de Poitevin sat on his horse, hidden in the trees, and watched the flames beginning to lick the wooden palisades of Stafford Castle. Moments later, a large party of prisoners appeared roped together—even from this distance, he could see by their blood-spattered clothes that they had been beaten. He recognised some of the minor lords and courtiers from the court of Powys, but with shock, he saw that the man on his own pushed to his knees at the front was King Maredudd. He scanned the rest of them as they appeared but couldn't see Prince Cadwgan anywhere. Undoubtedly, he had tried to protect his brother and paid with his life.

This attack and betrayal would be a huge blow to Belleme, for in one fell swoop, he'd lost his Welsh allies, who were to sweep down from the north. Maredudd had promised him several thousand men, but instead, Pantulf had triumphed here, and Roger wondered if they had underestimated Henry Beauclerc, for he must have orchestrated all of this. He could watch no more and, running his hands over his face, turned away to ride back to Bridgnorth while praying they would get there before King Henry's forces arrived to lay siege to the castle. He knew that positioned as it was on the higher defensive bluff, the castle at Bridgnorth could become a death trap for Belleme without the forces attacking from the north.

Several leagues away, riding west as fast as their horses could travel, was Prince Cadwgan with twenty remaining cavalry. He had become suspicious that morning when he found that Owen, the Welsh mercenary, had gone in the night. He disliked the man but had to admit he was not only cunning but also a survivor—he bounced like a ball from one side to the other but emerged unscathed—and now, they had fled in the night. He could see it was a sudden decision as they had left the tents and much else behind. *What did he know or find out?* he had asked himself.

Like Daegal, he walked in the early dawn amongst Iorwerth's men; not many could meet his eyes, and the answers to his questions were vague, giving nothing away. An hour later, Iorwerth's force of over five hundred men rode out to launch their attack on Shallowford. Cadwgan even joined in with the cheers and raised a hand in farewell, but he then raced to the hall to share his fears with the King. But Maredudd wouldn't take them seriously.

'Iorwerth needs this victory. He would not betray his own family,' he insisted. However, Cadwgan had seen the hatred in Iorwerth's face and thought it was all too likely that he would.

'I am going to ride after him to watch his attack; I will send a messenger, but heed my warning, Brother, I do not like the feel of this.'

He followed at quite a distance behind, but soon, he could hear the sounds of cheers and shouts. Hope sprang in his heart that Iorwerth had been loyal and true to his word and had already attacked and chased Pantulf and his men away. They rode quietly through the trees, and then, Cadwgan rode ahead with only his captain to look down on Shallowford. What he saw sent a chill to his bones. Pantulf was greeting Iorwerth like a long-lost relative, and the cheering was from the King's men, celebrating his brother's betrayal. He sat staring in disbelief for so long that his captain had to nudge his knee.

'Sire, they are mounting up. We must go, or they will find us here.'

Cadwgan turned his horse away, and feeling the wetness on his cheeks, he brushed the tears of betrayal away. They galloped south, having sent a messenger on ahead to warn the King. As they neared Stafford, he realised it was hopeless, because he could see how Iorwerth would ride in, pretending to be a victor, being embraced by his brother before he thrust the knife between Maredudd's ribs. They were a league away from the castle when Cadwgan reined in and turned to face his men.

'We ride for Mathrafal. We must protect the royal court and our families. We have warned King Maredudd. He will now close the gates and hold the castle against them. We have done what we can.'

With that, they had galloped away, leaving the King of Powys to his fate. As he bent low over his galloping horse's neck, Cadwgan told himself that, like Owen, he was a survivor. He was not so much running away as saving his life and those of his cavalry. He swore he'd make Iorwerth pay for his betrayal.

At Stafford, it had happened as Cadwgan had foretold, but

Iorwerth did not kill his brother; he took him captive and paraded him in front of the hundreds of men in the meadows, who had been ready to fight for their king. He cleverly told them that he would not kill his brother, but that he knew it was Maredudd who had betrayed them, that none of them wanted this war he had forced them into, and that they all could return to their homes and farms once the Montgomerys had been defeated. He swore it would now be over in a month.

He brought the King's chests of silver forward and climbed on the cart beside them. He threw back the lids and, lifting handfuls, let the coins flow through his fingers like a silver waterfall; the eyes of the men followed the coins.

'I promise that every man who fights for me will receive two pieces of silver, but if you decide not to, you are free to go empty-handed back to Powys.'

The murmur and rumble that spread through the ranks rose at this declaration, and Iorwerth could see some angry faces, so he nodded to his captain to blow the horn. At that, the castle walls filled with Pantulf's men while his captains rode from behind the castle to swell the ranks of Iorwerth's men.

'However, if any of you decide to take up arms against me, we will kill you. So, who is with me? Who wants the freedom to go home in a month with silver in their hands?'

At this, a huge cheer went up from his and Pantulf's men, slowly spreading outwards. Iorwerth saw a few men lay down their swords and walk away. He knew there would be some men who were still loyal to Maredudd, but he let them go. He was triumphant; there would be no stopping him now. They would ride to defeat the Montgomerys, and the throne of Powys would be his.

11th August 1102 – Bridgnorth

Robert de Belleme was alone in his solar. He often preferred solitude. He never sought company and had few friends. Roger was in Stafford as planned, and Arnulf was mustering his Irish allies into position. He was satisfied that his strategy was coming together. The steward had delivered two messages to him just as Fulk of Lisours had been admitted.

'What news on Henry's forces?' he asked, keen to know when to unleash the attacks he had planned down to the last detail.

'They are still about seven leagues distant, Sire. The recent heavy rain has slowed them considerably.'

'Unfortunately, Fulk, as you know, it works both ways, for it slows the forces coming to support us,' he said, waving the knight to a chair while he read the messages.

He found Fulk very useful. The man was experienced in warfare and grasped things quickly—qualities that Belleme appreciated. However, his eyebrows flew up as he read the first message, which had a second message hidden beneath it—unusual on a bird. He read it again, and then he frowned.

'Bad news, Sire?' asked Fulk.

Belleme shook his head and read both messages through for a third time.

'No, it's a very unusual request, but I'm not sure I'm minded to grant it.'

Fulk sat and waited while Belleme stared into the distance, deep in thought.

The problem was that Belleme knew Sir Nigel D'Oyly to be an influential and useful man to have on his side, and he did hate Robert de Courcy. However, by acceding to his request, he was helping the son of a man he also hated—a man fighting against him with his Horse Warriors—for he knew all about Conn's affair with Rohese de Courcy. Chatillon had advised him to bury the feud with Morvan de Malvais, but it had rankled and burned inside him for so long that it was difficult to put aside. However, Rohese was a Grandesmil, a family always loyal to Duke Robert, and that's what swayed him. He looked across at Fulk.

'Do you still have that ghost of a man who can flit in and out of the enemy camp at will, day or night?'

Fulk laughed. 'Yes. He pretends to be a pedlar; he has one of those blank, nondescript faces that is easy to forget. Do you wish to use him?'

Belleme explained that he needed him to take an urgent message to Edvard of Silesia and handed him the thinly rolled slip of paper hidden beneath the first message.

'I will see to it immediately,' he said, too well-trained to ask Belleme why he was contacting such a notable figure on the King's side.

Meanwhile, Belleme crossed to the table where he'd laid out his maps and notes. Henry was still far enough away for him to move some of his forces closer, but still out of range of Henry's scouts. He had at least five hundred men with him in the castle, another hundred in front of the gates, and a thousand or so in the fields on the further side of the river close to the bridge. Due to the position of Bridgnorth in its peninsula of land, it would be impossible for Henry to attack the flanks or rear; it would have to be a frontal assault. This meant he'd be leaving himself open to attack on three sides; this was Belleme's chance to finish Henry Beauclerc once and for all. He was positively buoyant at the thought.

Two hours later, everything had changed.

Belleme's brother, Roger, panting and white-faced, came running up the stairs and burst into the solar.

'We are undone, Brother, by treachery and betrayal. Prince Iorwerth has gone over to the enemy, taking his five hundred men. He and Pantulf attacked Stafford Castle and captured King Maredudd. We were forced to flee before they saw and turned on us,' he gasped.

Belleme clenched his fists and let out a roar of rage, followed by a barrage of foul abuse at Iorwerth. Roger let him rant, watching him limp back and forth, but he knew that his brother had a mind like no other regarding strategy. When he calmed, he would find a way through this, or they would all hang for treason.

However, by the next day, when Henry's forces arrived, Belleme had still hardly said a word, locking himself in the solar, and Roger was beside himself with anxiety. Finally, he opened the door, and he and Fulk entered.

'What do we do, Brother? Our forces are protecting the front of the castle, our cavalry are in the forests to the rear, and Arnulf is to the west with our Irish allies awaiting your orders.'

Still, Belleme didn't answer; he stood at the window, staring at the spread of Henry's forces before Bridgnorth. Then the horns blew, and a group of knights rode forward under the flag of parley.

'Go and listen to their terms, Roger. However, make sure they understand that we will not accept anything from the Oathbreaker and do not admit that I am here in Bridgnorth, while I decide what I intend to do.'

Roger felt more encouraged as he rode out to meet Henry's envoys. Like his brothers, he refused to ever recognise Henry as king. He took Fulk of Lisours and half a dozen knights with him, all dressed in finery, pennants flying, and horses caparisoned in their colours and badges.

It was Henry Beaumont, Earl of Warwick, who led the entourage and who opened the talks.

'King Henry is inclined to be generous; he has promised the Castellan and the knights who surrendered at Arundel that he would allow the Montgomery brothers to surrender, make their way to the coast and take ship for their lands in Normandy. I presume you are the mouthpiece for the Earl of Shrewsbury. So what say you to this offer?'

Roger sat for some time and stared at Warwick before he answered. He smiled as he saw that it made some of Henry's knights angry at this insult to their lord and king.

'Firstly, I am the mouthpiece for the people and men of Bridgnorth who have done nothing to deserve this attack and siege. My brother, the Earl, is not here. Secondly, we do not recognise Henry Beauclerc, Oathbreaker, as the King of England, as he stole his brother's crown.'

Henry Beaumont was slightly thrown by the news that Belleme was not here in Bridgnorth; the King wouldn't be happy that he had yet again escaped, and it begged the question, where was he? Was he attacking somewhere else while the King's forces had been drawn and tied up here?

'We thought you might refuse, so King Henry gives you warning—that if you have not surrendered in one week, he will show you that he is his father's son, for he will hang every living being, from servant to knight, inside that castle when it falls.'

Roger de Poitevin heard the sharp intake of breath at this from most of the knights around him, so he laughed in

Beaumont's face.

'Now Henry Beauclerc shows his true colours to the people of England. What price of his Charter of Liberties if you will hang the old woodturner and the local blacksmith because they were inside the castle? Henry is a cunning and ruthless man, guilty of murdering his brother, William Rufus. We see him for what he is, and I assure you that we Montgomerys will fight to the last man to protect the innocent and defenceless people of England inside that castle.'

At that point, Fulk and the other knights gave a rousing cheer, for they were brave words that shamed the King and his envoys. They turned and rode back into the castle, but although he tried not to show it, Roger de Poitevin was in despair. Belleme had to take control of his still considerable forces or they would all die here in Bridgnorth.

11th August 1102 – The King's camp, south of Bridgnorth.

Conn was with Rhodri, waiting for De Clare to return from the parley with the Montgomerys. They had hardly seen the Welshman since the incident in the oak grove; he kept himself to himself and stayed with Gracchus or Synnove, who had stayed by his side when they moved to Warwick. He never mentioned what had happened to Crick, and neither did anyone else, but Conn looked at his friend with new eyes as he now realised what he was capable of. Rhodri, always sensitive to the atmosphere, could see that Conn was on edge and hoped it was not because of him, but he stayed quiet. Over the last year, he learnt that Conn would tell you his concerns only when he was ready.

De Clare, however, as he dismounted with Serjeant Fox, immediately saw the furrowed brow and concern on his younger friend's face, as he asked how the parley had gone outside the castle. De Clare removed his coif and gloves and stared at his friend; he could see that Conn was distracted, as if he already knew the answer and didn't care either way about the Montgomerys. This was so different from the resurgent, focused Horse Warrior, determined to end this war since he had discovered his son was alive and in France.

However, De Clare obediently relayed what was said, and Conn gave a low whistle at the news.

'So the bird has flown. But truly, none of us ever expected Belleme to roll over and surrender. He did the same thing at Arundel; he'd been gone for weeks when they discovered he was not there. How long can he keep running, and why is he doing this when he has considerable resources in men and money?'

'It may be that he has just left Bridgnorth because he received the same news as we did, before we rode out to the parley—Stafford Castle has fallen, and our friend Prince Iorwerth has kept his word to us and joined forces with Pantulf. We believe Belleme's Welsh allies are now in disarray, which plays into our hands here.'

Conn nodded, but he still seemed to have something else on his mind. De Clare led him to one side as Rhodri and Serjeant Fox returned to the men.

'Are you going to tell me what is wrong?'

Conn took a few moments before he answered his friend.

'You may not have noticed as we were busy setting up camp, but Edvard was in deep conversation with a peddler for some time. Then, he came striding over and told me he must leave urgently. When I asked, he would not tell me where he was going or why, which is in itself unusual. He said he would be gone for several days, but he swore he would be in Shrewsbury the night before the 15th of August, which is only three or four days away, De Clare. We may find that we must do this without him, but he is supposed to deliver the ransom to free Georgio, which has gone with him in his saddlebags. We cannot let this go wrong now, as we are so close to bringing it to an end, and we must be there to rescue him and kill Owen. I cannot imagine what Georgio is thinking, for he can only believe that we have abandoned him.'

De Clare put a hand on Conn's shoulder to reassure him, as he could see the pain in his eyes.

'I trust Edvard, as I know you do; if he says he will be in Shrewsbury, he will be there. He is another one who loves you like a son. But if the worst were to happen, Georgio has one of England's most feared Horse Warriors fighting for him, along with Gracchus and your men. Serjeant Fox and I may come in as a poor second, but I promise we will also be there, and our men will have ringed that abbey and town so no one will get out. We will rescue Georgio and there will be nowhere for them to run if they have hurt a hair on his head.'

Conn felt reassured as he clasped arms and thanked De Clare; he had been by his side since he returned to England and had become a firm friend. He admitted that his fears about Edvard had kept him awake all night.

'It is not like you to be rattled by anything,' he said, narrowing his eyes at Conn and wondering if he'd told him everything.

'I think it was the suddenness of the departure and the expression on his face. I had not seen that look before—as if he was avoiding my eyes. Also, the urgency; something somewhere is amiss for him to leave so abruptly. I cannot but think that he is riding into danger,' admitted Conn.

'Edvard is well able to look after himself as we have all seen, time and again. I presume he took his men with him?' Conn nodded.

'Put your mind at rest by remembering that Edvard is Chatillon's man, for all that he has been placed at our beck and call for some time. Chatillon takes priority, and if he summons or orders him, then Edvard must go wherever he sends him. But he will return—he always returns,' De Clare said, reassuringly.

The man in question had ridden for over twenty-four hours. He and his men had changed horses twice; silver in hand had ensured them the best available mounts at the inns. The worst thing for Edvard was not knowing what he was riding into, as Sir Nigel's message told him to ride south urgently to rescue Lady Rohese—but rescue her from what?

He had not dared share this with Malvais; it needed careful handling, and he could imagine the effect on Malvais of such a message, especially so close to the reckoning to come in Shrewsbury Abbey. Suddenly, Edvard shook his head as everything fell into place, and he realised this was happening since De Courcy had come across Crick, where he'd been humiliated in front of the King and courtiers. He was planning revenge—not on Rhodri, for he was now very afraid of the druid, but on Malvais, and the one way he could hurt *him* was by hurting Rohese.

Edvard prayed they would be there in time, as there was still some way to go. He pushed his horse into a gallop.

Chapter Twenty-seven

11th August 1102 – Bicester

Fortunately for Rohese and Lady Adeline, the two manors in Bicester had been owned jointly by the d'Ivry and D'Oyly families. Of the two, Adeline preferred Wretchwick to Bicester, as it was a smaller manor, but less bleak and martial in its decoration. Also, it had lovely walled herb and vegetable gardens laid out by D'Oyly's wife, which included a rose garden. Once the bailiffs had been seen, the manor courts held, and the business of the estates finished, they were enjoying their days of freedom from the bustle of Oxford. It was a warm day, and they sat in the arbour's shade. Adeline loved these last weeks of summer before September brought its colder weather, and she could see Rohese slowly recovering her bloom from what had been a dreadful year for her. It was the age-old tale of someone loving a man she could never have. She knew Rohese was still deeply in love with Conn Fitz Malvais, but it could not be. It was an impossible love because of who she was: the wife of the Royal Steward and a lady-in-waiting to the Queen. At times, she could see the sadness in her younger sister's face.

The sound of a commotion broke in upon their peace. It

was in the manor house, and the raised voices echoed along the stone flags of the old hallway that led to the garden. Moments later, a young man burst through the doorway, closely followed by the protesting steward, William, and the young groom, Dicken.

'We tried to stop him from disturbing your peace, my lady, but he insisted on seeing you,' protested the steward, glaring at the young man.

It was only as Adeline walked forward, shading her eyes, that she recognised the young man from Oxford.

'Tom? What do you do here in Bicester? Is something amiss in Oxford? Dear Lord, is it Sir Nigel?' she asked, concern in her voice.

Rohese put a hand on her sister's arm. She knew how Adeline felt about Sir Nigel, although she tried to hide her feelings for him. A clearly exhausted Tom dropped to one knee in front of them.

'My lady, I have done my best to get here, but you must not tarry once you have read this—men are coming to take the Lady Rohese, and I believe them to be hot on my heels as I managed to overtake them a league or so back,' he beseeched, handing her the missive from Sir Nigel.

Rohese paled and raised her hand to her throat in alarm as she realised what was happening. This was what he'd threatened her with during his last visit.

'It is De Courcy. This is my husband's doing as he swore he would punish me,' she gasped.

After scanning the message, Adeline looked stunned, but then she turned to Rohese, took both of her hands and nodded.

'Yes, it is him, and we must leave here before they arrive. William, saddle our horses and have them taken down to the meadow. Dicken, go to the kitchen and tell the cook to quickly pack us some basic foodstuff and wine for a long ride. Be quick and bring them down to the meadow. Rohese, run upstairs and pack a few items of clothing to fit into a saddle bag. William, bring our boots and our heavier cloaks into the hall. We must leave immediately.'

While Rohese carried out her instructions, Adeline followed William into the hall and placed a hand on his arm. She'd known him since she had come here as a young bride.

'These men will likely come here shortly. Take your time to answer the door. Be as authoritative and pompous as possible, but do not put yourself in danger or risk your life on any account. Tell them that the ladies are out visiting sick tenants but will be back for dinner. Delay them for as long as you can, then take the cook and Dicken and run and hide in the mill.'

He nodded but then dropped to one knee to press her hand to his forehead. He'd served Lady Adeline and her family for nearly forty years since he first came here as a manservant. He'd never betray her; they would have to kill him first. Rohese came running down the stairs with the small bags. They pulled on their riding boots and were gone without another word. William followed them out and watched them run across the gardens, through the gate, and down the meadow. He closed the gate in the wall and bolted it. He crossed himself, praying they would get away.

Tom waited with Dicken and the three fresh horses. They mounted, waved farewell to Dicken, and crossed the shallow stream. They had ridden up the bank and into the safety of the trees on the far side when they heard the sound of hooves. Adeline looked back in alarm, but Tom chivvied them on. The men had reached here even quicker than he expected, so they had to use the little time they had wisely.

'You know this area and these lands, my lady. We have to ride to Gloucester. Sir Nigel has arranged for someone to meet you there to help you hide and escape, but as you see, De Courcy's men will be on our heels. We need to ride hard and fast, staying off the main roads and tracks, for they will pursue us.'

Adeline nodded and led the way, heading west through the woods and out into the fields beyond, while Rohese looked back in alarm. It was her they wanted, and she didn't doubt that De Courcy would set up a hue-and-cry once he learned that she'd run. She'd never forget his face, twisted with anger and hatred as he forced himself upon her. He wanted her to suffer, to be locked away for the rest of her life, but he wouldn't care if she was killed in this hunt; it would probably suit his plans to marry again. Fear of what he could do with his influence and money made her stomach clench in fear. No matter who was helping them in Gloucester, her husband could easily find her and drag her back.

It was very late. The moon was high, heavy clouds had appeared, and it had begun to rain when they finally stopped to rest and water the horses that were beginning to stumble in the dark, after being pushed across rough terrain. Rohese ached in every bone in her body, and when she slid to the ground, she found her legs were so stiff and cold that she could hardly stand. Adeline took her by the arm and led her into a large open-fronted barn. There was deep, clean straw in one of the animal pens, and they gratefully sank into it, stretching their legs with their backs to the wall as they watched Tom water and feed the weary horses. Then he unpacked the food and wine and brought it to them. Adeline insisted he took a large share, as she knew he'd saved their lives by riding hell for leather to Bicester, and forcing them off the main roads and wagonways into the fields and woods.

'Do you know where we are, Tom?' asked Rohese, while tearing a chunk of bread to go with the cheese she was now relishing.

'As you saw, I chatted with the shepherd we let pass with his flock. We are on the old Roman road, now a drover track, not far from Gloucester, on the outskirts of a village called Barnwood. Sir Nigel told me that we must find the Abbey of St Peter, which is not far from the river, and we will claim sanctuary there. A cousin of his, Abbot Serle, will be expecting us. We will be safe there for a while. Now, let us snatch a few hours' sleep as we need to ride on before dawn.'

Unfortunately for the two women, Tom had sat on the grass and talked to Dicken while they waited with the horses. Young Dicken was very excited by this sudden flight and asked several questions while holding Tom up as a hero. This made the young man stand a little taller as he watched the women running towards them, so he carelessly mentioned the long ride ahead of them to Gloucester.

When Dicken reached the Great Hall, he found two hard-faced men questioning William, who was doing his best to keep them at bay. Dicken backed up the story of the two women visiting sick tenants and made to leave, but he was told to stay put; they didn't want anyone warning the women. However, after an hour, the men became restless and asked where these cottars lived. The older of the two saw the significant glance that passed between the two servants. They tried to force more information out of William, but he stuck to his story despite their threats and vicious blows.

Dicken was a shy youth, not quite seventeen, and as he saw the blood and bruising on William, he became more frightened. It only took them holding a dagger to William's throat for him to blurt out that the women had gone, but he did not know where, and he shook with fear as they transferred their attention to him. The first punch broke his nose, and as his blood spurted onto the hall floor, the other man viciously twisted his arm up his back, forcing him to his knees as the dagger appeared in his face. It was over in moments, as Dicken begged for his life and William's, and told them the women had ridden for Gloucester. To his relief, the two men had gone, running for their horses, leaving Dicken, blood dripping onto his smock, to cradle William's bruised head and shout for help from the other servants.

The older of De Courcy's men had been a serjeant for nearly a decade. He knew Lady Rohese, and part of him was sorry for her, but he had a large pouch of silver at his belt, which was his alone if he found her and delivered her to Wytham Abbey. He was also a man who took pride in completing any order or task. He had chosen his companion because he'd trained him; he never refused an order, and he was good with both his fists and his weapons.

The only thing that perturbed him now was not knowing who had warned the women that they were coming. Who was with them, and why were they going to Gloucester? They had left the manor at Wretchwick and galloped after them onto the main road leading to Gloucester. However, it was not a good road—a wide, rutted wagonway that wound up and through the hills. They stopped briefly to question the locals at every village they came across, but no one had seen two women and a man. Whoever it was that was leading them, he was clever, keeping them off the roads and out of sight. It was impossible to know where they were, he thought, staring intently out at the rolling countryside and forests as if they might appear. He shook his head and waved his men on as this was pointless.

The one positive was that he knew where they were heading. She wouldn't go to the castle, for Walter of Gloucester was the King's Sheriff and a friend of De Courcy. He would not hide her and he might even agree to give him more men to search the town once he told him of his quest and orders. So that left the inns, abbeys or houses of other friends, and, from what he remembered, Gloucester was not that big. They wouldn't waste more time searching on the road—they would ride for Gloucester, and he'd wait for them there.

The 12th August 1102 - Various Locations

As Morvan de Malvais rode north towards Normandy, he had felt a wave of anticipation at first, but now, as he crossed the border into Normandy, he was feeling the first tingle of apprehension. He had not been in Duke Robert's court in Rouen for many years—his choice, preferring to stay at Morlaix developing their warhorse bloodlines, spending time with his family and, when called on, riding out to protect the borders of Brittany.

However, he had followed, with interest, Robert's invasion of England to take back the crown from Henry Beauclerc. Like others who knew the Duke well, he'd been shocked that Robert had given in so easily to his brother at Alton when he had an army twice the size of Henry's forces.

As he galloped towards Rouen, Morvan admitted to himself that he was flattered that Duke Robert yet again needed his help, for he'd grasped immediately the dilemma Robert found himself in. If he attacked Robert de Belleme's castles in Normandy as he was being ordered to, he might please King Henry, but he would make an enemy out of one of his biggest supporters. What if Belleme won in England and defeated Henry—which was just as likely, as Belleme was the better warrior, experienced and ruthless, and with endless wealth? Then Robert would find that instead of his brother, he now had a vindictive and bitter enemy on the throne of England, for with Robert's betrayal, Belleme wouldn't offer the crown to him—he would take the crown for himself and then turn on Normandy. Should that happen, the situation would become highly dangerous.

He slowed his horse to a walk as he thought it through. Robert de Belleme may have given up on the feud between them, as Chatillon believed, but once he knew he was advising and helping Duke Robert, possibly against him, then all that would change and place his son, Conn, in the firing line as well.

He had to come up with a solution for his friend, Robert, that played off both sides—a dangerous and possibly deadly game for both him and his friend Robert.

∽⊶∾

In Bridgnorth, Robert de Belleme had listened to Roger de Poitevin's description of the parley with the Beaumonts, which had initially filled him with rage but then inspired him to come out of his self-inflicted limbo to act. His brothers, Roger and Arnulf, were right in what they said—they had wealth, they had thousands of men and still had their Irish allies. He couldn't sit in his castle at Bridgnorth and brood when he had a war to win and a king to defeat and kill. He shared his plans with them and watched the excitement and satisfaction leap once again in their faces.

When darkness fell, he and his brothers ran across the large cobbled courtyard at Bridgnorth and down several steps, opening a heavy wooden door to what appeared to be a storeroom. At the back, there was a small door with a heavy iron ring that looked as if it was an old wine cellar.

Belleme had learnt his lesson at Arundel Castle, and when he'd reinforced the wall and towers at Bridgnorth with stone bases, he'd also built a long, secret tunnel out of the castle. It was well built, with wooden props and beams, but it was also low and damp, and they had to run along it doubled up in places. However, in no time, they were emerging in what appeared to be an old, dry well in the woods. As he climbed the rope ladder, Belleme heard the soft thudding sound of the trapdoor being barred below them by one of the defenders left behind—no going back now.

He followed his brothers in quietly climbing out of the well, keeping low and darting glances all around in case his enemy had placed sentries or scouts. They were not far from Henry's camp, and he could see the flickering light and smell the smoke from their fires in the distance, surrounding the front of his castle. They ran low to the ground across the open glade to the thicker undergrowth and made their way silently down the slope to the river bank where two men were waiting, crouched in the reeds beside a boat.

Following the current, the oars dipping gently into the water without splashing, it didn't take long to reach the opposite bank where Belleme's captains were waiting in the trees. They had received his orders and had secretly moved their men out hours ago whilst leaving all the campfires still lit. Belleme gazed up at the sky; the rain had stopped, the clouds were clearing, and a watery moon occasionally appeared as he glanced back at the dark silhouette of his castle. He had no regrets about leaving it and abandoning his men; it was necessary, he thought, as he mounted his horse and, with his brothers, Fulk, and his knights, they galloped towards Shrewsbury. He'd take Henry Beauclerc on in battle in the open fields, not holed up like a rat in a barrel.

The clouds covered the same moon as Tom, the squire, trotted along Gloucester's dark, narrow streets, clinging to the walls of the buildings in the shadows. He'd left the sisters with their horses in an old, dilapidated, wooden workshop by the river. Now, he had to get into the abbey, which would be difficult late at night. But it was crucial that he got to Abbot Serle to tell him they were here in Gloucester and needed help. He knew that all abbeys employed male servants, and hopefully, they could be sent to help him protect the women when he moved them into the safety of the abbey. As expected, the large gates were firmly shut, but the walls were old, and the mortar was crumbling, creating several footholds. In no time, he'd climbed onto it. He sat astride and scanned behind and ahead for any sign of pursuit and, seeing none, dropped soundlessly into what seemed to be the gardens. As expected, there was no sign of life anywhere—it was well after midnight, and he knew the monks would have retired to their cells.

He was running, bent low, along the paths between the herb beds when he thought he heard something. He stopped, glancing around and behind, not sure where the sound had come from. Although he froze and waited for what seemed a long time, the sound did not come again, and he could see nothing in the occasional light of the moon.

He finally reached the corner of the main stone buildings, and he pulled himself upright to lean against the wall, letting out the breath he had been holding. It was precisely as he put his hand on the corner of the wall to look into the yard beyond that the blow fell, and he dropped like a stone. Behind him, De Courcy's serjeant gave a grunt of satisfaction—he vaguely recognised the young squire and didn't doubt that he'd sing like a bird to tell them where the women were hiding. He was confident that in no time at all, he would be heading for Wytham, the Lady Rohese tied on a horse behind him.

While Tom's body was being dragged into a stable by De Courcy's men, in Owen's camp in Penkridge, Georgio di Milan was sitting, arms wrapped tightly around his knees, gazing up at the same sky.

His ankles were still in irons, and he was shivering, as he'd been soaked through today, and the night air was growing chilly. He believed it was Thursday. Tomorrow would be Friday, a fast day, which meant there were only two more days before Sunday when he would be in the abbey in Shrewsbury, dead or alive.

He had to believe that Malvais knew about this, that his friend would be there, ready to try and save him. he knew Owen, Rhys, and Daegal were sitting together tonight, planning what would happen in the abbey, but Georgio was too far away to hear anything but the low mumble of their words. He thought he'd been building a bond with Daegal O'Brien, for he'd seen sympathy in his face at times that he thought he could make use of. But for the last two days, the Irish warrior had avoided him completely, which didn't bode well.

He closed his eyes and prayed as he had never prayed before that they wouldn't kill him before they took him into the abbey. He longed to see Conn again, to grip arms with him, to know that he was there in Shrewsbury Abbey for him, even if it was as he breathed his last at the hands of Owen or Rhys.

Author Note

Robert de Belleme, the Earl of Shrewsbury and head of the powerful Montgomery family, despised Henry Beauclerc, whom he called the usurper, and was determined to remove him from the throne. England was plunged into civil war after the Montgomerys were declared outlaw following the Easter Court in 1102. Undoubtedly, King Henry faced a formidable challenge in taking on this influential and wealthy family. The Montgomerys had the resources to buy allies and, more significantly, possessed extensive military experience, a strength that King Henry lacked. Fortunately, Henry had the support of the Beaumont brothers, which helped to level the playing field.

Henry demanded that all his lords and knights provide him with men and summoned the fyrd to increase his numbers. This tradition dates back to Anglo-Saxon times when the kings expected and imposed military service on every able-bodied male, sometimes only in certain counties, sometimes across the country. However, it was limited to forty days, as these men were needed on the land. There has been past criticism of this 'army of pitchforks,' who could not stand against armed and mounted knights or regular soldiers, but with the long pikes in their hands, they could prove useful. King Henry personally involved himself in training to show the men how to use pikes effectively.

Henry initially had some lucky wins, especially with the help of Robert Beaumont, who executed Henry's strategy of capturing Belleme's castles one by one. However, Robert de Belleme, with the support of the powerful King Maredudd of Powys and his brothers, was not concerned about losing castles like Kimberworth and Mexborough. His main goal was to engage Henry in battle, knowing he could defeat him once on the field. Belleme's brother, Arnulf, also brought hundreds of Irish mercenaries from his father-in-law.

However, things did not go according to plan for Belleme. Prince Iorwerth of Powys betrayed his brothers by joining Pantulf, and in one fell swoop, he lost most of his Welsh allies, who numbered thousands of men.

Prince Iorwerth took his older brother Maredudd captive and handed him over to King Henry. Many of the lands he had been promised for such an act did not materialise and were given to Norman lords such as Sir Philip Braose instead. Iorwerth broke with King Henry in 1103; he was captured, put before a tribunal and imprisoned until 1110. Meanwhile, Cadwgan triumphed as he became the sole ruler of Powys, not in Norman hands.

Everything is not tied up neatly at the end of this book, but it is the fourth book in a series about our tattooed warriors. There are a series of cliffhangers, half of which are historical: Robert de Belleme is indeed heading for a showdown with King Henry at Shrewsbury; Pantulf, Iorwerth and the Welsh troops are heading south to join the King and bolster his forces; in Normandy, Duke Robert is indeed in a quandary, having been ordered by his brother, Henry, to attack Belleme's lands and is unsure what to do. As for Rohese de Courcy and Georgio di Milan, you must read the next book to discover if either of them survives against unlikely odds.

Sarah J. Martin

October 2024

Glossary

Anchorite – A religious recluse who has withdrawn to lead a prayer-orientated life, usually in a cell attached to a church.

Bailey—A ward or courtyard in a castle. Some outer baileys could be huge and encompass grazing land.

Boon – A favour.

Braies - A type of trouser often used as an undergarment to mid-calf and made of light or heavier linen. Usually covered by chausses.

Caparison – A cloth covering laid over a horse for protection and decoration.

Castellan – Responsible for the administration and defence of a castle.

Chausses – Attached by laces to the waist of the braies, these were tighter-fitting coverings for the legs.

Cist – A stone-lined grave.

Close-stool – A stool having a seat with a hole, beneath which a chamber pot is placed.

Coif – A flexible chainmail hood, which would cover the throat, neck and part of the shoulders.

Dais – A raised platform in a hall for a throne or tables, often for nobles.

Destrier – A knight's large warhorse, often trained to fight, bite and strike out.

Doublet – A close-fitting jacket or jerkin often made from leather, with or without sleeves. Laced at the front and worn either under or over, a chain mail hauberk.

Doxy or Doxie – a woman regarded as sexually promiscuous.

Fyrd – An army raised from a lord's manor, freemen and villeins pledged to fight for their lord.

Give no quarter – to give no mercy or compassion for the vanquished.

Hauberk – A tunic of chain mail, often reaching to mid-thigh.

Hoardings – wooden extensions to palisades for additional protection or for walking inside the fence.

Kine – a group of bovine animals, cattle, oxen etc.

League – A league is equivalent to approx. Three miles, in modern terms.

Liege lord – A feudal lord, such as a count or baron, entitled to allegiance and service from his knights.

Marcher Lords - These were nobles entrusted to guard the border between England and Wales. King William I created three new earldoms to do so: Hereford, Shrewsbury, and Chester. (March is an Anglo-Saxon term for a border.)

Missive – A letter or longer written message.

Motte – The large high mound of earth created by digging the deep ditches or moats for a Norman castle. It took time to settle; hence, wooden keeps were built before being replaced with stone once the earth was compacted.

Palfrey – A highly valued lady's light, smooth-gaited horse.

Palisade – Sturdy, high wooden fence surrounding a Norman castle.

Pallet Bed or Palliasse – A bed made of straw or hay. Close to the ground, generally covered by a linen sheet and also known as a palliasse.

Pell – A stout wooden post for sword practice.

Penny ordinary – A cheap meal on offer in Inns and drinking establishments. It would be whatever was cooking in the pot that day.

Pike – A long thrusting spear.

Pottage – A staple of the medieval diet, a thick soup made by boiling grains and vegetables and, if available, meat or fish.

Prelate – An ecclesiastical dignitary.

Retainer – A dependent or follower often rewarded or paid for their services.

Serjeant—The soldier serjeant was a man who often came from a higher class. Most experienced medieval mercenaries fell into this class; they were deemed to be 'half the value of a knight' in military terms.

Solar—The family uses this private room on the castle's second floor, which has south-facing windows that let in light and warmth.

Spavined – a type of joint disease that affects a horse's hocks.

Tow-headed – Having very light, almost white, blonde hair.

Vavasseur – A right-hand man, more than a servant.

Vedette - An outrider or scout used by cavalry.

Vellum - Finest scraped and treated calfskin, used for writing messages.

Character list

Fictional characters in *italics*

London & Winchester
King Henry I
Matilda of Scotland (Queen)
Henry Beaumont - Earl of Warwick
Robert Fitz Hamon - Baron of Gloucester
Anselm - Archbishop of Canterbury.
Robert de Courcy - Royal steward
William de Courcy - his son
Nest Ferch Rhys - Mistress of Henry I

Tamworth
Conn Fitz Malvais
Gracchus - Serjeant of the Horse Warriors
Serjeant Fox – De Clare's right-hand man
Edvard of Silesia - Chatillon's vavasseur and friend
Rhodri ap Gwyfd - White druid & Welsh horse whisperer
Robert Beaumont – Count de Meulan & Earl of Leicester
Gilbert Fitz Richard de Clare - Baron de Clare
Philip de Braose - Lord of Bramber
Urse d'Abetot - Sheriff of Worcester

Tickhill
Fulk of Lisours
Lady Muriel de Busli
Robert de Bloet - Bishop of Lincoln

Kimberworth
Sir Geoffrey de Ware
Lady de Ware
John de Ware
Synnove - Rhodri's woman
Wilken Crick — mercenary employed by De Courcy
Kenric — Sir Philip's squire

Stafford
Owen ap Cynan - Welsh mercenary leader
Rhys ap Tegan - Owen's captain
Maredudd ap Bleddyn - King of Powys
Iorwerth ap Bleddyn - Prince of Powys
Cadwgan ap Bleddyn - Prince of Powys
Raoul de Tosny — Lord of Conches
Daegal O'Brien — Irish mercenary, Captain of De Tosny
Sir William Pantulf — King Henry's man

Oxford
Nigel D'Oyley - Castellan of Oxford
Adeline d'Ivry - Elder sister of Rohese
Abbot Columbanus of Eynsham - Benedictine
Rohese de Courcy - Wife of Robert de Courcy
Tom — the squire

Bridgnorth
Robert de Belleme - Earl of Shrewsbury (Head of the Montgomery family)
Arnulf de Montgomery
Roger de Poitevin (Montgomery)

Chester
Georgio di Milan – Horse Warrior
Brother Alphonse

Morlaix
Luc de Malvais
Merewyn de Malvais – his wife
Morvan de Malvais
Minette de Malvais – his wife (Ette)

The Chateau – Chatillon sous Bagneux
Piers de Chatillon - Papal Envoy & Assassin
Isabella de Chatillon- Wife of Piers
Gabriel & Gironde – Twin sons of Chatillon
Dion Ui Neill – Finian's widow
Daniel – Chatillon's captain
Ahmed – Physician and apothecary
Darius Fitz Malvais – Son of Conn
Mishna – Edvard's wife

Neauphle-le-Chateau
Anton Dubois – Le Sanglier – Bailiff
Le Sudiste – Leader of raiders in Rambouillet Forest

Others

Amlawdd ap Gwyfd – Chief druid, Rhodri's grandfather

Duke Robert of Normandy

Sibylla of Conversano – Duchess of Normandy

Pope Paschal

Map

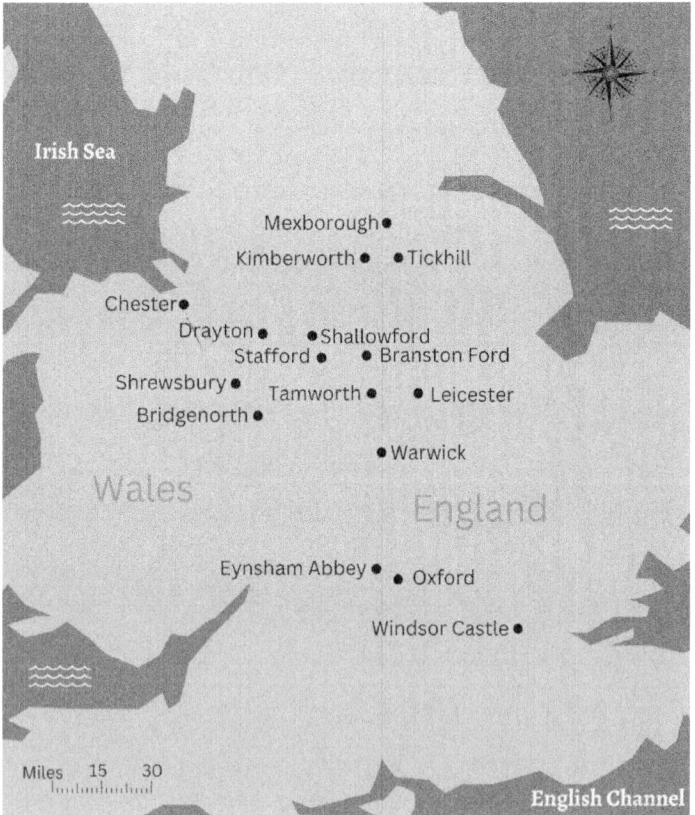

Other books by SJ Martin

THE BRETON HORSE WARRIORS

The Breton Horse Warriors series follows the adventures of our hero, Luc de Malvais, and his brother, Morvan. It begins in Saxon England, during the Norman Conquest and travels to war-torn Brittany and then Normandy. Luc de Malvais is a Breton lord, a master swordsman and leader of the famous Horse Warriors. He faces threatening rebellion, revenge and warfare as he fights to defeat the enemies of King William. However, his duty and loyalty to his king come at a price, as his marriage and family are torn apart. He now has to do everything he can to save his family name, the love of his life and his banished brother...**but at what price?**

THE PAPAL ASSASSIN SERIES

The Papal Assassin series follows the adventures, life and times of the darkly handsome swordmaster Piers de Chatillon. A wealthy French noble, the young, influential Papal Envoy of several popes and a consummate diplomat, he spreads his influence, favours and threats around the courts of Europe.

He is an arch manipulator, desired by women and feared by men; he is also a lethal assassin used by kings and princes alike. His adventures take him back and forth across Europe in the turbulent seas of politics and intrigue in the 11th century.

Meanwhile, an array of enemies plots his downfall and demise. With the help of his close compatriots and friends, he manages to keep them at bay, but time is running out for Piers de Chatillon, and danger draws ever closer to his beautiful wife, Isabella and their children.

THE TATTOOED WARRIOR SERIES

Conn Fitz Malvais, Horse Warrior, has fled after the traumatic murder of the woman he loved; she died in his arms. Blaming himself for her death, he rides to the Byzantine Empire, a thousand miles to the east. Meanwhile, his friend, Georgio, frantically searches for him, following a faint trail.

It is the year 1100, and it is easy for people to stay lost as Conn disappears into the vast and dangerous city of Constantinople. Here, he signs up to fight for the Emperor Alexios. The commander of the Emperor's forces recognises the Horse War-rior's talents and gives him the daunting task of controlling a troublesome, large crusade from Lombardy. This crusader camp is unruly and volatile; many of them are scum from the slums of Milan. They begin to rebel, attacking the local villages; Conn fails to stop them, but he is forced to deliver harsh and brutal punishments afterwards.

Meanwhile, in Normandy, Piers de Chatillon, the Papal Envoy, is weaving his political web to help Duke Robert regain the crown of England from Henry, and he needs Conn to return. He summons him back, unaware of the dangers he and Georgio are now embroiled in for the Emperor.

Conn has several enemies in the crusader camp, including

a vicious Lombard knight who leads the rebels and wants the Horse Warrior's head in revenge for his reprisals against him and his men. This knight plans to carry out a daring attack with hundreds of rebels on the Emperor's palace in the city, and they decide to lure the Horse Warrior into a trap to kill him. His friend, Georgio, hears of the plot, but it is far too late, as Conn is already in the city.

About the Author

I have adored all aspects of history from an early age, but I find the lawlessness, intrigue and danger of medieval times fascinating. This interest in history influenced my choices at university and my career. I spent several years with my trowel in the interesting world of archaeology before becoming a storyteller as a history teacher. I wanted to encourage young people to find that same interest in history that had enlivened my life.

I always read historical novels from an early age and wanted to write historical fiction. The opportunity came when I left education; I then gleefully re-entered the world of engaging and fascinating historical research into the background of some of my favourite historical periods.

There are so many stories out there still waiting to be told, and my first series of books, 'The Breton Horse Warriors' proved to be one of them. The Breton lords, such as my fictional Luc de Malvais, played a significant role in the Battle of Hastings and helped to give William the Conqueror a decisive win. They were one of the most feared and exciting troops of cavalry and swordmasters in Western Europe, fighting for William the Conqueror and then for his son Duke Robert.

My second series of novels is based on a captivating character from the first series. My readers clamoured for the ruthless Papal Envoy, Piers de Chatillon, to have his own series, and so the Papal Assassin series was born. It is amazing how an immoral, murdering, manipulative diplomat and assassin can seize the imagination as he cuts a swathe through Europe. Undoubtedly, he is an enthralling and mesmerising character; I will be sad to let him finally go.

I hope you enjoy reading my books as much as I have enjoyed writing them.

S.J. Martin Author | Facebook
Twitter/X
Instagram
moonstormbooks.com/sjmartin
sjmartin@moonstormbooks.com

Printed in Great Britain
by Amazon